"Thomas Laird's new novel *Desert Storm Heart* leaps out of the Conradian darkness of the Gulf War after a gore-thirsty Marine brings his murderous rage back home to America's heartland. When he meets his match in the Chicago detective Will Koehn, a fellow Marine, a battle of wits commences in private and public. Laird offers a brilliant psychological portrait of a depraved, driven murderer and his enlightened pursuer."

Thomas Palakeel
Professor of English, Bradley University
Peoria, Illinois

"Encountering a particularly nasty villain (or three), in Thomas Laird's *Desert Storm Heart* we're hooked by the mystery—and the cruelty—of those who wield power in war and civilian life, but mostly by our own curiosity for Detective Will Koehn's lifestyle. How can a man with a healthy disrespect for the bad guys manage his own private life so badly? Deep in his heart, does he want a family, and to straighten out his 'woman trouble,' or does he just want to put a bullet in the bad guy's back?"

James Manlow
Author of *Attraction*
Bournemouth, England

"Just when you thought it was safe to return to Chicago...Thomas Laird's latest crime thriller packs a punch to the gut, and dissects the heart of an Iraq War veteran turned Chicago cop."

Dr. Dean Lawson
Assistant Professor of History, Chowan University
Murfreesboro, North Carolina

www.parkgatepress.com

Desert Storm Heart

www.dionysusbooks.com

Also by Thomas Laird

Blue Collar and Other Stories (1994)

Cutter (2001)

Season of the Assassin (2003)

Black Dog (2004)

Voices of the Dead (2006)

The Underground Detective (2012)

To my beloved wife Marsha, who has returned me
to the land of the living.

To my children, Kathy, Anne, and Andy, and to my
grandsons Michael and John, and to the junior member,
Margaret Renae Laird, my granddaughter.

To Matt Fullerty, who wanted to go one more round.

And to the memory of Robert Raymond Laird, my father.
He was a man, all in all, and we shall not see his like again.

Desert
Storm
Heart

A Novel of Chicago Streets

by

Thomas Laird

Dionysus Books / Parkgate Press

Publishers Online!

For updates and more resources, visit
Dionysus Books and Parkgate Press online at

www.dionysusbooks.com
www.parkgatepress.com

Page layout by Dionysus Books
Cover design by Dionysus Books

ISBN-13: 978-1-937056-64-3

Library of Congress Control Number: 2013936350
Library of Congress Subject Headings:

Chicago (Ill.)--Fiction
Chicago in Fiction
Crime--Fiction
Fiction
Fiction--Psychological aspects
Police--Illinois--Chicago--Fiction
Sex crimes--Fiction

First Edition (worldwide) June 2013
[Parkgate Press: Dionysus Books reference number: 016]

"That snowstorm is a sandstorm and I'm stuck in it and I can't get out and somebody's gonna kill me and I'm looking for them. And that's what it is to me. To you, it's a snowstorm."

Dan Brown
Veteran of the Persian Gulf War, 2013
(Operation Desert Storm)

Desert
Storm
Heart

1

Kuwait, Desert Storm

S he'd been shot through the right eye, and the left had been scooped out, perhaps with a blunt instrument. Maybe with a spoon. Was that out of *King Lear*? I got a 'C' in Shakespeare in Brit Lit in high school, so I could be wrong.

It's the same MO as the first one. The rapes and murders had happened after Iraq folded its tent, after we'd reached Saddam's front door and didn't kick it down. But our Fearless Leader in DC had been in the Army Air Corps in WWII, and he sure as hell hadn't been a Marine. Patton would've run Baghdad over with his tanks, but Desert Storm had ended at the portals of the Evil City (depending on whose side you were on).

I work for the Naval Criminal Investigative Service (NCIS) after having served four years in the Corps, the beloved Crotch. I work Violent Crimes, including Homicide, of course.

This guy blinds them perpetually with a shot from a .45 automatic, and then he plucks out the other orb with something like a spoon, as I said. He must be using a rubber during the rapes, our Medical Examiner says, because he leaves no trace of semen.

He also leaves no witnesses. He's killed their families as well. Four victims the first time, and three the second. He shoots them and then he hangs them inside their dwellings. He finds a beam, or something on the ceilings, and he harnesses them in the main rooms of the houses. Both of the families were well-to-do. Not oil barons, but well-heeled Kuwaitis. The strange thing was that there was no evidence of theft in either of the homes. He doesn't take anything.

Except their daughters' innocence, and their lives. The girls were thirteen and sixteen. The latest victim was the youngest, the thirteen-year-old. She was the prettier of them, too. She would have become a beautiful woman if he'd allowed her to live.

My tour has come to an end. I'm going back to San Diego, before I go home to Chicago. I'm leaving with a sour taste in my mouth because I have not found that murderer/rapist from Kuwait. I know he was a Marine. I know he was one of us. From all that we'd discovered, Pete Donato (Pete was my partner in NCIS) and I know in our guts and in our heads that he was a jarhead, like the two of us used to be who worked Violent Crimes in Desert Storm.

I always found it more than a little ironic that we'd come to liberate Kuwait, and then there were criminals in the Crotch who killed little girls, raped them, and maimed them.

I always thought it had to be an officer who did the kids. The .45 would be unusual for a non-commissioned leatherneck. It's possible he was a private, but I think he'd be ranked higher, since he'd have more mobility if he were, say, a lieutenant or captain or above. That was just my gut talking because anything is possible in a war. It wasn't much of a war, I know, but Desert Storm was the conflict I was involved in.

My brother Sammy picked me up in San Diego, and we drove all the way home to Chicago in my bro's '87 Camaro. We stopped in Las Vegas, got very drunk, and drove home in a semi-stupor. Luckily, we didn't get hauled into jail. Getting arrested after Desert Storm would have been too ironic, even for me.

I didn't know exactly what to do when I arrived at Back of the Yards, my family home. We lived just blocks from Comiskey Park in an all white enclave, another chunk of humor, seeing that Chicago is heavily populated by Blacks and Hispanics. I come from German/Austrian stock, but I'm proud to say my ancestors bugged out of Deutschland in 1908, long before Hitler started his Thousand Year Reich. My father, George, was in WW II. He was in the first wave at Normandy. He survived, of course. He never talked about the landing. My mother told me his history, because he never talked about his war.

I promised myself I'd never talk about mine, either, even though Sammy has already started the interrogation on the way home from Las Vegas. I wound up telling him about the dead girls in Kuwait. It was almost eerie; it was almost involuntary. It spilled right out of my lips and into Sammy's ears.

"You never caught him, Will?"

"No, Samuel. We never did."

"Are they still investigating?"

"The NCIS is very stubborn. Yes. I'm sure someone's still after him."

"You sure it's just one guy?"

"No. But I'm fairly certain it was a lone perpetrator."

Sammy is taller than I am, and I'm six-two. He's about six-six, a basketball and football player. Played at Illinois in the Big Ten, left tackle. He goes about 270, fifty pounds heavier than I am. I played wide receiver in high school. They offered me a ride to Illinois for football too, but I went into the Crotch right after I graduated from a Chicago City College. The Corps further educated me. I started off as a Military Policeman, and then I tested out so high I was able to land a spot in NCIS, a fairly elite crew of cops.

I'd solved every homicide I was given, until this last sweetheart showed up in Kuwait. That's why I felt frustrated about leaving NCIS and the Corps to come home. The problem was, my dad was in the hospital with a heart murmur, and our mother, Sammy's and mine, was in the home with Alzheimer's. Someone had to take care of Dad, and Sammy's going back to school at Illinois for his MBA. I had to take care of the old man, and I felt privileged to receive the job.

When I finally got back to my beloved Back of the Yards, I found out that the old guy had recovered fully and that I could've stayed with my job. I almost felt like re-upping, but for some reason I knew my time in the Marines and the NCIS was over. It was time to move on.

So I entered the Police Academy the September after the summer I returned from the NCIS, in 1992. I scored high on their exams, and I spent only six months in the streets in uniform. They sent me for more training, and within twenty-four months I had a detective's shield. I worked Robbery/Car Theft for twenty months after that, and then I got my spot in Homicide. My Captain, Ray Pearce, says I progressed up the chain faster than any young copper he'd ever known. It was an honor coming from Capt. Pearce. He was a Medal of Honor winner in the Vietnam War, and he still is a legend in Homicide.

"Detective Koehn?"

It's pronounced 'cane,' like the walking stick or the stuff sugar comes from.

"Sir?"

"I see in your jacket that you had one red-liner you never resolved, back in the shit."

He's referring to Kuwait and the rapes, of course.

"Yessir. One unsolved case."

Pearce is a medium-sized man with sparse hair on top. It's a chestnut brown. His most outstanding feature is his piercing green eyes. They're almost like a jungle cat's eyes. I imagine they could stab through any dark alley, out at you. He's what they used to call nondescript, except for those two green orbs.

"Too bad they didn't let Schwartzkopf do his thing. Too bad they didn't let him fuck Saddam up thoroughly."

"Indeed, Sir."

I felt a slight grin take shape on my lips.

"You play any ball, Will?"

"Football, Sir. Yessir."

"Calm down, kid. You're out of the Crotch. Just call me Captain. Or Ray, if no other brass asses are around me."

"Yessir—I mean, Captain…. Ray. I'm sorry. Old habits, Sir."

"It's all right…. This multiple rape thing. Still fucking with your head?"

"Sir?"

"Come on, Will. Tell me."

I look into his green eyes. They won't allow a detour or a lie.

"Yes. I have nightmares. Not about the combat I saw in Iraq. We went along with the jarheads on convoys, sometimes. We saw what the war did to those poor bastards trapped inside it.

"Like I said. The convoys and the unsolved murders gave me some bad dreams. I went to the NCIS shrink and talked about it."

"And what did he tell you, Will?"

"That the crimes I told him about gave him fucking bad dreams too."

I still have those nightmares. I think there'd be something wrong with me if I didn't.

I remember the stench of those kill scenes. The heat was terrible. Both of the victims were wealthy enough to have air conditioning in their homes, but the perp had shut off the air, intentionally, I know. He wanted them to decompose quickly. Probably to make us sick. Likely it was a power thing, too. Here's what I'm capable of, he was telling Pete and me.

Pete heaved on the two scenes, and he never apologized. He came prepared with Vicks and a mask at the two sites also. The Vicks made me sick, so I gagged on both, but not enough to blast chow.

Mostly, I remember the girls. I remember the maiming of their youthful faces. He couldn't just ravage them. He had to destroy them as well. Then he shot and hanged their families, probably before he killed the teenaged girls. That's my theory, since the families' time of death was more than an hour before the rape/murder vics.

I have bad dreams. I see oil smoke above the desert floor. I see oiled up, dead sea birds on the beaches, and sometimes a few miles inland. I see suffering Arabs, innocent of the war, blown up and burning on the roadsides. I see weeping, fatherless and motherless children all along the highways, searching for an adult to shelter them. No one comes for them.

Just as no one came for the two girls and their fathers, mothers, and brothers and sisters.

Yeah, I have bad dreams. I wanted to tell Captain Pearce all about it. I wanted to tell Sammy and that well-built babe of a shrink in Kuwait. I wanted to tell my dad about it too.

"How was it, on the beach?" I asked him about two months after I got back from Desert Storm.

My father is the source of our size and our athletic ability. He's six one and built like the veritable brick shithouse. Huge shoulders. Still has a slim waist. Thick thighs, bulging pecs and arms. No fat, no waste. A tough old man whose body refuses to wither.

"What beach?"

"Mom's the one with the Alzheimer's."

He smiles.

"Smartass."

He smiles again. Even his jaws are muscular.

"You were close enough to the shit. So I guess you deserve to hear.... I stopped believing in God the morning after the first wave at Normandy. I was alone on the beach with dead men all around me."

And he won't say anything else.

In October in 1994 while I'm in Homicide, my partner Jack Clemons and I get a call to the far northwest side. It's a well-to-do, almost suburban neighborhood. A brick house, good sized backyard. Shady trees. Americana. It's July, and it's hot. Huckleberry Finn should be rafting down the eternal Mississippi. A murder on this day should not be possible. It's fragrant. It's summer. I'd rather be at Lake Michigan, in the water up to my neck.

The child is twelve. Her right eye is missing. It's been gouged out. Her left eye has been shot away with a large-caliber bullet, I'm guessing. More than guessing.

Her parents are hanging from two light fixtures. One in the dining room and one in the adjoining living room. There is arterial spray against the walls. I figure they were shot cowering up against that living-room wall, and then he hanged them after they were dead. It took considerable strength to hoist the father's body up to that fixture—the killer has to be fair-sized in order to do that kind of lifting. Almost too strong. Weight-lifter strength.

Jack Clemons is my age. Early thirties. Medium build, but wiry. Thin black hair. I'm guessing his mother was Italian. He's got that swarthy kind of handsome face that reminds me of a young Dean Martin. His father's name sounds like Gael—Irish or Scot. The name was Dermott. Jack is also shorter than I am, by about two inches. I'm about six-two, and I go a little over 200. I put on weight since high school.

"What is it?" he asks as we go outside for some air and as we let the ME finish up inside.

"It's that prick I was after in Kuwait."

"Say again?"

I explain the whole story to him.

"He's followed me home."

I have no dreams tonight. I'm awake in my bedroom in my father's house. I can hear Dad gently snoring in his recliner chair in the living room. Lots of nights he doesn't make it into bed because he misses my mother. We see her every other Sunday at the home. It's all either of us can take. Sammy's back at school, getting his MBA. He can't go to see Mom at all. It tears him up too bad, so I won't let him come home from Champaign to see her anymore.

I get up and walk into the living room and find my seventy-two year old dad sitting in his chair, his legs up, the TV in front of him on with no sound. When he sees me, he clicks off the tube with the remote.

"Have a seat."

"I couldn't sleep, Dad."

"I never sleep anymore. Not so you'd notice."

"I'll leave you alone, Dad. I'm sorry."

"Hell, sit down on the couch. Join the night watch."

2

I get replays of Kuwait frequently—three or four times a week. They come at night, but not always. I'll be staring off into thin air, and then the video runs right in front of my eyes. The only way the scenario ends is when Jack Clemons, my partner, or anyone else, distracts me.

"What're you looking at?" he asks me as we revisit the murder scene of the Milan family on the north side: Sandra Milan, 12, John Milan, 40 and Amanda Milan, 39. The usual yellow crime-scene tape is all around their brick house, and today we are canvassing the neighbors, who will of course have heard nothing. Someone must have heard the loud retort of the .45 handgun that he used to finish all three of them off, but they will have confused the gunfire with traffic noise or with some other sound of the city they've learned to live with.

Jack and I receive no help from the nearby neighbors. We almost never get any aid from them. Mostly, they don't want to get involved. It's like the military—it ain't my yard, a Marine will always explain when asked if he knows anything about a crime done to someone else.

We drive to the morgue. The doctor, Dr. Fandel, is waiting for us, and he's standing next to the remains of Amanda Milan, the mother.

"Asphyxiation. No broken neck. She was unlucky," the ME pronounces.

He's short and dumpy and unflappably calm. He's explained his demeanor at the morgue logically:

"No one bothers me at work."

He walks over to John Milan's corpse.

"This one was luckier than the other two. His neck was indeed broken. Neither of the gunshots killed the parents. He simply disabled them so they couldn't put up a fight. He made them bleed so he could handle the hangings. The child was killed by the shot through the eye."

"As usual," I say.

"Pardon?" Dr. Fandel asks.

Jack is eyeballing me too. I can feel his gaze on me.

"This is the same MO as a guy I was after in Kuwait in Desert Storm. We never caught him."

"And you were saving this information why?" Clemons demands.

"I wasn't positive until the doctor confirmed the manner of death."

"But you already knew?" Jack says.

"Yes. I'm sorry, but I had to be sure.... You two are the first to know."

Captain Pearce is next to be informed. And standing next to him is Pete Donato, my old partner from NCIS. He's in Marine uniform.

"I'm still with NCIS," he tells me as he shakes hands.

"You got here fast," I admit. I introduce Jack Clemons to Pete.

"I came here from New York. He did two more in New York City, just like Kuwait, and from what the FBI shared, just like the triple homicides you two are doing now. The Milans. I was just talking to Captain Pearce about it. He wasn't sure why you didn't tell him about our boy when you saw the scene and the vics, and I explained we always waited for the ME's verdict before we connected dots on multiple homicides."

"I still love you, Will," the Captain grins. "Next time, inform me immediately, ME or no ME."

"Done," I apologize.

"So?" I ask Pete as we sit down around the Captain's desk here in Homicide.

"Same same. The eyes. The adolescent young teenaged females. The rapes minus the semen. The hangings. Everything is repetitive. Same caliber gunshot wounds. This guy is happy with his script. It's working, so why should he change anything? He leaves next to nothing, as you know."

"The new scene here was immaculate," Jack adds.

"He's what the book calls an organized killer," Pete says.

"You talk to the profilers at Quantico?" Captain Pearce asks.

"Yessir," Pete tells him and us. "Nothing we haven't already heard…. White. Male. Twenty-five to forty years old. Solitary. Seems ordinary to those he comes in contact with. The rest you know by the numbers. Will and I were trained at Quantico by those same profilers."

"Why is he moving?" Pearce throws out. "Just to remain elusive?"

"Why'd he move here? It's a big enough country. But Kuwait is tiny, and we still couldn't grab him," I say.

"He came for you," Pete says. "He was one of us. I'm convinced he was a Marine. Probably an officer. I think you had him pegged, down the line. But there were lots of commissioned Marines in Desert Storm, in our area of operations."

"True enough," I answer.

"So now what?" Jack queries.

"We keep after him until he lets us fuck him up. He does want to get caught if he's trying to come here to get in my face."

"You have an idea who he might be?" Pearce asks.

"I had several candidates. None of them came up as winners in the lottery," I tell my boss.

"Who were they?" Pearce again demands.

"I'll write up that list for you, Sir. Then I'll see if I can begin to track them. But it's been years since Desert…"

"Get me that list ASAP. Captain Donato is here to assist the two of you."

Pete and Jack and I go to Fatso's on Fullerton on the North Side for a schooner of Old Style—but Pete opts for a Coors.

"That Chicago beer has an aftertaste," Pete explains.

"LaCrosse, Wisconsin, bro," I correct.

"But everyone in this city thinks it's the nectar of the gods," my old partner smiles as he wades into his schooner of Coors. "We are off duty, are we not?" he asks with a grin.

Pete has attracted the attention of the denizens of Fatso's. It's mostly a copper bar, but it has its female groupies too, like all police taverns. A blonde and a brunette have taken notice of my good-looking ex-partner. I know they're impressed because I am too.

"You're a Captain, huh?" I ask.

"Everybody fucks up. Even the hierarchy in the Crotch. Yeah, I'm a Captain. I deal with Violent Crimes only, these days, and apparently someone higher up has a hard-on over our killer, Laughing Boy."

"I have the same woody he does, for this guy."

"I think I suffer from the same affliction," Jack Clemons joins in. "Who were these guys you suspected?"

"A captain and two lieutenants," I tell my current partner. "They all set off the bells and whistles from the profile. None of them has high grades in dealing with their own troops. Each is a solitary. And the only reason they're ranked as high as they are is because they performed bravely in the field in Desert Storm. The Marines don't hand out the awards freely, but these three have their share of the chest fruit salad.... Captain Benjamin Anderson. Lieutenant Carl Thomas. And Lieutenant Philip Brandon. Sociopaths in training all, but never a single disciplinary action was taken against this trio.

"They were my three likely candidates for multiple murderer of these girls in Kuwait.... And now the twelve year old and family here on the north side."

Fatso comes with our second round. His real name is Billy True. He's a Native American, an ex-Burglary dick and a vet of the Vietnam War with a Bronze and a Silver Star for Valor. He's also missing his left arm, but he wears a prosthetic arm and hand, and you don't notice the missing appendage until he displays it for you. Billy is a Lakota Sioux.

He is also skinny as the proverbial rail, hence the name "Fatso."

"We ever going to make this prick?" Pete asks as he sips his second fishbowl of Coors.

"Fuckin' A," I tell him.

But there's no grin on my lips when I say it.

We lie in bed staring at the cream-colored ceiling in her bedroom. We always make love in her apartment because I'm self-conscious about doing it at my dad's house. I intend to get my own place soon, and there's really no reason for me to stay with the old man any longer since he's completely recovered. He takes care of himself, cooks for me and for Sammy whenever my kid brother's home from school.

"Mary."

"What?"

"I just like saying your name…. Mary. Okay?"

She smiles and rolls over to me.

She has startlingly blue eyes. Natural red hair—auburn, in reality. Natural, because it's the same hue all over her, I'm saying. She's not very busty, but she's well-shaped. I like her body because it's comfortable. Not angular or hard where it shouldn't be. We fit well when we have sex.

I don't think she loves me, but I love her and I always have. I think she's very fond of me and I think she'd like to get serious. But right now her career comes first.

She gets up, throws on her bra and panties, and then she puts on a severe black pantsuit.

The last item of business is to strap her shoulder harness on and to attach her FBI ID to her belt.

"I can't discuss an ongoing case with anyone. You know that."

We have drinks and dinner at The Marquee. It's on the far northwest side, in a good neighborhood where we don't receive many homicide calls.

The lights are low. I want to tell her I love her again, but I don't because I know she won't reply with the correct response. I know she can't because she can't lie. It's what I love about her, and I know it's the reason she'll never rise in the system of the Federal Bureau of Investigation. You have to have some bullshit to fertilize the pasture, as my old man says.

"I've told you who I think might head the list of suspects. I already crossed the line for you, Mary."

She stares at me from behind her Tom Collins. It's a hot day in late July, and I think I might order a Collins too.

"Do you trust me?" I ask.

"Don't go there," she warns.

"My partner from Kuwait came back to help us. The NCIS is cooperating. Why can't you?"

"I don't know any more than you do. All I know is that they've got the list you gave Captain Pearce."

"That's all you know."

"Yes, Will, it's all I know."

"But you wouldn't tell me if you knew anything else."

She drinks another swallow of the Collins.

"Don't do this, Will. Don't try to compromise me, because if you do..."

"I know. I know what happens then."

I never see her again is what happens.

There's a 10 x 12 manila envelope waiting on my desk the next morning.

I open it up. There's a photo of an alive Sandra Milan. She's obviously terrified of the photographer. She seems to tremble even though she's frozen in the moment in this picture.

16

I turn the photo over. It has an inscription, but it's done in cutouts from newspaper print.

HELLO, WILL. ARE YOU HAPPY I'M BACK?
SEMPER FIDELIS

The envelope and its contents are delivered to the FBI. The package came via US Mail. Our mail boy put it on my desk, just as he puts all my mail there, daily. The postmark was from a northside station not far from our downtown headquarters here, near the Loop.

The results come back very quickly. Two days. No prints, no leads. The envelope can be purchased at any place with a 'mart' on the end. The sender used gloves because the only prints belonged to postal employees, none of whom had ever been to Kuwait or the Middle East.

We begin searching for the two lieutenants and the captain. The captain wound up dead in Iraq at the end of Desert Storm, but the two lieutenants left the Corps and wound up in parts unknown. We are tracing them via the perfunctory paper trail, but neither seems to have ever established a line of credit.

We study their military jackets. They are not related. Apparently had never met in Desert Storm or anywhere else.

But it's the no line of credit that disturbs me. For an American in the Nineties to have no credit cards.... Something is out of joint. Jack Clemons and Pete Donato agree with me. Something is wrong with this picture. We cannot find either of these elusive Waldos. No paper trail usually displays a taste for solitude. They don't want to be found, and I'm wondering if maybe I selected a winner in the Kuwait Killer lotto. We've got two possibilities that we like now, at least. The dead captain cut down the field.

But the fact that my list might not include the real killer sinks my stomach. There is nothing to do, though, but persist. Pursue these two names on a list. Names written in red, just like the unsolved murders on our white board in the Homicide headquarters. Names in red. Suspects to be located and interviewed.

I'm hoping to locate both of them before we find another dead female child and her equally dead family.

3

We spend hours searching the paper vapor of Carl Thomas and Philip Brandon, late of the US Marine Corps. Both lieutenants, both highly decorated, both loners with borderline sociopathic traits that flew underneath the radar of the Marine guidelines for the term 'lunatic.' Neither ever got caught doing anything that would achieve them the Army's status of Section Eight—nuts. They were careful boys. They always behaved in front of the brass, obviously, and each of them distinguished himself in the short-lived combat that was Desert Storm. So the Corps had no cause to send them to the loony farm or to bust them and send them back to the States to push pencils in Quantico. They were sent to the fray and made leaders of men, and it wouldn't have been the first time for psychos to be leading the troops.

Carl Thomas came home to Davenport, Iowa, and then promptly disappeared. We call the cops, state, county and city, in his hometown, but they have no idea of his location. Lt. Carl Thomas is a white male, 26 years old, five feet ten inches, 172 pounds of trained lean mean killing machine. I'm still wondering if his kills were relegated only to the enemy in our War. I'm wondering if he's a murderous pedophile who decimated whole families, entire clans, here and in Kuwait.

We find out he has a sister in Peoria, Illinois. It's a drive of three hours from Chicago, but Pete and Jack and I feel useless hanging here at headquarters.

We take the Stevenson, I-55, all the way down to 116 and head west and south, meandering through some podunk Midwestern small towns en route. We stop at a McDonald's for lunch, and I buy two cheeseburgers and a Coke. Jack opts for the chicken sandwich and fries, but Pete indulges in coffee only. We squeak a leak, and we make Peoria in less than three hours.

Doris Calvin (her married name) is divorced with two grown children. When she opens her north Peoria door—it's an upscale bi-level brick and wooden siding mix—we see she's got a headache or an attitude. She's mid-forties, slim with a decent rack, and her face has a peeved look to it. It'd be a pretty face if she weren't pissed off or hung over.

She checks our IDs before she allows us in.

Her ex-husband, she tells us immediately, is having the house watched for "boyfriends" because he's trying to nail her for adultery.

"The cheap prick."

She has photos of two athletic-looking teenaged males above her fireplace on the mantel. The house is tastefully decorated, with expensive furniture cluttering her living room.

"I'm not a cheater," she explains. "You're here about Carl…. Is that right?"

We prepped her over the phone. If we'd come unannounced, she likely wouldn't have answered the door. We go in and sit down.

"Yes," I answer. "We're here about your brother."

"He was a war hero. What's the problem?"

She has her chin thrust out at me, telling me to take a pop.

I'd really like to slap her, but I'm not the type.

"We're here investigating a case." Pete tells her. He's dressed in civvies, as he has been except for the first time I saw him back in Chicago.

"And the case regards what?" she demands.

19

If she ever relaxed and got rid of her sour face, she might be very attractive, even though she's a bit old for us.

"Homicide," Jack informs her.

"Do I... I need a lawyer?"

"No one's accusing you or your brother of anything," I say. "We just need to ask him some questions regarding his tour in Kuwait."

"Were you there?" she asks me.

"He and I both served there in Desert Storm," I point to Pete.

"So you know about what Carl went through."

"We were policemen there."

"Okay. Then you know how some of these guys come back and then they want to take off on their own to get themselves back into one piece, then," she says.

Her eyes are welling up.

"We need to talk to him right away," I say.

She studies me again.

"Is there someone I can call to verify your IDs?"

I hand her my card.

"Call Captain Pearce at that number."

She goes immediately to the phone. It takes under three minutes. I look at my wristwatch to time her.

"You seem for real.... He took off for our grandfather's cabin in Wisconsin. It's not far from LaCrosse."

She gives us the directions, and I write everything down. Then we drive back to the city to ask the Captain if he wants us to do a road trip. He nods and tells us to get our shit together.

The trip from the city takes five hours. The cabin is in a micro-town twelve miles from LaCrosse. We have Jack's Explorer. We figured the roads might get rough. They are, indeed.

None of us figured he'd still be there. There was no phone to call. The sister said he didn't have a telephone. There's no number registered to his mailing address, here in Wisconsin, and so he has truly isolated himself from the world, and I'm beginning to wonder if the hangover sister isn't telling the truth after all.

The Yamaha bike is parked outside the door. If he's running, he's looking for a showdown right now, I'm figuring. So I unstrap my Nine. I have it so it's ready to pull.

Carl Thomas comes out onto the porch of the sturdy-looking log cabin. It appears to be well-maintained. Someone's done work to keep it up.

He's a strong-looking young man, a determined set to his jaw.

"My sister said you were on the way."

"I thought there was no phone here," I say.

"I have a radio. Short wave, for emergencies," he smiles.

The smile is crafty, intelligent. I don't like the son of a bitch *now*.

"Come on in," he tells the three of us.

I look at Pete and Jack, but their faces are blank. I can't read what's going on inside them.

The interior is spartan, unlike the cluster of furniture at the sister's house.

He sits us on a spacious leather couch, a three-seater.

"You've come here why?" he asks. The same leering grin is on his mouth.

"We're investigating the deaths of some Kuwait nationals. And an American family, as well," Pete declares.

"Why are you talking to me?" he wants to know.

"We're investigating Marine officers who were in the vicinity of the Kuwait nationals," Pete says.

"You think I killed some of the indigenous personnel."

He grins again, and I want to severely bitch-slap him. I know now why his men despised him and why the company shrinks were a little dubious about his stability.

I checked him out with the military, and he's clean. Things might have been a little less confusing for me if he were a registered offender, but then he certainly wouldn't have made it into the Crotch, let alone

21

achieved the rank of lieutenant. He's sly enough to have avoided having any paperwork done on him. He passed the psych evaluation too, obviously. I'm thinking he always knows the right answers.

I tell him that his area of operations in Kuwait would have placed him near enough to the two female vics and their families in order for us to be interested in him, then and now.

"I looked you up, overseas, but I had no evidence to interrogate you," I tell Thomas.

"Then why am I talking to you now?"

He's sneering again.

Pete lays his arm across me.

"Because you want to cooperate. You want to do the right thing," Pete says to him.

"Of course I do," he smiles again. But this time it's his affable smile. He has perfect, straight, white teeth.

"Can you account for the following days and hours?" I read him the dates and the times.

"I have no idea. It was long, long ago."

No smile, this time.

"Maybe you ought to try and remember," Clemons chimes in.

"You already know where I was. It was logged in, back then."

"But you had time on your own. You could've gone off on your own."

He eyes me. Still no smile.

"That'd be hard to do without a vehicle. And there's always paperwork with vehicles," he says to us.

"A lieutenant can sign out a Jeep without too much difficulty," Pete says.

"Someone would have seen that Jeep in the vicinity of the killings, no?" Thomas grins again.

If he were an opossum, his back would be raised now.

"Maybe. Most of the Kuwaitis shuttered the places up at night for security. It was a dangerous place at the time."

"Yeah, I remember. I was there too."

"You're fishing.... Isn't that what the NCIS cops would've called what you three are doing now? And there are lots of sport fish in this vicinity.... But I'm not one of them. If you have any other questions, you need to talk to my lawyer."

"I think that'll do for now," I respond. "But I'd appreciate it if you'd let us know of a change of address. I'd hate to have to bother your sister again. Looks like she's going through a bad time of her own."

"You go to her house again and I'll slap a suit and a restraining order on the three of your asses."

"Knock yourself out," Jack tells him.

The three of us rise and leave Carl Thomas's premises.

"I'd like to shoot him, whether he did the girls and their folks or not," Pete admits.

"But you're not a murderer," I remind him.

"I'd like to shoot him in the face," Jack says.

We laugh briefly.

The Captain wants to know the story. We tell them we have no story, but that we like Carl Thomas as a suspect.

"Because you found him unpleasant?" the Captain asks.

"He's too slick," Pete admits.

"He's very oily," Jack adds.

"Not grounds for an arrest," Pearce concludes.

"No, Sir," I agree. "But he's worthy of our interest. He was there when it all went down. They were all accessible in his area of operations. He'd be a poster child for all of our profilers. You'll see his picture next to 'sociopath' in the Webster's."

"Very adroit, Will, but still nothing of weight with which to swing Mister Thomas from the scaffold, no?"

"You're correct, Sir."

"Then dig his shit out from under him. Where it stinks, there's shit. Am I right?"

We grin at the boss, and then we get the hell out of his office.

Philip Brandon has no family. There's no one to contact. We check with the local constabulary in Refuggio, Texas, his hometown. They contact us with the Texas Rangers near Victoria, Texas, and the Rangers say he had left a forwarding address for his government checks. Brandon was wounded, and therefore he has disability checks from the G sent to him monthly. The checks have been sent to an address in St. Louis, Missouri.

We arrive in St. Louis on a wet, muggy August morning. It was a seven hour ride this time. But the good news is that there's no sister to tip Brandon off that we're coming.

His address is for an apartment near The Hill, an Italian neighborhood in St. Louis. It's a lot rougher-looking than Thomas's sister's hood. We get eyeballs from some of the Black and Hispanic teenagers who hang on some of the corners as we drive to the location.

When we arrive, we ring his bell. He lives in the upper of a two-flat. His name is on the bell, so we know which button to push.

No answer after a dozen rings by Jack Clemons.

We ring the lower apartment, and we receive a quick response. A guy in a Dago tee shirt sticks his head out of the door.

"What the fuck is it? I work third shift, goddammit!"

He's fifty, maybe. Balding, pooch stomach… And now a blonde female sticks her head out next to his.

"Joey… Who're dese guys?"

We show our IDs.

"Jeez Chris'," the man utters.

"You know where the upstairs tenant is?"

"Why you wanna know?" the blonde says.

The male shoves her back inside.

"Sorry. She don't trust strangers in this neighborhood."

"You the landlord?" I ask.

"Yeah."

"Let us in his place."

"Got a warrant?"

"Want us to get one and bring the local gendarmes with us? That blonde looks a little underage," Jack says.

"You guys are outta your jurisdiction," he smiles.

"Good. We'll be right back," I warn him.

He huffs out some air.

"Shit, let me get some pants on."

4

Kuwait, Desert Storm

*T*he girl cringes when her picture is snapped. Her parents are dying, bleeding against the living room wall where they were shot. Hasim, her father, looks at the girl from his propped up position with a pleading look on his face. Her mother is already unconscious and she's lapsed into shock. Her feet quiver and shake, and the girl, Kali, knows Marta, her beloved mother, is bleeding out.

Her photograph is taken once more, and the sound of the click makes Kali, the adolescent, scream. She feels the slap just seconds later, and then she hears the snap of the gun pointed at her head.

She dares not look up. She knows what she will see.

Then she hears the roar, and her head flies back against the wall and the force of the gunshot crashes her head into the plaster behind her.

5

His apartment is squared away, military. No debris, no trash, no waste. The bed in the bedroom is made so you could bounce the quarter off the blanket. The pillowcase is white and immaculate and freshly laundered.

A Marine lived here or still dwells here. There are clothes hung in the closet, but not many. Brandon doesn't appear to be extravagant in his apparel. He's downright cheap. Tee shirts you could buy from a mart, tennis shoes, blue jeans—nothing for a night at the Ritz-Carlton.

He has no job that we could find out about. He must be living on his savings from a previous job as a security man in Edwardsville, Illinois, just across the border from here. In the few years he's been back in the States, there haven't been many jobs, and he seems to wander from city to city in about a three hundred mile radius. He doesn't meander too far from the St. Louis area, which he calls home.

"There's nothing here," Pete says.

There is nothing here, nothing incriminating. Brandon and Thomas and Anderson made my list from an initial roster that included thirty-seven possibilities. The thirty-seven were officers who were in the vicinity of the murder of Kali Kazim and her mother and father in Kuwait. The list dwindled to twelve when the second kill occurred. Only a dozen were left in the crime area for both murders, and my list melted to three when I read their psycho profiles.

Of course, I may be all off. The killer might be a non com, but I just think it would be much more difficult for a private or a lance corporal to wander off by himself and then whack families of civilians in Kuwait. He simply wouldn't have the opportunities to go it alone that a higher-ranked personnel would. That's my theory, and as the wiseguys say: *I could be wrong.*

We leave the apartment. Joey, the greaseball landlord, says he has no idea when and if Brandon is returning. He says all he knows is that Philip Brandon hangs at a bar on The Hill known as Pookers.

Pookers is a biker/gay bar. There are women inside as well, and some are with male escorts, so I figure Pookers is a mixed scene. It attracts people from the wild side. And there are apparently all kinds of hitters and switch hitters in the joint. It's dark, lit with red bulbs. There are strobes running across the ceiling. It takes a few minutes for my eyes to adjust. I see Pete and Jack blinking, too.

I approach the bartender on the far left side of bar slab. He's bald; he has multiple piercings in his face and ears. It must be a bitch for the guy when he heads to the airport.

I take out a photo of Philip Brandon. I show him my badge. He's not impressed. He says he knows this guy, but Brandon isn't here at the moment. I tell him we'll take a look for ourselves.

Out of the corner of my eye, I see a figure dashing for the rear exit, back by the johns. Pete has already joined the chase. Jack is right behind me, and the three of us bolt out the back door.

It's early evening, and the light is becoming dim, just before it's fully dark outside. We're racing down an alley in hot pursuit of a male who's got the speed of a sprinter.

We're gaining on him anyway as he bolts around the corner from the alley, and suddenly we're in a small public park.

Just as suddenly we're surrounded by six males, all white, it appears in the dimness. All bald. All displaying the glint of facial piercings. I can't make Brandon in the group. They walk toward us. I see there's no one else in this neighborhood playground that has trees surrounding us on all sides. It's as if the park had suddenly erupted from the earth like some island volcano. We were on a sidewalk, and abruptly we landed in this copse, an island of green in the middle of concrete and blacktop.

I show them ID.

"Can't read," the middle one says.

They're good-sized men. Leather jackets on a sweltering St. Louis evening. No shirts beneath the jackets.

Pete has his Nine unholstered.

"Fuck off," he tells them.

"We got guns too," the same thug replies.

"Reach for it and you're dead," Pete tells him.

Jack and I have our Nines palmed now.

"Nobody has to get shot," I tell the six leathered punks.

"I don't need a fuckin' gun, do you?" the same guy spits at me.

He wants to dance.

"Forget it, Will," Jack says. "I say we shoot the cocksuckers."

They're not laughing anymore.

They take a few steps back.

"That's good with me, sweetheart," I tell the bald, iron-pocked banger.

Now I've done it, and Pete sighs loudly.

"Shit," Pete laments. He knows what's coming.

"Look. We didn't mean nothin'," the mouth says. He's trying a graceful retreat, but for some reason I'm balking at just letting them go.

I hand my piece to Pete.

"You armed?" I ask him.

"Look. I told you...."

"Do you squat when you piss, sweetheart?"

That sends him flying at me. He can't look bad in front of his boys.

He tries to tackle me and bring me to earth, but he succeeds in getting an elbow alongside his temple that flattens him face first in the grass. I'm on top of him before he can scramble away. I flip him over and punch him in the face twice, shattering his nose. I can hear him gurgling, and then I see the blood, and it's black in the dimness of dusk. I slap him three times, and then I rise and find his ribs with the toe of my shoe. I hear an audible crack with the third blow, and then Pete is dragging me off.

"You're under arrest," Jack tells them. He dials his portable phone for the local Mounties, and we wait just under eight minutes for them to arrive.

The St. Louis police are a bit out of joint that we arrested some locals out of our jurisdiction, but when we tell them about the case we're involved with, they become much more cooperative. They allow us to interrogate the six gangbangers, with one of St. Louis's homicide dicks in attendance with us.

One by one, they deny knowing Philip Brandon, until the fifth banger sits down with us. We can see he's frightened, that he was just going along for the ride when we got accosted in the mini park.

"Look. I know Brandon. He came running out of Pookers and found us where we always hang. Then when the three of you run up at us, he keeps going, right out of the park. Johnny is always looking for shit. I don't want no trouble."

This one is younger than the other five. He might not be eighteen.

"What's your name?" I ask him.

"Terry. Terry Larson."

"Why're you with these assholes?" Lt. Mark, the St. Louis cop, asks him.

"Johnny is my older brother. I'm... I'm in college at SLU."

"SLU?" Pete asks.

"St. Louis University," Mark explains.

Mark is sixty, thin, with a full head of white hair.

"Maybe you better go back to campus," the St. Louis detective tells him.

"You know Brandon?"

He looks at me hesitantly.

"Sorta."

"Well?" Jack probes.

He looks at the four of us nervously, as if he wants to bolt the interrogation room.

"We're looking at Brandon for the murder of young girls, here and overseas," I explain.

"I don't know anything about any murders. Shit… I know Philip is strange."

"Strange?" I ask.

He looks at all of us suspiciously once more.

"Yeah, as in weird. I think he's into kiddie porno. Shit like that."

"You've seen this stuff?" Pete Donato queries.

"I've seen some of his mags. Makes you want to puke. I don't like being around him."

"He a friend of your brother's?" I ask.

"You're not going to mess with Johnny any more, are you?"

"No," I smile.

"Because I thought you were gonna kill him."

Lt. Mark shoots me a look.

"He got aggressive. He charged me," I shrug.

Mark smiles his approval.

Johnny isn't nearly as fearful of us. He's talked to lots of cops before.

"You on probation, right?" Mark says.

"Yeah."

"So you're going back," Mark smiles.

"Why? He beat the shit outta me! You oughta be cuffing him. But you won't because he's one of your bros."

"You're looking at aiding and abetting a possible murderer, Johnny."

I look right into his ruined face when I say it.

"Who? Philip?"

"Could be," I answer. "And if you tell us where to find him, I'll drop the charges and ask the Lieutenant here to let you walk."

He watches my eyes to see if I'm lying about letting him avoid the penalty of assaulting a police officer when he's already on pro.

"Philip lives near The Hill."

"We already know that, numb nuts," Pete tells him.

He stares at Pete and Pete returns the glance in this brief pissing match.

"How did you get to know him?" I ask.

He shifts nervously in his chair. His eyes are already black, and he's going to need cosmetic surgery on the beak. He's breathing heavily from the bruised or broken ribs, as well.

"We supplied him with the shit he reads."

"Porno? Kiddie porno?" I ask.

"Am I gonna take a hit for this shit too?"

"Not unless you suddenly go deaf and dumb," Jack warns him.

"Yeah. He has strange tastes. Young girls. You know? He likes them before they bleed on their own, if you know what I'm saying."

"You like little girls too?" Mark demands.

"Fuck, no! I like my stuff legal, and that's no bullshit either. I'm not some teeny-bop faggot, if that's what you're saying. I ain't no pedo-whatever."

"No. You're a solid citizen," Pete smiles.

"Look. That's all I know. He hangs with us because I know where his supplier lives. I'm just the middle man with him, and that's the fuckin' truth, I swear."

"You're going to need a nose job," I smile.

He doesn't smile back at me, this time.

We wait in Brandon's apartment near The Hill for twelve hours. Then we figure he won't be coming home any time soon, so we go back to the stationhouse and see Lt. Mark. He says they'll be happy to look for Philip Brandon, and they'll be happy to call us down to St. Louis if they nab this prick.

We head toward I-55 North, and then we drive the whole long way home.

Brandon has vanished. Thomas remains in his Wisconsin hideout. We still have nothing hard and true on either man, but at least we know Brandon has the taste for adolescent females. The three of us understand it's no guarantee he's a murderer as well. He might just be a voyeur of porno mags. That's a felony when it comes to kiddie porn, but it doesn't nail the bastard who killed all these entire families.

I want to bring Thomas to Chicago for questioning, but I've got to come up with something evidentiary in order to do so. Cops can be sued too, just like private citizens. The burden of proof is on us, of course.

I'm rerunning the scenes from Kuwait and Chicago in my head as I sit at my desk and peer out my window that overlooks the Loop. I'm never bored by the sights I see on the streets beneath my cubicle here. The other side of the building has a prettier vista, Lake Michigan, but I like the buildings that lie outside. I like their size and their design and their vertical strength. A shrink might call it sexual, the vertical, phallic thing, but I just consider it powerful and awesome in appearance. Chicago is no frail sister. It's the "city with big shoulders" that we read about in grade school. I never liked Carl Sandburg, but he got it right about this city.

Kuwait looked nothing like home. The heat of the day could literally wither you. The cold of night could freeze you solid. It was a country of extremes, the way all of the Middle East is, I think.

Philip Brandon and Carl Thomas. Two suspects. But that's all they are right now. And all the time we spent looking for them both might have been wasted effort. We could be looking at the wrong guys—there's always that possibility.

But I'm liking Brandon more all the time.

That's when the call from St. Louis comes ringing through on my desk.

6

They've located Philip Brandon at last. So the three of us pile into the navy, unmarked Ford LTD and we head down south I-55 once more.

Brandon has been arrested for possession of child pornography and is awaiting bail for release. Since he has no family, bail has become prohibitive. He told Lt. Mark that he has a government check coming that would help him get the ten percent that he needs to get himself sprung. The check has still not arrived, however, so we finally get a break on Brandon.

He's a medium-sized blond, about five feet ten and maybe 165 pounds. Hazel- colored eyes that seem to sport a flash of green. He's a very handsome man, the young ladies might say. But his bedside manner sucks. He won't look any of the four of us, including Lt. Mark of the St. Louis PD, in the eyes.

"We were in Kuwait together, several years back," I tell him.

"So I hear," he whispers, almost inaudibly.

"Speak up so the recorder can get all this," Mark instructs him.

He smiles, but his eyes are on the table top, here in the interrogation room. The same room we questioned Johnny and his SLU brother in.

"You remember Kuwait?" Pete asks him.

"Yes."

His eyes stay on the table top.

"You have a whereabouts for any of these three dates?" Jack asks him as he slips him a sheet of paper.

"Got no clue. It was a long time ago."

"You would've remembered these three days," Pete answers. "You were a busy boy on them all."

"I didn't kill anybody."

"Who said you did?" Pete smiles.

Philip has his eyes trained downward.

"You wouldn't lie to us, would you, Lieutenant?" Pete asks.

"I'm not in the Corps any longer. Haven't been since I returned to the world."

And now he looks up at all four of us. He smiles again.

"Two families," I tell him. "And at least one, here in the World. You know anything about it?"

"No. Nothing."

"You ever read *The Scarlet Letter* ?"

"No. Why?"

"I thought everybody read it in high school. But I went to Catholic schools and we figured we were better-read than the other public school kids.... Anyway, a preacher named Dimmesdale knocks up Hester Prynne, a married babe, and then she takes the weight—no one knows *he's your daddy*, get it? And seven years goes by and Dimmesdale's sprung for the crime of adultery, which in old Boston is a hanging offense, and you can't cop a plea, they string you from the gallows tree.

"After seven years and after skinnying out considerably, Dimmesdale pukes it up on Election Day in front of the whole town. But by then it's too late. He strokes out right there. However, he gets all that shit off his soul.

"Isn't there some shit you'd like to live without, Philip?"

He lowers his eyes from mine. He smiles at the table. I think I see him rolling his eyes upward. He's trying to freak the four of us out.

"Boo!" Pete yells at him. He doesn't flinch.

He keeps staring at the table, smiling, only the whites of his eyes visible.

There will be no confession. We have no evidence. The only time Philip Brandon is facing will be for the child pornography, if he does any time at all.

We get in the blue Ford and we hightail it back to our home base, north on I-55.

Thomas and Brandon are drifting away from my grasp. And Mary is no help. I try to get her to throw some scraps my way from the FBI, but nothing is forthcoming.

We go to movies. We go to dinner. We make very passionate sex together, and then I leave well before dawn.

"Maybe we should stop doing this," I proffer.

"Why? I think we get along."

"I can't believe I'm the one talking about a relationship," I tell Mary.

She sits up in bed and displays her small but well-shaped breasts.

She knows it works.

"We have a relationship. We go out and we sleep together and that's all there is."

"You're the perfect woman. Ask Oprah. So why am I bitching?"

"Exactly. We're not going here anymore, Will. It's too exhausting. You know I have my job. I know you have yours. We both know that cops get divorced at a record percentage, and you further know I'm not going to set me and you up for failure."

"You're so sure we'd be a washout."

"Yes," she declares. "It's the nature of the beast, and the beast is law enforcement…. Look, don't we get along?"

"We get along, yes."

"Don't we have something special when we're together?"

"I want to go to sleep *and* wake up next to you. Is that so unthinkable?"

"How long would the good times roll, Will?"

I don't have an answer.

"You looking for guarantees? Because if you are, they don't run them off the presses," I say.

"How very glib, how droll."

I give it up for the moment.

"We had to let Brandon loose."

"Inevitable," she replies. "No evidence, no bust."

"How very glib, how very droll," I throw back at her.

"We don't have anything on Thomas or Brandon. There. Are you happy?"

"No. I'm not," I tell her.

Then I put my hands behind my head and she gets up and gets dressed and gets ready for work at the Federal Bureau of Investigation in the Loop where I met her almost six months ago.

"When are you going to move out, Will? You don't need to babysit me anymore, you know."

"I know, Dad. I like it here. I don't like living alone."

I'm loading the dishwasher from dinner. There are only two plates, not enough for a load. I'll turn the thing on at breakfast.

"You need to be on your own."

"You kicking me out?" I smile.

He laughs.

"Never happen. You stay as long as you like. I just don't want you to think…"

"I know, Dad. You're fully recovered. I know."

"This case still bothering you?"

"Yeah."

"Thought so…. I know you don't like to bring work home. I didn't like to do it to your mother, either."

"I can talk. But there's nothing new. The two guys I like for the killings are home free. We had nothing on them—or anyone else—back in Kuwait, and we've got even less on them here in Chicago. Whoever's doing these kids is smarter than I am, it looks like."

"Bullshit."

"You really think so?"

He laughs again. That's two more laughs than I heard out of him since before my mother succumbed to Alzheimer's, a few years ago. He used to laugh all the time, back in the day.

"I know how smart you are. I raised you and Sammy. Your mother didn't birth any stupid sons."

"I'm glad you think so, anyway."

"Stop whining. It isn't like you."

Now I have to laugh.

"That's better," he says.

"We need to look at Thomas again to show him we haven't forgotten him. I think I'm about to get transferred back to a ship," Pete tells me.

"They giving up?"

"They never give up and you know it. But they'll have me doing other cases. You know how it goes at NCIS."

We're sitting in my cubicle in homicide. I'm looking at my favorite sight, the buildings and the panorama outside our building here in the Loop.

"Let's take a drive to Wisconsin again."

I agree. We go find Jack in fingerprints, and then we head toward the blue LTD and the north country.

Seven hours later, it's 1:00 P.M. and we've arrived outside Thomas's cabin, the one he's borrowing from his late grandfather. His Yamaha is parked outside.

After a half hour, he comes loping out the front door and waves at us. So we follow him out to the highway. He rides the bike into Walworth, a small town five miles up the road.

He gets off the motorcycle and he goes into a small convenience store. Five minutes later, he comes out with a plastic sack of what appears to be groceries.

This time he doesn't wave to us. He just mouths one word:
"Harassment."

We stay the day and return to Chicago seven hours later, at 4:00 A.M. the next morning. Pete and Jack both hang it up and head home. I head for Mary's.

"Where've you been? It's six…"

"Wisconsin."

"What were you…. You were shadowing Thomas?"

"Yes."

"To what end, Will? Jesus."

"I guess I'll go home."

"Grow up."

"Am I behaving badly?"

"You're beginning to obsess on a perpetrator."

"That's a bad thing to do."

"It is. Stop being a wiseass…. I have to be at work at 11:00 a.m. We've got some time to spend, but I'm not going to hear you bitch about how impossible these murders are. All murders are impossible, until you solve them."

She smiles. I can't help but kiss her. I can't help but love her, even if she has no such feeling for me.

"You'll catch him," she says after I roll off to her left. The sheets are almost as sweaty as we are. It's late August, and she does have air conditioning in her apartment. The problem is that she sets the thermostat at 78 degrees. I'm far too hot-blooded for the setting.

"You'll catch him," she repeats.

"You really think so?"

"If you don't, we will," she grins.

"So," Captain Pearce begins. "It's dead end again."

"At the moment," I tell him. Jack sits quietly. Pete has his orders to return to North Carolina where he'll board a ship for parts unknown.

"We don't call it a cold case, even though it's been more than three years, back to the Middle East. If they really are connected to our newest murders, here in the city. I want you to go at it like it's isolated, like it isn't connected to your other two homicides in Kuwait. Try a different angle, even if it isn't true. Maybe it'll give you a different perspective on the case. Critters that don't adapt die."

"He did the two over there and the one here, Captain."

"Could very well be," he tells me. "Just give it a shot, okay?"

"It doesn't appear we have anything to lose," I reply.

We canvass the Milan neighborhood once again. We come on a little stronger at the neighbors this time. Florence Jankowski, two doors down from the Milans, now remembers she saw a motorcycle come down the street about 12:30 a.m., the morning the crime was committed.

Mrs. Jankowski is about eighty, but her wits seem sharp.

"I remember it because my cat Lilly was in heat and I went out to the living room to shut her up.... I looked out the blinds and I saw a motorcycle pulling up to the curb down by those poor people's house. The Milans."

"Right," I tell her.

"I noticed the motorcycle because it came up so quietly. Usually they make all kind of noise, but it was like he was being quiet on purpose. Like he didn't want to disturb anybody."

"Did you see a license number?" Jack asks.

"With these eighty-year-old eyes? You're joking," the old girl grins.

"Any idea of the make, the brand of bike?"

"Do I look like a biker chick to you, son?"

7

Carl Thomas goes off the screen. The cops in Walworth County in Wisconsin have been shadowing him in cooperation with the FBI and us in Homicide, but they lost sight of him eighteen hours ago, and there's no one occupying his grandfather's cabin at present.

Mary tells me about the disappearance without my asking.

"I can't believe you're offering intelligence to a lowly Chicago cop."

"Don't grovel. This is just cooperation, the way my boss told us it was."

"You can't be softening to me, can you?"

"I've already compromised myself by sleeping with you. I shouldn't be involved with any law enforcement people."

"But you're *involved?*"

"In a manner of speaking, Will. Don't make more of it than it is."

"Oh, you can count on that, Special Agent Janecko. I won't make anything of it at all."

She rolls over and shows me her tits. The blinds are closed, and the sunlight is blunted from making an appearance in her small studio on the near North Side, here near Clark Street. She lives among the whacked out and the spaced out and the very far-out denizens of Chicago.

"You want to ruin all this by giving me a ring and proposing?"

"Some women might think it was an honor for the asking."

"You really want to blow this right out of the lake water."

"I love you, but I know you don't love me back. It's called…"

"Unrequited love. Jesus, Will, you'll move me to tears."

"I love it when you're sincere."

She kisses me and smiles.

"Give me time. Maybe I'll soften. No promises.... But you'd better not."

"Better not what?"

"Soften, dummy. What do you suppose?"

We take another excursion north, Jack and I. Pete is headed back to North Carolina and parts unknown.

We search Thomas's cabin illegally. We didn't check in with the local constabulary. They could arrest us for breaking and entering, but, sometimes, extreme circumstances... And so on.

"I'm stealing his laptop," Jack tells me.

"For what?"

"I know a private hacker."

"He's probably got everything encoded. He's not stupid."

"He left the laptop, Will. That was stupid."

"It means he's probably coming back. We could get in some serious shit over that laptop."

I'm smiling at him as he unplugs it from the wall.

Jack's hacker friend is Cyril Finnegan. He's a North Side booster and a computer geek and hacker deluxe. He remains at large because he helps us all the time, but he knows he's in the shit if he gets caught. He knows we won't help him if he gets caught in the commission of a heist or a hack. Other than that, our burglary people have been turning the blind eye when they can.

Cyril is a short, heavy, mid-forties man. He has wispy gray hair that barely covers his pate in what was used to be called a hyacinth bang.

"This shit is a challenge. He isn't using common passwords, like birth dates. This prick must have something to hide, boys," Cyril tells us.

He lives alone in the top apartment of a three-flat with his empty aquarium. He told Jack he always kills his fishes. He's divorced, with two small children and a large dose of child support which he rarely pays.

"You have nothing for us, in other words," I tell him.

"Sorry, Will. Sorry, Jack. This one'll take a while, I'm thinking."

"This miserable son of a bitch might be slaughtering little girls and their families, Cyril," I explain.

"I'll go as fast as I can. But you know I can't make any guarantees, anyway.... Why can't you take this laptop to your FBI buddies?"

He knows we're not friendly with the Feds, but it's a fair question.

"Because the fucker is as hot as your Aunt Fanny's pussy," Jack tells him.

"I don't have an Aunt Fanny, but I get it," Cyril smiles.

The calls come in to Captain Pearce the day after we deliver the laptop to Cyril. There have been murders similar to ours in California, in a place called Auburn in northern California, and in Wilmington, Vermont. A thirteen-year-old female was killed with a brother, seven, and their mother and father. The female was shot in the eye, but the other orb remained intact. The parents and brother were shot and then strangled with barbed wire. No prints. No fibres. No semen in the sexually-assaulted girl. The above happened in Auburn, California.

The other girl, fourteen, was shot in the eye also, but this time the other eye was scooped out and stuck in her mouth. Someone snapped the mother's and father's necks after shooting them both. There were no siblings involved in Vermont. The FBI has sent us this information because of the similarities in MO, of course.

Now we know the new cases were not Thomas and Brandon. We have confirmed sightings of both men in Wisconsin and St. Louis on the dates of the recent homicides on either coast, which occurred two weeks ago. They couldn't have been that far away that fast, not even via jet. The timelines just don't work for either of the two.

"Maybe it's just coincidence," Jack points out as we sit in my cubicle in Homicide.

"You don't believe that any more than I do."

"Then how did they fly around and do all that damage—either one of them?"

"Maybe they had help," I say.

"You think it's a gang?" Jack smiles.

I'm not smiling.

"That's rather out there, isn't it, partner?" Clemons tells me.

"Yes, it is. You have a better idea?"

"Dumb coincidence."

I'm still spinning my wheels on the shots to the eyes, to the blinding of the vics.

"You ever seen the play or the movie, *Equus?*" I ask Jack.

"No."

"It's about a kid who blinds horses. It's fairly kinky."

"I don't think I want to see it, either."

"It's not one of those flicks you go back twice. It ain't *Casablanca,*" I smile.

"Why'd he blind the horses?"

"I don't exactly remember, Jack. But I know a guy at Northwestern who might understand it."

"These aren't horses he's blinding, Will."

"Maybe it's about the blinding, though."

"You said you pursued that with a Navy shrink," he says.

"I don't think he liked me. I don't think the doc was all that cooperative, especially to an NCIS investigator. He got thrown out of the

Navy for incompetence, which leads me to believe his assessment might be somewhat faulty."

"Why didn't you try another shrink?" Jack asks me.

"I was on my way out of the Corps and the job when it went down. Never had the chance."

"Why didn't you try a local headshrinker?"

"I wanted to catch this prick the old-fashioned way. I guess I'm just stubborn. My bad, Jack."

Dr. Kurt McGowan teaches Comparative European Literature at Northwestern University in Evanston, Illinois. He's a sometime actor as well and so is very conversant with theatre. He knows the play *Equus* quite well, he tells Jack and me in his office on campus. Northwestern is the picture postcard of a college campus. It lies near Lake Michigan in a dreamlike, wooded, wealthy neighborhood.

"He blinds the animals, some say, to shelter them from the cruelties of this world. 'See no evil,' get it?" McGowan smiles. "Who knows? Maybe the young man in the play is just an evil son of a bitch."

McGowan looks like an actor. Hollywood good looks. He's in his early forties, tall, about six three, and he reminds me of a leading man type....

"He might be exploiting their innocence. That's a more standard interpretation," he tells us. "Like most heavy theatre, it's got endless possibilities. You can pick one, really."

I tell him about the MO in our cases.

"Sounds to me, if you want my amateur opinion, like this guy is blinding them from the horrors of this world—Isn't that Pacino's speech in one of the *Godfather* flicks?"

"You got me hangin', Doc.... But it sounds like a possibility. He does the blinding thing on all of them. This is confidential information, so I know you'll be discreet."

He smiles at me. I've used his expertise a few times previous. He can keep his mouth shut, and he never talks to the press about our conversations.

"Have you talked to a licensed therapist?"

"I'm going to, Kurt," I tell him.

"I like my theory about blinding the girls to the evil of the world."

"Even though he does the worst evil *to* them?" Jack asks.

"You are dealing with a nut, right?"

Jack laughs at his bluntness.

"You might characterize him thus, yes," Clemons smiles.

"Rational people don't rape and murder children or adults. But he's rationalizing his evil deeds when he takes their sight away, even if it is mostly a symbolic gesture, seeing that he's killing them with the gunshots," McGowan says. "It's almost like *Oedipus*. The Greek rips out his own eyes so he can no longer view the unthinkable ugliness of his life. He has committed incest and he's murdered his own father.... Maybe this new guy has mommy/daddy issues."

McGowan stands to let us know he's got to go teach his summer-school class. I thank him for his time, and we leave.

We visit the staff psychiatrist, Dr. Evelyn Cramer. She's tall and blonde and has twenty years on us both, but I know we both consider her very attractive. She's not wearing a wedding ring, either.

But she's all professionalism. She doesn't give either of us any encouragement. I know it's just the sexist in me, but I can't help feeling drawn to her.

"I like McGowan's assessment," she says. Her face is dead-pan serious.

"I talk to him about profile issues from time to time. I took a course from him at Northwestern a few summers ago."

"You're in school?"

"Trying to get a Master's in American Literature," I explain. I should probably tell her that I'm mad about poetry. For some reason I want to impress this brainy babe of a shrink.

"Well, I think he might be right about this perp's longing to shield these female adolescents from the terrors of this life. He never considers the harm he's doing, himself. Perhaps he thinks he's guiding them to an afterlife of oblivion. Of dreamless sleep, without sight or consciousness. It's a bit of a leap, but this perpetrator seems to enjoy extremes. He doesn't just execute his victims. He includes a sort of ritual. That's why he maims them and then displays the family members' bodies with the hangings or the strangulations."

I'm staring at her legs. They're long and shapely. Like the rest of her. Then I feel the shiver up my backbone as her words finally sink into me.

"Ritual?" I ask.

I turn to Jack, but I think he's eyeing her chest.

"Gentlemen? Was there anything else? You know where I am if you need me. I'm available, since we all work for the same people."

She grins at us as if we're both young canines in the grips of doggie days.

"Ritual?" Jack asks as we sit at lunch at this North Side White Castle. He's ordered a half-dozen of these miniature "sliders," and I've ordered four. We both asked for Diet Cokes with the greasy hamburgers, the ultimate hypocrisy or irony, take your pick.

"I always thought the manner of the killing was important. I always knew that we'd have to pursue it, but I'm just as old school as you are, Jack. You place them at the scene, you nail them with hard evidence, and then no one gives a fuck *why*, except for the good looking MDs on the fourth floor, like our blonde goddess."

"I hear you. Motive is nice, but hard evidence is tastier."

"Your theory about a gang is bothering me," I tell my partner.

"Geographically, it's too farfetched."

"Not with modern communications."

"Meaning?" Jack asks.

"They're in touch. Pedophiles have chat rooms. They communicate frequently. Why not killer pedophiles?"

Jack watches a curvy waitress pass by. He has ketchup on his fingertips, and then he licks them clean.

"Most pedophiles want the sex, not the murder."

I nod and notice the two tiny mustard stains on my tie. I pick up the tie and study the stains. It's a new tie, dammit.

"True. But killing them guarantees their privacy, their remaining anonymous."

"She said, like McGowan, this guy—these guys—are extreme."

"It's getting more unpleasant, Jack. It's getting uglier every moment."

The curvy waitress walks by again. She has a copper streak in her hair. Jack licks his fingertips again. I'm thinking I need stain remover on my new fucking tie.

"Butt-uglier," he concurs.

8

I show the little love note to Jack.

"Why am I seeing this only now?"

"I apologize. I wanted to bear the burden alone, I guess."

"We're a dynamic duo, remember?"

He purses his lips as if he's suddenly disappointed with me. His eyes shift away from me, as if he's been insulted by my not trusting him.

"I recall. As I said, my fault. Won't happen again.... I ran it by Mary."

Jack knows about my love life, sort of.

"And?"

"Dead end. You knew it would be."

"Clever little prick, he is."

"Yes, indeed."

"Unless he and his buddy are in it together. Thomas and Brandon, another dynamic pair."

"It was on my mind, yes."

"How'd they pair up?"

"How does anyone pair up today, Jack?"

"The Internet, my dear Watson."

"Yep. Just like a lonely hearts club. Still no word from Cyril."

"I know. He says the standard codes are as fruitless as the tracking of that love note you received from one or both of them."

"These two are bright boys. It says so in their jackets. Both college graduates, both cum laude or higher. Both top ten in their high school classes. I'm amazed they joined the Corps instead of working the material, real world. Why the Crotch for those two?"

"License to kill. But I wish I knew why they've gone crazy, back in the world, here in the States."

Jack has no glimmer of humor on his handsome face. He's almost glum, somber.

"The Corps does teach you how to kill with great prejudice, yes."

"But, Will, you're supposed to kill enemies of the Republic, not little girls and their whole clans. There's the rub. Can't blame the green fighting machine for its aberrations. Every outfit has them. The Seals join the Navy to blow shit up. They say it just like that when they're asked. Can't keep the loons away from ordnance."

He stands up and looks out my window. He's glaring at the buildings in the Loop, rather than sending lasers at me. He holds his temper remarkably. It's his calm that disturbs me more than some kind of blow-up.

"I suppose you're right, but it doesn't make it any easier to swallow."

"What did Mary say, exactly, about the note from Laughing Boy?"

His cheeks turn bright red from the pent-up anger. But he doesn't let his voice betray what I know is welling up inside him. He paces from the desk to the window twice, and then he stops and faces me. I can see the skyscrapers through the window behind him.

"She said it was untraceable. Standard stock copy paper you could buy at any big outlet or department store. Newsprint from the *Chicago Tribune*. And guess how many copies of that paper come out every day?"

"So she has no wisdom to share with us?"

"Only that this guy is taunting me."

I feel the heat rising from my own cheeks. I should have answers for him, but I'm letting him down.

He paces back and forth between my desk and the window. I'm wondering if he'll turn around and leap at me like some pissed-off panther. The muscles in his cheeks have tautened to a near-explosion. I feel myself become rigid.

Then Jack suddenly loosens, and I feel my own tendons relax, slowly.

"He's taunting *us*, now, partner.... Were you a loner like this when you worked with Pete?"

"I don't think so."

I feel the tension in the room diminishing. He's got that affable, good-guy look on his face, at the moment. The face he shows to his lady friends, just when the moment has arrived. He's got me, and he fucking well knows it.

"That makes me feel all better, Detective Koehn."

This time he smiles when he says it, podna.

9

Kuwait, Desert Storm

The sky appears yellow, almost golden. The heat makes approaching figures seem almost horizontal instead of vertical. Ironically, the nights are brutally cold.

Neither of us is sickened by the appearance of the second set of corpses. We have seen too many bodies before, in the sparse days of Desert Storm. It was a war like no other. It was almost embarrassing. No one would count coup in this engagement. It was more like the proverbial ducks in a barrel. The kills came too easily. The Vietnam Vets found no honor in the conflict, other than doing their duty, as always. Semper Fi, motherfucker. That issue never changes. You go where they send you, and you kill the enemy.

It used to be my mentality too, until I joined NCIS after my hitch in the Marines was over. Then I went to plain clothes, once my training was done. Plain clothes is the attire for Pete and me as we fight the stench of death. A great many vets have written that you can get used to the sight of death, but you never get used to the *smell* of mortifying human flesh.

I suppose we should be moved at the sight of dead civilians, especially at the vision of the deceased young female, but we have been hardened to killing by the previous days we when observed the roadside carnage on convoys into Iraq and Kuwait City. It wasn't our chance to do any rifle time. The convoys were our only chances to get into the shit because both of us were too young for Vietnam, and there was no conflict on the horizon when we originally signed on with the Crotch, a couple years before then.

I look at the slaughter as if I were walking into a butcher shop. It's the way we were trained at NCIS. These are cases, not people. We cannot become emotionally entangled or involved. It would detract from our professional detachment, we were taught.

And it does make sense. If you're caught up in the gore and mayhem, you can hardly do the job properly. Civilians sometimes just do not fathom that we're not the Boy Scouts or the Red Cross. We don't fill up sandbags for flooded river rats every spring, and we don't go on camping trips to Michigan. In the Corps, we were trained to kill human beings, and now we're trained to find killers and to send them on their ways to hell.

I feel a twinge when I look at the ruined face of this adolescent girl. The gunshot from the .45 has blown away the back of her head. Skull fragments are scattered as if they were flung, all over the living room floor. There are blood stains on the walls and on the floors. There are even spatters on the ceilings.

Then there are the hanged family members. The father's face is swollen and dark purple. The mother's tongue is protruding hideously— it is purple and horribly swollen. And her eyes bulge almost out of her sockets.

Then I lose some of my detached air when I see the little boy's face. The color of his face is almost black, but his natural hue would've been light brown. It's that black death mask that makes my eyes sting. I'm becoming very angry, suddenly. I want instant closure on these cases. I want to see the murderer swing from the gallows. I want to see him before a line of executioners with rifles aimed at his head. I want to see him gasping in a gas chamber or fried by electrocution.

Punishment is not our task, of course, but I want to see him die multiple deaths in spite of all that Navy training for homicide investigations.

I have to go outside, into the dawn of the new morning in this fashionable neighborhood in Kuwait City. This is where some of the oil executives call home. They send their children to English-speaking schools. Their kids go to the States and matriculate at Harvard and Yale and Princeton and MIT and Cal Tech—all the best colleges, places Pete and I could never afford.

I don't begrudge them their money. I have no love for oil people or their offspring, but this goes beyond my preference for people. These murders were deserved by no one, no matter what their fathers do for a living. No one deserves to die the way these Kuwaitis did. No human creature needs to suffer as they did.

So I put an American face on each of the vics, and it gives me a better perspective on how to do my job. I know I'm not supposed to differentiate one dead body from another, and that way I will use my reason better. I will accomplish this task more efficiently if I do not assign individual personalities to the bodies laid out and hanged before me.

We saw other bodies on the roads. We saw the oil fires billowing from the derricks. We saw dead men and women scattered like ragdolls inside and outside their blown and burned vehicles. SUVs. Mercedes. Lexus. All the brands were in front of our eyes. All that money couldn't save some of them because we got there too late. No, it wasn't our fault that we couldn't arrive in time. But it didn't relieve the disgust and the horror of what we saw on those roads.

It gave some of us the *conceptual materiel* to meet and destroy the enemy, the Iraqis, Saddam Hussein and his personal crew. But it was a short war, as I said. That was the good news. We got it over quickly.

The bad news is the mess some of us made in our triumph. Yes, there are always messes in combat, but there is no explanation for these murders, other than one:

This, what we beheld on the crime scenes, was *evil*. I was not a practicing Catholic. I had been baptized a Catholic, but I did not attend very often, and now I didn't think I could ever stomach a Sunday in the pews. I didn't think I could father any children. Not with the carnage I'd been witness to. I couldn't expose an innocent to this kind of vileness.

When I was in grade school and high school, I think I was a typical adolescent and teenager. I played games, I dated girls when I passed puberty, and I went to classes. No one ever prepared me for this job. Not my regular teachers, not my NCIS instructors. Nobody explained the gut-wrenching nausea that holds you when you enter a killing zone like the one Pete and I were in the middle of.

It's the way it is in homicides. Yes, the stink of death is something you can never get used to. The conventional wisdom is accurate. But the sight of death gives you the willies, the nightmares, the night sweats. It's the picture show that remains with you forever. The frame-by-frame re-enactments stay with you for long after the bodies are bagged and tagged.

Col. Patrick Casy is our commander, our commandant. He's ex-Marine also, so he has empathy for us, for Pete and me, I think. He isn't the usual gruff prick you run into at headquarters. Our headquarters are aboard *The Intrepid*. When we have to see the boss, we have to meet him aboard that vessel. The intelligence area is aboard our ship. We travel to other places, but Kuwait is our current jurisdiction.

"You have suspects?"

He already knows I have a list that includes lieutenants and above, but he's not convinced our perp is an officer and a gentleman.

"Same as before, Sir," I tell him, after the salute.

"Cut the shit. We're all civilians here," he jokes.

"Yes.... Yes, Colonel," I grin. Pete is grinning also because we both like our boss.

"I am receiving the usual flow of shit from the top on this, as you might imagine," Casy informs us.

"I hear you, Colonel," Pete says, straight-faced.

"It's not our fault, but it is our problem, gentlemen."

There's no good humor on his face now.

"I understand, Colonel Casy. We're doing everything we can, but this guy is cute. He leaves nothing behind. Nothing but bodies."

"It is very bad public relations to murder and rape indigenous personnel, especially since we have come to liberate these motherfuckers."

Pete can't help but guffaw, but he sees Casy's genuine anger, and he makes himself cease.

"This is no joke, boys."

"I'm sorry, Boss. It's just the way you…. express yourself."

"Roger that. Excuse my levity, because there ain't anything humorous about this cocksucker and what he's up to. I'd like to scope him and smoke him myself. So you have to do the honors for me."

"That's an affirmative, Sir."

"Get your asses off this ship and corral this rat-fucking, mule-molesting son- of-a-fried-bean son-of-a-bitch."

We salute in spite of his informality, and then we disembark from *The Intrepid*.

I want to interview Carl Thomas and Philip Brandon and three other suspects, but they are deployed in a combat zone, so they are currently unavailable. I'm stuck on the notion that an officer has committed these atrocities because I know they have a greater length of leash to prowl about on, compared to lower ranked staff. Privates are more accountable for their every movement, but loftier staff can easily thwart SOP, standard operating procedure, and they can disappear from time to time.

I'm living in a barracks in Kuwait City. Pete and I share quarters with six other NCIS investigators when we're away from the ship. No one is home tonight as I head toward my bunk. I strip and flop in my bunk. I fall off into sleep immediately or almost immediately.

I'm awakened by a burning odor. I fling myself into a seated position on my rack, and then I hurl myself off, onto the floor.

I see the smoke—it's red, even in the dim light in our quarters here in the barracks that used to house combat Marines.

Smoke. It's a smoke grenade.

Someone approached me while I was asleep and set off a smoke grenade beneath my rack. I feel the tingle down to my sphincter.

Smoke. Just harmless smoke.

But it could've been a live fragmentary grenade. It could've been the real deal.

I almost want to piss myself, so I run into the head and relieve my bladder before I embarrass myself, even though there's no one here to see the stain on my boxer shorts.

Smoke. Fucking smoke. And he crept up close to me. Could have killed me in my sleep. He stealthed his way into an empty quarters—empty except for me—and he placed this grenade under my cot. The slimy piece of shit.

I feel like a rape victim. This prick molested me. I never even felt his presence. He's like the smoke of the bomb he put under my bunk. He's a ghost, he's vapor, he's fog.

Now he knows my name, he knows where I live, so he has to be in uniform to get past security outside.

I run down and talk to the guard in front of the barracks' entrance. I'm in my skivvies and nothing else. The young Marine flashes me a grin.

"Can I help you, Sir?" he salutes, even though he knows I'm plain clothes and an NCIS dick.

"Did anyone come through here in the last hour or so?"

"Just you, Sir.... Been quiet as a morgue," he grins.

10

Thomas was WIA, wounded in action, and therefore has a disability check coming in every month. We checked the mailman in Walworth for a forwarding address, but he didn't have one before we left Wisconsin.

It's very late summer when we get the call from the postmaster in Walworth, informing us that Carl Thomas has a new address, and it's a PO box in Chicago. We track the PO box down, and it's in a postal station on the near north side, not far from where Mary's apartment is. We have to stake out the box in eight hour shifts. The Captain figures that Thomas's flight constitutes probable cause to bring the ex-Marine lieutenant in for interrogation. We don't have anything to hold him on, but we can delay him with us for a while, at least.

We take the night shift. I ask for it because I don't think Thomas will want to venture out and about in the daylight. He's like one of those legendary vampires—he's a creature of the night. Night was when he did the girls and their families, with or without Philip Brandon, whom we are now also trying to trace.

It's a pretty downtrodden hood where his PO box is located. Lots of street dudes and dudettes. They come in various colors and nationalities; there is no preponderance of race or ethnic background here, on Clark Street, not far from Wrigleyville.

It's 9:40 p.m. We've been here since 8:00. We weren't supposed to come on duty until midnight, but Jack called and suggested we get dinner and then go on shift. We went to a McDonald's and came directly here after only forty-five minutes. Both of us seem to think Carl is going to come for his check. According to the Feds we called, it was sent six days ago. We called his bank in Walworth, and the check has not been cashed yet. He may not yet have endorsed it or picked it up. We'll just have to wait, at least a few days. If he's coming, I figure he'll come soon. He's not wealthy, and he has to eat, even if he is a creature of the night.

I've continually wondered why two bright sociopaths have turned out to be as worthless as they are. Maybe they're easily bored. Perhaps killing is the only thing that keeps them entertained. Intelligence is not always directed at productive endeavors. The smart ones are also the hardest to catch.

We listen to classic rock, some station that Jack picks out.

"You seeing anyone?" I ask him.

There is a lobby in front of the postal station. Post office boxes are available to walk-in traffic twenty-four/seven/365. All he has to do is walk right in.

"No. I assume you're still with the queen of the Feds," he smiles.

"More or less."

"Still keeping it casual?"

"Her idea, Jack."

"That's a flipside, no?"

"It ain't my idea."

A good-looking blonde, leggy and tall, walks into the PO. She walks toward a box—we can see her through the glass door because the inside is well-lit, to control the strong-arms and the muggers.

"What's the box number?" Jack asks.

"Twelve twelve," I reply.

"She seems to be in that vicinity, does she not?"

The box Thomas has is on the left side, near where the blonde is standing and fiddling with the lock.

"Let's go check her out."

"My pleasure," my partner says.

We get out of the navy blue LTD and walk across a streetlighted Clark Street. Traffic on the sidewalk right now is nonexistent.

I open the door and immediately flash my badge at the attractive, lanky blonde. She's wearing a halter top to maximum effect. She's generously endowed.

"What? What'd I do?"

My heart sinks a bit as I see she's still got the key in 1213, one box off.

"We thought you might be having difficulty," Jack smiles.

Then she relaxes.

"I didn't know cops helped ladies in distress at the post office," she flirts to Jack.

"We do all kinds of things you may not know about. 'To protect and serve.' It's on all the cars."

Jack notices I'm staring at him. But I walk out the door, leaving her with him inside. I walk back to the car and get in on the driver's side. Within a few minutes, my partner returns.

"Got her number, bro."

"Congratulations, Jack."

"I got her box open—no pun intended."

I have to laugh at him, and then we settle back for the long eight-hour shift to unfold.

Thomas never shows. Jack tells me he's calling the blonde tonight since we're off shift. It's our day off. We have to watch overtime, since Pearce is very strict about the abuse of it.

Mary is working late, on the next hot August night. There's nothing on TV, and my Dad has turned in early at 9:30 p.m. So I get in my Cavalier and drive over to Clark Street from our northwest side house.

McAdams and Corley are on duty, but I get out of the Cavalier and tell them to take a few hours' dinner break. There's no sense all of us watching for this asshole.

It's a half-hour later, 10:42 p.m., when the bike pulls up to the curb. It's Thomas. I call in for backup, but I see he's in a hurry, so as soon as I make the call for reinforcements, I'm out of the car and crossing Clark Street.

He's already on the way back out. He spots me, runs to the bike when I'm fifteen yards from him, and then he tears away from the curb as I reach out to haul him off the bike. I've missed him literally by inches.

I race back across the street and I jump in my Cavalier. I call his direction in with my portable phone. Then I take off after him down Clark Street. I see him stopped at a light just a block in front of me. When it turns green, he squeals his tires and turns left, and he's almost horizontal to the ground on his Yamaha.

My Chevy is no match for his motorcycle. If squads don't cut him off, I've lost him again.

But as he speeds toward the next big intersection, a red light stops him again. Of course I'm wondering why the hell he's stopped at a red light at all, why he hasn't flown through all the lights.

Then two squads have him pinned and halted at the next major intersection.

I arrive and jump out of my black Cavalier.

When he's turned around, hands handcuffed, I see it's all been a game. It's not Thomas. I look at the bike again. It's identical. It even has the same plates.

"What can I do for you officers?" the smiling biker says.

He looks like Thomas too, even close up. Same height, same color hair, same build.

"You have ID?" I ask. The two uniforms stand by their two squads, now, away from us.

"In my back pocket, Officer."

He's still smiling and I want to send his teeth into his stomach.

I take the wallet out of his jeans. It has a license that reads "Adam Johansen."

"You serve in the Corps?" I ask him.

"No. Never did. High blood pressure. Four F, you know?"

When we question him in the station, we find out nothing. He denies knowing Carl Thomas. But he has the paperwork showing that he legally owns the Yamaha that Carl rode first.

"Where's Carl?" I ask.

Jack is here now with me. I called him on the way to the Loop.

"I have no clue," he smiles.

"You lie once more, and I'll make you hurt but I won't leave any bruises," Jack warns him.

"I bought the bike from him two days ago. He comes up to me in a bar. He's starin' at me like I'm a long lost fucking brother of his. He says we could be fuckin' twins, we look so much alike. He tells me what a stroke of fuckin' luck it is, runnin' into me. I don't know this guy from dick, you know. But he keeps starin' at me like I'm some kind of fuckin' miracle or something, like it's his lucky fuckin' day. He's won the lottery. He says, 'You wanna have a real hoot, a real howl? I want to pull a prank on some friends of mine. Just drive your bike past the P.O., and watch what happens, next. You'll laugh your ass off.' And I'm fried enough to do it. So here the fuck we are, huh?"

We send fliers out to every bank and check cashing service within a twenty-five mile radius. We're betting he's here in the city.

We arrested wise guy Adam Johansen for obstruction of justice, and we impound the Yamaha as evidence in a homicide case. It's all bogus, and his lawyer will likely spring Johansen within twenty-four. I don't give a shit. I wanted to inconvenience him for messing with us, and this is my little gesture.

We'll have to hope someone eyeballs the real Carl Thomas, or that he'll take that check into a bank or a check cashing service. I'm inclined to think he's too sly to get caught. We couldn't catch him in

Kuwait; we may not catch him here. The sad truth is that sometimes these monsters get away with it. We're all familiar with the Zodiac killer, out on the West Coast. Sometimes they're too bright to get nabbed, and other times it's just dumb luck. We work under the law of statistics— most maniacs get jailed and smoked.

Mary is amused by the story of my false pursuit on Clark Street.

"I like the intelligent ones. I like the challenge."

"Yeah. He challenges us, so it means he isn't done partying."

Her grin vanishes.

"Likely you're right, Will. I'm sorry."

"It's all right. I understand what you meant. And he won't be able to meander about as easily as he did in Kuwait, or with his first job here in Chicago. Every cop in northern Illinois is looking out for him. At least we have that advantage."

"He could still strike again."

"Yes. He could."

"But you're correct. Everyone's got the dogs loose. Parents have been warned about keeping an eye on their daughters. It won't be such easy pickings. He'll have to be very careful."

I'm watching her pretty face, here in her bed in her apartment.

"What?"

"I was just thinking."

"What, Will? What were you thinking?"

"How."

"How what?"

"How he selects them. How he gets close to them. I couldn't come up with anything when I was working with Pete. I can't come up with it now. It's very frustrating."

"What did the Kuwait victims have in common?" Mary asks.

"Their age and the fact that they were Kuwaitis."

"Are you cracking wise?"

"It's obvious, yeah, but that's all we could tie to them. They were oil people, both families...."

"And the Chicago family? The Milans?"

"The old man worked for British Petroleum, BP. *Shit* ," I tell her.

"Could be coincidence, Will," she grins evilly.

"How do Carl Thomas and Philip Brandon connect to the oil angle?" Jack wonders aloud. "They have no family, no personal beefs with the petroleum crowd that we know of."

"But oil is the common denominator. It's no coincidence, like Mary joked about."

"No. It ain't no joke. Texas tea is involved somehow."

"Maybe."

"Maybe what, Will?"

"Maybe they're getting even for Desert Storm."

"Pardon me?"

"Maybe they're taking it out on the families of the petroleum barons," I say.

"Then why not hit the big-wigs? Why not hit the Saudis and the White House and the Congress? Why not hit bigger targets if you're making a statement?"

"I don't know. Maybe he's hitting mid-management, the little guys. Maybe he wants to throw a scare into the guys above, first. Who knows what this swinging dick monster has in his feverish little brain. Maybe he doesn't need a motive at all."

"No. You're right, Will. It's a starting point. It's a place to begin."

The check from the G is cashed at a northside check cashing service on Broadway and Jackson. We race toward the location, but the call was made twenty minutes after the cashing, so by the time we arrive, he's long gone.

We start to concentrate on Brandon again. It's the third week in August when Cyril finally calls us.

"I've cracked the motherfucker," Cyril says over the phone. "I own this son of a bitch!"

"The code was simple. I gave him too much credit. It was the same code they used in that movie *A Christmas Story*. Except it was a little refined. He was using letters instead of numbers. I got through on the clusters of vowels and..."

"Save it," I tell him. "It's all way the fuck over my head anyway. Just tell me."

We're in Cyril's apartment because he cannot be seen in the company of cops.

"They're a society-like thing. They have a chat room and they talk about the murders. They like brag about it, man. The dude in Vermont and the ape in California. And your two boys, Thomas and Brandon. They communicate, I'm saying. I checked out this chat room. They talk in that same code. They giggled gleefully, like, talking about tearing out those kids' eyeballs. It made me want to hurl, Will."

"They ever talk about why they're doing this?"

"It's a *strike*."

"A what?" I ask Cyril.

"A strike. They're calling it a fucking strike at the heart of the establishment."

"You mean it's about..."

"Everybody knows what Desert Storm was about, Will. No offense, I know you and that partner of yours, Pete, were both there. But it's about nothing but that black gold under the earth. And that's what it's

67

always about lately. They're striking at evil, they say. Drawing attention to the corruption that goes right up those fucking derricks."

11

We do some calling around on Thomas and Brandon. We talk to some of their college professors and a few of their high school teachers. Neither of them was well-liked by anyone who remembered them—and only a handful of their previous instructors actually recalled either ex-Marine.

What they said, by consensus, was that Thomas and Brandon were both intelligent, both argumentative, and that both of them were loners. What Cyril has given us is that they were picking out targets even before they entered the Corps. They had talked about the relative ease of taking out a family if that family wasn't wealthy enough to have hired security on their property. The Kuwait families were headed by men who were lower management of American oil firms. One worked for Shell in lower mid-management, and the other Middle Easterner worked for Amoco. The American, Mr. Milan, worked for Texaco. None of the four fathers could afford armed guards or electrical security on their grounds. That was Thomas's plan, apparently. Hit the low-level workers first, and then work your way up. It was the modus operandi for numerous series killers—you worked your way up the feeding chain as you got better and better at doing the murders. When you felt accomplished enough, then you'd worry about getting past security guards and electronic fences.

We have of course contacted petroleum products employees in the Chicago area through their employers and management. We've warned them to report any suspicious characters who hover near their homes. We've also told those with adolescent to young teenaged daughters to be especially wary. Jack and I didn't have to do much explaining about the young females because these guys read the papers too.

The FBI nabs a suspect in Vermont. They've taken him into custody, and they're bringing him to Chicago for questioning regarding the murder in Vermont and the killings here in the city. Mary is the bearer of the news. Her boss has allowed her to share the information with the Chicago Police Department, since the local crime is in our jurisdiction. Mary has simply bypassed Captain Pearce and told me to tell him. I told Mary about chain of command, but she simply shrugged it off.

"Consider this my gesture of good faith with you and your department," she smiled.

His name is Gerald Fahey. He's thirty years old, five feet eight, 155 pounds. He is not a veteran of any war. He was 4-F on account of deafness in his left ear, his jacket reads. We are allowed to attend his interrogation at the Loop FBI headquarters. Jack and I are also allowed to ask him questions when Special Agent Ted Delinski finishes his own line of queries.

After thirty-five minutes, it's our turn.

"How'd you meet Carl Thomas and Philip Brandon?" I ask.

He looks up at me and grins.

"You said you were going to cooperate, Gerald. Remember our little conversation about the death penalty? We still have one."

Gerald's face sobers.

"On the Internet. In a chat room."

"I know. We broke your code."

"So why're you asking me, then?"

"Why did you kill the young girl?"

"It had nothing to do with her," he says. "We were striking at the establishment. We were making a *point*."

There is no good humor on his face now. There is sober grimness on his visage.

"We were making a point against the corruption of those who abuse the fossil fuels on this planet. Those who make war for the control of oil."

"So you killed the kid, her two brothers and mother and father to make a point."

He smiles again.

"Gerald," Special Agent Delinski warns.

"But it's all true.... How many Americans died in Desert Storm?"

"Less than four hundred, in combat," Jack tells him.

"You make it sound like an insignificant number," Gerald replies.

"No. I was just answering your question," Clemons smiles back at him.

"And how many Iraqis were slaughtered?" he insists.

"In the neighborhood of a quarter million," Jack says.

"And *we're* murderers?" Gerald goes on.

"Yes. You're murderers. The others were casualties of war," I say.

"So were they."

The "they" means the family he wiped out in the Northeast.

"They were innocents. The girl's father was trying to make a living.... But anyway... You met on the Internet. You talked in chat rooms. So you might know where Carl Thomas and Philip Brandon are currently," I tell him.

"I discussed all that with the Special Agent here. I'll need to have my lawyer present before I discuss it with you."

"Your counselor told you to cooperate, Gerald," Delinski reminds him.

A look of bewilderment passes on this creature's face.

"All right. Okay."

"Death penalty, Gerald," Delinski repeats.

"But you said there were no guarantees," Gerald whines.

"That's correct. But being cooperative might help you at sentencing," the FBI agent explains to him again.

"We talk in code. Carl sent us the code by regular mail so it wouldn't get picked off the Internet.... He told us to always use the system when we talked in the chat rooms....

"I don't know where Carl is, but I think Philip is here in Chicago. I think he's planning on doing another one."

"Do you know who?" I ask.

Gerald shifts his ass in the chair. I smell his stale breath and his oniony underarm body odor. His brows are furrowed and his face looks intent on avoiding my stare. He's looking for real wiggling room.

"All I know is that it involves a middle management woman at Traders Petroleum. She's divorced, with two teenaged daughters. She works in accounting. And that's all Philip said. Carl planned this one. Carl planned all of them. All we did, in Vermont and California, was carry out Carl's scheme. I swear it. He thought everything up. He's the smart one. He kept insisting on how easy it would be, how no one would be looking for an assault on civilians. But he said anyone who takes money from the oil companies is an accomplice to murder all over this globe. And he's right. Think about it, and you'll know he's *right*."

Gerald has a natural leer on his face and a slimy grin to top his visage off. He's the kind of perp you wish you had in the days when rubber hoses were a part of a cop's repertoire. He shifts some more in his seat, and the ripe stink permeates the entire interrogation room. He's making me wish we could take all this outside.

The smile comes back on his lips, and the interview comes to an end.

We go straight to Traders Petroleum in Oak Park as soon as we're done with Gerald. We ask one of the office managers if they know who this woman is—divorced with two grown girls and she works in accounting. The manager, Theresa Mankowski, knows exactly to whom we're referring. Her name is Hannah Menke.

Hannah Menke is an attractive brunette in her middle age— perhaps forty-five. I'm thinking her ex-old man was a knucklehead for leaving her, if he's the one who took off first. I'm having difficulty taking my eyes off her, even though I'm in love with Special Agent Mary Janecko.

"Why are you here?" she wants to know as Jack closes her office door behind us.

"Have you read about the murder of the Milan family in Chicago?" I ask.

"Of course. Everyone...*Oh, my God!*"

Jack rushes over to her and helps her get seated in her plush office chair.

"You're okay," I tell her.

"I have two daughters. You're here because..."

"We have information that you may be a target for the people responsible for the deaths of the Milan family. But we're going to be near you until we catch them."

"Them? There's more than one?"

"We're not certain, but we think so, yes," Jack tells her. He's standing next to her, holding her hand. Only now does her natural color begin to replace the whiteness that covered her pretty face just seconds ago. She has short brown hair. You might call the cut severe, but I think it makes her even more attractive on close inspection.

"We've got people headed to your house right now."

They live, the three of them, in Oakbrook, not far from here. We have two squads looking in on the teenagers. They're at home, we found out. School is still out of session for both.

"No one's going to harm you, Ms. Menke," I tell her. "We're going to protect you for as long as it takes."

"Are you sure they mean to kill me? Us?"

I nod.

"But they're not going to. We know who they are, and they won't get near you. They thought you'd be an easy....target."

"Target? Us? *Why*, for Christ's sake!"

"Because of the company you work for.... It's a long story."

I explain what we've learned from Fahey and the Internet chats.

"That's insane," she says unemotionally.

"Yes, ma'am. It sure is."

"They're going to rape my daughters and murder us all because I work for a gas company."

I look straight into her eyes.

"Sociopaths don't really need excuses. They don't need reasons. If they were reasonable, they wouldn't be killing people."

She stares straight back at me. I can't help but feel the flutter of romantic attraction to this woman who has probably a decade on me.

"I've never had anything like this ever happen to me before.... Even with the divorce, it was nothing like..."

"He's not going to harm you. We'll catch him first. I promise you. And you'll never be alone, not you or your girls. I swear it to you, Ms. Menke."

"My name is Hannah. My girls' names are Bethany and Barbara. Bethany is thirteen and Barbara is eleven. Oh.... my.... God!"

She rises from her desk chair, and then Jack catches her as she pales once more and collapses.

The Menke house is in a fashionable part of Oakbrook. The lawns are large and so are the backyards. The house is perhaps twenty years old, and it's well kept. Brick on three sides with siding on the backside. There is a four foot above-the- ground pool in a fenced-in yard. But there is no security system, no electronic guard dog, and no real pooch either. There are just the three of them: Hannah and Bethany and Barbara.

Barbara, the eleven-year-old, favors her mom. She has short brown locks and her face is a double for Hannah's. She'll be a beauty some day soon. Bethany must resemble her dad. She has golden-blond hair. They're both good-looking, but not alike at all.

Jack and I are inside the house. Two uniform squads are parked a half block away from the premises here in Oakbrook, but the four patrolmen are a very short holler from us.

We stay in the kitchen after the Menke women have their evening dinner. Hannah asked us to dine with them, but we refused politely, saying we'd already eaten.

Which was a lie. We were both hungry, and I was going to suggest calling out for a pizza after the ladies had retired for the night.

There's a small portable color TV in the kitchen where we sit, and we've got some news on at very low volume. When the Menkes go up to their bedrooms on the upper floor of this spacious home, we'll reconvene in the living room. The patrolmen will be covering the area outside by foot, after 10:00 p.m. They'll be relieved, as we will, shortly after dawn.

At ten, Hannah Menke comes into the kitchen and announces they'll be heading off to bed. I smile at her and tell her we've got it under control. I don't think she believes me for a second.

At 3:00 a.m., I'm sitting in the kitchen alone. Jack's in the living room, keeping an eye on the front door. The air conditioning is on because it's late August, and it's hot and muggy.

Brandon would have to unlock an upstairs window for entry, after getting past the four uniforms outside. I wish he would sneak past them. I wish he'd climb through that upstairs window and then come downstairs here in the kitchen and catch sight of my nine millimeter in his face. I wish he'd try to escape so I could put six slugs in his back and then save Cook County some millions of dollars in trial fees.

But I know I just arrest them; I don't execute them.

The night passes uneventfully, and I don't think Brandon's coming. He's probably sniffed us out. Gerald didn't have the chance to tip him off to the fact that we know he's coming, so we should have surprise on our side. But his partner Carl seems to have that extra sense about danger. I remember the Yamaha biker and that futile chase. These pricks are sly, but just how cute they are is yet to be determined.

I'm thinking about the oil connection in Kuwait. I'm thinking I didn't recognize it there because everyone in those neighborhoods in Kuwait City seemed to be tied to petroleum and the big gas companies.

But when they pulled the job here in Chicago, it all clicked after I heard from FBI-Mary, and after all those years of missing something so obvious. If I were Captain Pearce, I could imagine him telling me it was an obvious mistake to be made—they were *all* about oil, back in the Middle East where the murders occurred.

I should have pursued it back then anyway. You're supposed to hit all the leads. But I didn't and now the Milans are dead. It's partly my fault, then. Maybe I could have nailed Thomas and Brandon in-country and I could have stopped the holocaust at the Milan house.

I know I'm being too hard on myself. But it's no use. I feel responsibility. I felt liable, culpable, even before we connected the dots with Brandon and Thomas and the two others, in California and Vermont. It might have been avoided, this last one.

It might have been, and that's what sticks, midway to my center.

12

Gerald is caught with his pantaloons about his ankles. He hasn't been as clever as Carl Thomas and Philip Brandon. (He swears he doesn't know the real name of the copy-cat killer out in Auburn, California.) He took a lick of his female adolescent's thigh. He left a saliva trace on her leg, and they've matched the DNA positively. It seems Gerald simply couldn't resist somehow touching the girl, flesh to flesh. So he's going to get smoked, and now he's being very cooperative, indeed.

But Philip Brandon remains in the shadows. He hasn't appeared anywhere near Hannah Menke and her daughters. We've been on shift three days straight—Jack and I doing the third shift, 11-7—and there hasn't even been a strange sound at night. And nothing doing during the other two shifts, either. Pretty soon we're going to be removed from keeping the watch here, and I know Hannah will be badly frightened when we have to leave. I'm becoming fond of her two kids, Bethany and Barbara, as well. I'm beginning to become overly fond of Hannah, too, and it's bothering my sense of professionalism, along with troubling my sense of loyalty to Mary Janecko, the woman I thought I was in love with.

She sits down with me at the kitchen table on this late evening in early September. The heat has still not fled the Middle West. It's been in the 90s the last two weeks, with no sign of relief, according to the forecasters.

She has spectacular brown eyes. They're her best feature. She is lanky and athletic-looking. She told me she works out in a gym four times a week—mainly to forget about her husband, Bob, the guy who left her for a younger woman of twenty-eight.

"He's an idiot," I blurt out, sitting across from this beautiful brunette.

"Pardon me?"

She breaks out in an abrupt guffaw. Her cheeks redden, and her eyes blaze directly into mine, as if I've come right out of left field at her. She stands, and then I see her legs are an outstanding feature of a very eye-catching package.

"I'm sorry. I shouldn't have said that."

"But you're right. Bob's an idiot."

We both laugh reflexively.

"I don't want to keep you from your work," she says.

She has amazingly full lips. Not too big, just full.

"You're my work. Remember?" I smile.

I think my face is aflame, and I'm becoming self-conscious.

"Will you excuse a personal question?" she asks.

"Sure. Go right ahead."

"Are you seeing anyone?"

I begin my fidgeting act. My fidgeting act annoys me as much as it embarrasses Hannah, apparently, because I've brought out a blush on her dazzling face. I feel like twitching some more, just to get her to stay that *alive*, radiant color.

"Yes, I am…. But I don't think it's happening."

"Why's that? If you don't mind talking about it. If it's too personal…"

"No. It's okay. She's a federal cop. She doesn't want us to get in the way of either of our careers."

I intertwine my fingers so I'll stop the spastic bit. I can feel the pulse of heat creeping up behind my ears. She never takes her eyes from me. And now I can smell her scent. I have no clue about women's fragrances. I have no idea what it is that she's wearing, but I know I'm in love with it. She smells like an acre of wild flowers. It's as if I'm out in that field, and it's April, and the rain has cleaned the air and everything is fresh and *breathing*.

"And you want it to progress."

I find myself staring into her eyes.

"Do you?" she asks again.

"I did. I don't know, now."

I look up and all I can see is Hannah. I'm locked onto her brown eyes, and there's nothing else in the room. I want to keep our eyes locked this way, but I have to break her spell or I'll get lost in her house and I'll never walk out of here.

"Good thing you didn't marry her, Will. Good thing you're sorting it all out before you commit. Maybe it's for the best."

I'm beginning to sweat. It's not that the room is hot. It's all internal combustion. She makes my ears and neck light up as if someone's standing behind me, torching the back of my head.

"Would you take him back?"

"Bob, you mean."

I nod.

"No. No way. That's over. I can't trust him, ever again. He wants a younger model, fine. To hell with them both.... That sounds mean, doesn't it."

There's a profound look of hurt on her, now. I've brought up the taboo subject. I've reawakened the anger in her, the betrayal, and I can see the passion of *hatred* flicker in her eyes. I've entered no-man's-land, with Hannah, and now there's no retreating.

"Not really."

"You were in the military?"

"Yes. Marines, for four years after I graduated college. Then I joined the NCIS, just in time for Desert Storm."

I stand up and walk toward the window. I look out at Oak Park, and I see the trees and sidewalks and houses that make this a suburb and a contrast to the gray ugliness of some of the barrios in the city just east of here. This is where people move to get the hell out of the nastiness of the blocks where I grew up. This is the reverse of the inner city where I do a lot of business.

"Was it bad?"

"It was short. I was a cop, not a combatant. But I saw lots of dead people, I'm sorry to say, and they weren't all job-related. We drove the highways with Marine convoys. It was pretty awful, actually."

Those convoys and bodies and horrors flash past me as I look out her pretty window at her pretty neighborhood. Oakbrook is a place to move *into*, not *out of*.

"I don't want to dredge up bad memories."

I'm still deep inside her eyes, and my color must be scarlet, right about now. She has to have noticed my flushed face.

"You're not. All the shrinks I've talked to, all the profilers I've met, have told me it's good to talk about it occasionally. I don't want to bother you with war stories, though."

"I don't find you boring at all."

I have to look away from her. And then I raise my eyes toward hers again.

"You mind a personal question?"

"No. Not at all."

"Are you... dating anybody?"

Her smile is warm. I don't feel humiliated, not as I thought I would, asking a damn-fool question like the one I just posed.

"Are you asking me out, Will?"

I try to answer, but the words won't come out.

"That would be unprofessional, if I were to.... You know. Ask you out."

"You could wait until you don't have to babysit the three of us any longer."

"Are you serious? Or are you just teasing me?"

I think they call it an impious grin. She shows me that glimmer of a smile that is teasing, but not mocking. She gets up and walks to the opposite side of the room as if she's trying to size me up better. I feel almost lonesome when she walks away from me.

"Why? Because I'm so much older than you?"

"You're not old. I've never thought you were anything but.... beautiful."

"My. What a lovely thing for a homicide detective to tell me," she grins.

She starts floating my way. I don't see her steps, but I know she's somehow closing the distance between us. It's like a magic trick, like levitation. I'm trying to figure out if it's an optical illusion. She's the sorceress, and I'm just the bewildered audience.

"I'm not.... I'm not just saying it. I mean it. If I weren't on the job...."

"When you're free, when you can maintain your professional detachment," she smiles, "you know my phone number. And you know where I live and work. I don't see a problem. Do you?"

I want to touch her now. I want to embrace her and kiss her right where she sits, three feet away from me. Somehow I find some self-control, just before my rocketry explodes.

"Who are you, Will?"

I gaze up at her, and I'm befuddled. I don't understand the language she's throwing at me. It doesn't sound like English. It sounds like some mysterious concoction of musical notes that I can't read.

"Excuse me?"

"What do you like to do? Where've you been—other than the Middle East?"

"I like reading. True crime. Crime fiction. I like historical stuff too.... Never been anywhere except for Illinois and California, where I did boot camp in the military. Never seen Europe. Flown over it. Seen the Atlantic from 25,000 feet. That's it."

I blush like a schoolboy whose teacher just asked him to recite what he did on his summer vacation. I have no idea what to tell her, next.

"What'd you do in school?"

"High school?"

She nods. I have the strong urge to come right over the top of this table to her.

"I played baseball and football. I had a scholarship for football, but I hurt my ankle and knee my freshman year at college."

"Did you date much in college?"

She's grinning mischievously once again. She's playing me like a keyboard. Her fingers are running up and down me, but she's never laid a glove on me. This trick is all done with her brown, intense orbs.

"No. Sports and school didn't leave much leftover time.... But I wasn't a monk, either."

"Nothing serious, at the University?"

She's smiling again, and I think I'm coming unglued.

"Nothing very serious. A few girls, here and there."

"When did you meet this federal cop?"

I'm being slyly interrogated, now. She ought to work with Jack and me, downtown. She's very bright, very sly. She's toying with me, and I'm loving every damned second of it.

"About six weeks after I got on Homicide."

"She works for which branch?"

"FBI. She's a special agent out of the Chicago branch."

"You really in love with her?"

That was a subtle, but penetrating slice. She knows she's stuck it into me, and there's almost a look of glee on her face. It's not malicious. She's just...She's simply probing, until she finds that lump or mass that she's seeking.

"I'm starting to wonder.... I mean, she has such different dreams from mine."

"What do you dream about, Will?"

"That's a line from *Red Dragon*," I laugh.

"Pardon?"

"Thomas Harris. The guy who wrote *The Silence of the Lambs*. He wrote *Red Dragon* too. It was the first of the Dr. Lector books, I think."

"You read a lot of crime stuff?"

Her interest seems sincere. The playful look has become sober.

"I read serious writers, sometimes. Cormac McCarthy, F. Scott Fitzgerald—And I'm a huge fan of William Faulkner.... I'm boring you."

"No. No you're not. I find you absolutely fascinating."

I believe every word she utters. She can make no false moves. Maybe she's hypnotized me, and the next thing I know I'll be barking like a fucking dog, as if it were some Vegas act. But there's nothing false in her inquiry. She's genuine, the real deal, and I find myself opening up in front of her like some time-lapsed blossom.

"I think you're very interesting too."

"Why don't you sit next to me?"

I stare at my hands on the table top.

Then I rise and sit on the chair next to her, on her right.

She leans over and kisses me and puts her hands behind my head, and then she kisses me again. Her lips are as firm and as pliant as I knew they'd be.

"We shouldn't."

"You're right," she smiles sadly. "But you've been very good to the three of us. And I am way too old for you."

I kiss her this time.

"Bullshit."

Then I kiss her again. And I hear Jack Clemons tromping toward us from the living room.

I hurriedly re-take my chair opposite Hannah Menke.

"Everything copacetic?" Jack grins.

I know there's Hannah's cherry red lipstick on my mouth, but I don't dare to try and wipe it off.

"We're excellent," Hanna tells him without turning around toward him.

Jack smiles at me and turns and heads back through the swinging kitchen door toward the living room.

"We've been caught," she grins slyly.

"Not much gets past him."

"If you're embarrassed by me…"

"Don't you even say that."

"Okay."

"I'll call you."

There is bemusement on her lovely face. It's as though she's heard this somewhere, several times. The notion that she thinks it's a line, that it's all bullshit, enrages me.

"Good."

"You don't believe me?"

I feel the flush of anger surge toward my face. I try to control it, but I can't resist it. I know she's reading my anger, and I see it tickles her to push every goddamned button I have.

"No, Will. This is just a brief encounter, just an infatuation with an *older* woman," she smiles.

"Bullshit. Again. You're wrong. Wait and see. I'll call."

"You will?"

"Wait and see."

She smiles again, and I want to jump at her once more, but this time my better sense takes over.

"You're not supposed to become involved with case people, Will," Jack grins.

"Yeah. Right."

"You going out with her?"

"Mind your own fucking yard, Jack."

"Absolutely...White Castle?"

"Why not?" I tell him.

It's one of the frequent hangouts for police in the city. They're open twenty-four, 365, which makes them popular on that count alone.

We frequent the Castle on Fullerton, not far from the Outer Drive. In September you can smell the lake and the dead fish on some of the beaches.

He orders six cheesesliders and a coffee; I prefer the Diet Coke with my five cheeseburgers. They're called "sliders" because they slide in one way and they slide out the other way. You don't eat the damn things when you've been partaking of alcoholic beverages, but after getting drunk they're irresistible. This dawn, however, I'm quite sober.

Jack doesn't ask me about my magic moments with Hannah Menke, and I know he doesn't give a shit about the question of professional detachment when it comes to my on job behavior. Getting involved with people does happen from time to time, no matter what kind of a hard case you might think you are.

I know I shouldn't call Hannah, but it was that bemusement in her eyes when she told me she knew I wouldn't. She thought I was taking her as a lightweight, as someone who was offering herself out of need.

But I knew that wasn't the truth of the matter. She touched me somewhere deep. It sounds like maudlin romance, I know, but she just got to me.

Maybe it was just her immediate availability, maybe it was her brown eyes.... Who the hell knows? But when you really feel something electric happening that deep down--

I have to call her anyway, just because she thinks I won't. And I know how bad that sounds, but it matters to me that I don't disappoint her.

She's got two almost-teenaged girls. A ready-made family. We've got no chance to make it work. Two different worlds. And she is a decade older than I am. There's that to think about even if I told her age didn't matter.

It didn't matter when our lips connected. There was more of a connection than just our mouths.

I have to think this out rationally. I've got Mary. She expects me to keep showing up at her place, and she's even shown signs of softening toward the relationship business. But why should I have to work so hard to talk her into it?

I was never interested in casual connections—not in high school or college or now. I've never liked to be around anyone who didn't know exactly what they wanted in life. Love, work... It didn't matter.

I knew I wanted to enlist in the Marines after the university. I knew I wanted to join the NCIS and become a cop. And when I wanted out of the G, I knew I wanted to come home and be a homicide detective. I could see my life unwinding clearly. I never had difficulty with goals and knowing where I was headed.

Then Mary clouded the whole issue. She kept me at arm's length, telling me to slow down and savor whatever it was that we had together.

And now Hannah enters the scenario. She seems more serious. She seems like she knows exactly what she wants as much as I do. Which makes her very appealing to me. And her ten years on me makes no difference to me at all.

When I'm fifty, she'll be sixty, of course. Will it matter?

The answer rings out immediately:

No. It won't matter. I can see myself in the future with Hannah, although I know it's all extremely premature.

Maybe she'll shoot me down if I do call her. I shouldn't. Not while we're still babysitting her and the kids.

Then I'll wait. I'll assuage my professional dignity and I'll wait.

Wait until we collar Carl Thomas and Philip Brandon and the phantom in northern California, too. When we've got our creatures of the night behind bars, I'll give Hannah Menke the chance to send me to earth in flames.

I can't think of a prettier way to go.

13

*M*issing in action are the men who are the walking dead. Some men stay missing. Their bodies are never found. Some others find ways of reappearing when you least expect it. They'll walk up to your front door and surprise you by saying: "I'm home." They simply reappear, like that.

Sometimes these walking dead don't come home at all. They take circuitous routes back to their native soil. They might make their ways home by way of foreign continents, foreign countries, alien cities and ports. As Mark Twain said it—the reports of their demise were highly exaggerated. All it takes to vanish is a plan. All it takes to pop back to life again is money and smarts. If you've got both of those, you can outwit almost anyone. They think you're dead; it's the world's oldest con. Again, it was my favorite writer, Mark Twain, Sam Clemens, who had his boy Huck Finn pull that scam on Pap. All it took was a little hog's blood and a few hanks of Huck Finn's hair. Then the whole town figured Huckleberry was history. That he'd tanked it forever.

Granted, some disappearances are more difficult to achieve than others. You have to have red herrings to pull the gag. You have to employ misdirection to achieve the desired results. It's the oldest smokescreen in the business; nothing is ever as it seems. The magician has you looking in one direction, and you're leaving yourself wide open for one hellacious sucker punch.

You don't even have time to duck.

14

Mary keeps talking more and more about getting serious. Then I have visions of spending serious time with Hannah Menke. With Hannah there is an upside and a downside, and it's the same thing: She has a ready-made family, two teen aged daughters, already there, already with a father in this world. What would I become for them if I married Hannah? I know I'm way ahead of myself because we haven't even gone out yet. I haven't even called her.

It might also become a little obvious to Special Agent Mary Janecko, lying next to me here, that something is brewing on a new front. Much I can't get past this bright federal cop. Not much at all. I have no poker face when it comes to dealing romantically with women. I can keep a straight face with females when I'm on the job, but when it's on my own time, I tend to be a little too much of an open book. They can read me, I mean.

The FBI continues the chase in California for the as-yet-unnamed perp who wiped out that family near Auburn. Gerald swears he doesn't know the West Coast guy's name. He knows Brandon and Thomas because they actually met up in Milwaukee. It was a setup from the Internet, once the other two killers had returned from Desert Storm. The three of them actually planned the killing in Chicago while they were in

Wisconsin before Gerald took off for Vermont and did his thing in the Northeast.

There is no trace of Carl or Philip. They have gone to earth. Neither the FBI nor the Chicago PD can get a handle on either man. They leave no paper trail because neither man is using a credit card with his right name on it. Thomas's sister is no help. The local police near her have interrogated her twice, and the second time she lawyered up, and now we're "harassing" her if we try her once again.

The surveillance at Hannah's has come to a halt, now that it's the third week in September. We don't have the manpower or the overtime pay to continue, according to Captain Pearce. Pearce is more than disappointed that we have to pull back on Hannah and her two kids. I'm a little distraught myself. Now I have no official excuse to head over there.

I was becoming fond of her girls, also. They're not the little princess types. They both have their shit squared away, it seems to me. They look you in the eye, and neither of them is catty to the other—or to me or to their mom, either. They seem well-behaved and respectful. I sometimes see myself being able to handle daddy-hood with two nearly grown stepdaughters. It's a fantasy I envision, from time to time.

Then I come back to reality, shacked up here with Mary, sharing a sweaty bed with my FBI lover, the same lover who has warmed toward the notion of taking all this to another level.

"I want you to meet my parents," she offers.

"Meet who?"

"Mommy. Daddy. You know? The heads of my clan?"

"Sure. Yes. Why not?"

"Don't sound so brazenly enthusiastic, Will."

"I am.... Enthusiastic, I mean.... You want to meet my dad?"

"Let's see how it goes with *Adventure Number One*, with my mother and father. Okay?"

"Sure. Absolutely."

Then before I can generate any more false energy, she starts it up with me. And I have no defense against her. She's unrelenting. In fact, she's always been sort of the instigator or aggressor in bed. I rather liked it when we first started making love, but now I like it to be my idea when we couple—at least some of the time.

"You aren't coming here again," Hannah Menke says. Her eyes are filling.

"Not officially. No."

"Unofficially?"

"I don't know, Hannah. I really don't."

"Why don't you know?"

"I'm involved with someone."

"Oh."

She looks away.

"But it might be going down for the count…. I'm not sure."

"So maybe you'll give me a call if this other thing doesn't…"

"Hannah. Please. You have no idea how this is tearing me up."

"You don't look torn up."

"I don't show what I'm thinking. Not when I'm on the job."

"I thought you were no longer an official presence here."

"Please, Hannah."

"You're right. I have no right to talk to you this way. I want to thank you for all you've done for the three of us, Detective Koehn."

"Hannah…"

"You need to go now. You really need to go."

And her Oakbrook door shuts in front of my face.

I get the call from Jack Clemons at three in the morning. I race out the door at my dad's house, I jump in the Cavalier, and I take off to meet my partner.

My heart has quite literally risen in my throat as I enter Hannah Menke's home. I walk past three other Homicide detectives as I go into her house here in Oakbrook. I see the splintered front door.

When I reach Jack, in Hannah's kitchen, I ask him.

"Where are they?"

"Upstairs," he answers.

I turn and run up those stairs to the upper level where the bedrooms are. I walk into Hannah's master bedroom.

No one there.

I walk into Bethany's bedroom next door. Still no one.

All that's left is Barbara's room.

Hannah is sitting on the bed holding a daughter on either side of her. The three of them are quivering as if they're lapsing into shock.

But they're all three *alive*.

The female detective, Joan Georgopolous, smiles at me and then leaves the bedroom and shuts the door as she leaves.

Hannah looks up.

"I heard him break in. He kicked in the front door. The security system went off and the signal went right to the Oakbrook Police and they were here in three minutes. Whoever it was must have heard the alarm, and he took off.

"I'm buying a gun," she tells me.

"Don't," I answer.

"Will you live here with us and protect us?"

"Hannah..."

"I know. You have a job to do. So I'm buying a gun, and I'm going to send these two to lessons so they can shoot him in the head if he ever comes back."

"I'm very sorry I wasn't here to help, Hannah."

"You can leave now. I don't think whoever it was will be back for a little while."

I can't think of anything to say. I can't come up with an apology. It's too lame to tell her we ran out of man hours to watch her home. She already knows that excuse.

I'm going to watch her house from out on the street the next few nights on my own time, just to make sure she's safe, until she's got the door fixed and the security system back online. I won't tell her, though, because she's angry with me. I led her to believe I'd be here for her—and not just professionally. I made her think I'd be around when she needed me. Instead I was home asleep when Jack made the call.

So I get up and walk out of her room before they take the three of them to the hospital to treat them for possible shock.

I work four to midnight on shift. I spent midnight to dawn out on the curb, about a block down from Hannah's house. I make regular passes on foot around her premises, but I don't come too close so that I won't trigger whatever electrical security system she's got. At least the bells and whistles don't go off as I circle the place.

I think about the fear on her face, and then I want to find Brandon and Thomas and shoot them both. We have a very good circumstantial case against them with Gerald's testimony about the Internet chats and the physical meet in Milwaukee. Our DA thinks he can convict them both of the Chicago murders with what he's got. Confessions would be the clincher, but I'm thinking neither Thomas nor Brandon would tell the truth about what they did in Kuwait and in Chicago. They'd never give it up; they'd make us dig to smoke them both.

Which is fine with me. I want to throw a full shovel of dirt on both of their graves. We still have the death penalty in Illinois.

I sit outside Hannah's lovely home, and I remember my anxiety on the way over here on the night of the attempted break-in. Jack didn't tell me they were alive. He was en route himself, and there was no time for details. There was just the rush to get there and see for myself.

On the third midnight-to-dawn surveillance, I knock on Hannah's door.
"Yes?"
She looks very tired, drawn.
"Can I come in?"
"It's one o'clock in the morning."
"Please let me come in, Hannah."

92

"I don't think..."

I kiss her and take hold of her before she can further remonstrate with me.

"Maybe you'd better come in, after all."

I look down into her eyes as I enter her. Her breath escapes softly from her parted, full lips. Then I kiss her and lift her off the mattress, and I'm joined completely with her. I feel her tightening inside, and then she gasps.

"You're sure the girls are sound asleep," I grin at her.

"I've got the door locked. They can't get in," she smiles hazily up at me.

"I can't do this again," I tell her.

"Why not?"

"It doesn't feel right. It feels a little awkward, with them in the next couple rooms down the hall."

"So are you saying we should meet for a four hour nap?" she laughs.

"No motels, no. But I live with my father."

"So it's the same deal at your place."

"Yeah. But I was talking about moving out into my own apartment. I'd hate to leave the girls alone here, right now."

"They stay with their dad, every other weekend. Even though he's an asshole and doesn't deserve visitation rights."

Then the anger passes her beautiful face, and she looks up at me.

"They go to their father's this Friday night and they don't come home until Sunday evening. The bastard still loves both of them, I have to admit. Even with his new twenty-eight year old ho."

"So, am I being invited?"

I slap my hands against my thighs, and then I feel my fingers gathering into a fist. I feel like a rejection is imminent. My face flushes, embarrassingly. I can sense the deep red.

"You are."

My hands unclench. The heat is released from my cheeks. The temperature is quickly back to normal.

"I'm off shift on Saturday. I could come here at midnight on Friday when I get off work."

"Don't you get called in for cases at any hour?"

She smiles coyly at me. She thinks I'll come up with some lame excuse and that I'll let her down. Her grin is almost *evil.*

"Maybe the bad guys'll be reasonable, this weekend."

"What about the other thing?"

She shows me all her lovely pearlies, now. She's having fun, dangling me over the open pit barbeque. The flames heat up my mug, again.

"Other.... You mean Mary?"

"Her name is Mary?"

Her visage goes to a pout, suddenly. Now she seems to be on the defensive.

"Yes.... Yeah, I guess I'll have to talk to Mary."

"You're not marrying me, Will. We're just getting to know one another. Don't get so serious on me."

I'm being lectured by an *older,* worldly woman. She has her hands on her hips, and it's as if I'm back in the seventh grade with the ancient Mrs. Monaghan, the geography teacher.

"You're not serious?"

"Are you questioning me?"

She smiles.

"I don't mean to.... I just don't get into casual things—at least, I try not to."

I force my blush to dissipate. I'm telling my facial temperature to cool it, also.

"We'll just have to see, then, won't we, Will."

She kisses me again, and then I have to put my pants on because I can see the first darts of dawn piercing her blinds.

15

The St. Louis cops are keeping an eye out for Brandon, but there have been no sightings.

And I'm beginning to wonder if Thomas might be dead—accident, perhaps suicide, although he's not the type to take to the idea of suicide, I don't guess.

The conversation with Special Agent Mary Janecko, FBI, did not go well. I did all the smart things: I took her to a big restaurant with lots of people there, but she made a scene anyway, throwing ice water on my lap. It gave several customers a big laugh, but it made me look like a fool, on the way out, who'd just pissed his trousers. Apparently my "informant" at the Bureau has now become a dry well.

I knew it wouldn't be pretty. I always had an idea that Mary had a vindictive streak. She simply never showed it until now. All her talk about becoming committed apparently was just that—talk. We never moved to any other level than bed partners and lovers. It's all a moot point, now that I've left her.

I had trouble all through high school when I dated because I never wanted to float. I wanted to find someone who really liked me, even loved me. It never happened. We'd go out, we'd become romantic sometimes, and then she'd flit off to be with someone else.

I joined the Corps after college because they practice fidelity, just like the famous Marine slogan, *semper fidelis*. Those two Latin words were what attracted me to the Crotch. But when I got into the Marines, I noticed it was just a slogan, just a cliché, to a lot of the men in the service. All there was was cynicism—it was every man for himself, a lot of the time. In reality, I mean. Everybody said the words, but I didn't see many guys living them. It's like the Secret Service, which I had aspired to join until I got into the NCIS instead. The guys who protect the President really would take a bullet for the Boss. I would've been like that, had I made it into that branch. I felt that way for my country, and a lot of the guys I grew up with in the city thought I was a fool. I was a romantic, like that Spanish idiot, Don Quixote. Jousting at windmills.

Because I believed that justice was attainable, that our cause was right. Because I believed in the American Dream. The young guys I came up with all became pessimists or cynics. They told me this country would go down, and that like every other world power, we'd flame out over the course of history.

I refused to buy it. Not because I'm some idealistic pinhead who believes what the Establishment tells him to believe. It's just that I really do love this country. I love what it stands for in spite of all its glaring blemishes and shortcomings. I'm not a shiny-eyed moron. I know all about the evil on this globe. I've seen it, personally, in the Middle East and right here at home. I'm not a right- wing bible thumper, either. I have no religion. I was baptized a Catholic, but I've never practiced. My parents never dragged Sammy or me to church. If we wanted to go, they always said they'd take us and drop us off. But they never went, themselves. We put up a tree at Christmas, and we hunted for eggs on Easter when we were little, but Mom and Dad never did the hypocrite route by attending mass on Christmas and Easter to become C and E Catholics. They gave us all the right words about right and wrong without the evangelism bit. My Dad gave up on God after World War II. My mother said there was a reason she divorced Him from her life as well, but she never elaborated. Sammy and I grew up without knocking off gas stations or murdering the neighbors—or even cheating on school exams. So I guess we were raised properly.

My dad loved America too, but he never waved any flags, and neither have I.

But I'd take a bullet for my country, and I don't give a shit if no one but me believes it.

I watch Hannah's house on my own time. I spend some time with her when the kids are with their father. And I've told Dad that I'm moving into an apartment.

"Does that mean you're not gay after all?" he said from behind his newspaper.

I've made arrangements to move into a New Town flat this weekend. It won't take much to move me. All I've got are my clothes and my books—and of course my nine millimeter weapon, holster, bullets and badge. And one Detective's ID, too.

I cart my three suitcases to the second-floor flat with the help of Jack Clemons. It helps that he drives a Ford 150 truck. I asked him what the hell he needed a full-sized truck for when he lives by himself (only about a mile from here), has no wife or kids (whom he knew about) and isn't a handyman/construction kind of guy.

"You never know," was his cryptic answer.

We get me moved in in an hour and forty minutes.

"You own nothing," he smiles as we sit on the couch in my furnished, three room apartment. Bedroom, kitchen/dinette, and living room. Fairly spacious for $750 a month. And Hannah is coming over tonight to christen the bedroom, she says.

"No. Just a few clothes and those."

I point to three boxes of books.

Jack goes to the boxes and opens them.

"Jesus H. Christ," he grins at me.

"Fucking poetry," he laughs.

"It's not *fucking* poetry," I inform him.

"Robert Frost, Lawrence Ferlinghetti. Who the hell are these guys? I mean I heard of Frost, but..."

"Those guys are called 'The Beat Poets,'" I explain. "Allen Ginsburg and some of the others. But I've got Walt Whitman and Emily Dickinson, too."

"Did your brother leathernecks think you were a little odd, with all this shit?"

"I never shared my literary tastes with anybody in the Corps. I read this stuff on my own time. I even wrote some poems in college. Got a few published in the college review, as a matter of fact, asshole."

"Now you're showing me your vindictive side."

"I learned it from my ex-girlfriend, Mary."

Jack looks at his hand and smiles patiently at me. He always seems amused with my love-life.

"I never liked that bitch, Will."

"Speak kindly of the departed."

"She ain't dead, Detective."

He grins paternalistically at me, and suddenly I want to whack him. I can feel the tension gathering in both of us, even though I know he's trying to be funny.

"To my life she is. She threw water all over my crotch at Spinoza's."

Spinoza's was the popular eatery I took her to when she doused me.

"You should have shot her in the head."

"Sure, then you could come cuff me, Jack."

"I would've given you a twenty-four hour jump to cut out of town.... Are we done here?"

He looks back down at that same hand, and an evil grin returns to his face. I can't help but like the asshole.

"Yes. Thanks for the help.... What's on your mind?"

He looks around the room as if he's looking for a long-lost relative.

"This thing is becoming colder as we speak."

"You mean Carl Thomas and friends."

"Yes, Will. Exactly. I don't like the stink in my nose."

"What's troubling you?"

"You mean other than the fact that those two fucks are running free?"

"Sometimes the bad guys get away with it. I had to live with that three thousand-pound primate on my back in Desert Storm after they whacked those two families over there."

I glare at him as if I don't believe he'll ever know what I know, because he's never seen what I've seen. It's not his fault he wasn't in Kuwait, but I'm glaring at him angrily, anyway.

"I don't like what this Gerald told us. The whole conspiracy thing, to kill up the tree, working your way up the echelon in the oil game. It just sounds too whacked out."

Now he's pissed off, too. His jaw is thrust out at me pugnaciously, as if he wants me to take a swing at him. He's almost in that fighter's stance. It's the way he holds himself when he becomes combative, I've noticed.

"Guys kill people because they hear little voices telling them that God's telling *them* to *smite thy neighbor*. So what's so nuts about getting even with the gas people?"

"It sounds like…. terrorism, is what it sounds like."

His rage is beginning to boil over. I see his hands clenched as if he really *is* going to take a whack at me.

"This country hasn't been attacked by terrorists. Yet."

"I can't see it happening, either."

He slumps out of his fine anger, all of a sudden. His shoulders go lax, and an unexpected chill takes over the room.

I look at him in the eyes.

"I don't want to go there, Will."

"Nobody else does, either. Right now we're after two killers. I don't really give a shit why they killed all those vics. All I want to do is stop them from doing it again."

"Motive does matter. I don't give a damn what you say."

"That's always been pretty obvious to me, partner. And I like a guy who thinks for himself anyway."

"Yeah. Right…"

He looks at my boxes of books.

"Poetry? Jesus Harold Christ. *Poetry.*"

He waves, and then he walks out the door.

First there was a list of a dozen solid suspects, back in Kuwait. Then the list dwindled to three. Captain Benjamin Anderson, Lieutenant Carl Thomas and Lieutenant Philip Brandon. Anderson was eliminated when he was presumed dead in action, KIA, killed in action. The body was never recovered, but his vehicle, a Hummer, was so severely burned that nothing but fragments of the hood remained; the heat from the explosion was so hot it damn-near melted everything down to cinders. His dog tags were thrown from the blast, as were his scorched combat boots. That was all they could find to recover of his body and the two other Marines in his vehicle. There were only particles of the lance corporal and the gunnery sergeant who were signed out with the vehicle. No one recovered anything until two days after they'd gone missing. It was presumed they'd run into a booby-trapped vehicle in the road, but they were out in the boonies outside of Baghdad, so no one witnessed the blast. They were due at their camp, just three miles from the home of Saddam Hussein. They never made it back to their tent.

I liked Thomas and Brandon in-country because of their borderline profiles from psych records. Neither of them was outright Section Eights, but they were loners. The Corps has its share of loners, and I'd always qualified as one before I joined NCIS just before the shit broke out in Desert Storm, but these two were different kinds of outcasts. They seemed to know where their boundaries stood—neither man had any kind of military offense on his record. They were clever fuckers, I'm saying. They never went too far, but they were always on the edge, their superior officers had written in their personnel jackets. Both of them were a little too good to be true, it seemed to me. I was running on instinct with Thomas and Brandon, but I really liked them for those multiple homicides then, and I still liked them, even though we had a nut's word that they did the Chicago slayings.

Organized killers. Series murderers. Serial killers. *Serial killers.* Madmen who weren't so mad as to leave incriminating evidence behind. Smart assassins, left no forensic evidence.

Left only suspicion in the mind of a young NCIS investigator whose job was Crimes Against Persons/Violent Crimes. Violent crimes, as in murder.

Even the Soviet Union was beginning to admit it had a problem with these kinds of predators. They'd always had series killers, but they liked to say it was a "western" phenomenon, not something a communist state had to suffer.

Jack was right. The scent was becoming faint; the trail was becoming obscured. The longer a homicide went unsolved, the colder the case became. Thomas was mist. Brandon was a phantom. Jack was becoming anxious to break this thing open, not to mention the anxiety level our Captain Pearce must be burdened with.

I never felt the pressure of having red names on our white board in Homicide. Some detectives lived and died with their percentage of solved cases, but I tended to look at my load as a challenge, not a percentage. I'm not a bean counter, and perhaps I'll live to learn to regret it. The word has always been "quota." It's like a car salesman. If you don't move the merchandise, you get shit-canned. Same is true in homicide.

I've been lucky that my red names are far fewer in number than my black names. I do have a high solution ratio—85%. But what matters to me most is what's on the table before me now.

Someone kicked Hannah Menke's front door down and scared the hell out of her and her two daughters. Someone killed two entire families in Kuwait on my watch and got away with it. Somebody killed a family in my hometown of Chicago, and he's still at large. All the above bothers me, and if it's obsession with my work… I don't know how else to play the cards I've been dealt. I give a shit about the victims I have to speak for. You can call that idealistic, fine. The day I stop caring about cleaning up the messes they leave, maybe I'll become a security guard in a bank or a night watchman.

Homicide has a high burnout rate. Numbers. Fucking numbers.

What are the odds we ever find Thomas and Brandon? What are the odds that neither of them did it and Gerald is a lying piece of shit who needs severe psychiatric therapy for his pathological lying problem?

Doubts. Self-doubt. It comes with the job. Make a wrong move. It's like step on a crack and you'll break your momma's back. My mother's not dead, but you get my point, I think.

I lost my personal contact with the FBI, true. But I got Hannah in return. I think I came out ahead. The days don't seem as leaden and dark anymore. They actually seem more hopeful.

Unless I start to obsess on those two pricks out there somewhere. And it might be more than two, if you count the guy who did the family in California. And who knows how many more of them there might be, if Gerald was in fact telling us the truth about this "Internet mafia."

Series killers. Serial killers. Organized killers. Call them whatever you like. I was after Carl Thomas and Philip Brandon in spite of my partner Jack Clemons's doubts about their reasons for killing. Do it for oil. Do it for money. Do it for the Holy Grail. Do it for whatever you like.

All those victims remain dead, and payment has come due.

16

I go to Jack's softball game in Orland Park, under the lights. It's Chicago-style, sixteen-inch slow pitch—no gloves allowed. It's an older guys' game, at least on the mound and in the infield. The younger guys, like Jack Clemons, are the speedsters in the outfield. Jack played minor league baseball in the Cubs' organization, Class A, before he was injured and quit and went to college and then became a policeman and later a Homicide. He's got a girlfriend at the game, but I've met her before and I really don't want to get into any more conversations with her. She's a little unhinged, I think. Last time I went to one of Jack's softball games she told me she was going to recruit six Jews and return with them to the Holy Land. I asked her if she were Jewish herself, but she got all huffy and explained she was a "Christian, of course." So I let her sit by herself on the third baseline. I sit in the bleachers behind the plate. They're better seats, anyhow.

Hannah couldn't make the game because it's Bethany's birthday, and both sides of her family, her ex-husband's and hers, are going out for pizza and cake and ice cream. Bethany doesn't seem all out of joint about a birthday party at her teen years. She just goes along with it all because she loves her mother and doesn't want to break Hannah's heart. Hannah thinks her daughters will remain forever young, like the Bob Dylan song.

I humor her about it. She was very excited about Bethany's party, and who am I to poop on it?

Jack's team, The Jesters, out of Orland Park, lays into the Generals, a crew out of Tinley Park, another southwestern burb. It's 12-1 in the third, so I become bored and I start taking in the scenery. I like to look at faces in the crowd.

Then I see Carl Thomas standing out on the first base line, about 20 feet from the right field foul pole and the fence. He's got shades and a yellow tank top, and he's pretty far from me, but I know it's Thomas. I've looked at his photo in his jacket often enough. When I'm sure he's staring right at me, I get up slowly and walk down from the top of the home plate bleachers. I don't want him to think I'm headed his way. I take my time on the short descent, and then I casually head toward the concession stand behind the bleachers. I go up and order a Diet Coke, and then I swivel my face toward the right field line and I see Thomas still standing there. I'm wearing shades too, so I think maybe he doesn't know I've caught sight of him yet.

I turn with my Diet Coke and head back toward my seat, but when I get to the bottom rung of the bleachers, I place the cup of soft drink on the seat and then I burst into a sprint toward Carl Thomas, and several people in the home plate seats gasp as they see me tear down the right field line.

Carl finally makes me as I'm headed at him, and he pivots and races to the right field fence. It's a six foot chain link, but he's over it like a high jumper in competition. When I reach that same chain link, I have to struggle and grope to clear it, but I overcome this hurdle, and I'm after him.

There is another softball diamond opposite Jack's, and there's a game going on right now. I've landed in left field. Thomas is galloping across their infield, ahead of me.

When I make it to the adjacent field's shortstop, the bull moose of a softball player *tackles* me.

"The fuck you think you're doin'?"

"I'm a policeman," I tell the giant who's pinned me to the grass behind short.

"I'm after a felon, so get the fuck off me!" I bellow.

"How I know you're a cop?"

"Let me up."

He finally relents as the other two teams begin to circle us like Native Americans around a wagon train.

I get up and take my ID out of my pocket. They take a quick look, and then I burst through their circle.

"Sorry, man!" I hear the apelike shortstop yell behind me.

There's another fence behind this field, back of home plate. It was the direction Thomas was headed, at least. I scale it hurriedly.

There's a large copse in front of me now, but there's no sign of Carl Thomas. The trees are thick. There are oaks and thorny elms and maples, and they're bunched so tightly together that I can't make out an entry.

And then I see a tiny dirt path off to my left. There are tall oaks on either side of this little slit. If Thomas entered these trees, I'm thinking he had to do it here. The underbrush is too thick for him to have made his way at any other starting point.

I take off down the path at full speed. My legs aren't bothering me, even after going over the top of two fences and even after being tackled by a Dick Butkus look-alike back on the second ball field.

I'm running as hard as I can, and my wind is still there, but I know he's got too big a lead. So I stop. I have to place my hands on my knees. My wind has suddenly betrayed me. I'm not the athlete I used to be a decade ago. Sammy'd think I was falling apart if my brother saw me right now.

Then I hear a rustling off the path. Suddenly I stand erect.

I'm not armed. My nine millimeter is in the trunk of the Cavalier, back at the parking lot. I didn't want to carry it because it's too hot, even though it's mid-September. The 90s won't depart and give way to all that Canadian air up north.

I'm the veritable sitting duck here. He can see me but I can't locate him. It's probably what he planned. He decoyed me. He knew I'd seen him all along, and he was just waiting for me to pursue. Stupid. Very stupid. Poor field tactics. I should have called for backup as soon as I made him out there in right field. I should have called in the troops, goddamn it. Now I might get myself shot in the process, as well. He has me. The advantages are all his. He knew where he was going all along, and now I'm going to die in a wood next to a softball diamond. Maybe they'll all hear the crack of Thomas's weapon, anyway.

The rustling continues. I think about climbing this tree next to me, but the trunk is thorny. It's a thorny elm. I begin to run into the underbrush when I hear a voice calling me.

"Will! Goddammit! *Will!*"

It's Jack Clemons in full softball regalia—and he's armed with a wooden baseball bat.

I stop in my tracks and turn. Jack has halted by the path, and he's waiting for me.

"Are you going to come on out here?" he asks. He's nearly out of breath, himself.

I walk out of the ground cover. I know I must be covered in poison ivy or poison oak, and I begin to scratch reflexively.

"Jesus fucking Christ. Where were you headed?"

"Thomas. It was Thomas."

"Where? Where the fuck…"

"He's gone. It's just for chuckles and grins. He's fucking with me."

"He could've fucking *shot* you out here, goddammit, Will!"

"My piece is in the car."

"Yeah, I guess."

We stand quietly here, both of us trying to regain our oxygen.

"I'm in the middle of the fucking game, and I see you streaking down the right field line. But I never saw him, Will. All I saw was you, tearing like hell toward that fence."

"You think I'm making this shit up?"

"Take it easy. I'm on your side, jackass. Take it easy…. Let's get back, huh?"

When we've got our collective winds back, we begin the long walk back to Jack Clemons' softball game.

The envelope sits on my desk at work. I know who it's from without even opening it. The 9 X 12 is postmarked Chicago, so he is here in the city for real. It's from Carl Thomas.

Inside is a single sheet of typing paper, plain white. Standard size. It has a crayon-rendered picture of a bull's eye, and in the center is my name—Will Koehn—glued to the spot. It's made from newsprint. There is no other message.

Captain Pearce is very concerned and irate.

"Why didn't you tell me about the first little message?"

"I thought it might just be a crank."

"Very lame, Koehn."

"Very lame indeed, Sir. My apologies."

"Apologies don't feed the bulldog, Will."

"Aye. I mean *yes, Sir.*"

"You will not withhold any viable information or evidence from me again, young man. Am I being clear?"

"You are, Sir. Very clear."

"He's in town," Jack tells me as we eat dinner at White Castle once again on the four-to-twelve shift.

"Master of the obvious," I grin at him.

The lovely smell of fried onions permeates the already greasy atmosphere. The smell of the ground beef is all over us. It is delicious, this high-fat heaven.

"He can't stay under forever."

"Maybe. He's stayed cleared of me since Desert fucking Storm," I remind Jack.

A waitress walks by. Her upper lip has a slight mustache over it, and I can see the beads of sweat that have clustered above her mouth. The windows are fogged with the heat of the cooking inside and the humid air outside.

"Well, he's clever. You have to hand him that."

"Yeah. I know all about this prick. I know he scored a perfect on his SATs. I know he had a full academic ride to Stanford and he passed it up to go to some small college in Ohio. I know Brandon is almost his twin—astronomical scores on both the ACT and SAT, and a full scholarship to UCLA. Smart pricks, both of them. Officer material. Right?"

The guy sitting down three seats from us is wearing a 1940s fedora. Too bad he isn't also wearing a zoot suit. The hat makes him look like he's arrived here fifty years too late.

"You don't need to get pissed at me, partner. I'm still on your side."

"I know, Jack…. I'm sorry. I'm venting. That's what Mary used to call this shit."

"*Fuck,*" the guy with the boss fedora mutters. It's barely audible, but he said it loud enough so the waitress with the mustache heard him as she lays down his platter of sliders. Apparently she didn't remove the onions from his hamburgers, as he requested.

"If they're so goddam smart, how come they're criminals?"

"Gerald said it was about evening up with the *man*, getting square with the Establishment."

Jack grimaces as he sips at his coffee. He looks as if he's swallowed arsenic, the way his face is all twisted up in pain.

"You believe Gerald?"

"No," I tell him.

"Then why are they killing these people, these young girls? They all were involved in oil."

He's got his "demanding" pose with his body language. He's ordering a response from me. Next thing he'll do is stand up in that boxer's stance.

"They have that common thread. But it doesn't seem right. It seems too…too plotted out. Everything they've done has been by the numbers. It's too obvious of a plan…. Does that make any sense?"

My mouth goes dry. I see the bodies in Kuwait again. Suddenly I'm transported back to all that ugliness.

"You're talking about misdirection, Will. Yeah, I get it."

Jack's face goes serious. He's lost his wisecrack, Homicide attitude. He can't joke away this case, the way we both try to from time to time, just to lighten the air we breathe.

"It's like a come on. It's as if they have this false scenario they're running at us to keep us going the wrong way. I don't have anything to back up my impression, my take on this, but I think they're running a gag on us, a game."

"Why?"

"Yeah. Indeed. There it is. Why, indeed?"

My life with Hannah continues to intensify. She spends weekends here when I have time off, and sometimes she comes over during the week when her mother can stay at the house with the two girls. Neither of us wants them to be alone any more, or at least until Brandon and Thomas are taken down.

We don't talk about marriage because the divorce is too fresh in her mind, but I have nothing else on my mind—except the two elusive rapist/murderers who occupy my sleeping and waking moments.

I want to make a commitment to Hannah, and I've had it on my mind ever since I burst into her home that early A.M. and kissed her and took her to bed for the first time.

I don't broach the subject of matrimony because I'm afraid to scare her off. I can see she's wary of my intentions, but that doesn't stop things between us from being more intense as the days of September burn into the chill of October. Sooner or later it'll flood its way out of my lips. I'll ask her to marry me in spite of reason. I know she wants to go slow. But going slow is what I tried with Mary, and I saw how that all unwound at the end.

She's loveable. She's sweet. She has a mild temper, but it's there when she's riled. I don't see me marrying a passive-aggressive woman.

My mother was that way with my Dad, and it drove him nuts sometimes, but he loved her so much he overlooked it.

Hannah is definitely assertive when her back is up. And what a pretty back it is. And the rest of her is not bad either.

We laugh together. She likes poetry, too. I never expected that from a certified public accountant—she passed her CPA ten years ago, she told me. She likes the Beat poets that I enjoy. We don't mesh on every single item, but we do have more in common than just the lust. The lust is good. You need it to be in love eventually, I figure. It'd be boring if you didn't have the hots for your old lady. It's a necessary ingredient for something that lasts.

But you need respect and concern. You need to want to do for the other. You need to want to take that bullet for your partner—your partner in Homicide and your partner at home, too. I want to *do* for Hannah Menke. I want to be there to protect her.

I want to take care of her daughters too. I've also come to fall in love with both Barbara and Bethany. I almost look at them as if they're my own kids, although I'll never expect them to call me Dad. They've already got one of those.

But I'd take a bullet for those two. I know it deep inside myself. I want us to be a family. Even though this has all happened in a hurry, something deep down resonates that it's all true, it's all right.

I'm hoping that I feel this way forever, and I'm hoping that Hannah does too. Even when they clank the doors shut on Thomas and Brandon, I'm hoping she'll still need me.

I know how it is with me. I guess I am a damn fool romantic, but I'd give it all up for those three. All they'd have to do is ask.

17

Aguascalientes, Mexico

*T*he trick is to sell the cause. It's simply marketing. To the men who were recruited in the States, it was Big Oil. Down here, it's the Government in general. These are not the guerillas up in the mountains. These are the college boys from Mexico City who want to get at the corruption that keeps la gente down— keeps the people down. It was the same for Zapata at the turn of the 20th Century, except that he was dealing with the hill people, the mestizos, the Indians. They were the dark-skinned denizens of the rugged country, the men who carried machetes because they couldn't afford guns and ammunition.

It's almost easier to recruit them here, in central Mexico, because they're still Zapatistas at heart, even if they are university students on the Internet fighting for justice by murdering their fellow countrymen.

I always look for young men who have a taste for very young girls. I indulge in their rape fantasies. I talk to them about power. Power is the real issue. Not oil, like that lie I use in el norte. It's about power over persons. The young girls just titillate them into more murder, more mayhem. It's a rush like any other high- velocity drug. It makes you swell, it makes you erect. The adrenalin flows wildly as you watch their terrified eyes. They watch horrified as their family is strung up. They watch in disbelief as they see their last sight before they are blinded and then butchered with a final blast through the leftover eye. Then there's true darkness.

The cop in Chicago was after me back in that short-lived desert war of a few days. He searched for me but he could never lay hands on me. I was too elusive, too intelligent for him. And I don't even have to kill Will Koehn to exert my power over him. I can have someone else kill him if I like. All I have to do is toy with him, as a kitten is toyed with by a boy with a piece of string.

Perhaps I'll have his new bitch executed along with her two daughter-bitches. I'd like to be there to see them hanged as the mother watches, just before she gets blinded. Yes, this time I think we should alter the scenario so the mother gets one eye plucked and one eye blasted to gelatinous goo. I'm sure I can have all that arranged.

I know Koehn would love to catch me just so he could sit in on the interview with me. He'd love to hear the Department shrinks proffering their questions at me:

Did you have issues with your father?

Did you hate your mother?

I never knew my own parents. I was raised in foster families. All very loving, I suppose. But the first pair shied away from me when I was twelve. All the family pets kept on disappearing. They never caught me at it, the poor souls, but they suspected I was severely ill. They simply couldn't prove it because I toyed with the Social Services counselor, a pretty woman named Delores. She couldn't come up with a name for what I have, but she could see the anxiety on the faces of my petless foster parents, and so I was given up to another pair of foster parents.

When I was sixteen, Janice, my second foster mother, died of a coronary. It was called "natural causes." They never found out what induced the shock that caused her massive heart attack, but my foster father, Daniel, went back to Social Services and claimed he couldn't handle me any longer, so they dumped me on a Beverly Hills lawyer. He gave me a lot of room, he and his second wife, and I didn't want to rouse any more suspicion about me, so I behaved until I was eighteen. I went away to college at USC, and I graduated Summa Cum Laude in pre-law, which tickled my foster dad. But then I broke his heart by joining the Corps. Because of my grades, I went to officers' candidate school, and from there…

It's just history.

The Corps loved my anti-social attitude. All the way from boot camp through officer's training, they thought I was a natural cold-blooded killer. And they were smarter than any Social Services bitch.

I wasn't mistreated during my stays in those foster homes. I suppose the animals in that first home didn't deserve what they got and neither did the mom with the heart attack in the second household, but you have to learn your trade from the beginning, through experience. You have to learn to improve as you work.

The Internet is a godsend. It was my way of reaching out and contacting men just like me. We're sort of an unofficial fraternity.

I read about Leopold and Loeb when I was in pre-law. Darrow was brilliant in their defense. I'd like to hire Darrow if they ever do close in on me— but they won't. I'm too separate from the fray. I always knew how to distance myself from trouble.

That's why I'm in Mexico, beginning a new false cause. I find the oil ruse boring, now. The others do not, but I do. I'll keep on trying to enflame them with my scheme to terrorize oil companies by murdering low level drones. I'll keep on telling them that we're just practicing, just perfecting our art on our way to the powerful overlords of black gold. Oil is an incredible boiling point for the young, easily-indoctrinated and the insane. Not that I think my co-conspirators are necessarily nuts. It makes it easier to evangelize them, though.

It fascinates me how supposedly intelligent men can be so easily brainwashed. The Chinese and the North Koreans experimented with brainwashing in the Korean War. Hence the book, **The Manchurian Candidate.** *Richard Condon fabricated and exaggerated, in his novel, but some of it rings true. The power of suggestion is incredible, to a certain kind of human creature. When I reached out into cyberspace, I had no idea that I'd get as much cooperation. Not with murder, anyway. It's the ultimate prey, afterall. The human being. Killing a dog or a cat or a parakeet or any mammal or reptile cannot come close, by comparison. There is no excitement like it in the rest of the world.*

Getting away with murder. There's nothing on its level. Nothing.

This is a beautiful part of Mexico. The climate is temperate. Aguascalientes means warm water. There is indeed a warmth here. In central Mexico you don't have the crush of humanity that Mexico City has. Mexico City reminds me of Los Angeles, except there are even more Mexicans south of the border in Aguascalientes.

I can find perhaps ten or twelve kindred spirits on the Internet, and these young men are very happy to do murder to clean the pestilence that is the government. We speak in code on the computer. I teach it to them after I find out their addresses. Then I mail them the code so that I'm untraceable. I use a post office box that is at least a hundred miles from where I am, and each time I send a letter with the code, I use a different post office box.

It spends some gas, but I'm not a fanatic about oil. My friends in the north are a bit balmy about fossil fuels. Oil is simply a boiling point that I employ in order to get them to do the killings.

Personally, I have no desire for sex with young females. I prefer older prostitutes. I have never killed a whore, either. Why deplete the numbers of women who actually endeavor in honest labor? You can't argue that they supply an important service to mankind. No, I have no urge to rape little girls. It's all a throw-in, to keep Will Koehn et al off the real track. He's so busy looking for pedophiles that he'll never raise my scent in his nostrils. He'll be too busy chasing others, in Illinois and in California.

It's unfortunate about Gerald. But I have no fear of our Eastern brother. He does not know my real name, nor does he know my whereabouts. None of my killer fraternity knows who I really am. Not even the men who served in Desert Storm know who I really am. They might attach a name to me, but that doesn't give up my real identity.

Desert Storm seems a thousand years ago. It seems a whole world apart from where I am now, and it almost is that far away.

Maybe I'll give up this pursuit in the years to come. The odds are not with me if I continue. Perhaps I shall quietly fade into the woods, like some jungle beast that has natural camouflage. You never know. Maybe I'll fall in love with a non-hooker, I'll marry, settle down and have daughters of my own. Stranger events have occurred.

Jack the Ripper was never apprehended. He always remained elusive and greasy.

Too chancy. You go on scene, you leave a little something behind. I was amazed that didn't take place in Kuwait. No fingerprints, no DNA, nothing. A cold trail. Two cold cases.

I can imagine the frustration that Will Koehn and his old partner from NCIS must still feel, knowing we're all still out here. Then he might imagine we're just one. But we are legion. He'll never embrace the scope of this venture. It's *really too bad I can't write it all down. Some of it is fiction—killing low level oil workers and their entire families and making it appear that the oil cartel is somehow responsible.*

No, I am responsible. I am a mature man, and I take accountability for what I do. I did it. No question about it. I was the brains behind the scheme.

Now I am a few thousand miles from Detective Koehn and Detective Clemons and that war hero boss of theirs, Captain Pearce. I might as well be in a different solar system.

I have Gloria coming to visit me in an hour. I have the tropical white suit and I have the straw hat with the broad brim and the orange hatband. I have the white shoes of a gringo, too. It's what everyone expects me to wear, here. So I don't disappoint anyone. I dress as they expect a Norte Americano would dress.

I like Gloria. She's an Indian, she's dark, and she never says anything, before, during, or after. I pay her in pesos, and I come away from her feeling refreshed and relaxed. I come away from our encounters feeling sane.

Which psychiatrist or philosopher said that the only time a man is truly sane is the ten minutes in afterglow, right after the orgasm? I can't recall, but there is wisdom to those words. I could never kill any living thing after having sex, but the impulse always returns quickly after those ten minutes.

Killing is the way of nature. It is only in the human community that we indulge ourselves with the comedy of glorifying anti-violent behavior. We ignore our civility frequently, but we like to repeat and recite the fairy tale about the sanctity of life. There is nothing holy about life. We are killer organisms. We kill to eat; we murder to survive. We destroy life to celebrate our way of life. It is all hypocrisy, and the Church is the worst hypocrite of all. These pompous celibates with the red hats preach non-violence, but they have perpetrated most of the mayhem on this planet. Check out Northern Ireland, the Middle East, and the genocide of the Native American. Manifest Destiny was simply a façade for mass murder. It indulged our lust for manslaughter. Whack them for the American Dream! What an ungodly hoax!

Gloria is coming, so I will be too, soon. It only takes about twenty minutes for her to have me speaking in tongues. What the languages are, I have no idea. Speaking in tongues is not a phenomenon relegated to religion. There have been numerous cases of people talking in long-dead languages for centuries.

The first time it happened, my initial foster mother threatened to have me evaluated.

115

But then, her mynah bird disappeared from its gilded cage, never to be seen again. She got the message and told her husband, my foster father numero uno, that Tweety or Whoever had simply flown away, right out the living room window.

The miracle would have been that bird flying through a screened window. He did not, however, question his quivering spouse about the mynah bird's disappearance any further.

Gloria is ringing at my apartment's doorbell, so I ring her up to my third floor apartment in this very modern apartment complex. Once inside my door, she wastes no time disrobing. She leads me into the bedroom in this central air-conditioned, cool apartment, and she sits me at the foot of the king-sized mattress and she begins felatio on me hurriedly. Once I am erect, stout, she hops aboard my lap and I am deep within her. She tightens on me, and I come almost instantly. She keeps on lunging downward at me until I am flaccid and harmless.

Then I bend down and bite her nipples, until they perk and turn darker wine-colored then they were when we started all this. I nip at them repeatedly.

Until she smiles. And then I let go of her and she disengages.

She sits on the bed and I watch her masturbate herself to orgasm. She throbs at least three times before she's finished.

Then she throws her clothes back on. No underwear. Just a white cotton skirt and a short-sleeved white blouse. She wears cheap flip flops on her feet, the kind you can buy at any store for a few dollars. Gloria is not a well-heeled whore. She's a working woman with no husband and three teenaged sons.

I give her fifty American dollars—twice what she normally receives. She doesn't smile, however. She never does. I don't look for any good humor on her attractive Indian face. Smiles are not what I'm paying for. I'm paying for service. She comes through, so I have no complaints.

When I left the military, it was difficult at first, but I adapted well, as I always have. I joined the Marines to become an efficient killer. I'd killed before, but I wanted to perfect my technique. The military trains you to kill the enemy only, of course, but that doesn't mean you can't use the training for other purposes. Lee

Harvey Oswald is a famous case in point. The sniper at the University of Texas is another. There are other examples, as well.

The Corps taught me discipline, something I only knew by instinct. Plan. Prepare. Execute. Have your escape route ready. Disappear. Vanish inside the crowd. Those are talents the military developed for me. I learned them well. I had good teachers. They were brutal instructors, but the lessons were permanently engraved inside me.

I had no desire to kill Saddam Hussein or his troops. I had every desire to kill those families in Kuwait. It's what I signed up for. Killing was a daily event in a war. What better way to get away with murder? We were in a war zone. Death was everywhere present. Loss of life was commonplace. Murder was sanctified by our own government, just the way it always is when a country declares war on anybody.

And what is it to God if I help dispatch a few more souls to Him? In the course of history, what can it mean to my own soul, if I have one, that I have increased the supply of fresh corpses on their way to heaven?

18

She's sitting at the booth in Denny's, waiting for me. I sit down opposite her. I haven't seen her look this good in a very long time.

"Will."

"Mary."

Her face is solemn and unreadable. I always have trouble trying to guess her mood.

"You said you wanted to talk to me," I tell her.

"Yes. I did."

I feel as though she's about to lay waste to me with something devastating. Maybe she'll tell me she's pregnant. But she'd never make a mistake like that happen to her. She's careful. She's smart. She's on the pill.

"What can I do for you?"

"You don't have to come on that stiff, Will. I'm not going to make another scene."

Now she's become stiff, like a porcupine raising its back at you, quills at the ready.

"I wasn't thinking. Yes, I was."

She has that damnable freshness that makes me want to grab hold of her in spite of our current situation. Her breasts stand out against her tight, ribbed turtleneck sweater. Her lips are plum-colored and they're disturbing and devastating me.

"Cannot tell a lie, no?"

"I can tell lies. But I never did to you."

"How's the new lady working out?"

"It's progressing all right."

I'm being very much distracted by her fragrance. I have no idea what she wears, after all the time we spent together, but it's subtle and sweet, and I can't take my eyes off her white, delectable throat.

"Anything serious?"

Then she smiles at me.

"Oh. I forgot. Everything is dead-serious with you."

"I laugh at things. I laugh at things all the time."

"What do you laugh at, Will?"

There's nothing amusing happening inside me, now. But I can detect the flush of self-consciousness and embarrassment she arouses in me for still wanting her as badly as I do.

"I thought you wanted to talk to me about something."

She looks down at her clear-polished, short fingernails.

"Yes. I do. They've caught the hacker who procured the victims for Thomas and Brandon."

She's checking her nails fastidiously, as if the edge on those nails can never be finely-honed enough to please her.

"The guy who found the victims?"

"Yes. They even think he might have been used back in Desert Storm. Apparently he knows Carl Thomas from way back in cyber history."

"He hacked into the personnel files of those oil companies."

"It seems to be the case, yes. We've interviewed him several times and explained the penalties for accessory to murder, in multiples, and he's become very concerned about his own longevity.... But he still appears to be hesitant about naming names. All we could get out of him was the names of Carl Thomas and Philip Brandon. I was at those interviews, Will. I think he's holding back."

"Holding back what? Holding back how?"

"I think he thinks if he keeps that ace of spades up his sleeve that he'll have better bargaining power at his sentencing. I think he might have all four aces up his shirtsleeve. It's just my impression. Maybe. I could be wrong."

"You're saying he knows at least one more name. A very important name."

I want to feel my tongue inside her warm and pretty mouth. I want to taste her lips with my own, the way I did, not so long ago. I feel the temperature in here going up, although I know it's my own body heat that's rising.

"That could be it. Or it could just be a feint, you know, a false jab, to make us think he knows more than he does. These hackmeisters are an arrogant lot. They think their little machines are going to take over the world."

"He might have something there, Mary."

She puts on a pouty face that she knows will distract and arouse me. It's the competitiveness in her.

"You think there's another player involved who we haven't spotted?"

"I think it's possible."

"Meaning?"

I look at my own fingertips. She thinks I never laugh. What the hell does *that* mean?

"There was a Captain Benjamin Anderson we looked at, back in Kuwait."

I feel the clench of my teeth down to their roots. It becomes painful as I hold the clamp tightly.

"And why aren't you still interested in him?"

She is now the prosecutor, with the accusatory jab at me.

"Because he's dead."

"I love ghost stories, Will."

Her sarcasm drips all over me, head to toes.

"There are no ghosts."

"You sure? Not even the Holy Ghost?"

She's grinning at my obvious discomfort. I want to take her by her hair and flatten her.

120

"He was blown out of his boots in Iraq, and there was nothing left but his dog tags. The whole scene was ignited with a small fire bomb, and they finished it off with Willie Peter."

"Say?"

"White phosphorus. The shit burns and burns and it makes big holes wherever it lands. There were three guys in that Hummer, and there were only ashes left of the other two Marines with Anderson. They couldn't ID any of the three after the intensity of that burn. And none of the three were ever seen again."

"So why are you still interested in Anderson?"

I'm tiring of the berating, but I can see she's loaded with energy. Her tank is still filled, and she's not about to let up on me.

"I wasn't—until you fed the fire with this stuff about another player being involved. I always liked Anderson. He had a fucked-up family background, foster homes and so on, but he didn't have anything incriminating in black and white in his jacket. He was another brilliant student.

"One of his DIs wrote, though, that looking into his eyes was 'like looking through a pane of glass.' He said Anderson was unreadable. And drill instructors are paid to read their platoon of pukes. It's their job to know their guys.

"Anderson was a wild card. You never knew where he was, in the deck. You follow me?"

"You're talking about a borderline sociopath, Will. Yes?"

She's instructing me. She's patiently sticking the analytical knife in my chest, and she's loving every minute of this.

"Not borderline. No. This guy was very clever, very sly. Those are my kinda guys, in series killers. The dumbasses hit you with a fry pan and then get caught because they sit there on scene with blood all over their dago tees."

"He's not a dumbass?"

"None of the three are—or were. They're all bright boys. Cutie pies. And I don't buy the oil theory as a motive, not for one goddamned second."

"Then what was their motive, even if Anderson is really dead?"

"They did it for the hell of it."

121

"Come again? I don't think Dr. Freud or Dr. Jung would buy it."

"They're thrill killers. They do it for the buzz. They do it just to get away with it. They're just laying down a false track with the oil thing."

The thought of Anderson distracts me for a moment, and my desire for Mary is on the wane. Suddenly my own heat starts to plummet. I can feel the room chill, all around us.

"That was the other thing."

"What?" I ask her.

"We just had a message from the *Federales* in Mexico City. They've come up with two dead families of their own."

"Same MO?"

"Not quite. This time the youngest girl was assaulted and murdered, like ours, but currently they all had something called a Panamanian necktie done to each of them, along with the final hanging. The girls were both propped up as if they were watching their family members being strung up."

The Panamanian necktie is indigenous to the drug gangs in South and Central America. The deal with their tongues being yanked out of their throats and tied around their necks is their new signature. The eyes thing has been replaced.

The author remains the same, however.

I look at Mary and I feel a rise of temperature, but only briefly. The arousal is replaced by something sad, something gloomy and morose. I feel emptied out.

And hollow.

"What about this guy Anderson?"

I remind Jack about the Captain being one of my "big three" suspects back in Desert Storm. Then he recalls our original conversation about Anderson.

"How'd he get out of the Middle East?"

"That, Horatio, is the question."

"Who the fuck is Horatio?"

I want to explain to him about Hamlet's best friend and sidekick, but I wave him off, and we head to the archives.

I open the yellowing folder I have kept on my investigations in Kuwait. I made copies when I left NCIS, even though I was supposed to leave everything aboard *The Intrepid*, my last ship in the Navy cops.

I read again about his foster homes. I see how his first set of adoptive parents couldn't handle him, somehow, so he was transferred to another home. In the second house, the adoptive mother suffered a massive heart attack and died not long after Anderson entered the household. The bereaved second adoptive father also could not handle the Captain, so he was sent packing to live with some attorney.

Anderson went to college, was brilliant academically, like his two playmates, Carl Thomas and Philip Brandon, and then, like the other two, he entered our beloved Corps. Anderson, however, went to a "brand name" university. In the Marines, he apparently was learning to hone his anti-social skills, as all killers are encouraged to do from boot camp onward. But it appears that these three could not step back into their own humanity from all the brainwashing about kill zones and fields of fire.

Perhaps killing the enemy wasn't enough. Or perhaps killing the enemies of the Republic was never the idea for them in the first place. The military has spawned its share of nut jobs. We don't own the license for that kind of thing. Postal workers have had a bad track record from time to time, as have medical doctors. The theory remains hot that Jack the Ripper owned a surgeon's bag and a surgeon's skill, and he paid no attention to "first do no harm."

The Captain could not have survived the blast in Iraq, the one that melted his vehicle and his two co-riders to ash or less than ash. It troubles me, however, that no trace of his DNA was found on scene. It troubled me back in Desert Storm. It troubled Pete Donato, my partner back then, as well, but there was no physical evidence nor was their anything circumstantial about his "demise" that pressed us to pursue him.

Unless he really is the walking dead, a zombie. Anderson was not from the Islands, nor do we have any idea that he practiced voodoo, so that theory flies in the light of reason.

The alternative is that he faked his death to escape the war and to flee his crimes before we really had a chance to talk to him face to face.

The Oedipal thing about the blinding of the girls would be something a smart guy like Anderson would pull. I read he took a number of classical literature courses as an undergraduate. It was the same thing I discussed with the teacher back in Evanston at Northwestern. The Captain would be familiar with Sophocles, of course. Oedipus blinded himself, gouged out his own eyes when he discovered he had mated with his biological mother and that he'd murdered his real father at that legendary crossroads. He blinded himself because he could not bear looking at the world he'd been fated and born into. Something like that, if I recall my own lit classes at all.

Greek tragedy. Has to be a holocaust by the time it winds up. There have to be dead bodies scattered all over the stage. It's like a requirement of the genre. That's what my teachers taught me, back in college. Shakespeare pulled the same numbers in his tragedies. The corpses fill the stage before the final curtain.

If I don't catch Thomas and Brandon soon, there'll be more dead people popping up in the local scenery. Now they're cropping up south of the Rio Grande. He's tweaking the MO. He's using the necktie instead of the Oedipal *modus operandi*. It's still the same perpetrator. I think Anderson really is alive.

He got out of Iraq. I'm betting he has money from the lawyer, his third foster father. He behaved like the model son in that household because it was to his best interests to keep straight. He was just letting it build up after the first two foster failures. Smart prick. Bide your time. Wait. Let the pressure cooker heat until the urge becomes unbearable. As it did in Kuwait. As it did here in Chicago, and as it likely occurred in Mexico. *Mexico lindo*.

I'll make some phone calls to the lawyer. I'll fly to LA if I have to so I can face to face him. I think Captain Pearce is good for one or two round trip tickets to LAX. Jack likes Southern California, anyway. He has relatives in Burbank.

David Crowley is the lawyer, now retired. He lives in one of those mansions, not houses, in Beverly Hills. He lives among the rich and infamous. Notorious. Whatever you want to call these face-people from La La Land. I liked seeing the Hollywood sign on the side of the hill as we drove the rental over here.

We get out of the Chevy and walked across his enormous, manicured lawn, and he greets us at the door as if he were expecting us. We did call, so that's why he's waiting for us.

He takes us into his elegant estate, and Jack and I join him in what he calls his "California Room." It's glass-enclosed, it's air-conditioned, and it has a full bar.

David Crowley has sandy, thinning hair, but he's in peak condition. I'm certain he has a trainer, making sure no blubber defaces his athletic, fit frame. He is Hollywood handsome too. He's one of those sixty-year-olds who ages well—like corked wine.

"You're here to talk about my son, Benjamin," he smiles.

"Yes."

Jack is silent, perusing all the goodies in this "California room."

"My foster son is dead. I don't really understand why you're…"

"I think…. We think your son might be alive."

"Excuse me?" he smiles. The teeth are straight and white and feral. This guy must have been a shark in the courtroom. He has that winning air about him. I'll bet he never settled. I'll bet it always went his way.

"I think he might have deserted and got out of the Middle East. But I think he must have had help, and his only possible source for that kind of money would be you."

"That's absurd."

"It's called accessory to a murder, in this case accessory to multiple murders."

"I think it's time for you two to leave."

125

"We can have the LA Police take you in for questioning. I know you know your rights, Counselor, but if you have information on the whereabouts of Benjamin Anderson, once Captain Benjamin Anderson, it'd be to your best interests to divulge that knowledge right now. Because if we find out you financed that desertion, we'll be back, or someone more local will be."

Jack stands, and then I do, and we leave the "California Room."

"Maybe Anderson really is dead, Will," Jack says as he takes the earphones out of his ears on the flight back to O'Hare from LAX.

We were in Southern California for all of sixteen hours. It didn't give us much time for sightseeing.

"No, he's alive. He's not close to Dad, though. My guess is that he's in Mexico, killing new folks. You know, expanding his repertoire. He's adjusting his technique, tuning it up for some big opus. It's like he's in training."

"And maybe he got blown to snot, back in Iraq."

I smile at my partner, and then he plugs himself back in to his onboard movie.

"Nope. This fucker's a zombie. A walking corpse, straight out of the grave. The undead," I grin.

Jack hears me through his soundtrack.

"*Boogedy boogedy*," he says, straight-faced.

19

The FBI got a phone tap okayed in Peoria, Illinois, and Carl Thomas made the mistake of calling his sister there, and now we have a number in Tinley Park, a southwest suburb.

The Feds want to join us on the raid in Tinley Park, and it's good etiquette to say yes, since they did the legwork in Peoria with Thomas's sister. Jack and I and six uniforms head from The Loop toward Tinley Park at 9:45 P.M. We've waited until dark, and we've been assisted by the Tinley Park cops in clearing the nearby houses and apartment buildings. They said they'd do it quietly, and when we arrive forty minutes later, the area seems tranquil. There are streetlights on these blocks, but the lighting remains dim. We pull up to the curb in our unmarked LTD, and the uniforms park a quarter block down behind us.

The address is 1616 Melborne. He's supposedly on the uppermost of a three flat apartment building. The name on the box is Smythe, I see, as we pass the mailboxes in the hallway. The entry is locked, so Jack uses his illegal burglar pick to pop it open in seconds. The three FBI special agents accompanying us, two men and a woman, are not enthused with Jack's picking the lock.

"Son-of-a-bitch was broken open," Jack lies to them over his left shoulder.

Then we ascend the flights of stairs to the third floor, guns drawn. We're all wearing vests, Feds included. We're all carrying nine millimeter weapons, but the FBI woman carries a pump shotgun.

She doesn't appear soft or feminine, either. I imagine she's used the shotgun before. She has the look of a hunter on her plain, not un-pretty face. She simply looks like a female cop, I'm saying. The two males are standard, buzzcut Fibbies, both wearing dark suits underneath their vests.

We arrive at Thomas's door. The two uniforms pass by the FBI personnel and Jack and me. They're the ones with the swinging sledge. I stop them, and I listen by the door, but I don't linger, because I don't want to get shot at through the door. I've had that happen in my NCIS career, and pulling out splinters from your face is no joy. The vest only protects your chest and torso. Nothing stops the damage to your melon.

I hear nothing, so I shout through the door as I stand with my back to the wall.

"Thomas! Police! Open the door! Now!"

Jack aims his weapon head-high at the door.

Still no sound.

I nod at the two uniforms with the swinging sledge.

They take a fierce backswing, and then they splinter the door and its frame with one mighty blow. We're through the entry, and we crouch, guns pointed into the darkness. We search the living room first. There appears to be no furniture. The place looks barren, less than spartan.

Our next stop is the bedroom. Again, no furniture, not a single stick. No bed, no anything.

The FBI agents are into the kitchen, after we split up by the bedroom. The woman calls for us. We see the light she's turned on in the kitchen. The Feds are surrounding a man lying on the floor in a pool of his own blood.

It's Philip Brandon, and he looks like he's just about tapped out.

We rush him to Mercy Hospital, back by the Loop. The paramedics arrived at the Melborne address within ten minutes, so Brandon is still breathing, but just barely. He's hanging on by a spider's thread.

They hurry him into ER, and then the ER surgeon dismisses us. We post two uniforms by the room in which they're examining him. Jack and I head for the cafeteria because neither of us has eaten since 11:00 A.M. this morning. I get a Diet Coke and a wrapped submarine sandwich. Jack opts for coffee and a cheeseburger.

"Do you have hypertension yet, partner?" I smile at him as we sit in a booth.

"Not yet, but I'm working on it," he smiles back at me.

"Do you think he'll live long enough to talk to us?"

"No. I think he's four quarts low."

"Gunshot, don't you think?" I ask.

"You'd think. Ripe big hole under his right shoulder. Large caliber, maybe a .45. Might be a .38 magnum. Ballistics will tell all."

"I'm betting on the .45."

"Yeah. It sounds logical. You think Thomas shot him?"

"Thomas was the guy receiving those calls at that address, according to the tap. The FBI says he identified himself to his sister from Peoria."

"Could have been anyone else?"

"Maybe, Jack. But I think it was Thomas."

"Why shoot his fraternity brother—the oil Mafia hitman?"

"Family feud. Who the fuck knows," I say.

I put down the sub sandwich. It's dry and tastes suddenly like ashes. We expected to collar one of our principals, and we end up with a stiff-to-be.

"One jump ahead of us, Jack, and I'm getting real fucking tired of it."

"I hear you.... But Phil might hang on after all. Give the piece of shit a chance."

129

"Hello, Philip," I tell the man lying on the hospital bed.

He blinks.

I look over to Jack and then at the tough-girl FBI agent who's here to listen in for the Bureau.

"How're you doin'?"

Brandon groans.

"You need a stronger drip in that morphine thing?" I ask him.

He looks right at me.

"*Get...out,*" he murmurs, just audibly.

There's a doctor watching the proceedings. He's eyeballing us very carefully. We've got all of three minutes.

"Who shot you, Philip?" Jack asks.

"Yeah. That's what I was going to ask you," I add.

"Get out," he says, a little louder.

"He left you for dead, guy," I explain. "Don't you want to make him pay?"

He looks at me as if something has registered.

"*He...came...back.*"

"Who? Who came back?"

He stares at me with an appeal on his ashen face.

"I was supposed to meet...Carl."

"Yeah. And?"

"*He came back.*"

"Who was it, Philip? Who came back? Who shot you?"

"I..."

Suddenly he shoots straight up in bed as if he's going to try and jump at me. The nurse who just now entered the room screams, and the doctor grabs her by the arm, holds her back, and then releases her and rushes toward Brandon, who's still having spasms on his bed.

The doctor yells for us to clear out and the nurse composes herself enough to help him get Brandon back down flat on the mattress. We all leave them to work on Philip.

Ten minutes later the doctor re-emerges and tells us that Philip Brandon has expired.

"What did ballistics say?" Jack asks me, six hours later. We're way over our regular shift, but Pearce wants us to locate the shooter.

"Forty-five, just like you said," I report. "But he picked up the casing and dug out the slug. Probably with a big knife, like a k-bar," I explain.

"No wonder he bled out."

"The ME said he did a nice job of removing the bullet. Almost surgeon-like."

"But he made him bleed a lot worse, digging into him."

"That was his intention, Jack."

Clemons grins at my sarcasm.

"Indeed," he smiles.

No prints on Brandon's body. In Peoria they bring in Carl's sister and threaten her with accessory to whatever crimes they can come up with, but she lawyers up and shuts up, and there's nothing forthcoming out of her.

Whoever shot Philip might have missed who he was really gunning for, I'm thinking. I'm thinking he might have come looking for Carl and found Philip there instead. Brandon and Thomas seem to have been a pair, so to speak, ever since Kuwait. One was always somewhere in the vicinity of the other. They were partners in the 'terror' plot against the oil guys, and they were true believers. The guy who shot them obviously has no sense of *semper fi*. He shot one of his own kind, it seems to me. I think it was the zombie from California. I think he was coming to fix Thomas before he fixed Philip Brandon. I think it was Captain Benjamin Anderson, recently deceased, who has come back from the land of the dead, like Odysseus in *The Odyssey*, to live once again in the land of the mortals after he'd learned the secrets of the Underworld. It's Captain Benjamin Anderson, recruiter of young maniacs like Carl Thomas and Philip Brandon and our boy Gerald from the Northeast. It was Anderson all along who was giving the orders, and now he's fixed himself up with a little trigger time, here in my hometown.

I kiss her once, then again. But I don't talk about Brandon or Thomas or Captain Benjamin Anderson or any of those spooks who've haunted my house. They don't have to inhabit Hannah's home too. I kiss her again, and then I embrace her tightly, here in my bed in New Town.

"The kids are with him?" I ask her.

The brown eyes grab me, as usual. Her torso is sweaty and slick. I run my hand down to her pubic hair, and she flinches, deliciously. Her body is lanky and elegant. Her legs are long and athletic—like a runner's legs. They're not overly muscled, just strong and sexy.

"I already told you twice. Yes."

"I'm sorry. I must have forgotten."

She sits up in bed.

"Bringing work home with you?" she asks.

Her lips are full, but not puffed, like some actress who visits the plastic surgeon. They're enticing, yes. They have the slightest tinge of scarlet still remaining after I've kissed the color off, for the last half hour of passion.

"Yeah. I guess so. I'm sorry."

"Am I safe, Will?"

I take her and pull her back toward me. She relents and lies down beside me.

"I won't do it again," I tell her.

"You say that all the time."

Her eyes have warmth as well as color. They bid me to keep coming closer. Then she takes her delicate, long fingers, and she runs her rose-colored nails down my right thigh. She's putting me in a very painful state of arousal. She takes hold of me and squeezes until I issue a mock protest.

"I mean it all the time."

"I read about Brandon being found shot and then dying this morning in the paper. How come you didn't tell me last night?"

"They're still out there. At least two of them. When we get them all, you'll be the first person I tell."

She sits back up and I breathe out.

"Don't hide stuff that concerns me and the girls, Will."

Her passion has been replaced by sober concern. She's not angry. Just disappointed in me, in all of us, I think.

"I tell you everything I *can* tell you."

"Are you telling me the truth or are you telling me what you think I want to hear?"

"I won't lie to you. But there are things I can't discuss. Not with anyone, Hannah."

She returns to soft. She rakes her lovely rose fingernails down both of my thighs, and then she kisses my calves and then moves her way up to my navel.

"Okay. Just so I know the rules."

"It's the life."

"That the way it was for you in the military? 'That's the life?'"

"I don't want to lose you."

She takes me in her mouth and a shock wave jolts me to my core. Then she rises back up quickly, just to let me know she's the lover in command, here.

"I don't want to lose you either."

"If I say what I really think, I'll frighten you off."

"Frighten me off?"

"Yeah. You'll say I'm going too fast."

Her arms are thin and lithe, a contrast to my thick and heavily muscled forearms and biceps. She's the lean one. I'm the ex-athlete who's thickening, year after year, lately. My legs are twice the size of Hannah's—but she insists she likes my bulk. She says I'm not really fat and that I never will be.

"Yes. You might do that, if I know what you're referring to."

"Well, I'm not going to go there tonight. This is all too short, so I'll save it for much later."

She looks out into the darkness of the pre-dawn from my front window that faces Clark Street.

"You really want to get all this serious?"

"Yes, Hannah."

I never want to leave this house. It exudes the same warmth and safety that I feel while I'm in her arms. This is a *safe* place. Nothing bad can harm us, here. This is my citadel, my safe place that cannot be stormed and taken. Hannah is the source of the comfort I feel when I'm with her in her home.

"So do I."

"You do?"

"Yes, Will, I do."

"How am I supposed to take that?" I ask her.

"For what it's worth. I love you, you know."

I aim those words right back at her.

"Don't bring your work into our bedroom again, okay?" she says.

And then she lies back down next to me.

Forensics can come up with no evidence. If it was Anderson, he left no trace. He just left a dying Philip Brandon in his wake.

We have federal wiretaps on Anderson's lawyer-daddy. Nothing has come up yet. I don't think it will. Anderson is too smart to get himself caught electronically. If he's living off Daddy's money, we can find no account. There is of course the off-shore solution for him. It makes it much more difficult for us to find a paper trail.

If I'm guessing right, because he disappeared in Kuwait, it will be very difficult for us to look into his disappearance from here. The Kuwait police are not very helpful and they are not very efficient. And like most countries we've 'liberated,' they don't have much use for Americans, either.

So we beat on, boats against the current . . .

Fitzgerald was one of my favorite authors. He wrote prose-poetry. His lines were lyrical and sometimes cynical, but you can't ignore the beauty of his words. I'm flapping against the current, myself. I'm trying to find at least two killers, one of whom is a rapist as well, and I haven't been able to come up with a whiff, not a single scent nor one solid trail. They remain elusive—that's why I thought of *The Great Gatsby*. Boats against the current. Everything seems uphill.

What does Anderson do next? He kills Carl Thomas. He killed Brandon because he thought Philip was stupid enough that we'd eventually nab him, and then we'd find out about the Captain's rebirth. He's burning all his bridges behind him. He's getting rid of witnesses before they can be caught and squeezed. Carl's next.

I have to find him before Captain Benjamin Anderson does. I have to find him before this "dead" man re-enters the world beneath us once more.

20

Bridgeport is an old neighborhood, one of the oldest in the city. It lies near Comiskey Park, home of the White Sox. Richard J. Daley was the Mayor for decades, and he lived not far from my father. I come to visit my dad often, even though I've moved out now. I get lonesome for him, as I always do, and then nothing can take the place of seeing him in the flesh. He's seventy-two, and so I know someday not too far off I won't be able to see him anymore. Death was something you could get used to by sight, but you could never get used to the smell of it, back in the Middle East.

That same smell greets me and Jack when we visit homicide crime scenes, here in the city. If the vic has been lying there for a while, it reminds me of the stink in Kuwait City and in Iraq.

I sometimes regret that I left the Corps for NCIS just when the shit hit the blades of the fan in Desert Storm because it would have been my only real shot at real combat. I've been shot at a few times trying to apprehend bad guys over in the war zone, but I've never had a bead drawn on me in the States yet. I'm kind of hoping I won't, also.

My dad looks just slightly grayer than he did the last time I was home, but he looks healthy. His color's good, and his posture is the same as always, board-stiff-erect. He must have a good supply of calcium in his bones, but I've never seen him drink milk in my life.

"When's Sammy coming home again?"

It's October, and I already know the answer.

"Probably Christmas," he says. "You know how busy he is with school and with his girlfriend."

His girlfriend's name is Megan. He's living with her in an apartment in Champaign, Illinois, home of the Fighting Illini and the University of Illinois. Sammy's got two more semesters before he gets his MBA. He wants to work in Chicago, and Megan wants to work and cohabit with him in the city, as well, he's told me on the phone. I don't have the time to visit him on campus now that I'm on homicide because we're always on duty and because of the rape/murder business that headlines our unsolved board in my office.

"How are you, Will? Really. How're you doing?"

I'm sitting at the ancient kitchen table across from him. The windows are opened because it's a warm day—60 degrees—and because George Koehn is a fresh air fanatic. He used to battle with my mom over opened windows off season, but the old man won every fight, and my mother got used to wearing a couple of sweaters in the house.

"I'm all right, Dad."

"Let me ask you one more time, without the perfunctory bullshit response," he smiles.

"I'm all fucked up. Better?"

"Why?"

"The job."

"The rape case you were telling me about? The one connected back to that little war?"

"Yes."

"And what else, Will? You can't be living your life without those damn personal entanglements. You've been watching *Oprah* again?"

He knows I rarely watch any kind of television. I didn't when I was a kid, either.

"I'm still with Hannah, if that's what you're getting at."

"Don't get angry, kiddo. I wasn't trying to make you mad."

"I'm still with her. And I know she's older than I am."

"When she's sixty. You know how that goes. You really want to watch her age? I had to watch her age in front of my eyes, and shit, she's only a little younger than I am."

"I can't help how I feel. Next time I'll screen them with a questionnaire. I'll have the age thing number one, just for you."

He laughs.

"She make you happy, Will?"

"Yeah. She does. Yes, she does."

"Then you take it from there. You're a big boy. You were a big boy even when you were little. I don't mean size. You were always more grown up than the other guys around you. Anyone could see that. You always knew your own mind. You weren't a follower, that's for goddam sure."

"Is that supposed to be a compliment?"

"Actually, it's a complaint. I don't ever remember you *being* a child. I remember you being smaller physically, but you were always like talking to an adult. It's as if you just skipped being a kid and went right to becoming an old fart in a young man's body."

I look down at my fingers.

"It's just that you never acted childish. You know what I mean? It made me, and your mother, worry about you some."

"You worried about me?"

"We thought you might turn into one of these whacked-out little shits. You know, prodigies or whatever. They said your tests were unusually high, the scores, I mean.

"You were always so goddam stone-serious, Will. I can't remember hearing you laugh after you passed twelve."

"I laugh, Dad. That isn't right."

"It isn't the way I remember you. You were as serious about football as you were about school, and you never had a girlfriend for very long, so I was wondering if you even *liked* girls."

"You thought I was *gay*?"

"Not really. I just thought you might be what they call anti-social."

"I don't have many friends. No."

"Jack Clemons a friend?"

138

"He's my partner. He has his own life and friends."

"Your partner from NCIS?"

"Donato?"

"Yeah."

"Same deal, Dad. We were on the job together. He's still in the Navy cops."

"Why don't you have any guy friends?"

"I don't know. I really don't. It's just hard for me to get that close to anyone."

"Was it hard to get close to this Hannah?"

"No. It wasn't. That's why I'm still with her, so to speak."

"So to speak? She isn't talking anything permanent?"

"She thinks I'll get put off because of her age."

"She's just being realistic, Will. And she's been divorced. You carry old shit with you whether you want to or not."

I can hear the noise from the streets outside. The sound used to put me to sleep when I lived here. On ship, I almost went section eight because of the quiet of the sea. All you had was the sound of the waves against the hull and the occasional outburst from some swabbies back from a shore leave. Mostly it was maddeningly hushed on board *The Intrepid*.

This is where I grew up. I played touch football and softball across the street in the playground of the elementary school I attended. My mother and father made it to all the activities I was involved in—Cub Scouts and Boy Scouts. Later they attended my football games at DeLaSalle High School, a Catholic secondary school not far from here. I was All City my junior year and All State in football my senior year. Then I turned down the chance to play in the Big Ten because I wanted to get my education and leave the game behind. I didn't want sports to interfere with my learning. All the guys I played with at DeLaSalle thought I was fucking nuts—a full ride to the University of Illinois. They thought my love of words was a little strange, also. I think they had the idea I was a little weird, even though I dated girls in high school and throughout college. I didn't do what everyone expected me to do. Not what my father or mother or brother thought I was going to do, anyway.

"You going to catch this piece of shit, Will?"

He was handsome once. I've seen the photographs. Full head of hair. Now he's got the male balding pattern on the crown of his head. His neck has acquired a little bit of turkey neck, but his chest and arms are still as powerful as they always were. Age has merely bent him, a little bit.

"There's more than one."

"You going to catch however many of them, then?"

He has the kind of internal power that a child always takes for granted. He's a rock, the way any father is supposed to be. But my old man was a survivor; he endured.

"Yes, I am."

"That's good to hear…. I always dreamed of becoming the sniper who blew the back off Hitler's head. But the dirty prick did himself in his bunker, or so the story goes. He was afraid the Russians were going to get him."

"I wouldn't have tortured him if I'd caught him alive. You know that? I would've given him a shovel, fed him real well, treated him like a prized bull, and then I would've had him begin burying everybody he was responsible for in those death camps. He never would've had time to take poison if I'd got him. I'd have kept him busy twelve hours a day. And then I'd make sure he was fed well and that he slept eight solid every night so he'd be able to dig graves every day of the rest of his fuck-faced life."

His eyes are distant, as if he's returned to Normandy. He's on that French sand, hearing the bullets buzz by him. He's seeing the tide turned red with American blood.

"This guy isn't even in Hitler's league, Dad."

"Sure he is. Killing one human being is holocaust enough. Just because Herr Hitler murdered millions doesn't make your guy or guys any less evil. There ain't no math in killing. One's as good as a million. One's all it takes to secure you a spot in hell."

I can see him pulling the trigger on *Herr Hitler*, right now. I can see hatred, murderous hatred, on my dad's face at the mention of the Nazi tyrant.

"Maybe you're right."

"I'm always right. I'm your old man."

A young boy on a bicycle goes flying by the front window. I can see him down the hall from the kitchen here. The leaves are only just turning to reds and oranges.

"You like your new place?" he asks.

"I like it when Hannah's there. I'm not so sure, when the place is empty except for me."

My eyes seem to focus more clearly when I say her name. I see a big smile on the old guy's face. He knows how I feel about Hannah. He's always had more than his share of intuition, regarding what was going on inside my brother and me.

"Will they let you bring in a mutt?"

"No pets, Dad."

His face saddens. A little liquid gathers in his eyes. He's a dog-lover, regardless of his bitching about the neighbors' barking hounds.

"Too bad. Dogs are good companions."

"How come we never had one, then?"

"Too much aggravation. We got enough goddam barkers in this fucking neighborhood. If it wasn't illegal, I'd shoot some of these bastards who let their animals yowl all goddam day. They're a nuisance, these people and their mutts."

"Can I do anything for you, Dad? Anything at all?"

He peers over at me. He's giving me his "patient" face. I'm being retarded. Slow. He's way ahead of me.

"You can take me to Burger King for a double Whopper with cheese."

"You don't like White Castle?"

"That place is going to kill you and Jack."

I've told him about my eating habits.

"All right. Let's go," I tell him.

"When do you have to be at the job?" he asks.

"I'm off 'til tomorrow night."

"Good. Then I'll take you out for a steak for dinner at Maggio's."

It's his favorite restaurant.

"Is it okay if I invite Hannah?"

"Hell, yes. I'd like to meet this 'older woman.'"

"I'm paying for dinner, and I won't listen to any of your usual shit."

He smiles at me because he knows I used to let him pick up all the tabs until I got this job as a detective. Then I vowed never to let him pick up a check again.

"It's a deal."

Hannah meets us at Maggio's. The restaurant is on the far southwest side, so I drive my father, and Hannah takes her car from Oakbrook. The girls are once again with their father this weekend.

She's wearing a summer dress that Irwin Shaw might have liked and might have written about. It isn't low cut, but it's very attractive on her. It's a forest green that accentuates her hair and face, somehow—I'm no fashion person.

"Hello," I tell her, and I can feel my face flush.

She gives me a kiss, and when I introduce my father to her, she gives him an affectionate peck on the cheek. I can see the old man blushing slightly, as he does when he's surprised or when he's moved by somebody or something.

"You're as pretty as he said you were. And I thought he might be exaggerating because he's in love with you, you know."

The old man smiles at her to take the pressure off what he's just suggested.

"He's told you about me?" she smiles.

The warmth has reached my ears, now.

"It's all he talks about—except for the job."

"I'm at the top of his conversation, am I?" she continues to beam.

"You are a very important personage, yes."

"That's very good to hear, because I love your son very much."

I look over at her as if it's the first time I've seen her face.

"Well, now that all the mush is dispensed with, you suppose we could get a drink in this goddam joint?" he laughs. "Tulio!" he yells out to his favorite waiter.

Tulio rushes over.

"What can I get you folks?"

"Two beers. And for the lady?" my Dad asks Hannah.

"I'll have a scotch on the rocks, with a little glass of ice water on the side."

Dad makes the order with Tulio, and the waiter rushes off. Maggio's is very busy tonight. All the joints in Oak Lawn are hopping on weekend evenings. We were lucky to get a table at 6:00 p.m. The place jams up after 5:00 p.m.

We finish our meals—Dad and I have the New York strip and Hannah has the salmon—and then we have another round of drinks.

"Once you get past all that dead-seriousness, my boy's a load of laughs," he cracks to Hannah.

"I don't think he's all that serious. I think it's all a big front, Mr. Koehn."

"My name is George."

"George," she smiles back.

I look over to her and I reach for her hand, and then I squeeze it tight.

"I think he's a deep well, yes. But I sure like the water," she tells the old man.

21

We search for Carl Thomas in the Chicago area. It's still possible that Carl might have shot Brandon, and that my theory about the Captain is all the stuff that nightmares are made of. I've told Jack and Captain Pearce about my suspicion, but until we can come up with evidence that Anderson is really alive, we'll continue looking for the one suspect we know is real and alive—the last we heard, anyway.

The FBI has questioned Thomas's sister in Peoria, and they've threatened her with obstruction, but her lawyer knows the drill, and they can't keep coming at her. She must know her phone's tapped, so listening in on her has provided no leads as to her brother's whereabouts.

There have been no more killings in Mexico that resemble the two that already took place. I'm wondering if Anderson is still up here. He's the type to try and take off when he smells a scent in the air. He's been tipped by lawyer-daddy in California by now, I'm sure, so he'd be dumb to hang around. But then there's the arrogance factor. It's the one card we still have to play on him. He's in this for the personal power play. He's not a fanatic bent on any political gain. It wasn't about oil or about who rules south of the border. It's about his ability to get away with murder right in front of our very eyes. He's trying to flaunt his power and his intelligence at me, as if this were a competition between the two of us—*catch me if you can*. First at the NCIS and now at the police in Chicago and the cops in Mexico as well. It's a muscle/testosterone thing, I'm saying: "Look at the balls on me!", he's declaring. You know, *catch me if you can.*

Gerald, the Vermont rapist/killer, told the cops in the Northeast that it was a typical topic for Carl Thomas to talk about the Leopold/Loeb case back in the 1920's. It was the case where Darrow got the two thrill killers out of an execution for the murder of a young man. He got them life instead of death. The thing that fascinated Thomas, Gerald told the police, was that they'd kill someone just to see how it *felt*. I wonder if Carl came up with that obsession all by himself, or I wonder if someone else fed him all that food for thought.

I love the Loop. I love this city for all its blemishes and for all its crazies and wombats and kiddie molesters and assault artists and conmen and crooked pols.... It's like the world's ugliest dog. He's so goddamned ugly that he's attractive. It's not that Chicago doesn't have its eye candy. The Sears Tower and the Tribune Building and the Art Institute and the Shedd Aquarium and the Natural History Museum and the Science and Industry Museum and the Planetarium and Wrigley Field and Soldier's Field and Comiskey Park and the Gold Coast and Lakeshore Drive and.... On and on.

If I'm able to take some time, I like to walk the Loop and its environs. I write poems in my head that'll never meet the paper and ink. I'll forget them in a few minutes, but I like hearing the words in my mind.

I drive down to Monroe Street and park the LTD in underground parking, because it's cheaper than the private parking joints. I can walk to the Lake or to the History Museum or the Art Institute from where I am right now. I think I'll head toward the Natural History building. It's only a good stretch of the legs.

It's late October, but the cold hasn't filtered down from Canada quite yet. It's still in the mid-fifties. Invigorating, the weather guys might call it. The air is crisp, most of the leaves have already descended to earth, and November is looking at us down the barrel. It can stay fairly comfortable until mid-December, some years. The scientists are talking about global warming, whatever the fuck that really means. *El Nino*, or some shit. Something about the warm winds coming off the Pacific—I never get it straight.

I can see the portals of the museum dead ahead. It's a Thursday, and there are school buses parked all over the lot to the left of the entrance. Maybe I should head elsewhere, but I had my sights set on seeing that pile of dinosaur bones that always fills the entrance to this hall of history. The dinosaur must have been huge, according to the size of his skeleton. I can't imagine the patience it must have taken to reassemble him or her.

I watch the MEs go over bodies with that kind of imperturbability. They take hours studying minutiae, just to get us the details of cause of death. They're better men than I am, *Gunga Din*.

It's eight bucks to get in, but I wait my turn behind a bunch of middle schoolers from the city. They're Black and Hispanic kids, perhaps fifth or sixth grade. The pretty little black girl in front of me has the tiny braids with all the cat toys tied on. I can't imagine the tirelessness of doing all that handiwork on her hair, either. Some people can simply *focus*. The girl turns and smiles at me with the most beautiful set of teeth I've ever seen. The kid just radiates at me.

We finally get our tickets, so I head right for the bones of the Tyrannosaur. He stands right before us in the middle of the entry hall. The little girl with the cornrows and the cat toys suddenly stops and begins to wail. Then her teacher, a black woman about thirty and very attractive, rushes to her and consoles her and finally gets her giggling when she assures the kid the Tyrannosaurus is good and dead.

I would have thought she was too old to be scared by a bag of bones, but who knows what scares people.

Captain Benjamin Anderson and Lieutenant Carl Thomas scare me. Philip Brandon used to frighten me. And Gerald was fairly spooky, too. Big bones don't do much for me except pique my interest in the dawn of creation. It's lucky that human types weren't around when these gigantic lizards were. I don't think our adaptability would've helped us much in one-on-ones with these pricks.

After wandering from gallery to gallery, I figure I've blown an hour and a half. I go downstairs to the cafeteria to get a McDonald's burger and a Diet Coke. My extended lunch hour is way over, although I really just took some time to wander away from the job. In fact, Capt. Pearce suggested I take some time. He said I looked like I was more haggard than usual. And Jack had to go to a dentist's appointment, so I was without a partner.

When I get in the long line at the museum's McDonald's, I feel the hair on my neck stand up. The dinosaur exhibition didn't make my skin crawl, but I suddenly feel a distinct chill rise up my backbone. I turn quickly—I do a 180. But there is nothing out of the ordinary behind me: just schoolchildren, scattered adults, and museum employees.

I get the Big Mac and Diet Coke and I head for one of the lunch tables. There are only a few seats available, so I don't have much of a selection. I sit next to a chubby Hispanic middle-schooler.

"My name is Felipe," he grins.

"I'm Will, Felipe. Glad to meet you."

He's got a little baby fat, but he's going to be a killer with the ladies. Dark brown eyes. Latin lover. He'll lose the chubbiness in high school, become an athlete, maybe a baseball player, and the babes'll be standing in line for Felipe. I can simply see it all in his childish face.

He goes back to his cheeseburger Happy Meal that all the other students received. He's next to his also-Hispanic teacher, and she's already dynamite. Very young, extraordinarily ripe. I try to conjure Hannah in my mind so I don't blurt something stupid to her.

I gobble the burger and down the Diet Coke. I go up to the pop machine for a refill, and then I put a lid on the cup and grab a straw. One for the road.

On the way up the up escalator, I feel that same ice on my backbone again. I whirl about, and then I see him. At least twenty people separate him from me, and I'm just about to get off this escalator, so I have to step out of the way.

It was Anderson. He was wearing shades and a Cubs baseball hat, but it was the Captain.

I take the nine millimeter from my shoulder holster, and I palm it. No one is paying attention to me. I thought I'd hear someone shriek: *"He's got a gun!"*

But no one is looking at me. I'm wearing a thigh-length black leather jacket, so the holster was concealed, of course, and my hand all but conceals the weapon.

I've got very large hands. That's why Illinois wanted me for a wide receiver or tight end. And my hands were very soft in football too.

He never rises on the escalator as I wait for him, so I look back down the upward-moving stairs, but I can't make him. I haven't got time to find the down escalator, so I begin to run down the up version. I have to weave among the ascenders, and some of them don't look too happy with a grown man bursting the wrong way past them, but I get down to the basement in a hurry. I'm still palming my piece.

I look all around the McDonald's serving area, where I started, but I can't sight him.

Then I see the Cubs hat and the shades at the far end of the eating gallery. He's about to leave, heading toward some other hall in the museum. I bolt toward him, but the wash of museum-goers slows me down drastically.

Finally I make my way toward his last sighting, and when I get into this next gallery, I see him departing, at the far end again. I run as fast as I can, zig-zagging between all these vertical bodies, and suddenly I think I'm gaining on him.

The strange thing is that he doesn't seem to be running away from me. He's moving fast, but he hasn't broken into a run or even a trot. It's as though this were a bad dream, and there's no way I can catch up with the monster/villain in my nightmare.

He's prodding me after him, but he's confident I'll never catch up with him.

He moves on to the Neanderthal exhibition, which is jammed with school- kids. I've still got the nine in my hand, and I've got my hands at my sides so I won't alarm the children or the adults in here. I don't have my portable phone because I left it in the LTD, and now I'm living to regret leaving it there.

He's going to get out of here because I don't have any backup. It's as if he knew I'd leave that goddam phone in the car. I only figured to be in here for a few minutes. I didn't figure on pursuing anyone.

He's taking me back to the Tyrannosaurus in the entry hallway. Now I know where he's headed. But just as I sprint into that hallway, I lose sight of him again.

And this time I know I've lost him for good.

"For once in this whole sorry business, I was right. He's alive. It was him. Shades and ball cap aside, it was Captain Benjamin Anderson. He's no spook. He's no zombie, he's no walking dead. The sad fuck is alive and humping. It was Anderson in the museum, Captain. I'm certain of it."

"How does this ghost get out of a war in Iraq, get himself back to the States, get into the country in the first place, wander around killing as he goes—maybe even in Mexico too, if you're right.... How does he get around to accomplish all these things?"

"He gets out of Iraq by way of Kuwait. There's lots of money in Kuwait," I tell my boss and Jack in Pearce's office, two hours after I put my tail between my legs and returned to headquarters from the History Museum.

"When there's lots of available cash, you can buy almost anything. He buys himself a berth on some small vessel and he makes his way back toward somewhere in Europe, where he procures documentation, a false ID, the whole bit. He flies to Canada, where immigration isn't the strictest, and his ID is good enough to pass him in. Then he filters down into the US, somewhere from the Canadian border, where they're not too vigilant about bogus IDs. And no one's on the lookout for this prick because he's already *dead*."

"Still, it's hard to figure he could just walk out of a war, Will," Pearce says.

"We've had AWOLs before. The NCIS goes after missing persons all the time. He sure wouldn't be the first guy to go over the fucking hill."

"You're certain it was Anderson?" Jack asks me.

"It was him, Jack," I confirm. "I've memorized the son-of-a-bitch's face from the photos in his jacket, and it was Captain Benjamin Anderson."

He let me see him. He's taunting me and telling me he can reach out and touch me, like the phone ads, any time he feels like it because he's slyer than I am. He's the superior intelligence. He has the muscle and the *cojones*, and he can tap me any time he feels like it.

Or he can put one in the back of my head any time he chooses, also. It wasn't just a message—it was a threat.

Now I'm worried about Hannah, once again. If he's been tailing me, he knows we're together. He also knows where my father is. He knows where we all live.

"I got a weird phone call today," Sammy says.

"Yeah? From who?"

I already know.

"He didn't say. He just said he wanted to let me know that he saw you at the museum.... Were you at some museum recently?"

"Yeah. History. Yesterday."

"So why is this idiot telling me about it?"

"He calls again, you put a trace on your phone. I'll pay for it."

"What the fuck's going on, Will? I haven't said anything to Megan about it, but..."

"Don't. Don't say a damn thing to her. But if anyone makes another call, call the phone company and tell them you want a trace on harassing phone calls and that you want to prosecute."

"You going to tell me?"

I explain to him about Anderson and about Thomas and about Brandon and about the beginning of it all back in Kuwait.

"Jesus. Can't you grab this bastard?" he asks.

"I will. Just keep an eye on Megan. Stay with her. Keep your locks locked. Get the trace if he calls again.... I don't think he will, Sammy. I think he's just fucking with me. There's only one of him, and we've got a lot of cops. We'll get him, so don't let him frighten you."

"Forget about me. How about you? Is he scaring the shit out of you, Will?"

22

I took them along for the ride, knowing the day would come when I would have to liquidate them both. I took care of my loose threads in central Mexico before I returned. Now I've got to meet up with Carl Thomas. Then I can go home to California and take care of that loose thread, near Auburn.

I was expecting Carl to be there when I went into that Chicago apartment, but it was just as well Brandon was there instead. It saved me hunting him down and shooting him. Not getting Carl as a result of coming to this city was a disappointment, but it only delays the inevitable for this second of my acolytes. I'll find Carl as I found Julio Guerrero and Jorge Montellano in Mexico City. They were both fervent anti-government, modern day Zapatistas, and it took no real arguing or cajoling to get them to do murder. Then I simply took care of the policia's job and I whacked them both, burned their bodies in a kiln, and dumped the ashes in the sewers of Mexico City. They are now flowing with the rest of that ciudad's flotsam and shit.

It was unfortunate that I was forced to leave Brandon's body in that apartment, but it would have been more difficult to dispose of after seeing the police clear the buildings around me. Luckily I was able to leave the apartment building with the downstairs neighbors before Detective Koehn and his entourage were able to come catch me in the act. They missed me by mere minutes.

I thought his sighting of me in the museum was very amusing. I hope it gave him a little cheap thrill as well. I have plans for Will Koehn. I've come all the way to Chicago for a three-fold purpose. I know Carl Thomas is somewhere close. I know Philip Brandon has already expired, courtesy of me. And I know Detective Koehn will not run from me. Other cops might very well take off on leave of absence, knowing they've become a target for a man like me who they will undoubtedly call "insane."

It matters little to me, a handsome young dog in his late twenties, what their analysis of my character turns out to be. I'm sure if they ever caught me I'd spend no time in a prison. In Illinois they have an institution called Elgin. It's where they keep the chronics and some choice acutes. The terms I use are no doubt old fashioned, but I'm an old fashioned kind of guy.

I know they'll be interested in my foster home upbringing. They will lay blame on the fact that my first two homes were headed by incompetent parents, and they'll suggest my legal-eagle foster father was a bad influence—especially if they ever find out about his cocaine usage and his bi-sexual proclivities.

All that is mere happenstance to me. Excuses are simply excuses. I am the man my DNA made me be. I assume my biological father, whoever he was, had some kind of misfiring chromosome that explains my unusual behavior.

When we killed the two families with those two young girls as highlights, I watched but I never participated. The only killings I've done are the men I've recruited to do the group assassinations. I was simply a witness in Kuwait and in Chicago and in Mexico City. I never got to see or join in the festivities in California or in Vermont. Those were long-distance assignations, but I did the details and the planning. I procured the hackers who located our participants—on the receiving end, I mean.

The young girl in the first job in Kuwait City took longer to die than the other girls because we had not yet perfected our technique. We were all learning on the job. So by the time the murders took place in Mexico, we were all very adept at our tasks. I was the director. Thomas and Brandon and the boys south of the border were simply my crew.

It's frightening even to me how easy it is to find someone on the Internet who is capable of most anything, including murder. The most foul of all crimes, according to the Bard, William Shakespeare. There are pedophiles in legion on the net, but you'd think killers would be rarer. In the military we were trained to take life, but even in the Corps there is hesitancy to pull the trigger, especially when it comes to civilians. I rather think there are lots of targets out there, people who need to cease breathing. Thomas and Brandon finally figured out the oil ruse, that it was simply a bone to throw at the NCIS in Kuwait and a red herring to toss to the police in this city, Chicago—and in the other sites where we did our community thing.

I rather Brandon and Thomas insane when they shot two adolescent girls, scooped out an eye on each, over in the Middle East, and then murdered and hanged the families of both victims?

I think not. The act was premeditated. We planned the killings out in detail.

We were very careful never to let anyone from the military see the three of us together in Kuwait City. I met Carl and Philip at Quantico in OCS before we arrived in the war zone. Then I had to make special arrangements for us to physically get together to organize the raids, as I called them. They had to technically go AWOL late at night, bring civilian clothes with them, and then I picked them up in a 'borrowed' vehicle from the base near Kuwait City. I could hardly sign a vehicle out legally without leaving paper behind me.

I drove us to the sites, over there, sometime after 2:00 A.M. on both occasions. We made certain that no American patrols swung by at the time we were active inside those two homes. The military is very precise with time, and so were we. In and out in forty-five minutes. The patrols were famous for arriving and departing on the hour. So we wedged our action between their scheduled pass-bys.

We were careful to avoid leaving traces. We policed up our Areas of Operations when the shootings were accomplished. Carl and Philip did the excavations of the slugs, we all three retrieved casings, and all of our work was accomplished with latex on our hands. No fingerprints.

When the boys took turns on the females, they used condoms that were buried later, not flushed so they could float back up in the toilets. No trace of DNA was left for Detectives Koehn and Donato to find and use against us.

We didn't press our luck over there. We only did it twice. The third operation could very well have been a charm for our pursuers. I know Koehn was looking at the three of us and at other suspects as well because I had informants at NCIS who didn't even know they were informants. I'd made a few connections in their outfit as a result of my rank. People talk, even people who are required to remain silent. It's amazing what a few drinks will do at some officers' watering hole that attracts ex-Marines who became Navy cops.

We showed no mercy on those two families in the Middle East, nor did we show mercy to the clan in Chicago. You cannot be weak when you accomplished what we did. You have to have resolve, and you have to have endurance and strength. Once you look at them as cases rather than human beings, it becomes simple to pull the trigger, easy to hoist them off the floor to asphyxiate them. Then you shoot them each, once through the forehead to make sure they don't miraculously survive the gallows.

Of course, they'll insist we're all insane. However, I know better. Philip was no madman, nor was Carl Thomas. I watched them follow instructions methodically. Neither man was ever out of control. They did things with a purpose; lunatics perform outrageous acts thoughtlessly. We are not mad.

Nietzche spoke often about the ubermensch, and he wasn't talking about the cartoon character from the comic books. No, the ubermensch wears no cape, nor does he leap tall buildings with a single bound. He is an extraordinary man, but he appears to be of the herd. His mundane appearance allows him to roam among his prey. He can hunt undetected and undisturbed because he is the neighbor next door. He seemed perfectly normal—every description of a series killer reads thus. They were always chameleon-like individuals; no one ever noticed them. They blended in with the crowd. They were not peacocks with brilliant plumage. Instead, they were ordinary birds, like sparrows. Worker birds, nesting and surviving like every other airborne creature. Occasionally, a bird of bright plumage might make an appearance in the annals of crime, however.

Except our wings are stronger, our purpose is far more resolute. That was why we soared higher. And if Thomas and Brandon and those two young Mexican men had to be eliminated, at least they soared high in the clouds for a time. They did what few dare to accomplish. They trod where no one is allowed to walk. It was almost like perusing the face of God in the burning bush on Sinai. They looked instead upon the face of the Fallen Angel, the Angel who should have ruled in Heaven. They elected the wrong guy to run this show. Satan understood and understands the human creature far better than the Creator with various names. Lucifer was far more psychologically attuned to us than God ever was or shall be. We are not good by nature. We are weak. We do not desire to do the right thing. We wish to do what is self-serving and pleasurable. What gives us pain is what determines the God-like scenario.

I'm no Satanist, but I'm a big fan.

I made my way by wired money from my attorney foster father to free myself from Desert Storm. Finding my way out of Kuwait City and out of the war was complicated, but not impossible—obviously, for here I am! I made my wait from the Middle East through various ports of call, and then on to Paris, and from Paris to Canada, and from the northlands back into the States, before I briefly toured Mexico. It only took money and the proper connections—all of which my third foster parent has plenty of. He defends scum, Vietnamese gangs in Los Angeles, New York and Chicago. He has advocated for the Italian Mafia in New York and Chicago, and he has done legal chores for the Russian Mob in Chicago and Detroit.... Oh yes, and for the Irish Outfit in Boston. He has done legal work for them all, but strictly for the money and for all that good-will publicity for helping the underprivileged in the inner cities of America. He's one helluva guy, my old man. All that aside, the Zurich account is the source of my funds. It is no legitimate bank, of course, so they are highly trustworthy.

I got my new identities from an excellent forger in Amsterdam, one of my stops prior to Paris and Canada. He works for the Vietnamese, primarily, so he is very trustworthy. I was warned not to eliminate him after he fixed me up. The Vietnamese have a very unique code of honor when it comes to whacking their employees.

I stayed in Canada only briefly. Perhaps six months. I am now John Charles Moran, but I can become Randy Jackson on demand, also. The Dutchman gave me alternate IDs. I switch off regularly.

I considered plastic surgery to alter my facial features, but I declined because disguises are so much cheaper. The fact is I hardly ever use beards or mustaches because I'm officially and legally dead. The Marines have declared me deceased, and no one argues their verdict since the Humvee was turned to ash on that road in Iraq, along with two unfortunate brother Marines who had to make my demise look authentic. I know Koehn was suspicious about the lack of remains in my case, but it's amazing the heat that Willie Peter, white phosphorus, can generate. He was smart enough to have his doubts, along with his partner, Donato. But Donato still serves in the NCIS, last I heard, and last I heard, he was back aboard The Intrepid , headed for Portugal, if my information is accurate. And it almost always is.

It's amazing what the various Mafias and Tongs can come up with if I come up with the cash.

My foster daddy does it for the money. Every fucking thing he does is cold-hearted and calculated. He can't bullshit me. This is the big-fish-eats-the-smaller-fish planet. We're all predators, but some of us have more finely-tuned skills. I was a killer before I ever reached the Corps. I've been a flesh-eater long before I partook of animal meat. I'm a cannibal, when it comers right down to it, though I don't literally partake of my victims' bodies. I just enjoy watching them fade out. I like looking at them as they evaporate in front of me. It's the ultimate muscle, watching them leave this earth. I have the power, and power is everything. All those adventures, getting out of Iraq and Kuwait—they were nothing, nothing compared to the adrenalin rush of watching one of my subjects be dismissed from this life. If I'd been David Crowley, I would've killed me. Nothing worse than a leech, no? But he was weak because in some weird way he had gained affection for me, and I suppose it was easier for him to support me financially than it was to have me waxed and disappeared. Here I am, so I guess you have your answer. I always sort of liked him, though. He gave me anything I wanted, and he stayed out of my personal business. I could have been incarcerated for statutory rape in my senior year in high school, but he maneuvered me out of trouble on that incident by paying off the girl in question.

There was also a Driving under the Influence thing that he got me free from, so I guess you could say he was a doting daddy.

I'm hunting the cop, these days, but I have my sights on Carl Thomas as well. I have excellent intel from the Russians in Chicago, and I'm sure they'll relocate Carl for me shortly. It's a matter of time before I find my young acolyte. Then I'll make him vanish, too. Killing a cop is a more serious matter, though. Even with my dad's connection here and throughout the world, murdering policemen is frowned upon. Draws too much heat; gathers too much publicity and attention. Usually someone swings from the yardarm for whacking a homicide detective, and I'd prefer I not be the swinger in question.

Getting away with it has always been the issue. You can kill anyone in this world, if history teaches us anything. Weren't those the words of wisdom according to Michael Corleone in Godfather II? *It's just a matter of proper planning. You can kill the Son of God and skip on it, if you're smart. You can liquidate two Kennedys, and maybe the right guys went down for it. Same for Martin Luther King. Did they really get the right shooter? Maybe. I know. Conspiracy theories are for the nutcases.*

But I know very well that justice is an illusion in this world. Pleasure is the real matter at hand. Not just sexual pleasure or the high induced by alcohol or other substances that produce a rush. Drugs and alcohol were a brief phase for me. I tried near-strangulations with a few hookers in Las Vegas, but nothing ever came close to the buzz of my current "occupation." I've got lots of money and nothing but free time.

Poor Will Koehn. He seems to be searching for himself. I watched him at the museum, looking for something, perhaps someone like me.

And all the while, his prey was his predator. I was right behind him, watching, waiting. There's no hurry to do him. If I did it right away, there'd be no building excitement, no buzz, no thrill. It's like premature ejaculation. Ruins the whole experience. It has to have a buildup that literally builds up before the amazing climax. No slam bam thank you ma'am in my trade. No, I get my money's worth.

I watched Thomas and Brandon kill three entire family units. I watched them be raped, shot and hanged. I watched the girls be blinded en route to dying. I watched the two younger men relieve the children of their flowers, of their innocence. It was something to behold, something you'll never see at the movies or read about in a book.

Call it evil? I call it the way of reality, the way of the authentic world. The powerful dominate the weak. It is the way our script is written. Darwin had it right, but it wasn't just in the animal kingdom that his theory applies, because we are indeed animals ourselves, clever beasts, but animals nonetheless.

Detective Will Koehn will be a challenge. I might even work my way through his family and his current lover, Hannah, and there was a serious connection to an FBI agent, I have been informed.

There are lots of bodies to walk over before I arrive where I'm headed.

23

His friend's name is Arkady Kormelov. Jack calls him Kady, but his girlfriends call him Arkasha. He's originally from Moscow, but he emigrated to the States in 1989, and so he speaks English fluently. Jack says he inherited his sense of Americanization from his paternal grandfather, who emigrated here after World War II. The grandfather actually had to be smuggled out of the Soviet Union because Stalin wasn't friendly to the notion of Russians going AWOL to America. The old guy got here, though, and his grandson Arkady dreamed of following the old man to the New World, and his dream finally came true in 1989.

The one unfortunate footnote to the whole saga of the Kormelov family was that Arkady was and is a member of the Russian Mafia, here in Chicago. They are not rivals to the Italians yet, but they're creeping upward because of their ruthlessness and their brutality.

Arkady came to know Jack because of a burglary investigation, back in 1990. Clemons and his partner caught the guy who boosted Arkasha's 1977 Mustang, and they caught him cold with the Mustang on his hot little hands. Arkady was not the type to allow the cops to do his own legwork, but he appreciated the speed and success of my partner and Jack's old partner in the apprehension of the booster and the return of the

'77 Pony. They became "friends" as a result of Jack's busting that car thief, and Arkady is the sort who never forgets a "friend."

In other words, he became Jack's informal informer, and when something goes down that doesn't connect to Arkady and his crew directly, he passes along information to Clemons. He's helped Jack a few times since the car incident.

We meet at the Denny's on Broadway at 3:30 A.M. It's almost empty, here in the restaurant, and that's why Kormelov agreed to the meet.

He's a big-boned, muscular man. No waste, no fat. He's probably 6' 3" and he's got a small waistline for a male. Broad shoulders, full head of black, straight hair with a blue sheen to it. I think Jack said he was Cossack. From the Steppes or some damn thing. The horsemen, you know, with the Russian wooly hats.

His eyes are a cornflower-blue. Odd color, but fascinating—especially if you're an admiring woman, I'm guessing. Jack says he does very well with the ladies , and I can see why.

"How you doin'?" Clemons says as he shakes his hand. The three of us sit in a booth in this nearly deserted Denny's. It's a twenty-four-hour joint, so it seemed ideal for our meeting here.

"I'm fine, Jack. You?"

No trace of an accent. Perfect English, just as Jack told me it would be.

"You think maybe you can help us, Kady?" Jack asks him as the waitress lays three menus before us. She's in her forties, a little mileage on her face, but the body looks good. No waste on her either. But the only one of us she eyes is the Russian. Then she walks away with her order pad after we're done with her.

"Help you? You know I'll help you, Jack.... This man got my 1977 Ford Mustang back to me in just four days. Did you know that?"

"He's told me. Yes," I answer.

"Your friend is a serious man like you, Jack?"

Clemons looks at me and smiles.

"Maybe he's a little too serious, Kady. He is in love with a woman ten years older than him."

Arkady Kormelov smiles at Jack and then at me.

160

"Older women are more patient with us, Detective Koehn."

He has gargantuan hands. They're hands that could snap a man's neck. When he talks about women, I can't picture him being gentle with a lover.

Jack has told him my name and apparently more than that.

"They know what they want and aren't afraid to tell a man. Now with a young bitch, it's always a fucking guessing game.... What can I do for you two fine policemen that won't get me fucked in my ass?"

Jack laughs out loud.

"You know our deal. I can't look the other way. I won't," he tells the Russian.

"I know our deal. I know how this game is played. But you might return me a favor, if it does not compromise either one of you."

He has a quick wit. He has natural, street-wise intelligence. I don't know if he's literate, too, but it wouldn't surprise me if Arkady were an educated man.

"What favor?" Clemons asks.

"Immigration. I have a cousin who wants to defect to this country. Do you know anyone in INS?"

Now we see the deal-maker. He does nothing unless it means gain, profit. The Russians truly have embraced our way of life in America. He's become an *entrepreneur*.

"Yes, as a matter of fact, I do," Clemons grins. "Been dating her, on and off, for a month or two."

Arkady smiles and intertwines his fingers and lets his hands rest on the top of the table. He's trying to come off like some goddamned State Farm Insurance man, some kind of actuary or salesman who does a routine job in this city, someone who goes home to the little woman and the tow-headed kids after a long day of hustling life insurance.

"This cousin is not affiliated. You know what I'm saying? She is eighteen, a concert-level pianist. Brilliant. Moscow Institute. All that happy horseshit. She wants to stay in this country, scholarships, and so on and so on. Can you help?"

He's the fucking "man of the year" at the lodge. He goes to mass on Sundays—Russian Orthodox, of course—and he gives big donations to the poor on the first Sunday of the month. I want to strangle this fucker with my bare hands. He's one step short of running for public office.

This cute prick knows Jack will help him, if my partner can. He wants to make it sound like Jack'll be doing the Russian a personal favor. Everything sounds so friendly that I'm waiting to see him pull out a knife.

"I'll do what I can, yes."

"Okay. Then tell me."

"We're looking for the man or men who raped the little girl and killed her family and her. You read about it?"

"Yes. I know the story from the papers," he answers.

"He seems to pop up from time to time in the city. If you can give us any information..."

Arkady has a definite look of inquiry on his chiseled face.

"Has this man, or men, got a name?"

"His name is Benjamin Anderson. The other man is Carl Thomas. One of them just shot and killed a man named Philip Brandon, who we think was involved with Thomas, and perhaps with Brandon, in rapes and murders in Kuwait City, a few years back, around the time of Desert Storm," I explain.

"That was a mistake for the United States. They were at the doors of that prick, Saddam. Anyway, you want to locate either or both men. I will see what I hear, but I must be very discreet in asking questions, you understand."

Clemons nods, and then the waitress brings us our early breakfasts. Then Jack sips from his coffee cup. There is a hush in the restaurant. I can hear the clinking of silverware, and I can see the waitresses bustling to their tables, once in a while. But the quiet is almost unnerving. Sitting next to this murderer is disquieting. His demeanor of civility sickens me.

I smell sausages and grease and the sweet smell of maple syrup, and it's all wrong. There should be the odor of the streets, the stench of where Arkady really lives. This is a family restaurant, and his only "family" is the thugs who do his crimes for him. But here he sits, like some kind of normal businessman. Nice threads and cool manners. I can still see the mud on his feet and the blood on his fingertips.

"These are very evil men, Kady," Jack tells him.

"The world is filled with such men," he tells us.

His hypocrisy is so blatant that I want to laugh in his face, but I don't want to screw up our little "trade." The sweet fragrance of the brewing coffee comes wafting at me from somewhere in the kitchen.

"These two are especially bad. The word is 'heinous,'" Clemons tells Arkady.

"In the Soviet Union I grew up with this type of individual. It was very bad in Moscow before I left. I left to follow my family over here. I do not apologize for the work I do. I've told this to Jack before, Detective Koehn."

"Will."

"Will."

He gives me a soulful, sorrowful look, and I almost believe him. But the feeling passes.

"And I also have no use for those who molest children. Killing might be sometimes necessary. But what those men did to those girls.... That was not necessary or acceptable, even to the people I deal with in my world.

"I'll look into it. I'll make some quiet inquiries. If I find out anything about the whereabouts of this Anderson or this Thomas, I will be in touch."

He rises, leaving his breakfast untouched. He drops a fifty in front of us for the bill and raises his right hand before Jack can protest.

"She's a very good waitress. Tell her I said so."

Then he leaves us as abruptly as he first sat down.

The FBI has an all points on Thomas and Anderson, as do we. The sighting of the Captain at the museum on Lakeshore was enough to prod Pearce into believing that Anderson is not among the dearly departed. The zombie has risen to the land of the living for our Captain. Now Anderson is an official suspect.

I've talked to Mary from time to time via private calls to her apartment. She wants to get together to "share the wealth" on this case, because she's been officially assigned to the rape/murder of the Chicago family. It is officially a series killing, so the Feds find a way to get involved, as they always do with headline cases. High profile murders, they're called.

I've talked to the CPD shrink too. Her name is Brenda Carlson, M.D.

"The profile you worked up is essentially accurate," she tells me as I sit in her tenth floor cubicle.

Brenda has strawberry-colored hair, very curly, very kinky. She has freckles and is in her early forties, like Hannah, and she's wearing no wedding ring. She's attractive in a *wholesome* kind of way. Sort of like a female version of Opie Taylor, all grown up. She looks like a farmer's daughter who ought to be wearing pigtails.

"He is a white mail, 25-40. He'll fit in among people. He won't make scenes. He will not be involved with spectacle of any kind. No, he's quiet and unto himself—until it comes to killing. Then he views it analytically, as if he were a scientist watching an experiment. His victims will be on the level of test rats, as far as he's concerned.

"He's a true sociopath. Someone who cannot fathom the evil he does. Or he is extremely adept at rationalizing his behavior. These people he's murdered were not human. They were objects. He might refer to them all as 'it.' It's typical to depersonalize his targets. It makes them things instead of people, like subjects in a case study.

"I know you've heard most of this before, Detective Koehn."

"Some. But this is helpful. Thanks."

"You're looking for a man who would pull off only one wing from a house fly. He would cripple the fly simply to make it suffer longer."

She looks up at me with her dimpled chin and her abundant freckles. It makes me want to hug her, until I picture that poor bastard fly of hers.

Sammy has received no new phone calls. But I drive down to Champaign to check on him in the second week in November. Megan is home in Decatur, Illinois for the weekend. I arrive on a late, drizzly Friday.

We go to the local college bar. Sammy buys us a pitcher. Beer is unusual for him because he didn't drink through all his athletic years.

We sit on stools at the bar. It's too early for the TGIF crowds. The beers are cheap, but not very cold.

"I bought a gun," he tells me.

I stare at him.

"Well, I did. I'm not going to let this son of a bitch…"

"You let us handle him. Get rid of the gun and get a loud dog. It's much safer."

"I don't like dogs."

"Does Megan know you own a piece?"

"No. I didn't tell her about…. any of this."

"She needs to be apprised."

"No, she doesn't."

"I know you're the MBA motherfucker, Sammy, but…"

"Don't pull the routine, big brother. This isn't a competition. You frightened me, and I don't like being scared. On the field you could take it out on someone with a downfield block, but you can't grab hold of mist, man."

"He's not mist. He used to be a captain in the Marines. He organized all this shit, over there and up in Chicago. He's the honcho. And I almost caught up to him back near the Lake."

I explain the museum incident to him.

"Your legs must really be going."

"Everybody's legs give out. They're the first equipment to become obsolete."

Sammy's face becomes ashen.

"You got years to go before yours go south," I smile at him. "Look, I didn't come down here to bitch you out. I came to see that you're okay. I don't mean to make it sound like I'm checking up on you, but I guess that's what this is…. What kind of a weapon?"

"A .38 police special. Got a good deal on it from a grad student here."

"So it's hot."

"No, *Detective* Koehn. It's all legal. Papers and everything."

"You don't need the hassle, Sammy. What if Megan spots it?"

"I've got it hidden."

"So how are you going to gain access if you need it in the middle of the night?"

He looks at me with a trapped glance.

"I'll figure something out. Don't fucking worry."

"I worry. I love you, asshole."

"Is this a brotherly fucking moment?"

"Call it whatever the hell you like, Sammy."

"Don't get pissed."

"Get rid of the gun."

"I'll sell it. Okay, all right."

"Give it to me. It'll be safer. You'll probably get entrapped selling it to an ATF asshole."

"All right. I'll hand it over to you."

"Good. Now buy us another pitcher."

Suddenly the beer's gone.

We ramble by foot back to Sammy's graduate-student apartment. He's got a nice, modern facility to live in. A one-bedroom apartment, fully furnished, lap-of- luxury stuff for a college punk and his lady-love. I wish I lived half so well.

I get back to Chicago on early Sunday morning because I go on shift at 4:00 P.M. I get a phone message at my apartment on the answering machine.

It's my father. He says to get my ass to Bridgeport ASAP.

His house has been trashed. It's a thorough job, every room, every corner of the house.

"I just went out to play bingo at the legion hall. I was gone until midnight Saturday, last night. I came home, and *this*.... "

There are no tears in his eyes, just deep anger. It's beyond anger, I'm thinking.

They've slashed the furniture and peeled off wallpaper. It's been done with extreme prejudice, a complete job.

I go next door to the neighbors', on either side of Dad, but neither neighbor heard a thing. It was all done methodically and by the numbers. So I go back inside my father's house.

"It's in the thousands," he says, his cheeks still crimson with rage.

"You still have insurance," I say.

"Who gives a shit? But yes."

"I'm so very sorry, Dad."

"Not your fault."

"I feel like it is."

"It was him, wasn't it?" he says, looking me right in the eyes.

I look back at him, but I don't answer.

24

He walked over the line with my father. He already tread too close when he sent me the little "messages." But the notes made from newsprint didn't cross over into the personal-vendetta territory. He fucked with my old man, and that was unlucky enough for Anderson. Now he's involved my brother, too. I've talked to Pearce about keeping an eye on my father and brother, and he's been very good about everything. It's all been taken care of.

I want to kill Captain Benjamin Anderson myself, and if it ever becomes possible, I will shoot him. Or break his fucking neck with my hands. Or throttle him with a coat hanger. Or kick him to death with my feet. Or stick him with a very large kitchen knife.

Whatever it takes, he's never going to trial, and I will make it appear to be self-defense. I know about crime scenes and what the ME and the CSI techs look for, and I will take plenty of time making sure I cover my own ass. But I will take Anderson's life if I have the opportunity. He's gone beyond cop-perp relations. It's become absolutely personal, and I look at it as nothing more than the moral imperative of protecting myself and my family. I know that it isn't kosher with the police and with the law itself, but I don't give a shit.

He's a dead man, and this time he will not rise again from the earth. This time I'll bury him deep, myself.

Hannah Menke is the woman with whom I want to grow old. Someone has already kicked down her front door and attempted to attack her and her two kids. That was also over my line of demarcation with Anderson. He knows who I care about, and he knows what pushes my personal nuclear buttons, but no matter. I have indeed decided to whack him myself. And I will not involve Jack Clemons in the move I make against Anderson. It'll be a solo operation. Just like *High Noon* when Gary Cooper nails John Miller, the bad guy, after Gary Cooper has already smoked the other bad guys. Then it becomes just the two—the protagonist and the antagonist, alone, just the two of them for that split second in the dusty street where all Western showdowns take place.

Sounds theatrical, I know, but it captures the mood I'm in. I should be struggling with the morality of taking the law into my own hands, but somehow, that ethical dilemma has avoided my conscience. It just feels *right*, putting a very large hole in Captain Benjamin Anderson.

"Forgive me, Father, for I have sinned. My last confession was-- Jesus, I can't remember my last confession, Father."

"It's all right," the priest behind the screen tells me. I don't even know his name, and I've never been to mass at St. Stanislaus, here on the northwest side. I've come by myself on my lunch break. Jack is in fingerprints, working on another case we're involved with. We have six other unsolved murders on our plate—besides the Milan murders—so we're too busy for me to linger here with this anonymous padre.

"I'm thinking of killing a man," I admit.

"You know that's at the head of the 'thou shalt not' list," the cleric says.

"Yeah, I know. But this guy really needs killing."

"That's a matter for the police, son."

"I *am* a copper, Father."

"*That's* not good, then."

"This man has threatened my family."

"And you want to protect your family."

"Yes, Father."

"Being a policeman, you know all about the wrongs with vigilante behavior."

"Sure. But I don't care. He trashed my dad's home in Bridgeport, and he threatened my younger brother in Champaign. And he tried to kick in my girlfriend's front door—or he had his partner do that one. She's got two teenaged daughters, and she lives alone."

"I see. That still doesn't excuse what you plan on doing."

"Somewhere in my head I know that's right. But somewhere deeper, someone's telling me to kill the prick."

The priest coughs, or guffaws, or something like the above.

"Thou shalt not kill is pretty straight up, I'm afraid. I don't think God was thinking 'flexible' with that rule."

"I'm sure you're right, but I can't see letting this guy go through the system."

"You're putting me in a real bind here, because I should report this even though I'm bound to secrecy in the confessional."

"I'd understand if you ratted on me, Father. It'd be your duty.... But it won't stop me. I'm going to kill him before he can kill anybody else. I can't let him wiggle away through the system, because I've seen smart guys like him do that magic act. His lawyer'll find a constitutional hole or something, and he'll squirm out of it."

"You won't kill him."

"Why's that?"

"Because you're a moral man and a Catholic. And more important, you wouldn't be here if you thought you were doing the right thing by assassinating this man. He may be the most miserable excuse for a human being, but you won't lower yourself to his level, and that's exactly what you'd be doing if you tried to exert justice by yourself. Now tell me I'm wrong."

I can't.

And I don't.

I help my dad put his house back together. The furniture was trashed, so the insurance paid for new stuff. We go to his favorite discount outlet in Oak Lawn on the Southwest side, and we buy everything brand-new. He almost enjoys the shopping spree until he remembers the way the place looked when he came home and saw the damage. New furniture will not replace his belongings because with older guys like my father the things around him *were* his home, not just the walls, foundation and roof. Anderson or whoever he sent to do all that did some lasting harm to my old man. His home was *invaded*, not simply trashed.

We sit on his new three-seat couch. It's a leather substitute, but it is pretty. He likes the look and feel of leather, and so do I.

"Maybe this guy did me a favor. The old couch was a piece of shit," he says to me.

"Yeah, but I grew up sitting on that piece of shit."

He looks down at his hands. And then he looks down the sofa, right at me.

"I never enjoyed pulling the trigger on the Germans. I knew some of them might be SS or Gestapo—you didn't get to pick your targets very often. But I looked at them simply as men. They never looked at us that way, Will. We were inferior cattle, as far as some of those supermen were concerned.

"We fought that war against their line of thinking, as I recall. So if you go after this son-of-a-bitch for vengeance, you're no better than he is, Will.... You listening?"

"Yes, I'm listening."

"I've seen that look on your face. You used to get that same look when you got pissed at someone in the neighborhood or on one of your playing fields. I know that look. You want to take care of things all by yourself."

He looks at me but I don't reply.

"Am I correct in my assessment, Will?"

"Yeah. You're right."

"And you're going to go through with it anyway?"

I don't answer this time, either.

"I didn't raise you to become a thug with a fucking badge."

And he walks into the kitchen for a bottle of Old Style.

Kormelov sits across from us in the same Denny's where we met before.

"This man, Carl Thomas. He has a liking for prostitutes who let him, how you say it? He likes to *bite*. You know what I'm saying?"

"Yes," Jack confirms.

"He is a pretzel. Twisted, this fuck."

"Yes," I add.

"He likes one particular whore that an associate of a friend of mine handles. She is a Russian, unfortunately, but I don't judge how a man or woman makes their bread. Her name is Nina Simonov. She lives at 412 Dempster Avenue on the northside. She does business in her residence there. My man says Carl Thomas has visited her several times in the last month. The last time he was there, he almost maimed this woman. He got carried away and bit her a few times. The friend of my associate says they beat this Thomas up and sent him to the hospital with a broken cheekbone—but the son-of-a-bitch came back for Nina again. This time he promised not to misbehave. So she tripled the fee, and the dumb bitch took him on again.

"Apparently he will return for the encore performance because he is, how do you say it? He is obsessed with this nibbling business. Nina doesn't care what kind of sex a man requires, and it is pretty obvious she's a very stupid cunt."

Jack smiles at him, and then he asks for a rerun on Nina Simonov's address.

We set up on the Russian woman's apartment with three shifts. Jack and I take the late shift because it's more likely Carl Thomas will be arriving at Nina's at a very late hour. He's been smart before, and there's no reason to suspect him of being rash. He'll show up when the streets are deserted.

As they are now, at 12:22 a.m. It is mid-November, and it's turned wintry. No snow, but there is frost in the air. We're wearing leather coats to ward off the Hawk, the northeast wind off the Lake. We turn on the Ford's heater, but neither of us likes to run the motor too much. The exhaust is a tip-off that we're staking the place out.

We listen to Jack's classic rock station until neither of us can stand the high energy of the music at this late hour.

We take turns dozing, but Jack's a snorer, and he bothers me when I hear him stop breathing every so often.

About 12:43 a.m., a man in a leather thigh-length jacket approaches Nina's three-flat, here on Dempster, just four blocks from the Lake.

I nudge Clemons out of a grunt and a snore.

"Show time," I whisper.

I call in for backup as our boy enters the doorway and buzzes Nina's apartment. She lets him in and we get out of the LTD with weapons drawn. There's no time to wait for backup, even though we know we've broken the cardinal law of stakeouts by proceeding ahead without the cavalry.

He's gotten away too many times before. Not tonight. Not on this watch of ours.

We get to the hallway. Jack punches the other two buzzers, not Nina's. The first floor buzzes us in. When we walk by the apartment, Jack tells an old lady who's grunting in Spanish to get her hoary ass back into her apartment.

"*Policia*," he explains to the old bat. She retreats and shuts her door.

Nina is on the second floor. When we arrive up the steps, her door is closed shut. I put my ear to the entry, but I hear nothing.

"We could wait for the swinging sledge," Jack whispers at me, in barely audible sentence.

I shake my head, and before my partner can protest, I put my right heel to the door, near the handle. The rectangle crashes open. We burst through and head, with weapons pointed in front of us, toward Nina's bedroom. It's a three-room apartment, so our choices of where it's located are very limited.

When we enter the darkened bedroom, Thomas snaps on a bedside lamp.

They're naked, and he's got a switchblade at her throat, and he's clutching the nude whore from behind. A small droplet of blood dribbles its way down Nina's throat.

"Great tits. But she's as frigid as a block of ice. You know?" Thomas smiles.

"Let her go and stand up," Clemons demands, his nine millimeter pointed directly at Carl's forehead.

"You shoot, and I'll cut her and sever an artery that'll kill her for sure."

"She's a whore. Go right ahead," I tell him.

Nina's eyes aren't much smaller than the tits he was talking about. They've widened hysterically. She must speak pretty fair English.

"Don't," she gurgles.

"I said, let her go," Jack repeats in an even voice.

"You'll shoot me anyway," he says, looking directly at me.

"Yes," I answer.

Nina gurgles, and her breasts bob as she struggles to avoid being pierced by the tip of his blade.

Now Carl's eyes become a bit rounder and a bit more enlarged. It's as if he finally believes I'm about to let loose a round regardless of what he does to the hooker. Jack is watching me now, as well.

My partner shakes his head.

"*Don't*," he mouths to me.

I look back at the naked man and woman in front of me, and then I shoot Nina in the right shoulder, and the bullet obviously keeps right on going through her and then into Carl Thomas's upper right chest, which forces him to suddenly release the knife.

174

Nina collapses forward onto the floor, off the bed, and Thomas is writhing in pain on the mattress.

I put my pistol's muzzle against his forehead.

"*Will,*" Jack pleads.

Thomas's eyes roll back in his head, and then Jack Clemons turns around and finds four uniforms bursting onto the scene behind us.

25

I'm put on paid leave until they investigate the shooting of Carl Thomas and the hooker I shot him through. Nina recovers nicely. Fortunately I didn't blast through any major arteries, and she will make it. Thomas, on the other hand, is more iffy. They give him 50-50 odds of making it. The slug did significant damage to his upper chest, but the surgeon in ER told me after his operation that Carl would likely pull through because of his generally excellent physical condition prior to my giving him a new hole to bleed out of.

Jack has already been interviewed by Internal Affairs, and from what he tells me, it went well after he explained that Carl was about ready to decapitate Nina with that wire clothes hanger. He thinks they bought his story, and when they talked to me I confirmed that I believed Nina's life to be in jeopardy, and I also believed a head shot to Thomas was highly unlikely, and so I felt shooting him through her would be my only chance to prevent one or two deaths. The three interrogators seemed reasonable to me. At least the three guys who asked me questions *seemed* understanding regarding the predicament we were in at Nina's apartment.

It'll be a few days before the decision comes down, Captain Pearce informed me, so I get a short vacation, which I'll be spending protecting Hannah and her daughters from Captain Benjamin Anderson, the lone perpetrator to all these murders. Carl's alive, but he won't be going anywhere for a very long time. We have him for nothing less than attempted murder on Nina, and maybe Gerald will help us put the finishing touches to the other homicide/rape raps on the son of a bitch.

I spend time with Hannah, at least when she's home from her job at the accounting office for the gas company. She returns to Oakbrook about 6:30 p.m. and then the four of us have dinner here, and then the girls do their homework upstairs, and Hannah and I watch TV and occasionally neck on the couch in front of the tube. We have to be careful the two young girls don't descend the stairs and catch us in the act, but they rarely come downstairs once they hit their rooms. They each have phones and computers, and they're busy with their own young-woman worlds.

We make love only when we're alone, at my place, or here when Barbara and Beth are with their father. I can't bear the lack of privacy when they're around, and Hannah feels the same way.

I'd ask her to marry me, but I'm terrified I'll scare her off or that she'll give me the brush the way Mary Janecko, my FBI lady, did. It's frightening what a two- letter word can do to you:

No.

I love her and I've told her so in spite of my trepidation about her rejecting me. I can't help but say it in and out of bed because it is simply *true*. I know I have a bad habit of speaking what I'm thinking, and it's put other women off, even before my FBI babe.

When I tell her tonight, she looks right into my eyes.

"You want to escalate this war?"

"Which war?" I smile.

I take my fingertips and trace her throat from top to bottom. Her flesh is warm and smooth. No imperfections. It isn't right, somehow, that there are no flaws on her perfect flesh.

"The war of the sexes," she laughs.

She touches my face with her slender fingers. The tips just glance against my cheeks, and a chill rises up my back. She keeps touching me as if she's reading me by her very contact with my cheeks and with my chin. Her eyes are a mist; they're so close to mine. I feel as if we're in some fog bank. The air is thick between us. The atmosphere is dense, and I wonder why I'm not having trouble breathing.

"If you mean do I want to get serious with you, with us, then the answer is affirmative."

"Very military. Very precise."

She's smiling warmly at me. She knows the effect it has on me. I want to drop the girls off at their Daddy's and head for a four-hour nap. But I will not leave them alone in the house. I've told Hannah that's not negotiable, especially at night. I will not leave them unattended.

"I love you. And, yes, I want to get very serious with you."

She kisses me.

"And the age factor?"

She smiles slyly at me. She loves to tease me until I have to grab hold of her and end my misery. I can only hold back from embracing her for a very short time, and she damn well knows my limits.

"Stop. There is no age factor. Stop reading that goddam *Cosmo*."

I can only fake being really angry with her. She plays me very well. She's in command, and she knows I want her to lead me on endlessly.

"You're not angry, are you, Will?"

"No. Not really. But I don't know how to make it any clearer that I don't give a shit how old you are, and I never will. And women outlive men all the time anyway."

She looks as if she's in her early to mid-thirties. She could pass for a peer of mine, age-wise. There are no striations on her beautiful face. It's as unmarked as her gorgeous throat. There are no telltale markers that suggest she's anywhere near her true age.

"I don't think I really have a problem with your age, Detective. You seem a lot older than most thirty-something guys I work around at the office. You seem too serious, sometimes."

"I get that a lot."

I blush at her insight. She knows me as if she's been with me for decades. Time. It's always about time, when we're together. But the truth is that the clock moves far too quickly when I'm near her.

"I'll bet. You've scared a few off, I gather."

"Yeah. As a matter of fact, I have."

"And you're afraid to scare me off, too?"

That teaser face is in place, again. Her lips part and she shows me just a glimmer of a grin. Her arms are crossed in front of her, and her breasts lie on top of her forearms, and she knows I can't help staring at that delicious pair.

"Sometimes."

"Like right now, Will?"

"Like right now, yes."

If I don't take hold of her soon, something embarrassing is going to happen. I'm like a schoolboy who's never been laid. But she takes mercy on me and embraces me, and the pent-up explosion within relaxes. Everything inside me relaxes, and I'm somewhere soothing, the moment her warm arms are wrapped about my waist.

She kisses me hard.

"It's Friday night. I have a sister, Franny."

"You never told me about Franny."

"I never told you anything about my family, other than those two upstairs and that bastard who fathered them."

"Franny?"

She giggles when I say her sister's name. I like her giggle. I like her laugh. They're both soft and casual and real. Her humor is just as genuine as everything else about her.

"My younger sister. She lives in Palos Heights. She's the girls' favorite relative. And the rumor is that there's a motel near her that specializes in four-hour naps."

She picks up the phone. Franny must be there because Hannah engages in a short, precise conversation.

"She asked me why I didn't bring them over before."

The girls agree to visit Aunt Franny without a struggle. It seems they really do get on with her. Franny is unmarried, once-divorced. She's a high school English teacher, and when she opens the door, I can see she's a miniature of her older sister.

Hannah tells her we're going to a movie and dinner and that we won't be very late. Franny already knows about the attempted assault and about the break-in at Oakbrook, so she's all for having the girls with her so they won't be left on their own.

Barbara and Beth protest that they're really old enough to take care of themselves without a babysitter, but they go along with the scenario because they are indeed fond of their Aunt Franny, who's a writer of adolescent fiction, Hannah explains to me. Franny seems to squirm when her older sister brings up her vocation beyond teaching.

"I wrote some poetry that actually got into print, in college," I tell her.

"A policeman/author, huh?" she beams.

I think I just made a new friend.

The four hours go by very quickly. It isn't enough time to make love to her. The full deal would take a few months in bed together without interruptions. I cannot seem to tire of her. When we finish, I want her all over again and almost immediately. There is none of that male, "well, it's been nice, and now I'm getting the hell out." It wasn't that way with Mary, either, although she seemed to like to get dressed and then go out and do something else in a hurry after we copulated.

There is nothing quite like holding Hannah after we've made love. There is nothing similar in my life to just being physically near her when all the fireworks have ceased. The interim between the couplings never takes very long, though. The passion is intense, even firier than it was with Mary Janecko.

It's hard to explain the *loss* I feel when I have to leave her. It's literally painful. I can't tell her that yet because then I know I'll scare the hell out of her. I'm going to have to follow Jack Clemons' advice:

"Leave them wanting more."

I have a hell of a time leaving her at all.

The Internal Affairs detectives have cleared me—with reservations. They said I might have waited for a clean shot at Thomas's melon, without plugging the prosty too. Since she's recovering, with my good fortune, they don't think she'll be prosecuting me for the harm I did her; Captain Pearce has reminded her of her probation for possession of heroin and other illicit drugs. She's agreed to live and let live, in other words.

They give me back my shield and my gun and I'm back in the saddle on a late November Tuesday.

We visit Carl Thomas at Christ Hospital on the southwest side.

"Hello, Carl."

"You shot me, you prick. I don't want to talk to you. Or him."

He means Jack.

"You don't have a choice," I tell him.

His public defender is standing right next to us.

He looks at the PD, and the lawyer nods at him.

"Talk to them, Carl. It might make a difference," the public defender tells him.

"What if I fire you and ask for another lawyer?"

"He'd tell you the same thing, Carl. They're after the big man in your thing."

"I don't know what you're talking about," Carl says, lying on his bright white hospital bed. There's an armed uniform standing outside the door.

"Carl. They have a witness who'll fry you in deep fat. Talk to them, Carl."

He's referring to Gerald, who's ready to squeal *sooey* for our prosecuting attorney.

"What's the *deal*, then?"

The PD now has clarified Carl's situation for him.

"You save your sorry life if you finger Anderson for us."

He smiles back at me.

181

"You mean the *oil terrorist?*"

"Whatever," Jack says. "You just testify that Anderson was behind the deaths and you might save your own scrawny ass."

"I could give it a shot with a trial. See if they believe that idiot you're threatening me with, whoever he is."

"You could get escorted to the gas chamber. Or maybe it's the electric chair, Old Sparky. I can't keep up with it, frankly, Carl," I grin. "But I know it'll be painful, especially those last few days before they torch you."

There's no smirk on his face any more.

"Well?" I ask him.

"I need to think about it," Thomas replies.

"The offer is null and void the second Jack and I leave this room, Carl," I explain.

Thomas looks at his attorney, and the PD simply nods.

"All right. All right. But I don't know how much I can give you. I don't know where he is right now. The guy floats. He's got money."

"Coming to an end, there, Carl. It seems the IRS has issues with Benjamin's lawyer-daddy. It was those same boys from IRS that put Capone away, and then Big Al promptly died of syphilis and other assorted ailments, and compared to Capone, Carl, you are very small potatoes indeed," I smile again.

"The last I knew, he was in the area. He's got a hard-on for you, Detective Koehn. He's had that stiffy since you began sniffing after us back in the shit, back in Iraq and Kuwait."

"Really?" I grin.

"I wouldn't be so cheery about Anderson wanting your throat, Detective. After all, he's still out there. And you're no closer to him than you were in the Middle East. He's very smart, very clever. You couldn't catch him then, and it isn't likely you ever will."

"Look, asshole, I'm touched about your concern for me, but no thanks. All I want is your confession and corroboration at trial. The prosecuting attorney here in Cook County has authorized us to offer you a shot at life in prison, which beats the shit out of the alternative. I'm betting that Gerald fries you after the jury hears about you and Nina and her near-death experience. I think our circumstantial case will bury your ass *without* any help from Gerald. What do you think, Carl?"

Carl doesn't answer. His court-appointed attorney just stares out the window at downtown Oak Lawn.

Now all we have to do is catch Anderson, which is like saying all we have to do is de-fang King Kong with a set of pliers. Finding him has been impossible since he staged his own death by burning up those two other Marines in Iraq. He's slipped past the radar ever since his "disappearance."

So Jack suggests we go back to Arkady Kormelov, one more time.

"I can't be seen with policemen so often," he says to Jack.

We're at Morlinka's Russian Tea House on Randolph Street in the Loop. It's a genuine Russian restaurant, Jack told me.

"I apologize, Arkady," Jack tells the muscular Soviet. "But this is even more important than scoring Thomas.... And your eighteen-year-old phenom on the piano is now headed toward citizenship thanks to my INS lady friend, no?"

Arkady grins at my partner.

"There you have me, yes.... All right. But one more favor and we are quits, yes?"

"Yes," Jack agrees.

"You are looking for a dead man. Am I correct in this?"

"Yes," Jack replies.

"Then how in the fuck do you find a ghost? Do you ask a priest? Do you go to a medium?"

Jack shrugs. I'm all out of advice.

"You know lots of people. People who are involved in illegal pharmaceuticals," Jack smiles. "Anderson's father made his fortune defending trash in the court room. He amassed millions. Someone who made that kind of cash must have done business in this city. They would know how to find Sonny Boy. Through his father, Kady. Am I getting warm?"

Arkady Kormelov shows us his fine white teeth. Now I see the predator in this charming thug.

"You might be warming up," he says, straight-faced.

26

*W*hen I arrive at the drop, my guy is waiting for me.

"This is my last trip," the young blond man with the wispy white mustache tells me. "Your old man is in the shit. The IRS wolf is at his door."

The two of us are standing in front of a park bench in Lincoln Park, near Lake Michigan. I can smell the water from here.

"What're you talking about?" I ask the young man with the silvery blond hair.

"Your old man is going to get arrested by the feds. It's any day now. Your cash cow is getting its fucking throat slit."

"You're lying. You're stealing my money for yourself. You know what I'll…"

"I'm telling you the fucking truth, man. They've caught Daddy messing with his tax returns. He's going down officially for income tax evasion."

"My father… My foster father is being taken down by…"

"You've grasped it, dude. Now give me my tip and I'm on my way and it's *adios* muchacho forever."

"Are you Mexican?"

"Who? Me? Are you fuckin' kiddin'? What's that?"

"This? Oh, it's called a k-bar."

"Now listen…"

Before he gets another word off, I stab him in the forehead. He staggers back with my military blade stuck in the space between his two eyes and just above the eyebrows. The tip must have pierced his skull and made its way into his brain, because his eyes roll, and then he collapses onto his back.

There is no one in Lincoln Park to observe the blond man's death. It's 3:46 a.m.., according to my lit Benrus watch. I drag his body into the shrubs behind the park bench, and then I see a male jogger approaching quickly. He starts to pull up and stop on the path in front of the bench. He sees me coming out of the bushes.

"Something wrong?" he asks.

I've got the k-bar palmed behind my back.

"I was out for a walk, you know? Couldn't sleep. And when I got where you are now I heard someone moaning."

"Is there someone back in there?"

"I think so, but I can't quite locate him in the dark. The street lamp doesn't do much good back here."

"Hang on a minute."

The jogger, lithe and wiry-looking, approaches the bushes and me.

"You say you heard what, where?"

When he's in front of me, I stick the k-bar in the small of his throat, and he staggers back the way the blond man did. When he falls on his back, I see a river of black blood rising from the gaping wound the k-bar has caused. I draw the knife out, and then I jab him repeatedly in the face until there's no face left uncovered in gore. The blood is of course all over me, so after I drag his body into the bushes, I wipe the blade on my sleeve and I head for the beach and the Lake. It's only a few blocks from here, and the sidewalks are deserted now. The jogger— what the hell was he doing, running at 4:00 in the morning?—and the wispy-mustached bagman are the only two other souls in my vicinity. It's as if the rest of the city is sleeping. The cops, the firemen, all the municipal workers… No one's here except for the three of us. And two of our trio is now very much elsewhere.

I continue down onto the beach and I remove my shoes and wade into the icy water. I rinse my hands and my face. I've got a jacket made of cloth that I'll get rid of. There is nothing I can see on my pants, in this dim light from the street lights that circle the beach's parking lot. The only spray from the jogger hit me from the chest up.

186

There is a pier nearby, so I walk out to the end of the pile of concrete blocks and I toss the jacket into the lake. I feel the chill from the wintry November air, so I hurry back inland. I run toward my parked Mustang, and then I make my way back toward the Stevenson Expressway. I drive south to Joliet. I get off at Route 30 and drive farther to the small farmhouse that my father's associates rented for me.

His friends are Italians. They are members of the Outfit. And they asked no questions when old Dad offered them some reliable legal advice in trade for the use of one of their safe houses. It's good to have connections like my father's, but it's also worrisome to hear the bagman telling me the IRS is about to incarcerate the old man.

I never knew the extent of my foster father's mob-related activities until college. Then he bailed me out of trouble a few times, and he made the complaints literally disappear. My old guy has very good connections in several of the major cities.

When I told him I was going to join the Marines, he almost had a seizure. He couldn't believe I'd want anything to do with the military; he was convinced I'd become an attorney in his mold. I thought of getting into the kind of "business" my good dad was in. It's very lucrative, naturally. But he was always very lavish with money whenever I wanted any. Later, he told me if he didn't give it to me it might be lost in a real estate deal some day, so he figured he'd rather smother me in cash than let the banks have it if he ever got unlucky with property. His generosity made me very popular with women at the university, and I had more than a few good drinking buddies.

I've never really been interested in the law or in the buying and selling of property.

Killing gives me all the buzz I need.

I watched the lights go out on the blond man at Lincoln Park. I watched the glow dim in the eyes of the jogger when he realized what was now intruding into the flesh of his throat. The facial wounds were all superfluous. They'll make the police think it was an act of rage.

I'm never angry when I take life. There is passion, yes. There is emotion. But there is never a point at which I lose control. I don't allow it. It's almost like a scientific experiment, every time it happens. I'm in control of life and death. A person passes me on the street, and I say to myself: "Is this the last moment of their existence?" I have control over their fates. I'm the manipulator of their destinies.

It's all in my hands. I've taken the controls from God, and now I am their lord and commander. Nothing in nature can stop me from sending them on their ways, dispatching them to heaven or hell or oblivion. It's in no one's hands but mine.

It is, as they say, a rush.

With limited monies, I'll have to limit my movements, as well. I sit on the leather couch in my Joliet farmhouse. I turn on the TV to a 24 hour newscast, but news of the two murders hasn't been reported yet. They may not find those two men for several hours. I've put them both in some thick foliage.

Yes, I will have to curtail some of my plans in the United States until I can come up with a new source of income. If my father doesn't get indicted by the IRS, perhaps he can connect me with the right Italians in Chicago or some other big burg. Or it'll be the Russians or the Vietnamese—I don't care, as long as I become liquid again.

I look out the front window of this small brick house that sits on twenty acres of fallow land. There are trees and bushes to conceal a lot of the outside of this home, so it's almost impossible to see me from the road that ends at a half-mile driveway that leads to the front door here.

I'm well concealed. It would take an informer to help the police locate me. This place is truly off the beaten path.

I was remembering my father's reaction to my joining the Marines. I recall the look of disgust on his face when he heard what I planned. He was in the Vietnam War. He only enlisted to further his political career—he thought, back then, that he would someday run for public office, but it never turned out that way. He fucked up, in other words, because he could've got himself wasted. But he survived in spite of his blunder.

My foster father was what you might call amoral, which is a good thing to be if you're an attorney. Then you won't mind defending people who don't deserve justice. It's a wonderful system we have in this country. Every piece of shit is equal to every other piece of shit—in theory, at least. Christ knows, the poor are fucked in this nation. But poverty and injustice do not interest me, either. I'm too busy trying to keep my face above the surface of the water. It's that struggle to keep breathing that makes living interesting. And being one step ahead of my pursuers always makes my life vital and interesting. I'm never bored. Only those who indulge in routine become mired in the mundane, the everyday. If nothing else, my life is exciting. Never a dull moment, my dears.

If I'm going to kill Detective Will Koehn and his brother Sammy and his father George, his mother who's in a home, and Will's mistress, Hannah Menke, and her two lovely, delectable daughters, Beth and Barbara, I will have to conserve all my finances. I will have to be sure to be careful with my outlay of cash, because that source of drachmas is quickly drying up, now that my war veteran old man has been stupid enough to become ensnared by the Internal Revenue Service. What an ignominious way to go—it's the same way that Italian, Capone, was smoked. By a bunch of fucking accountants. How dreary. How bourgeois. How vulgar.

I would have thought Dad would've liked to go down in a drive by at the hands of Dominicans or Cubans or some such Latin cretins. Like the movie Scarface, *with Al Pacino. Now the way Tony Montana went down is the way my old man should've dreamed it up for himself. But to be handcuffed by a herd of CPAs? Christ, it's just too funny.*

When I go, it won't be with a whimper, but with a bang, like in The Wasteland. *I'm a big fan of Machiavelli, and I'd much rather be feared than loved.*

It was I who kicked Hannah Menke's door down after Carl Thomas told me things were becoming a bit too dangerous for the both of us. I was going to kill him, but Philip was there instead, and I missed my opportunity to rid myself of a co-conspirator. Thomas would have been caught eventually, and eventually is now, according to the newspapers. And suddenly another dead man has become a "person of interest." That person is me, of course. They are "on to me," as they say.

How to do Will Koehn and crew before the rest of his boys get on to me?

I could lay low and wait for the heat to evaporate. I could use my remaining funds, such as they are, and purchase a new identity, complete with plastic surgery to totally alter my appearance. I hesitate to change my face because of the ease of disguising it, and I also have become quite accustomed to the countenance that greets me in the mirror every morning.

It was too dark to see that visage covered in the jogger's blood in the surface of Lake Michigan. If there had been a full moon, then I might have had the opportunity to see myself bathed in someone's blood. There is no equivalent snapshot in life.

I do not expect to go out unscathed when I do meet with my end. I expect a bloodbath ending. It's only just, only right, that I should burst into a crimson flame when I finally expire. I would prefer that that climax be put off for quite some time, but I do not fear extinction, I don't dread death. It is a part and parcel of this life. The food chain insists that the stronger creature consume the smaller and the weaker. Darwin was the poet of our times. His words are made true every time one observes animals in the wild. And how dare we consider ourselves higher in the life chain than a cheetah or a lioness? We're predators as they are, our eyes squarely in the front of our faces. It is ludicrous to suggest our nature is really any different from theirs.

Ah, there. I have waxed philosophical for long enough. I could never engage in such discourse in the Marines because my fellow leathernecks were far more interested in common pussy and even more common brew, beer. There was no one to talk to in the Corps, and that is why I decided to bug out and leave, go AWOL. The danger of such a move was also a consideration because the excitement of wasting Iraqis was becoming tedious too. It literally was like shooting ducks in the proverbial barrel. It was all too easy. Pulling off the murders of the Kuwaiti girls and their entire families.... Now that had a little more pizzazz to it!

The adventure of returning to the United States. The immigration back to my native soil. All very exciting stuff.

Now the old fossil, my daddy, has to shut off my life's blood because he wasn't clever enough to avoid some bright math students in the IRS. I feel like shooting the old son of a bitch myself.

Perhaps I needed a closer relationship to a mother-figure. That might have put me on the right and proper path. I might not have turned out murderous if I'd had a more tender tit to suck on. I'm not a fan of breasts, anyway. Women don't fascinate me, except as objects for the cat to toy with before it snaps the prey's neck.

Will Koehn is what someone might call my antithesis. He's a bit different from me. I wonder if he's religious, as well? But I've never seen him go into a church....

Oh yes, I saw him enter St. Stanislaus recently. But he didn't stay long, and it wasn't a Sunday, nor were there masses scheduled while he was there. No, but they did have a confessional listing on their bulletin board. So young Will must have been unburdening himself to a padre. Interesting. He's having a moral dilemma.

You might ask me: Why Will Koehn? My answer would be that I knew his type. I knew his kind, all my life. They were the children of privilege, but I'm not talking about money. They were the kids who had real parents. Those loveable moms and pops you see on television and in the movies. They inhabit my nightmares.

Maybe you think it's jealousy, and in a way you might be correct. But it goes deeper than that. Some of my foster parents thought I was mentally ill. That, however, is a pat and facile way to explain me away. I will not be dissected so easily, no.

Some might call me unnatural. I understand there is no fair play in nature. I understand that some children are born under lucky stars and are endowed with loving, biological parents and that some youngsters have the cruel fate of being passed from household to household like a pet cat that no one wants to keep, any longer. It brews bitterness, being handed about as I have. It's no great mystery why I'm the way I am. It is nothing but logical for me to be a furious man. I direct my spleen at God. He's the rotten son of a bitch who fated me with this existence, and now I have the divine purpose of getting even with the Bastard.

I don't need a fancy shrink to tear me into edible pieces to be devoured by the animals around me. You can see their predators' eyes in every bush. They lurk on the periphery, and you have to be strong and brutal to keep them at bay.

Why Will Koehn? He's everything I despise. And he's inherited everything he has through dumb fucking luck: a father, a mother and a brother. All of them tied in the blood.

All I can do to get even with people like Will Koehn is to spill some of that precious blood.

You see, it's what I do.

27

I take Hannah to the gun shop to get her outfitted with a handgun that will suit her needs. She's fairly petite, although she is in great physical condition. She does use a gym and she does run all the time—which I'm concerned about, for safety reasons. She insists running indoors at her club will be the only compromise she'll make for me because she says she won't allow Benjamin Anderson and his crew to take over her life. She has a point, but it still frightens the shit out of me when I think of her alone anywhere.

We go to a shop that a lot of cops use for their personal hardware. It's on the far northwest side, and the police come here because the owner, Art Michaels, is an ex-Homicide who is very scrupulous about his chosen business contacts. His paperwork and background checks are famous in this city.

"I suggest the .38 snub nose," he tells us. "She looks strong enough for the kickback, and it has the stopping power I believe you're looking for, Ma'am," he smiles at Hannah.

Hannah takes the piece in her hand.

"You know the most important rule," Art warns her.

He's a big, beefy Mick. Sandy-red hair and flushed cheeks. Very popular with the ladies, the legend goes, in the day.

"And that is…?" Hannah smiles.

"Don't point it at anyone unless you intend to shoot them dead."

Hannah colors just slightly.

"It just means keep the muzzle low or high unless you intend to use it. Don't let it sit where kids can get at it, but hide it where you can get at it quickly. You won't have time to lock and load in the middle of the night when you're half asleep. Because if that guy shows up, you know *he'll* be wide awake and ready."

He smiles to try and reassure her.

"I know this guy," he nods at me. "Ex-Marine. You probably already know that. Did you know he was NCIS?"

"Yes. Will's told me."

"Did he tell you he rose to Homicide in the shortest time in anybody's memory on the force? I was there thirty-five years, and I never saw anyone else move up as quick."

"He's very bright."

"Yeah. But your friend here has more than that going for him. He's a bulldog."

"Bulldog?" Hannah laughs.

"He'll never let go of this Anderson guy. I know this man's type. He's book smart, but he's street-smart too. Deadly combination. I'd say Anderson is a prohibitive underdog."

I feel myself blushing slightly, now.

"Don't be embarrassed, kid. I'm not trying to pump you up in front of this pretty lady. It's just the truth…. If I were you, Hannah, I'd forget the gun and let this guy take care of business."

"That's kind of you, Art, but I want her to have some insurance."

"Okay, then. We'll have to fill out the papers, but I'm betting this lovely lady's got no priors or even a jacket at all downtown."

"Not even a speeding ticket," Hannah smiles at this affable Irishman.

We take the .38 snubnose back into Art's personal target range. It's more like an oversized basement, below the store. He lets the cops try out their purchases here before they take their weapons home.

"Here," Art tells us as he hands us earplugs and goggles. "Safety first."

The basement is well lit and must be a hundred and fifty feet long and perhaps half as wide. He's got fluorescent lights all across the seven-foot ceiling.

The targets are at the far end, and I can see the padding behind the bulls-eyes that are there to swallow the slugs.

He shows her how to grip the piece.

"I'll be the teacher, today. It's like having a relative teach you how to drive," he explains to Hannah as he nods toward me.

Art has his son-in-law working the counter while we're down here.

He shows Hannah the proper firing stance. He tells her how to grip the snubnose .38, and then he takes the weapon and shows her how to load it.

"These bullets are called hollow-nose. They will make an enormous hole in whatever you hit. Preferably you'll stop him with one shot, but this is no competition, Hannah. Empty the piece into him, and if you can, hit him in the melon or in the torso, preferably the upper chest. Try for something vital if you have time, but if you don't, just unload this thing on him, and if that doesn't work, reload and keep firing until there's nothing left of the son of a bitch."

She giggles like a schoolgirl, but Art's not smiling back.

"I'm serious, Hannah. You're shooting to kill. You have to make certain he can't get to you because this man is absolutely evil, and those kinds of pricks don't die easily. Excuse my French, Ma'am."

She takes the pistol when he offers it to her. Our earplugs and goggles are arranged, now. She assumes the firing stance, and then she holds the piece two-handed, as he showed her, and without hesitation she pulls the trigger six times. Even with the plugs, you can feel the boom of the shots. The sound must be deafening to the naked ear.

She's hit the central part of the target five times. No bulls' eyes, but excellent for a first-timer.

"Jesse James, for Christ sake!" Art exclaims with a smile. "Nice shooting, Ma'am."

"Phenomenal," I add.

"You ever shot before?" Art asks her.

"Never. Not bad, huh?"

"If it was a crossbow, you'd be freakin' William Tell," Art laughs.

Detective Frank Menlow comes into my office the day after we got Hannah the gun. Art says we can pick up the piece in seven to ten days, when the paper comes through.

"Think I have a little something for you, Will," Frank says.

Frank is a young Homicide, late thirties. He's got kinky brown hair that is almost an afro, but he's lily-white, damn near anemic-looking. He only colors when he's pissed, I've noticed.

"Yes?"

"They found two bodies near Lincoln Park. Some street fuck and a jogger. The homicides seem connected because time of death from the ME was put at only minutes apart. And the bodies were dumped in the bushes, close to each other. But the point of interest is that we got a viable print off the arm of one of them. We sent it to the Fibbies, and they were able to match—It's your guy, Benjamin Anderson. He was a Marine, no?"

"Yes."

"Well, it appears that Laughing Boy is alive and breathing, and this time he wasn't as careful as he was on your vics. He must have been surprised by the jogger. I'd be. Who the fuck runs at that hour in the morning? Oh, it was around 4:00 A.M. Sorry. I forgot. This is my case."

Frank colors only slightly.

"But I knew you and Jack were on this, so I came here as quick as I could."

"Thanks, Frank. I really appreciate it."

"And the Lake coppers picked a bloody jacket out of the drink. Some idiot fisherman was trying to catch Moby Dick in December, and

195

the jacket hooked on his line. The water's only about eighteen feet deep by the rocks where this clown was casting, and he snagged it for us. The blood made him think he could become helpful to the department, the guy said. Good citizen.... Anyway. The dead man is ambulating once more."

We find out about the blond bagman. He was a junkie named Mark Madigan. He was loosely tied with the Italian Outfit, the Mafia in Chicago. He was of course not a member of the Mafia because Madigan is not quite Sicilian, but he was their gopher.

We bring in Vic Castigliano, a northside *capo*. We tell him it's for ID purposes on Madigan, and naturally he refuses when we contact him, but we explain about how easily all his northside eateries could get inspected by the Health people, and finally he agrees to come downtown for a session with us. Of course he brings his mouthpiece, Marty Parrie.

We show him pictures of Mark Madigan. He seems impressed by the shot of Madigan with a big slice in his forehead.

Vic is a blond Italian, a rare color of hair for southern Italians. Vic is one hundred percent Sicilian, seeing that he's a made man.

"We want to know if Madigan had any connection to this man."

We show him a military photo of Benjamin Anderson, because it's the most recent snapshot we have of our zombie.

"Never saw the man."

"Vic. Did we talk about the rats in your kitchens?" Jack Clemons says.

"That sounds a lot like harassment," his lawyer tells us.

"It is. Very illegal, probably. But you want to roll the dice and see if anything happens? Look, we're not after your client, Counselor, but we're very intent on locating this man, Benjamin Anderson."

"He the guy who did that family on the North Side? What's the name? Milan?"

"Yeah, Vic. You have an excellent memory for names. Tell us the connection between Madigan and Anderson," I tell him.

"You were the NCIS cop back in Kuwait. I read about you in the *Tribune*.... Maybe I should just roll those dice."

"Your crew like kiddie molesters, rapists who do little girls and their families for shits and grins?" Jack asks Vic.

"Watch your mouth, officer. I don't need that crap from anybody, cop or no."

"Cooperate and we'll let the FBI deal with you, unless you kill somebody in our jurisdiction," Jack smiles.

"You pricks are really hot for this guy?"

"Yeah. We're very interested in Anderson," I say.

Vic looks at his counselor.

"You think these guys are bluffin'?"

His attorney shrugs.

"All right. I don't know this kid personal. I know one of my guys uses him as a gopher guy. He's a fuckin' nobody. But there is a lawyer.... No offense."

He looks over at Marty Parrie.

"There is a lawyer who does business on occasion with some guys totally unrelated to me."

"Right," Jack grins.

"You're dubious about my veracity?" Vic smiles back at my partner.

"No shit," Jack grins again.

"Anyway. Where was I?"

"This lawyer-acquaintance of someone in your crew."

He stares at Jack.

"Everybody knows the Outfit is just a myth you guys and the papers concocted.... But anyways. This lawyer hails out of the left-hand coast. He defends some guys I know. So he has this nutty-fuckin' kid.... This is all speculation and rumor, you know. And this kid needs a place to crash. So the lawyer trades with some free, useful legal advice, and he procures a place out by Joliet for said fucked- up kid to hide out because the kid might have a few problems, legally speaking. Before the sonny boy can move around freely, he has to have regular doses of cash because he cannot use plastic on account of you fine fellows will pick up his whattayacallit, his paper trail. I wouldn't know about such things myself, being a legitimate businessman.

"This fuck-up, this Madigan, brought Sonny Boy his weekly allowance. That's all I know. And this is the end of the conversation unless you're going to pinch me on bogus charges."

"Where's the house near Joliet?"

"I have no idea."

He stares at me.

"One call to the Health Department, Vic, and by the time your fine attorney gets it all straightened out, how much in lost income?" I ask him.

"That is blatant blackmail," Marty protests.

"Fuck you, Counselor," I say. "How 'bout it, Vic? The hard way or my way?"

"Give me a paper and pen," Vic tells us.

When we finally find the house near Joliet, near Route 30, there is no one here, and it appears that no one has been here at least for a few days. The brick house is clean. No remnants, no garbage, nothing to point the way for us.

"This guy really is a spook," Jack admits. "We should have had him. First the fingerprint, and then the break with that Sicilian fuck, and I thought we might nab Anderson. Now he's vapor again."

I look around the room we're standing in, just inside the entrance.

"You can't even get a whiff of him. But the fingerprint was intentional, Jack. He was saying hello to us again."

We leave the scene with four cars of uniforms from the city and an additional two vehicles with six FBI reps inside.

It's a long drive back to the Loop. It's December and it's cold, but no snow as yet. I'm thinking about what I buy the girls and Hannah and my father and brother for Christmas. I can't even picture Anderson in my head right now. He's disappeared too easily and too often, so I can no longer conjure him on my internal video screen.

He's like a nineteenth century Apache. He strikes and he disappears magically into the mountains, and the cavalry and the *federales* can never capture him. He's slicker than Geronimo. They'll never snare him and make a circus clown out of Captain Benjamin Anderson. He's too elusive, too sly.

He's the phantom in your nightmares that always remains just beyond the grasp of your fingertips.

28

Christmas is rather solemn for most of those twenty-four hours at the hospital where Carl Thomas is rehabilitating from his wounds so they can stick him in a cage for the rest of his life if he testifies against Anderson and if we catch the Captain in the first place.

Not many visitors come to the wards, but usually there is a volunteer who comes dressed as Saint Nick. So you can imagine the surprise on the face of the uniform, William Demerest, who sees Santa Claus ambling toward Carl Thomas's room.

"Sir, the children's ward is down on two," Officer Demerest tells the oversized elf in red.

Santa never says 'ho ho ho,' but he keeps on coming.

"Sir…"

Before the patrolman can react, he finds the syringe stabbed deeply into his chest. Since it is 11:30 p.m. and the floor is clear, no one sees the thirty-three year old cop hit the floor. And no one is around— probably because the night watch is sharing some punch or some eggnog at the desk, all the way down the hall and around the corner—to see Benjamin Anderson enter Carl Thomas's room. Thomas opens his eyes only at the last moment to find that twice-used k-bar of Anderson's sticking in the middle of his forehead. Carl doesn't even have time to let out a yelp before he's dead.

Two more bodies on Anderson's scalp pole. But this time one is a Chicago policeman, which is intolerable to the CPD. The Chicago police have been noted for their corruption over the years, but killing one of them is definitely out of bounds for any criminal. When it happens, it's literally like the hounds being unleashed after the fox. Anderson had better submerge deep because everyone is on overtime to apprehend him. Captain Pearce has given us carte blanche to go after him now, no restrictions. Manpower has ceased to be an issue.

I have moved in with Hannah until Anderson is jailed or killed. She says the kids understand why I'm there and that they actually feel safer now that I'm around except when I'm doing a twelve-hour shift.

They feel safe even though their mom is toting that .38 snubnose in her purse. She has a license to carry it with her because Captain Pearce made it happen, under these special circumstances.

I don't feel safe, however. Not while he's still out there. With most perps there is no personal vendetta happening. They're just trying to stay as far away from me as possible.

Which is why Pearce has me and my family tailed, twenty-four-seven. Sometimes I can spot them and sometimes I can't. It makes me feel better when I can't pick them out.

Jack and I have been waiting to hear from the Russian, but it's silent. The only thing we learned from Vic the Mafioso was that Anderson's supply lines have been cut off. No one in their family will touch anything from the hands of David Crowley because he's about a week and a half away from incarceration, thanks to the IRS and the US Marshal's Office. It's getting closer to lockup time for Crowley every hour.

Arkady has gone into deep cover, Jack informs me. He's tried to contact the Soviet mobster, but to no avail. He's gone to earth, just like Anderson after killing the policeman and Carl Thomas at the hospital. He doesn't want anything to do with all the publicity and public attention. He likes to live in the shadows like all gangsters do.

The syringe contained an overdose of adrenalin. William Demerest had a quick and lethal heart attack.

For Christmas, I spent the afternoon with my father and the evening with Hannah and the girls. Hannah's family does Xmas on the Eve, so she had plenty of time to spend with me.

It feels awkward making love to her in her own bed, but she told me the girls have accepted me as "the man" in their mother's life. I still feel a little hincty about their being under the same roof, but I try to imagine us as being already married—although marriage has still not entered our conversations.

I thought about giving her an engagement ring on Christmas Day, but I thought it might be pressuring her too much, especially with the way things are. We're sort of enduring a siege, I call it. It hasn't been physical, but it certainly has been an attack emotionally and psychologically. That's the kind of thing Anderson was hoping for, all these 'psy-ops.' Psychological operations, they call them in the military. Win their hearts and minds by first grabbing their balls.

I won't let her talk about him on Christmas Day. I didn't tell her about Carl Thomas and our copper, but she read about them in the paper.

"He walks into a hospital just before midnight, and no one stops him?"

"I'm guessing he rode up in an elevator and changed into the red suit on the way up. The hospital was running a skeleton crew on Christmas. Only the really ill are in there on that day and night. So the staff tends to be a little more laid back than usual, unless there's a big accident or some other emergency. They're only human, Hannah. No one keeps their guard up all day every day, even in a place like that. All he needed was a chance for them to relax. Would you be frightened of Saint Nick?"

"I guess not. But you'd think the policeman…"

"It was Christmas Day for him too. A guy in a red suit. Maybe he's there to raise morale, late as it was? Maybe the copper was half-asleep on his feet from doing a double shift. Who knows?"

I'm not doing a very good job of raising her spirits. I start to think I *should* have proposed. But now when she's visibly shaken is no time for the normal things in this life like getting married and so on.

When I was at my father's house, I found him cleaning his old .45 that he'd kept as a souvenir from the Second World War.

"I haven't seen that thing for years," I tell him as we watch *A Christmas Carol* for the hundredth-something time.

"Neither have I. Not since 1970, when I took it out and cleaned it the last time. You were just a kid, then, Will."

"I remember it because I never saw a weapon in this house unless it was my own, since then."

"No cause to bring it out. I always felt safe in this neighborhood. Now I'm looking forward to that prick trying to come here for an encore. I'm not shopping for any new furniture or for any more replacement wallpaper."

"You won't have to because we'll get him before he has the chance to make a comeback."

"You have your finger on him, then?" my father smiles.

"Not quite. But there are ten thousand law enforcement people after Benjamin Anderson. His money train has been run off the rails, and now the Outfit won't have anything to do with the son of a bitch."

Tiny Tim says: "*God bless us all.*"

I miss Sammy, right now. He's with his girlfriend at her parents' house.

"I'm getting tired of this movie," George Koehn says.

The LA cops have made overtures to David Crowley concerning the whereabouts of his foster son, but to no good end. The lawyer seems to be willing to go down with the ship and one large rat, his son Benjamin.

We've reached out to the various gangs in town to see if anyone wants to trade a favor, but there are no offers out there. They really don't seem to know where our man is either.

He could be using disguises to move about. He could be going out only at night so he is more difficult to spot. It's not likely he's gone to a plastic surgeon because our department has those physicians pretty well blanketed—even the not-so-legitimate surgeons. They know that if Anderson contacts them they better be in touch with us immediately. Aiding and abetting is no joke in this city and state.

We've thrown out the net for one big fish, and sooner or later he has to get snagged in the lines.

New Year's Eve is when I take out the ring at Hannah's. I can't wait for the axe to fall on Anderson's neck any longer.

Much to my surprise, Hannah utters, "*Yes.*" I had prepped myself for a negative response, and I was going to tell her I understood why my timing was lousy, but she jolted me with a quick and definite affirmative.

"You'll make a big fan out of my ex. No more alimony. Nothing but child support until they turn eighteen."

She smiles and kisses me.

We're going to be married in June, as corny as it sounds to both of us.

The ring cost me three months' pay. It's a fair-sized diamond, but you would have thought it came from King Solomon's Mines the way she beamed over it when I slipped it on her ring finger.

"It's stunning. I love it," she declared.

The kids were with Dad on New Year's, so we made love on the couch. We fell asleep ten minutes after midnight. The emotion was a bit too much for both of us, I figured.

The sound came from her kitchen. We were naked underneath her comforter on the couch and the TV was still on without sound, but I heard the noise clearly and it jarred me out of sleep. Hannah mumbled something incoherent, but I told her to go back to sleep. She put her head back down on the pillow.

I got up and threw my jeans on and a tee shirt. I kept my weapon and holster underneath the couch, so I reached for them and retrieved them. Then I walked barefoot toward the kitchen. It was the room adjacent to the living room, so it was close by. There was not much light coming out from the crack where the swinging door swivels, but there was a dim glow from the nightlight she always keeps burning in there.

I shoved the swinging door open, and there was nothing there to shoot at. Just the stuff that belonged in her galley-type kitchen. Pots and pans hanging where they belonged. A sink with no dishes. Drawers for utensils of every ilk.

She has a security system, so if anyone enters the house, it should have gone off by now. There's a loud alarm that fires up inside as well as outside. No silent alarm for Hannah. She wants something to scare the shit out of any intruder.

I walk slowly through the room with my gun pointed in front of me, and I swivel to sweep the entire area as we were first taught to do in NCIS and then later in the Academy in Chicago. There is no one here.

So I try the study that is next, after the kitchen. I flip on the lights and find that nothing has been disturbed. I'm thinking that I would be able to smell Anderson's presence, but there are no unusual scents in the air. My hair is up on my back. It's as though I sense him, right behind me.

Next, I ascend the stairs toward the girls' bedroom. I check Barbara's room, and then Beth's. Still nothing. I look in the upstairs bedroom and the situation remains the same. It's deserted. No one.

So I come back downstairs, my gun finally lowered. I flick on the low wattage bulb farthest away from Hannah and the couch, and when I look up, I find my naked fiancée pointing a snubnosed .38 right at my noggin.

I raise my hands.

"Don't shoot me, darlin'," I plead.

"Jesus, Will! Where the hell did you go?"

205

"Thought I heard the boogey man."

"That isn't funny."

"No, it's not, Hannah. Lower the gun, huh?"

"Oh, I'm sorry. I'm sorry."

"It's okay. Hey."

She begins to cry.

"I can't keep looking for goblins in the dark, Will."

"You won't have to. You have my word."

I wrap us both in the comforter, and a bit later things get out of hand again on that couch.

January is a long month. Almost as long as March, I think. The three months before spring arrives are usually dreary, drawn-out matters. It's on the order of cabin fever. You get cramped up being inside most of the time. It seems like it's always snowing or sleeting or dipping below zero, especially when The Hawk swoops off the Lake from the northeast.

Northern Europeans are said to be prone to alcoholism, and part of the problem is relegated to the climate. I don't know how that works with the steep rate of homicide and mayhem in sunny Florida and temperate California, but there are those who adhere to the notion that the weather brings the loonies out to play.

Maybe. But it doesn't draw Captain Benjamin Anderson out to the surface where we can lay irons on him. He lurks just below. It's almost like Dante's Nine Concentric Rings. Anderson has put himself below ground, but we can't be sure how far he's descended. My preference would be the Ninth Circle where Judas is being munched on by Satan, but Iscariot never gets consumed. Now *there's* some frontier justice.... Too bad it'll go down easier for our guy if he's caught. I have the sick feeling he'll be placed in a mental institution instead of getting himself a firing squad, like the good old days in the military.

No punishment is really good enough for him. What would justice entail? Torturing him and then finishing him, like old English jurisprudence? The punishment is supposed to fit the crime. One of the most imaginative ones I remember reading about concerns putting a cage over a man's head with fiercely hungry rats inside it. That'd make one hell of a training film for thugs, wouldn't it?

The old man told me he didn't want me to join the ranks of those very same thugs, but it's getting more difficult all the time not to want to become part of that crew from *The Oxbow Incident*. The only difference is that if I were part of that posse this time, we'd be hanging the right man.

29

M y mother's name is Vivian. She is seventy-one years old, but she
might as well be six. She's been in the 'home' for more years than I
can remember, now.

I'm tracking a mass murderer, I'm engaged to a woman a decade
older than myself who has two young-adult children, my father's house
has been ravaged by that same above-mentioned maniac, and I've got a
"little" brother who's been threatened in a subtle way by that same nut,
Anderson. Then I have to make my semi-annual visit to my Alzheimer's-
destroyed mother. It's been a pretty fucked up six months, I'd say. The
only shining spot to date is Hannah and her daughters.

The visits are as brief as they are useless. Perhaps "hopeless" is the
word I was looking for, because my mother, Vivian, naturally, doesn't
know who the hell I am.

Her ward reminds me of the glaring whiteness of the hospital
walls in the movie *One Flew Over the Cuckoo's Nest*. Everything, indeed,
appears porcelain and bone white, as a lot of medical centers look. I have
always had an aversion for such places, but my mother seems to be
treated with patience and kindness here at Rosewood Clinic. The people
who care for her seem to actually *care* for Vivian. They talk to her gently

and calmly, and there has never been an incident at Rosewood to suggest their treatment of patients is any different after visiting hours.

"Am I dying?" my mother asks me.

There is no special emotion attached to the query. It's very matter-of-fact in tone.

"No, Momma, you're not dying. You're still a young woman."

"Where've you been, Bobby?"

"I'm Will, Momma. You have two sons. Sammy and me. I'm Will, your older son."

"Oh. I thought you looked like Bobby."

"I don't know a Bobby, I don't think."

"You look like Bobby."

I gaze around her private room. It's fairly spacious, with TV, double bed, wardrobe cabinet made of maple wood, sink, and adjoining bathroom. It's a very decent accommodation, it appears to me.

"I'm Will, Momma."

"I know. I was just kidding."

But there's no smile.

"You're the policeman, aren't you?"

She has her moments of lucidity now and then.

"Yes, Momma. I am."

"Do you catch killers?"

"Yes, I do. Sometimes."

"But sometimes they get away."

"Yes, Momma, I'm sorry to say they do get away."

"Caught any of those bad guys lately?"

"A few."

"That's good, Bobby. There are lots of terrible people in this world."

"I'm Will."

"Yes. Yes, I forgot. You're my older boy, aren't you?"

My mother has aqua colored eyes. She was once a very beautiful woman. My Dad used to tell me about all the competition he had before she agreed to marry him. She's tall, about 5' 9", and she never had any extra weight on her frame. She looked like a female distance runner, but not quite that severely skinny. More like a tall ballet dancer, I'd say. But when she trained those aqua-hued eyes at you, it felt as if you were in the crosshairs of a sniper's scope. She had that way of *engaging* you with her glance.

She was a schoolteacher, taught the sixth grade until she retired at sixty-two, almost ten years ago. It wasn't long after that that she succumbed to this disease. She deteriorated within three years to the point that Dad had to put her here where she could be taken care of round the clock.

"Bobby, you don't look too good. Is something bothering you?"

I don't argue about "Bobby" anymore.

"I'm fine, Mom."

"Your name is Will. I forgot."

"You look pretty good, though, Momma."

"I'm dying. You're lying."

"You're not dying, Momma."

"It doesn't matter. Not really. The daffodils will bloom again this year. They do every year."

"They will. You're right."

"I was never much of a rose woman. They live too briefly. Their beauty dies with too much rapidity."

My mother had a Master's degree in elementary education. She read a lot. I got my love of poetry from her DNA, it looks like. Now she can't read because she can't remember the sentence that she read before the sentence she's reading.

"Where's your father?"

"He's at home."

"When's he coming to see me? He never comes to see me."

"He visits you all the time, Momma."

"There are too many evil people in this world. Your father had to kill them all in the war."

"He didn't kill them all, Momma. He was a soldier, just one man."

"Then he *should* have killed them all.... I have a son who's a policeman. He used to play football, and then he became a policeman. He catches bad men. He's told me so."

I look out her window. There is snow on the ground. It has been an almost-Arctic winter to date, temperature-wise, but we've been spared the snowstorms. Mostly, we've received the light dustings that cover the earth and the concrete in the same bone-white as I see inside her room.

"Do you love me, William?"

"I always have and I do."

I can't believe how lucid she sounds at this moment. It's as if she's suddenly come back to Earth.

"Oh. I was just wondering."

And she looks out the window into the white world that extends past her window.

Jack Clemons is a ladies' man, regardless of his protests to the contrary. He has a girlfriend in the INS, but he has lady friends scattered all throughout the city. I'm surprised one or more of them haven't shot him because he plays a large deck of cards with all his "relationships." There's nothing predictable or uniform about Jack's female harem. They come in all colors and all sizes, as well. He isn't prejudiced against "big" women. He loves them all, all shapes and sizes, like the song in *Gigi*. Except they're not little girls. They're all adults, of course.

He has a fondness for the female sex that goes beyond "appreciation." He's a student of them, and I have to say he understands them far better than I do.

We're at Burger King on a snowier-than-usual Saturday morning in late January. The Holidays have fled, and we're entering the dregs of winter.

"You have to experience deep pain before you can fathom the feminine mind," Jack smiles at me.

He's got the Extreme Omelet Meal. I've gone with a Whopper with cheese. I can eat hamburgers any time, which frustrates and infuriates Hannah whenever I order a burger early in the morning when we're out somewhere.

"You can't know women unless you empathize with their personal agonies. My old man used to say, '*never trust a creature that bleeds every twenty-eight days but doesn't die.*'"

"That's spectacularly misogynistic, Jack."

"Is that a fucking word?"

He's got his merry prankster face on his puss.

"How the fuck do I know? But your old man was full of nineteenth century shit."

"You're probably right.... How's it going with the fiancée?"

He winks like a conspirator.

"Good."

"You sure you want me in the wedding party? A misogynistic fuck like me?"

Now he's leering at me with his wise-guy grin.

"Sammy's my best man because he's my brother, but you're the only friend I've really got."

"I am?"

"Yeah. What's so odd about that?"

"Because, Will, best friends tend to hang out together—outside of the workplace. We really only hang when we're on shift."

His countenance goes serious and solemn on me. His sincerity briefly takes me by surprise.

"So? We go out to dinner or we play golf or bowl. Isn't that what buddies do?"

"Yeah. Exactly. Didn't you have any bros in the Marines or in the NCIS?"

"No. Not really."

"What about that Pete Donato character?"

"He was my partner, but I stayed alone, over outside the World."

The World is here in the United States.

"You didn't hang with anyone when you were in the military or overseas in the Navy cops?"

"Not really."

"You sat around reading your gay poets," he says with a mock sneer on his face.

So much for the sad-faced, serious Jack Clemons.

Clemons has gay friends too. He's introduced me to a few when we'd be out in the city from time to time on dinner or lunch break. For a guy with archaic attitudes about women, sometimes he can surprise you with his liberality.

"Yeah, I sat around reading my fairy queen poets, Jack."

"You are a very hard case, Detective Koehn."

A redhead walks by who gathers my partner's attention.

"I like a woman with just a little too much clustering in her caboose."

"You are really lost. You really are a pig."

"I know. But I'm loveable. Just ask any of my *legion of love*."

I can only roll my eyes.

"Has this cocksucker gone under the ground for good?" he asks suddenly.

It's been weeks since we heard a word about Anderson. The Captain's anxious, I'm worried, and even Lover-Boy here appears genuinely concerned. Jack doesn't take our caseload to personal heart, he keeps lecturing me. Which is why he'll burn out far later than I will on this job. I'm beginning to believe him. Except that he's really a bullshit artist at heart, and not just with the girls in his life. He's a serious man hiding behind his feminine smokescreen. The guy *cares*, and he isn't about to snow me under with his bullcrap.

"No. Anderson is alive and thriving, if my guess is good. The only thing that's going to stop him is a fucking stake in the heart. That's the way all monsters have to die, Detective Clemons."

I feel a quick flush of heat in my cheeks.

"Do I detect a note of levity?"

"What do you do besides chase pussy?" I ask him.

"What else *is* there to do that is worthy of my time and toil, Detective?"

You can't make him stay serious for long. He shows those glittering white teeth to me again.

"You have a point."

"I work with wood."

"You *what?*" I ask.

"I work with wood. Can't I do something untwisted in my little life?"

"What kind of woodwork?"

"I make flutes."

"Now you're fucking with me."

"No. I make little flutes and I give them to kids in the street, mostly. I give them to hospitals and they give them to children also."

He's staring at me as if he's giving testimony under oath.

"Are you whacking me, partner?"

"I like having whacking done *to* me. Not a big fan of servicing others that way, Will."

His face is absolutely deadpan, so I think he's being upfront with me.

"You make little flutes for little kids."

"Yeah. You know about idle hands and the devil.... When I have loose time, I carve them. Bet you didn't know I majored in music in college, played a pretty mean recorder, too."

"Now you've gone way over the top of the lid, Jack."

"But it's all perfectly true.... You've never been to my apartment, have you."

"No. Why?"

"I've got my Kimball baby grand in the living room of my little abode."

"Really?"

"For true.... And here's the kicker. I have perfect pitch."

"What's that?"

He explains that he can tell by listening if a note is being played or sung on key.

"Only a few dudes have that gift, buddy."

"I believe you.... How come you never told me any of this shit before?"

He leans aggressively toward me as if he'll pull the truth out of me yet.

"You never asked. I didn't think you cared to hear about any of that."

"Well, you were wrong, Jack."

"Oh, God. What've I done now? Have I *humanized* my poor fucking self?"

"Just about. It's like I never knew *anything* about you."

"Please, Will. You'll be holding my fucking hand, next thing you know."

His expression of mock contempt makes me laugh out loud.

"Not likely, partner."

"You ought to come over with Hannah, sometime. I'll play some Chopin for you both."

Then he returns to the solemn, artsy-fartsy Jack Clemons. It's like he splits his personality before my very eyes. He's a magician, sort of.

"And who're you going to bring to the concert?"

"I don't play for the ladies. I play for myself and for select audiences only."

"You don't play for your women folk?"

"No, Will. It'd overwhelm them. It'd be vastly unfair."

It's like he's come alive before my eyes, now. He was just another cop with a badge, even though we'd been working in close quarters together for months.

"I don't get why you held back for this long," I tell Clemons.

"Look. My old man was a Vietnam vet. He was a lifer in the Army. Rangers. Very tough individual. He always talked about how he never got close to "fngs." Fuckin' new guys. He always thought it'd hurt too much to get attached to another grunt, so he held back with the personal history stuff. You follow?"

"Yeah, I do. But I wish I'd known all this before."

"Point is, Will, you know it now. I mean, am I right or not?"

30

*S*weet hitchhiker.

    She can't be more than twenty-two-or-three. She has auburn hair to her waist, and the freckles lightly dot her face. A pretty girl, all in all.

    I couldn't risk using the BMW that my foster daddy procured from his Italian friends in Chicago. By now they have all deserted him, seeing that he is persona non grata *with the IRS, that infamous band of hooligans that rid the country of Alphonse Capone. The name "Capone" puts my father in league with crime's heavyweights. I'm not sure if he's deserving of that high-level association.*

    The driver's name is Carrie Anne. She picked me up on US 80 on my way out of Joliet on an early Wednesday morning. Carrie tells me she never picks up hitchhikers, but she asked as if I were the strong silent type who might serve as a bodyguard for her on her long journey. I was more than happy to accommodate her.

    "You're not one of those serial killers, are you?" she grinned as we headed for parts west on the Interstate.

    "Do I look like a bad guy to you?"

    "You're a very attractive man," she blurts.

    "Why thank you, Carrie."

    "You don't carry much luggage."

She's referring to my single duffel filled with my belongings now resting in the backseat of her 1994 Escort.

"I travel light."

"You look a bit well-dressed to be a hitcher."

"I enjoy the challenge of getting places without the cost or the hassle."

"What's your name?"

"William. People call me Will, though."

"I like that name. Will."

She smiles with the same kind of gushing sincerity she handed me a little earlier.

"Where exactly are you headed?"

"Los Angeles," *I tell her.* "Beverly Hills, to be more exact."

"I don't mean to pry. Sorry."

"It's not a problem, Carrie. Really. Ask away."

"What do you do?"

"I'm an exterminator."

"You kill bugs?"

"No. I take care of bigger pests than that."

"Like what?"

She has her eyes half off the road, and since traffic is fairly heavy this morning, she's making me just a wee bit anxious.

"I don't want to distract you," *I tell Carrie.*

She turns her head toward the west.

"What do you do?" *I ask so she won't turn moody on me. We've got over 2000 miles to travel together, if I don't kill her out of boredom, dump her body in a truck stop, steal another ride, and keep going to La La all by myself.*

I'd rather talk to her, though. I've been leading the solitary life too long lately. The only contacts I make seem to disappear before my eyes. I look forward to seeing if I can be with people without murdering them.

"I'm a graphic designer. I've got a job waiting for me in LA."

"Good for you."

"What is it you really do?"

"I was going to be a lawyer. You didn't buy that exterminator joke?"

"I'm not stupid, Will."

"No. I can see you're not. You're very bright."

"And I don't want you to think I'm some desperate female, either. When we stop, we'll be sleeping in separate rooms."

"Of course. The thought never crossed my mind."

And the thought really never did cross my mind. I have no intention of coupling with this silly bitch. I just wanted to see how long I could go without throttling her. I might be able to make it to David Crowley's house in Beverly Hills without actually liquidating this dumb cunt.

We approach California on the third day on the road. We've crossed a desert or two; I can't recall which bodies of sand because I spend most of the time sleeping so I don't have to talk to Carrie anymore. She bores me, but not to the point of homicide. Besides, with all the cops looking for me having a female at the wheel driving as a pair is perfect cover. I suspect that Detective Koehn and his crew think I'm still in Chicago or the area. Which is fine for me because I want to let Koehn's personal pressure cooker build up to a boil. And then I want him to forget about me. I want him relaxed before I visit him and his entire family. And before I meet up with his wife-to-be, the beauteous Hannah and her fair daughters. I have special plans for those last three females.

We descend the state of California until we reach Los Angeles and its spider web of highways and freeways and interstates. Carrie winds up being a skillful navigator. She's received excellent directions from her new employers, whoever the hell they are, and she drops me off at David Crowley's gate three days after we began our little odyssey together.

I thank her for her company and for the ride. She was true to her word about separate motel rooms en route. We stopped twice. I paid for the rooms, and she was surprised when she saw I paid in cash. The guys at the motels were used to plastic, but they took my bills without too much eyeball-rolling.

It's hours before dawn. I press the buzzer at the gate.

"It's not the IRS, Jason," I tell the security guard.

My foster daddy hired Jason when I was in my late teens. Jason was a Marine sniper who served in Vietnam, which is why David hired him, I think. Old ties to an even older war. And Daddy lost his war; we didn't.

"Hello, Jason," I greet the security guard.

"Hello, Mr. Anderson," Jason replies. But there's a dubious look on his face. He knows the police want me. He, however, will not drop a dime on me because he's discreet. Discreet to the tune of six figures a year for watching Daddy's gate. He might be worried that his job is coming to an end, what with my father's IRS difficulties, but he's probably waiting for the results to come in. I don't know what other job a high school graduate like Jason could find that could come close to his current salary.

My handsome, sandy-haired dad opens the door.

"You're taking a very stupid chance by showing up here," he says to me.

"It's dark. They think I'm still in Illinois."

He brings me in and quickly shuts the door.

"At least you had the sense to come here late."

Very late, indeed. It's 2:20 a.m., Western time, of course.

If there are surveillance people on the street, I didn't see them, and Daddy's estate is very well concealed from the other homes down his street. Not to mention that his spread occupies three acres. In this part of LA, a lot this big is a bit unusual. But I think I made it past Jason without being observed.

I don't plan on lingering here long.

We go into his expansive study. There are law books galore. The classics. The usual collection of fine literature adorns his massive bookshelves. He sits at his large oaken desk with an impossibly perfect shine to its surface. I sit where I always do, opposite from David.

"What do you want?" he demands.

"Money."

"I sent you fifteen thousand."

"I'm broke, Dad."

"Don't call me that."

"Have we lost our connection?" I grin.

"The day you did murder. Yes."

"Then why do you have anything further to do with me?"

"I took you in. I told you I'd take care of you. I went beyond any reasonable bounds of doing things for you, Benjamin, but here it stops. They are going to catch you, and now you've come to my house, which makes it aiding and abetting a fugitive."

"You already abetted and aided me."

"Here it ends, as I said."

"I need money," I tell him.

"I don't like the demanding tone," he tells me.

"I've always had that tone with you, David."

"You're a blackmailer and a murderer."

"I'm the little boy you brought up in this lap of luxury."

He looks around his study. He appears trapped and trying to find an avenue of escape.

"How much?"

"Whatever you have in that safe behind you."

"I can't. I need every dollar. I'm trying to get out, tonight."

"You're going to run from the Feds? And how will you do that?"

"That's my business."

"No. It's mine now too, Daddy, since I'm back here in the friendly confines of home."

"You've never lived here. You've never really lived anywhere. You went from this house to the military like a disease, infecting anything you've touched."

"Such lofty morality from a drug Mafia mouthpiece."

"I never murdered anyone. I shot at men in a war, but I never..."

"You defend scum."

"I'm not a good man, but I'm not a..."

"Monster?"

He studies me. Then he taps his fingers on the top of the oaken surface. "How much?"

"Everything you've got."

I show him the .45 caliber Colt, now.

"I'll give you whatever you want. That isn't necessary."

I aim and shoot him in his left shoulder. The shot is not meant to kill him. The blast knocks him out of his swivel chair onto the floor behind him. When I reach him, he's flat on his back and bleeding heavily.

"Don't, Benjamin. Please..."

I walk out of the study and make my way into the garage. He has several large gas cans that he uses for the upkeep of his gardening devices, mowers, and weed whackers. My daddy is the consummate gardener. It is his passion.

I take two of the five gallon gas cans back into his study. His face is considerably paler now.

There is no danger that Jason has heard the retort of the .45 because this house is very well insulated. In fact, Daddy's study is well sound-proofed. Only a slight chance he heard the crack of my pistol.

Daddy is bleeding out.

I begin pouring the gasoline all over him. Then I douse as many of his fine books as I can before my pipeline of fuel depletes.

David Crowley is groaning at me.

I already know where the safe is, just behind where he lies. So I go to the panel, and I press the hidden button, and the bookcase swivels about, and there it is. I know the numbers because Daddy has allowed me to watch him, since he has always feared that he'd need me to secure him funds for just such an occasion as the attack of the accountants at the IRS.

Eureka! The old man has stuffed his larder with something close to a half million in American dollars. Sometimes he has British pounds stashed here because he loves flying off to London, but my luck is with me because it's homeland currency this early morning.

I unload all the clothing out of my large military duffel. Then I put as much money as I can inside the bag. Fortunately, David has concealed thousand-dollar bills and hundred-dollar bills, along with a smaller collection of twenties and fifties. So I'll be able to use the smaller denominations to make my way out of California and then head back east, where I have unfinished business.

And then it's perhaps back to sunny, warm Mexico lindo. Not back to Aguascalientes, of course, because that might be asking for trouble. The Mexican cops frown on rape and murder, and they have my likeness undoubtedly posted everywhere in that vicinity now, and I'm also determined not to go through plastic surgery. For one thing, you can't trust the doctors, because I've been in the headlines lately. For another, I'm not a big fan of personal agony. I don't like being in pain. Hurting is something other people should do. It's not for me.

I look down one last time at David Crowley. I show him the little lighter he uses for candles and for his fireplace. Then I light it and place the tip of the flame just above his shoe-tops. The stink of the gas is almost overwhelming.

"Benjamin, don't," he pleads.

I light him up, and his body flares like an explosive torch. He screams as the flames run riot over him. Then I quickly go to the bookcase and I apply the fiery end of the small wand to some of his literary collection. The bookcase explodes, and I have to jump back, grab the duffel loaded with Daddy's cash, and I have the .45 palmed, all as I'm sprinting for his front door. The flames seem to follow me, and I barely make it out his entrance.

Jason has smelled the conflagration, and as I approach him, I raise the .45 and shoot him once in the forehead. The back of his skull is blown behind him, but in the dark, the blood looks black. I can't see the usual pink and white profusion of brain-matter.

I hurry toward the front gate, punch in the code, and the big barrier opens more slowly than I'd like it to.

David Crowley has a security system that will no doubt alert the police and fire department automatically, so I have to run for it. The duffel is heavy with my money and my weapon, but this burden is not too heavy to bear, and I race away from my father's burning, ruined estate.

31

March is harsher, with the white stuff. We get three inches apiece on each of the first three days of the month. It makes getting around the city interminable. The streets are clogged; the Stevenson and the Eisenhower and the Ryan and the Kennedy are fucking nightmares. The plows can't keep up because the snow just keeps on coming.

On the twenty-eighth day of March, the weather relents and the plow guys make the most of the respite.

The news of the bonfire in LA travels quickly to Chicago, so we hear about David Crowley's death just hours after the fact. The gas cans were found—or at least remnants of them were—and the fire inspectors relay to the cops here and in California that the blaze was no accident. And the next day, they scooped up enough of Crowley to find a bullet hole in the charred-broiled shoulder of the owner of the mansion that was torched. Prints won't help us because Anderson left fingerprints all over the house in which he once dwelled. A jury wouldn't have much use for that kind of evidence.

But everyone knows who called on the Mafia mouthpiece. The LAPD and the CPD have no doubt it was our boy and his own, Captain Benjamin Anderson.

Then the girl who gave Anderson the ride from Joliet to the West Coast comes forward. She positively IDs Benjamin as her road partner for three days on Interstate 80. She says she dropped him at Crowley's front door early in the morning on the day Crowley became fried rice.

So we have him cold, pretty much, for his father's slaying and for the killing of the security guard, Jason. Gerald is still in the wings waiting to rat him out even though he never actually met Anderson in the flesh. The circumstantial case is pretty solid, our prosecutor insists. I'm not so sure. I've seen good criminal counselors blow gaping holes in circumstantial and hard evidence cases. That's why they make the big money and that's why they dwell in large estates in the ritziest locations in California and on Long Island.

I'd rather see the Captain's corpse in the morgue. Then I know that if there is a God He'll do the right thing to him when it comes to handing out genuine justice.

We have other cases on our load. We have two seniors murdered in the inner city. They were both petty heists gone dirty. They had their wallets stolen, both of these black geezers, to the tune of $12.36 total for both. The bangers who did them were pissed the take was so small, so they smoked both old men with a shot to the head apiece. We catch the bangers in six days. They're both multiple time losers in the hood. We even get a couple of standup citizens to rat them out. Eyeball witnesses. Both old guys were shot in the street in the cold, harsh light of March in the city. So they both go black on our boards after a short posting in red.

We have a welfare mommy who suffocates her two-month-old daughter in her own breasts because Mommy winds up being bi-polar, and the shrink says she was severely depressed at the moment she asphyxiated her own kid.

We have a teen driver, aged sixteen, who knocks down a priest on the southwest side and damn near cuts the padre in two, killing him instantly. We find out he's got a bench warrant on two other DUIs.

The list goes on like that. Benjamin Anderson is the aberration. He's the "high-profile" murderer that the media always wants to know about. They don't ask about all those other murders because they regard these demises as too "mundane." Too ordinary. So they don't get the press.

But they're just as dead, and the crimes against them are equally heinous. Everybody knows we're the last resort. We're the guys who speak for the dead. It's been well-documented in fiction and in fact. It's one of the reasons I became a policeman. I'm an advocate for people who no longer have a voice. They might have lawyers, but attorneys won't keep on coming after the felons responsible for their non-existence. Lawyers have billable hours to deal with, and I understand that. They're businessmen, like most everybody else out there in the charge-as-you-go world.

Cops aren't exactly like that, however. We do a lot of research and investigation off the clock—at least, the best policemen do. And homicides are extremely reluctant to let a case go frozen solid. Some pursue perpetrators even after the coppers' retirement. The stories are legend about detectives who just won't quit, just won't let go.

I won't let go of Benjamin Anderson now, and I won't release him any time in the future, should he still be running free out there. I'll be after him until they close the curtains on my life, if he doesn't die first.

In early April, I'm still living with Hannah. I'm a fixture in her house by now. I'm giving up my lease on the Clark Street apartment in the summer when it comes up. I'm betting that we'll really tie the knot in June and that I'll be a resident here eventually. So there's no point in hanging onto my own flat. I'm not going to sublet, though. I think I want to hang onto it until the lease runs out just so I have somewhere to go to if things don't turn out the way they appear to be turning out.

Because everything just gets better and better for Hannah and me. I get closer to Barbara and Beth all the time. Beth has even been calling me "Dad." It feels rather strange when she does call me that, too, but I rather enjoy it. I haven't gotten to that level with Barbara yet, but our relationship seems solid. We get along, all four of us. We're a family, and I love the sensation of being a cog in that familial wheel.

"You still love me?" she smiles hazily in afterglow, here in Hannah's large bed.

"What do you think?" I tease.

"I think you'll tire of me," she groans softly.

I roll away from her.

"Hey? I was only kidding? Hey?"

"I wish you'd stop that kind of kidding."

"Some day you're going to develop a sense of humor, Will Koehn."

I roll back to her.

"You think?"

"I think, baby, yes. I think," she smiles.

We start at it all over again.

We have that security system in place at Hannah's. I chipped in to enhance it to top grade, too. At first, she resisted my donating to the cause, but I explained it'd make me feel more comfortable if she had state-of-the-art in the house, since I was now an inhabitant. So she finally agreed, and we have a quality system in place.

The girls, however, are still never left alone here. Hannah still has the snubnose .38 in her purse or in the bed stand at all times, loaded with hollow points that'd blow a hole in a raging rhino. I keep my weapon under my pillow. I also keep a .25 automatic strapped to my ankle when I'm out of bed and when I'm dressed. Otherwise I keep it under her pillow when we're asleep.

There is nothing new on Anderson's whereabouts. The Staties in all 50 in the Union have his picture in their patrol cars. He's a feature snapshot on the Net. He's on the FBI's most wanted list. I know Pete Donato and the NCIS are still after him for murder and desertion raps. Interpol would love to snare him should he wander abroad. Scotland Yard is aware that David Crowley owned three townhouses in the London area, and one farmhouse in Scotland. Defending thugs pays well, as everyone knows.

No one has seen a hair on the Captain's wholesome looking scalp, word is. Word is there's no word.

So Jack Clemons reaches out to his Russian buddy one more time, now that we have the news the Russian's been spotted on the streets again.

"Kady. It's been a long time," Jack smiles as he shakes the Soviet's hand.

"Not long enough," Kormelov says.

"You don't sound friendly tonight," Jack tells him.

I let Clemons do all the talking with Arkady Kormelov. It's his connection, after all.

We're at that teahouse again near the Loop.

"If I had anything on this Anderson, I would tell you," Kormelov explains after the waiter has departed the table.

"I think you know something and you're holding back," Jack explains.

"Are you going to bust my balls and start talking about deporting Russian girls who play the piano?" Kormelov says.

"I don't punk out on my deals, Kady. How about you?"

The Russian waits until the drinks have been delivered. He is drinking tea, of course, but the two of us shocked the waiter by ordering diet soft drinks. It just isn't *done* in a *tea*house, apparently.

"This man has connections with the Italians. I could get into major complications for telling you this, Jack. The father, the one who was incinerated, was very well-hooked-up with the guineas. You're talking to the wrong man. The only guy I knew in this deal was that son of a bitch Carl Thomas who liked to chew on cunts. Now if there's nothing else..."

"Who do we contact?" Jack insists.

"You are becoming difficult, Jack."

"Was that a threat, Kady?" Clemons grins.

"I would never threaten a policeman. I'm a businessman, and you know this."

"Okay. Who?"

"Jimmy Zags is the man you want to talk to."

Jimmy Zagnarelli lives on the far southwest side. He "owns" six pizza joints, but his real living comes from whores and loans and union deals and drugs. The FBI has a full dossier on him, but they still can't clamp him in irons because to date he's been too careful and too smart. He does it the way the old mayor of this town accomplished it. He let other men take the fall for his misdeeds.

We meet him at Linguinis on 87th and Pulaski. It's one of the few southwest side neighborhoods that hasn't gone Black and Hispanic. It's mainly Polish and Irish and Italian. White Sox territory. Cub fans have their asses handed to them in this hood.

He's about five feet nine, and he must go about 185 pounds of muscle. He's thick, but not fat. He wears the usual pinky ring on his right hand, and he's got a big ruby ring on the wedding-band finger on the left hand. His hair is oily and curly, and it looks like your own hand would get stuck if you ever tried to put your fingers through his top mop. Jimmy Zags smells of the garlic they use in his restaurant. His breath is foul, too, when you approach him. He's appropriately slimy.

He has those guinea cupid's lips, as well. They're thick and way too red for the rest of his swarthy face. It's as if he's grinning malevolently all the time. His expression only changes when he smiles and shows you his white, feral teeth.

"I know you?" Zagnarelli asks me.

"No. I know someone who knows you, though," I explain.

We sit in a booth, the three of us, including Jack.

"I don't know what the fuck you're talking about, but I gotta make nice with Homicide or you'll call those health cocksuckers. Am I right?"

"If you say so," I smile at him.

"What is it? I'm a businessman."

The cook comes out of the kitchen behind us and he yells out for someone named Gino to "get the fuck back in here!" Jimmy Z stares over at the cook, and the guy in the white tee shirt and white pants beats a retreat back where he came from.

The waitresses are uniformly big-breasted. They all wear old-fashioned piled up hair, and they all have very unnatural hues, up top. They wear low-necked blouses, and they give all the customers a free shot at some gigantic tits. I'm betting Jimmy Zags hand-picked all of them.

"Benjamin Anderson."

"The guy who waxed the little kid and her family on the North Side. And he torched his fuckin' old man too—I read the fuckin' papers. I went to school, but I don't wear suits except to impress the hoos."

He grins, and you can almost see the evil in the perspiration on his upper lip.

"You had connections to David Crowley. You had money muled to his foster son so he couldn't be tracked with a paper trail."

"Prove it, Officer."

He purses those cupid's lips, and his face takes on an obscene appearance. He makes you want to get up and get out of here.

"If I could prove it, you'd be downtown in the shit already, and we all know it. So let's cut through the bullshit, *Jimmy Z*."

"Here comes the health department."

"Here comes the way it is," I tell him. This time Jack's the silent partner.

"You don't tell us this guy's general location, we're going to be very unsympathetic toward you when you get nailed for aiding and abetting a wanted fugitive. This is high profile, *Jimmy Z*, and all your connections are going to bail on you like you're AIDS when we get done explaining to the local citizens how the wiseguys were helping out a kiddie rapist."

He folds his hands on the table here in the booth. He sucks his teeth, and then he produces a gold toothpick. He proceeds to pick his teeth. Then he stops and stares at both of us. He's going to stonewall us. He's going to outlast us in a pissing contest.

The place reeks of olive oil and mozzarella. The ripe odor of garlic permeates our atmosphere. It's as if we've been transported to Little Italy in New York.

"I've heard about you, Koehn. Hardass. Can't do business with you. Straight-arrow motherfucker. Never cracks a smile. Like one of those Pistol Petes in a fuckin' Western."

He leans his head toward me until I can smell the stench of that garlic in my face. He keeps leaning aggressively toward me until his nose is barely a half foot from my own. He's trying to cow me, so I lean even closer, back at him, until our beaks nearly touch and until he's a blur in my eyes.

"Okay, hardass. We set this guy up with a place out near Joliet. You already know it but you can't prove it. He had a vehicle also, but he left it in a garage on Tuohy. I'll give you the address. The last I heard he was in California, calling the shots at a fuckin' family barbeque."

There's no smile on his acne-scarred and thick-lipped Mediterranean puss.

"You have no idea of his whereabouts," I say.

"Somewhere between LA and Chicago would be my guess.... Look, if I hear, I'll call you."

"By the way, that business about not calling the health department on you? I was lying. Keep your toilets filled with Clorox, asshole."

We rise from his booth and leave.

"You gotta learn to play nice with the wiseguys," Clemons laughs as we return to White Castle for yet another dose of Ready-Mix to our arteries. The sliders are too good to turn down, though, so we keep coming back. Especially when it's midnight shifts. And especially when it's February and there's not even a hint of spring in the frosted air outside.

These places remind me again of that famous painting with the denizens of a coffee shop in the dead of night—by that artist Hopper.

White Castles are places to go to when you have no other place to go to. Cops come here a lot, but so do all kinds of other lonely people who're searching a spot open long past midnight.

I worry about Hannah and her kids when I'm working third shift. I worry about her in spite of her new security rig and her .38 with hollow points that'd flatten the Frankenstein creature. I worry about my father and brother. I worry about anyone connected to me.

Jack has noticed my increased tension on the job.

"I know it's not because you need to get laid," he leers at me after gobbling four cheesesliders without a breath.

"Thanks for your concern."

"You're letting him get to you."

"And Anderson hasn't got to *you?*"

"Not like he has with you. Of course it's understandable, seeing that my family, such as it is, hasn't been touched by this motherfucker."

"And what if they had?"

"My mother's dead. My old man left us when I was fourteen. I'm an only child. Most of my relatives are coots who're ready to die anyway, so his pickins are rather lean with me, Will."

"I see."

"Look. I'm just saying. Don't let him get *that* far into your head. Because once we do nail him, there might not be anything left worth having. That's all I mean, Partner. Fact is, I'm becoming rather fond of your silly ass."

He goes back to his three remaining cheesesliders and inhales them in rapid succession.

32

We find the car at the Tuohy Avenue location. There's nothing inside, however, that appears to be of any aid to our locating Benjamin Anderson.

The funeral for David Crowley has already taken place yesterday in Los Angeles. There were plenty of his peers at the burial. Crowley knew everybody who was anybody in the legal trade, so there were plenty of flowers and a line of expensive cars headed into the cemetery.

I have to believe that Anderson is making his way back to Chicago. I know he's setting me up with all this waiting, but the trip to California was to get some money together for his personal "siege" against me, and perhaps against my family as well. I've been on the phone with the cops in Champaign so that they'll keep an eye on my brother and on Megan too. They were very cooperative and said they'd send extra patrols by his apartment complex every day with the help of the University's campus police. The Chicago cops are keeping tabs on my father and on Hannah (and me), and on my mother in the nursing home where she lives. So I can't bitch about the precautions they're taking. They've been very good about everything. Everybody knows about the cop fraternity from television and the movies, and it's one of the few accurate things about the police, coming out of Hollywood. We indeed do take care of our own.

We're keeping a special eye (and wiretap) on Jimmy Zagnarelli also. We're thinking Benjamin might try to re-open his lines of communication with the Outfit guy who helped him in the past. Zagnarelli wasn't about to give us any help, but we had to talk to him.

Five hundred grand was missing from the safe at Crowley's, according to the insurance man who took care of David Crowley's estate. And the LA detectives got some intelligence from one of their mob moles that said David Crowley kept a very interesting ledger which had some explicit and damaging information about the Mafia guys that Crowley made a fine living out of defending. We figure Benjamin Anderson might try to peddle the ledger to Jimmy Z's people, since Ben will need spending money fairly soon.

We're only guessing about the content of that missing "ledger," but we figure it's not about family recipes.

I'm also betting that he'll pay cash for a vehicle and that he'll use some of his bogus IDs that Zagnarelli's people fixed him up with to travel this way. I'm betting he won't use Interstate 80 or any other major highways or interstates to arrive here. He'll be careful and he'll take his time. It only adds to his tactic of putting me and us at our ease, making us begin to believe that perhaps he's not coming back here at all. He'll think we figure it's all too dangerous for him to return to Chicago with all this manpower poised and ready for his renewed attempt to kill me and mine.

Waiting equals anxiety. But it can also add up to carelessness. You just get tired of *anything*. After a time, you gradually let down your guard.

It might happen to anyone else, but I have one virtue if I have any: Patience.

I learned how to "hurry up and wait" in the military, just as the Captain did. I can sit still for hours in a surveillance without twitching.

I have to. My survival and my family's might depend upon it.

Jack plays Chopin for me and for Hannah, and surprisingly for Jack's lady INS agent, Sheila Marshand. Sheila is a truly dazzling woman even though she is not what a photographer might call cosmetically beautiful. Her nose is too large and her hips are perhaps a bit too wide and her breasts might not be erect enough—yet, all in all, she's very sexy. And I know Jack concurs in my estimation of Sheila.

He's playing some etude or other on his Kimball baby grand, the one he told me about. He's very good, at least to this untrained ear. After he finishes the Chopin, we go out to dinner together.

We try a Czech place not far from Jack's New Town apartment. The food is excellent and the ambience of the place makes it seem as if we've been transported to Prague. I can almost see Kafka hanging out here. They have the red and white checkered tablecloths and the wicker-backed chairs. I can't pronounce the name of the meal Clemons orders for us, but we leave the ordering to him since he's been here a lot. Our trust is rewarded with a great meal. It's unbelievably tasty, and everyone agrees that it's delicious.

We walk out into the chill. Spring has not crept up on us yet in Chicago. It's still as if it's late January, except that the snows have ceased and the temperatures have risen to the point of clouds producing a cold rain that doesn't freeze until later at night. Then you have to beware of iced-over byways and sidewalks. But the temperature is in the upper thirties tonight, so we can walk about with some confidence.

I liked Sheila and so did Hannah. She's younger than Jack and me, but she seems very intelligent and extremely personable. Jack has begun to date her exclusively, a first for my partner. Playing Chopin for her made it clear to me that he's serious about her.

We walk back to his apartment. My hand grips the bare flesh of Hannah's hand, and I can feel the cool of her skin. She squeezes my hand from time to time, and by the time we say good night to Clemons and Sheila Marshand, I'm ready to go hunt down a justice of the peace and get this thing legal and consummated.

We drive back to Oakbrook, kissing and mauling each other at every intersection with a red light, regardless of nearby cars that might witness our unabashed lust for each other.

We barely make it out of my Cavalier and into her Oakbrook house before we begin to disrobe hurriedly on the way up the stairs to Hannah's bedroom. Luckily the girls are once again with their father, so we'll have no embarrassing scene with the kids on the stairway.

We're halfway up the flight when I grab hold of the banister for support as she hooks her right leg over me and lets me join her here. I feel her heat as we come together, and she climaxes as soon as I enter her. But I'm able to withstand that irresistible desire to flood her with my seed at the beginning of our coupling.

She is able to hang both legs around my waist, now, and I let go of the banister and begin to ascend the last few stairs to the top landing that lies in front of the bedrooms. When I struggle to get us to the upper floor, I stand still as she undulates atop me. Her hips lunge at me in an insistent rhythm. Finally I let us settle to the floor where we make love in the traditional fashion.

"I want a baby with you," she whispers.

"I want what you want."

"Well, I skipped my pill tonight," she grins.

"Good foresight," I grin back.

She urges herself up at me, and then I can no longer control the tide. It happens quickly and intensely, and Hannah smiles up at me as she wastes me lovingly.

I take her to target practice regularly, three times a week. I have all my stuff out of the Clark Street apartment, and I'm fully moved in. I have to keep the Chicago address, though, because I have to live in the city to work for the cops. It's a rule we have that I never thought about until I considered moving in here and ditching the flat in New Town. Jack tells me I can either lie about my residence or keep paying for the place on Clark Street. I think I'll opt to just renew the lease. Unless Hannah wants to move to the city after we're married. Which I don't see happening. And I have to admit that I love it at her place. So I'll keep the apartment and reconsider subletting it. Maybe Sammy, my brother, might want to live there after he graduates.

I'm not giving up my job or my badge; that much I know for sure.

I still see the crime scenes in Kuwait sometimes in my dreams. Things like that are not so easy to turn away from and leave forever. They haunt you and stay with you as if they happened to you personally, which in a way they did. It is difficult to remain aloof and separate from the madness I witnessed in the Middle East. The madness I'm referring to is not limited to the murders I investigated. It includes the terror of those criminal investigations as well. You cannot harden yourself to make things impersonal, just business, no matter how tough or military you might consider yourself. If there is a shred of humanity inside yourself, you suffer at the sight of what "human" beings can perpetrate on one another. If you don't show that reaction on your face or with your body language, then it manifests itself in your subconscious and in your dreams. That's the way it happens with me. For all the cool I try to transmit on my exterior, I pay for it all on the inside.

So I return to Kuwait to those dual scenes of misery and lunacy. I see what Benjamin Anderson and Carl Thomas and Philip Brandon spawned as a result of an Internet conspiracy that was supposed to have some political meaning—to Brandon and Thomas, at least—to explain its ferocity. Now we know it was all slight-of-hand on the Captain's part, but knowing why doesn't relieve the nightmare he created and executed.

How could someone supposedly human, like Anderson, grow into the *thing* who mutilated at least three young girls and the beast who destroyed the girls' families as those dying children watched?

I could spend the rest of my career and the entirety of my life trying to unravel that ultimate mystery: *evil*. Why is there such a grand dose of it in our world? Better minds than mine have gone full tilt trying to fathom the causes of such despicable human behavior.

Blame it on the devil and his demons. Say it's the work of the indifference of the cold, materialistic, spiritually-depleted society around us, and still it gives us no comfort to know *why*.

I've read a lot of the Russians. Especially Dostoevsky. He went into that black ocean in *Crime and Punishment* and in some of his similar stories. Raskolnikov was an axe murderer in *Crime*. He hacked up an old pawnbroker to steal her goods and then spends the rest of the novel trying to free himself from his conscience before he ultimately confesses to Porfiry Petrovich, the detective. Then he goes to Siberia for seven years and it is suggested by the author at the end that Raskolnikov has been reborn by his love for Sonia, his hooker significant other. The book's a classic psychological study because it explores the psyche of a killer, but it doesn't cop out by making Raskolnikov a fucking nut! He was deadly *sane* when he wasted the old lady pawnbroker. He couldn't explain his crime away with "madness" as a plea!

I wish it would become the same scenario for Benjamin Anderson, series murderer. I wish he would have a conflict with his conscience and then come find me and confess and get himself thrown into a hole for eternity, if, by some legal loophole, Illinois refuses to execute him. I don't really care anymore if he gets the death sentence, of course. I wish it would work out neatly, as it does in the storyline of *Crime and Punishment*, where the bad guy comes to justice.

Justice seems fainter and more remote as each day passes in my real world here in Chicago. This is not St. Petersburg, and there is no literary logic and logical denouement here. Bad guys get away with murder, and the old truth about the longer a case goes without closure.

Dostoevsky dramatized murder, as all writers do. Real murderers sometimes avoid the justice and the closure that novelists give us, the readers, and knowing all that scares the shit out of me no matter how much I'm aware that you can't catch them all.

This one has to be nabbed. He can't slip through time's fissures. *He has to be stopped!* I know Clemons is right---it is counter-productive to obsess about him; but I have no choice. Too much is at stake. Too many lives are involved. Sammy and my father and Hannah and her girls. My mother. Myself. He has no right to dangle this noose over our heads, but it's dangling, nevertheless.

"Will you come to school and talk about what you do?" Beth asks me.

I have to think it over for a beat.

"You want me to frighten your classmates? And how're you going to explain our...relationship?"

"You're my mom's fiancé."

"That sounds cool. Say it again."

She smiles and I'm hooked. Show and tell day for her is next week. I'll have to get a couple hours personal time to make the appearance for her, but I never really considered turning Beth down.

This is domesticity, except for the anxiety and dread business that is mutely present in our lives. We go shopping on Saturdays and we buy our necessaries at the Mart place and at a local meat market. The only things which distinguish Hannah and me from all the other shoppers at both places are the automatic in my shoulder holster and the .38 snubnose in Hannah's purse.

I've taught her to wrap the handles of her purse around her elbow so that some street booster doesn't snatch the bag and the piece out on the curb somewhere. So far, she's done everything I've suggested.

We bring the groceries back home and we prepare our meals at noon or at six in the evening. We go out to movies as a family, sort of, and the girls go to school every day, and we go to our own jobs, and it's all very ordinary.

The girls know the danger they're in because I've talked it over with them. I am very proud of the stiff-upper-lip they've assumed. And I don't think it's false courage. I think they're just as strong as their mother.

Except no one else in the neighborhood is being sought out by a Marine-trained murderer. We have that one distinction, all to ourselves.

33

*I*nteresting man, Detective Will Koehn. He's shaken up his routine by changing his route to the Loop every day, and I'm sure he's watching for a tail, although he's being followed by a police car with two plainclothesmen inside. They don't appear to be taking any pains to stay out of sight, probably because they want to discourage someone exactly like me from following the homicide investigator and ex-NCIS dick.

I wonder if he's had some warm family get-togethers, lately. I'm wondering if he's been over to his father's place and if he's had a cozy meal with the patriarch. Maybe he's been down to Champaign to visit his brother, the ex-jock, and his sweet little live-in mamasan. It's almost saccharine, the way they all relate to each other so lovingly. Makes me want to puke, every time I think of them. It's like a fucking Norman Rockwell cover for The Saturday Evening Post.

I remember the NCIS policemen as having little paunches at the belly. And they wore gray or navy blue suits so it was easy to pick them out in a crowd. They all looked like junior FBI agents. They came aboard our ships and told us not to shoot the indigenous personnel in Kuwait or in Iraq. It was all anyone could do not to laugh at them, but they were so solemn in their duties that we withheld any merriment, more or less.

I have trailed after the good detective on earlier occasions, notably the foray to that Lakeside museum. Now I have to be careful to alternate the three *vehicles I have been supplied with by one James Zagnarelli, capo of the Chicago Outfit and certainly no fan of Koehn's. Will apparently tried to muscle Jimmy Z into helping the cop locate me. Since I laid fifty large on the wop, I am now back in his good graces. He's found three "rental" cars for me, and none of them are hot. They were paid for in cash out of the fifty Gs. He said he wanted to see the policeman dead for the insulting way he talked to him at one of Jimmy's restaurants. I was more than happy to pledge my help in making his wishes for Will Koehn come true.*

She lives alone in an apartment. She has no current paramours that I have been able to spot. I was expecting Koehn to come visit her, but apparently their relationship has been severed. Still, they were at one time a hot item. He made frequent visits to her home here, and it was pretty obvious that they were having some kind of horizontal boogie joy together. It's got to hurt when he hears I've killed her.

I come up her stairs at 2:12 a.m. She's been settled in for at least four hours. I'm sure she's an early riser, having watched her for three consecutive days, now.

It is mid-April. It is false spring, my favorite time of year. Today, on this early morning, Mary Janecko gets hers.

I pick her lock quickly and quietly, but she's clever enough to have a chain on her door. I have to use my pincer device to open the chain before the door swings all the way open.

Inside it is pitch dark. The bedroom must be off to the left, down her hallway. I wait a beat to progress toward her, and then I walk softly down that hall. The bathroom door has been left open, and there is a dim nightlight on inside. It helps guide my way toward the last door, which has to be her boudoir. There are no other choices left.

I crack open the bedroom entry and walk in stealthily. I hear no sound, and there is no light inside. I see a shape on the bed. I take the k-bar out of my pea coat, and then I inch toward that form. When I reach the bedside, a light snaps on behind me.

"Noisy little bugger you are," she says.

241

I turn and see a woman dressed in navy blue sweats pointing a nine millimeter handgun at my face.

"Drop the blade," she tells me.

Very demanding. I like it.

I drop the k-bar on the floor. It thumps softly on her thick carpet.

"On your knees," she says.

"No," I reply.

"Pardon me?"

"No."

"I'll kneecap you, you son of a bitch."

"Go ahead. I won't kneel."

She looks at my knees as if picking a target. I'm standing next to her nightstand. The telephone lies on top. It's a pink "Princess" phone, and it tickles me to know it's in her bedroom.

She moves slowly toward the telephone.

"Back up," she orders.

So I back up.

She's within three steps of the nightstand, and I have my shoulder blades against her papered wall.

When she takes one more step toward me, I lower my shoulder and charge her. The weapon explodes with a shot, and I feel a searing stab in my right shoulder. It knocks me backward, but while I'm on the floor, scrambling, I grab hold of the k-bar. She appears a bit woozy from my tackle, and she doesn't see the blade in my right hand. I try to sit up, and I see her staggering sideways, the piece pointed toward the floor. I lunge out at her with everything I can muster, and I succeed in leaping far enough forward to spear her left foot with my knife.

She screeches in horror and in pain as she sees the handle of the k-bar quivering on top of her foot. She tries to raise the barrel of the nine millimeter toward me. I'm on my back again, and I know I'm bleeding heavily, but when she tries to aim the gun at me again, this time she falls back on the bed behind her.

I rise to my feet. I hear footsteps outside her door, and then the footsteps recede and go away down the hall. I want to take that gun or the knife and finish her, but I don't have time. Someone has already made the call to the police by now, and I've got to get the hell out of here.

I'm driving with crossed eyes. I finally make it to a phone booth on Crossplains Avenue. I swoon my way to the phone and find some change, and then I dial the number. It's after three in the morning, and fortunately, I'm able to prop myself up in the booth for thirteen minutes, as I make it on my watch, and then Jimmy Z's man appears in a Lincoln Town Car beside my booth.

It costs another thirty grand for him to get me medical aid. He's put me up in another safe house near a farm in Mokena, not far from the Joliet site that I inhabited once before.

"This is it, Anderson," *Zagnarelli himself tells me when I wake up and find him and a woman standing by my bed.* "Your goodwill has run out. I don't give a fuck about your money, and if you rat me out with the cops, I'll cut you into ground chuck myself. Are you getting the picture here? Because you'll be flat on your ass for a few weeks. You've lost a lot of fuckin' blood. Helene, here, is a nurse—or she used to be. She'll watch over you. And as soon as you're walkin', you're the fuck outta here. Capeesh?"

I nod. I feel like throwing up.

"Good. You better disappear forever this time, asshole. You stabbed a fuckin' FBI agent. You killed a cop. Your life expectancy was up yesterday, asshole. I'm havin' no more to do with your sad ass. I hope I make myself clear. You and Koehn are quits as far as I'm concerned. Go kill people somewhere other than Chicago, or I'll do their job for them. You follow?"

I nod again.

Helene is a good-looking nurse. She's in her early forties, and she shows me that's she's carrying a .22 pistol just in case, as her boss, Jimmy Z put it, "I get frisky." *She says she'd be happy to cap me herself, but she has orders to do so only in self-defense.*

243

Since I have no weapons of my own presently, and since I'm as weak as a wounded rabbit, Helene has all the cards in her hand. I'm not interested in killing her, anyway.

But I might try recruiting her.

After four days—we're in the third week in April now—I'm regaining strength. This ex-surgical nurse has sewn my wound and told me it was superficial in nature, regardless of all the bleeding I did on the way over here. She says Jimmy Z had to torch the car they transported me with. The car I was using was towed away from the phone booth and burned to the ground as well.

"You are a very pretty woman," I tell her.

"You tell all your victims the same thing?" she smiles at me.

"I didn't kill those girls and their families. I just watched."

"You are a very twisted young man," she grins.

"I must be like a lot of the people you 'work' for."

"I'm not a whore. I just do medical work for Jimmy's associates."

"The kind of work he can't hire from a regular hospital, right?"

"You have grasped it, Mister Serial Killer."

"I'm no such thing. You've got it all wrong."

"Sure. And that's why that FBI lady splattered you in her bedroom. You're just misunderstood."

"Can't we be friends, Helene?"

"If you take one step toward me for any reason, I'll pop you with this Saturday night widow-maker. You ever seen what a .22 does to a piece of meat?"

"I'm conversant with firearms, yes."

"Are you conversant with brain-dead as a minimal injury from one shot to the noggin with this handgun? It's the Mafia weapon of choice, killer."

"Again, you have me all wrong."

"Step off that mattress and you'll never have to worry about being misunderstood again."

"I think we've come to terms."

"I'm giving you some morphine so you'll sleep and shut the fuck up, Anderson. By the way, I don't like you. You aren't charming at all."

She sticks me with a shot, and a chill follows the fire of the hypo.

I dream of oil fires in Iraq. I see flames shooting up from derricks. I see charred bodies along the highways, most of them native bodies, not American. I see the faces of those two families in Kuwait. I see their surprise as Carl Thomas aims his rifle at them and as he makes them cower on their knees before the three of us—Brandon, himself and me.

Their eyes seem to roll back in their skulls even before the fun begins. The first little girl faints as Thomas tears her clothes off. There can be no greater insult to a Muslim than to see his daughter deflowered before his very eyes. I don't participate in the rapes or the shootings or the hangings. I watch. I'm an observer. I'm the director of this scene, not a participant. They are all actors performing my script. I have orchestrated this home movie, but no one is filming it. Too many so-called "series killers" make the mistake of taking mementos of their killings from the sites. They want reruns of the deaths so they can watch them over and over.

Far too dangerous. I have a wonderful memory. Total recall. I don't need films or videos or tapes to help me replay what happened inside those two homes or inside the Milans' house in Chicago.

We lingered for a few hours inside all three sites. We enjoyed ourselves. Thomas and Brandon were covered in their victims' blood, so they both showered inside the homes and even did their own laundry in the houses. All three families had wonderful facilities for our cleanup. We walked out of each place immaculate, as if we'd simply been on an early-morning visit to our own relatives.

The images remain with me even today, here in this dreamscape, this morphine-induced teleplay that I'm watching right now.

"Hello, Helene."

"Hello, yourself."

"You married?"

"You kidding? Three divorces."

"Kids?"

"You striking up a conversation, Captain?"

"I was in the Marines a long time ago."

"And you went over the hill, Jimmy told me."

"Jimmy a vet?"

"Are you kidding? Does he appear to be retarded?"

"Anti-military, right?"

"No. He's very patriotic—when it comes to turning a buck."

"My, what a cynical young woman you are."

"You trying to make nice with me?" she grins.

"Sure. What's it been? A week?"

"Too long. You're becoming a bore."

"I apologize."

"Not your fault, Captain. I've worked the psych ward before I got hired for my new position with Jimmy's friends. See, you crazy bastards become repetitive after a while. You all try so hard to sound sane."

"You mean, you doubt my sanity?"

"Oh, no. I know *you're out of your fucking mind."*

"That's very harsh, Helene."

"Save it, sweetie. I've still got the weasel-popper in my purse, and I still don't like you any better."

"When do you think I'll be able to leave?" I ask her.

"You mean, before the FBI bursts in here and grabs you?"

"You're a very humorous and very pretty lady."

"They're going to find you eventually, you know. Jimmy isn't going to help you any more, but he might just kill you.... How do you know I'm not a hired assassin?" she smiles.

"Why would you have waited this long, then?"

"Good point. You're almost as bright as you think you are."

"How bright is that, then?" I ask.

"Bright enough to quit trying to snow me. I've been overwhelmed by men far slicker than you, darlin'."

I guess the battle has been lost, and as any competent battlefield commander knows, you take your losses and cut for higher ground. Helene has won the battle, but she hasn't necessarily been victorious in the campaign.

Not quite yet.

34

Mary Janecko has nerve problems in the foot Anderson skewered with his knife. She'll likely have some difficulties with severe cold. There might be numbness in any weather, her doctor warned her after the surgery. She'll be on extended leave for a few months, at least.

I see her at Mercy Hospital, near the Loop. Her color is better than the first time I was here, which was the day after I heard she'd met up with Anderson in the flesh.

"I have never been as frightened in my life, Will, and I've charged through a few doors hunting down fugitives. But he was in my *apartment*, Will, waiting to try and kill me. If I hadn't heard my front door being picked, I would've taken a long time to die."

"I'm very sorry, Mary. I wish I'd been there to kill the son of a bitch for you."

"For us all," she smiles.

"Is there anything I can do for you?"

Her face is white, almost ashen.

"Come back."

"That, I can't do. I'm sorry, Mary."

There is moisture clustering in her eyes, but she doesn't cry.

"I know. Actually, I'm happy for you. You found a serious woman. That's what you were always looking for."

The dam breaks, and the droplets wander down her cheeks.

"You're a serious woman, too. Any man would be lucky to have you."

She smiles, even though she's weeping.

"That's the kiss of death when a relationship goes south, Will. 'Lucky to have you.'"

"I didn't mean…"

"I know. I know."

She tears up. Today is the first time I can remember seeing her *vulnerable*. She was passionate in the bedroom, but she never allowed her emotions off the leash any other time. She was the consummate Fed—always under control.

"He came into my home. He's trying to get at you through the people around you, so…"

"I know, Mary. They're all being watched."

Her eyebrows shoot upward, and she looks genuinely frightened.

"Who the hell was watching *me?*"

I hang my head because I've got nothing with which to assuage her anger. She ought to be pissed. Someone *should* have been keeping watch over her, her being an armed special agent or not. She was open to attack, and we should've had someone there. I feel personally responsible for an error in judgment that could've cost her life.

"It's my fault, Mary. I should have included you on the list I gave to Pearce."

"Out of sight, out of my mind, right, Will?"

"You've never been out of my mind."

"Really?"

"Really. I didn't stop caring about you. I never stopped loving you, either. It just didn't…"

"I must sound like a whining little ass to you."

She tightens her face. Her lips become taut. I can see white lines at her cheekbones.

"Stop it. Don't be silly."

"I don't usually get this way."

Her cheeks color deeply, now. I've caught her being vulnerable, and I know she's very angry about it.

"I know, Mary."

"It's not very professional, my behavior, is it."

As soon as she looked defenseless, she commands herself to get it under control. Now her brows are raised determinedly. She will not allow me to see her appear weak.

"Cut it out. You're just as human as the next federal agent."

She grins.

"You have a way…. You just have a way."

"This is really going to sound lame."

"What is?" she asks.

"I'd really, truly, like to be your friend."

She looks up at me and the tears gather once again.

"Don't cry anymore, for crissake," I laugh.

She laughs with me.

"Okay. Friends with a homicide detective?"

She sniffles, but her face lightens up just slightly.

"Friends with *me*, Mary. Just with me."

"Like that movie—can a man and a woman be just friends?"

"Why the hell not?"

She wells up again, and the facial cloud bursts.

"Why're you always so goddamned *sweet*, Will?"

"You deserve better than I gave."

"You underestimate yourself, buster."

Then she takes my hand and squeezes it tightly.

"Catch that miserable bastard. That's my first request of you, buddy-boy."

"Done," I tell her.

She looks at me with just a slight edge of suspicion in her lovely eyes.

The FBI frowns on their people being assaulted and stuck with knives. They send out six agents from the dark recesses of Quantico. All six are specialists with series murderers. They are all profilers as well as experienced field agents. They're housed at the Loop office, and Pearce has informed us that we're to extend all courtesies to them.

And Pete Donato has returned to Chicago. He's in civvies, as NCIS people usually are. He looks like one of Mary Janecko's FBI brethren. Gray suit—but no paunch. The haircut is absolutely GI.

I re-introduce him to Jack Clemons.

"Glad for any help we can get," Jack tells my one-time partner at the Navy cops.

"I'll try to stay out of your way.... He's become as high profile as you can get, and the only way he could get more altitude is flying into the stratosphere. Benjamin Anderson has now achieved superstar status," Pete tells us.

"I want someone to finally figure out why he ordered the rapes, in the previous killings, I mean," Jack asks suddenly.

"He's not the typical pedophile, and he never joined in," I answer. "Thomas and Brandon did the girls to achieve power. The usual shit for these guys. But I don't think any shrink we've talked to about them thinks they're genuine, by-the- numbers, kiddie rapists. The kids are being done to let the families see just how helpless they all are in the presence of Anderson and his dynamic asshole duo. At least that's my best guess. I could be wrong, as the old joke goes."

"I don't think you're in error," Pete tells us. "We've been through the misdirection with the oil business. It was the first tie that we suspected until we remembered that *all* those Kuwaitis in that area are in the oil business. Then Anderson just continued the feint here in Chicago. He was playing us like he was playing Carl and Philip. He supplied them with motive, the way Hitler provided the Reich with the fantasy about the Jews owning everything. Unite with a negative cause. That's what the Little Corporal did, and it worked for a while.

"And then Benjamin went south of the border and continued his bullshit smokescreen with a couple of Mexican nationalists who were dying to become true believers. Benjamin Anderson's greatest talent is to locate fanatics of any hue to band together for his own purposes. He paints them a patriotic picture with all this savagery, and Genghis Khan rides again. And these fucking computers make the distances go away. He had people on both coasts doing his bidding. Dracula just had to rely on close-quarters mesmerism."

Jack looks down on his own hands. He's sitting across from me, as Donato is, in my cubicle here near the Loop.

"So now we think we understand the prick, but it doesn't make him any closer to the gallows pole."

Pete watches my Chicago partner, but he never blinks at either of us.

Hannah wants to take me out to dinner. We go to Rinaldi's on Cermak. It's one of the best Italian eateries in the city. I don't know how she was able to swing reservations, but she accomplished it.

The place has the traditional red-and-white checkered table cloths with the wine bottles atop each squared table.

I get the fettuccini, and Hannah goes for the linguini Alfredo. The food comes quickly, and it's as good as advertised.

"I've got some news for you."

"What?" I ask.

"You might find it a bit disconcerting."

"You're pregnant."

She looks shocked that I've guessed her major announcement.

"I didn't know we were trying," I apologize.

"I'm on borrowed time, Will Koehn," she frowns.

"Stop the older woman routine. Women are having kids a lot later than you."

She displays her calming smile. Hannah puts me at ease with the warmth she glows at me. She summons all that balmy comfort whenever she feels like it.

"You're really sure?"

"Yes," she smiles.

I get up and move next to her on her side of the booth.

"Don't cry."

"Hormones. Shut up, Will."

She laughs to show me she's not really angry.

"Want to move the date up?" she asks.

"Sure."

"When?"

"Tonight," I answer.

"Where?"

"Vegas," I smile.

We call her sister to watch the girls. We've got twenty-four hours to get this thing done. I call Pete and Jack and let them know I'll be taking a little personal time—about twelve hours. I've got the time stored up from all the overtime I've put in on Anderson *et al*, so Pearce hands me his blessings.

Hannah calls the girls after she calls her sister to go babysit. The girls are thrilled and want to fly out to Las Vegas with us, but Hannah explains we're too rushed, so the kids agree they shouldn't tag along with us. They're too happy for us to throw a shit fit.

I buy our bands in Vegas. We pick out the least vulgar chapel to get married in, and the service is over in fifteen minutes. I promise her a church wedding in June to come through with the wedding we'd planned, and she agrees.

We stay at the MGM, but we don't have time to gamble. There's only enough time to consummate the marriage, again, and then we're back on the plane to Chicago, sixteen hours later.

We make out aboard the Southwest jet, and we get blushes from the female flight attendants. It doesn't slow us down, though, and I ask Hannah if she'd like to join the mile high club. She slaps my cheek playfully, and I begin kissing her again.

The newlywed husband is back on the job ten hours later, doing a twelve with Clemons and assisted by Pete Donato and the six FBI guys. We have a major confab in the Captain's office.

"Anything at all new and startling?" Pearce asks us all.

The FBI crew just stares. Six males and no females. All suits, and three have the required paunch and all have the near-crewcuts.

"Same place we got stalled at three days ago," Pearce complains.

"We have nearly exhausted all of our sources," Special Agent Franco throws in.

"What about your street rats, Jack?" Pearce asks.

"I think he's back with the Italians," Pete Donato counters before Jack can answer.

"Why's that?" Pearce wants to know.

"His crispy-fried daddy was tight with the goombahs, with the Outfit. Will and I think that book that was missing from the safe might have been a righteous 'book of lists.'"

"Well?" Pearce asks. "What the fuck are you waiting for? Squeeze our swarthy friends by the balls and win their fucking hearts."

The "squeeze" begins immediately after the big meeting in Pearce's office. The FBI and our own people start dragging in anyone with a connection to Jimmy Zagnarelli. They haul Jimmy Z in again as well. The idea is to make everyone in his crew very uncomfortable with the notion of aiding and abetting.

"The fuck is this guy?" Jimmy Z asks in our interrogation room downtown.

"I'm Peter Donato. I work for the NCIS."

"You're a swabbie in a fuckin' suit," Jimmy counters.

Pete never answers.

Zagnarelli's lawyer is present, naturally.

"Nice suit," Jack tells the counselor. I don't recognize this mouthpiece for the wiseguys. New player.

"This meeting is bordering on true harassment," the attorney protests.

He's young, maybe thirty-five. *Gentlemen's Quarterly* good looks. Dark, slicked-back hair. No facial hair. Looks like he works out regularly in some club.

"This meeting is beyond that border and I don't give a shit," I tell Zagnarelli and his man.

"Pardon me?" the cover-boy mouthman asks.

"Fuck off, Counselor," Jack says in a bored drawl.

"You charge *Mister* Zagnarelli or you release him."

"Are you through with the rote shit?" I ask him.

He doesn't reply, this time. He's getting better at this game. A fast learner.

"We know you're in contact with Benjamin Anderson. Don't bother denying it. And when we squeeze the right guy in your outfit, your crew, we're coming back for *you*. End of conversation," I announce to them all. I get up from my chair and leave the interrogation room. Jack and Pete look over their shoulders at me as I depart.

"The fuck was that all about?" Zagnarelli says out loud as I'm out the door.

35

*H*elene is warming toward me. It takes just a week. We're holed up together here outside the city, so when we get tired of cable TV and magazines and the radio and newspapers, we wind up talking in spite of her grave reservations about me. I try to tell her the rap on me is bogus and that the only reason I'm in trouble is because of my recently departed father—foster father, that is.

"So you're just a victim of circumstance," she grins slyly.

"You don't believe me."

"You can knock off the con-job. I've heard better, on several occasions."

"And you don't mind being cooped up with a serial killer?"

"Most of Zagnarelli's crew come under that category."

"So you don't have a moral problem, tending to a bad guy like me?"

"Not really. Would I be here if I did?"

"But you still have that .22 in your handbag."

"Always," she smiles again.

"I could really use a massage—on the good shoulder, I mean."

"Long as you stay seated. Long as you don't try to get cute. Because I'll shoot you, honey, and I won't even blink."

"You're a hard woman, Helene."

"Not so hard. Just cautious. It comes with the territory."

"I understand.... And why would I ever want to hurt you?"

"Why would you want to hurt all those other people?"

"Now there's a good question."

"I read about the little girls."

"The other two men I was with got out of control. You may not believe this, but I tried to stop them."

"All three times?"

"You've done your homework, Helene."

"It's a lost cause, Ben. You're not going to go for a rerun on me."

"What do I have to do to convince you I'm harmless, when it comes to you?"

"I've read about women who marry guys like you when you're in prison. I never understood them, until I got to know you a little better. But I don't think I want to get that close to you. No one seems to survive very long when they do get around you."

"That's all history. I can't do any of that anymore."

"Why? Did you find Jesus?"

"No! It's just too risky."

"I can't believe it's out of your system. I've read about you guys in journals. You always have a taste for it. It never goes away."

"It has with me. I just want to get out of here and disappear."

"From what Jimmy tells me, you've got enough to live comfortably on for the rest of several natural lives."

"He's right.... But still. It gets lonely here. Just the two of us. And you're too frightened of me to let me get close to you, Helene."

"There. You've grasped it!"

We laugh together.

"He must be paying you very well," I tell her.

"It beats forty hours in a hospital. Yes."

She always has that handbag with the pistol close at hand. A very bright girl. Not the type to be convinced by flattery, so I don't go there.

"I think Jimmy Z wants me dead."

"You do?"

"Sure. I've got a little book with lots of information on him and his crew. He'd really like that book, and he'd really like me dead."

"So why doesn't he kill you, then?"

"My father has attorney friends in Chicago. Several friends. And one of them has that little book, and that lawyer has instructions to hand it over to the Chicago Tribune *and to the State's Attorney—a copy to each, of course. It would put Mister Z in a very bad light, I'm afraid. He and all of his associates."*

"So you're a blackmailer, too."

"Is that bad?"

She laughs with me once more.

"I could almost believe that you're not a killer at all. But then I'd be thinking with my pussy and not with my head."

I find myself aroused suddenly. I haven't felt this way about a woman since the whore in Mexico.

"I have an idea."

"You do?" she queries.

"Tie me up on the bed. But be careful of this shoulder."

"I'm a nurse. Remember?"

"You mean you'd consider it?"

"I mean I'd have the gun in hand throughout."

"Sounds very exciting."

"Sounds dangerous, to me."

"You'd have the gun and I'd be strapped to the bed."

She stops to consider the proposal. I should say proposition.

"Is money a factor?" I ask.

"I'm not a fucking whore," she tells me, with a grim look on her middle-aged face.

"I'm sorry. I didn't mean that. I know you're not like that, Helene."

"Okay, then."

We sit and watch each other for a few moments.

"I have the gun. You're tied securely to that four-poster. Right?"

"Exactly," I agree.

"You blink, and I shoot you right in the fucking head," she grins again.

She has me knotted to the four-poster bed. The knots are tight and secure, too. As promised, once she gets naked, the Saturday night shooter is in her right hand. She's taking no chances, just as she said.

I know she'd pull the trigger. I can see it in her eyes. She's been around Zagnarelli long enough to sniff out a con. She's been with guys who've pulled the trigger or shoved in a blade before.

"Maybe I should charge," she grins as she gets on top of me and guides me inside her.

She has a much younger woman's body. Erect breasts, no waistline, trim hips and ass. This is the kind of frame my Mexican prosty had. A working girl who's kept herself in shape. I doubt she's ever had children. No telltale sags that I can spy.

She thrusts herself heatedly on top of me. The naked nurse with the palmed pistol has excited me even more than my pro, south of the border. It's the notion that she might pull that trigger on me that has me revved up. For Carl Thomas it was the nipping and biting factors that got him where he wanted to be. For Brandon it was adolescents who threw him into a sexual fury. Everyone has his boiling point. With me, it has always been jeopardy—even if I was only a witness to the murders and rapes. The chance of being caught, and then getting away with it, has always been the catalyst to my arousal.

Now she begins in earnest. The thrusts are faster and more regular in rhythm. She holds her left breast with her free left hand; the .22 is in her right.

I can't withstand it any longer, and I climax violently inside her. I can feel her tighten and go off just after I do.

She rises from the bed, all sweaty and wasted. She nearly wobbles as she gets to her feet. I'm still connected to the four-poster.

"You're my first serial killer," she laughs. "I think Jimmy's guys I've been with have all just been glorified boosters. They'd rather steal than fuck, too."

"I think my arm is cramping up."

I wince severely to make my point.

"Sorry," she apologizes. But she shakes her head and smiles at me.

With one violent swing, I rip the injured arm free, and then I punch her right between the eyes. She goes down like a stunned steer. I quickly untie my other hand and my feet. She's groaning on the floor, but she's still semi-conscious. The pistol came flying loose, off to her left on the carpet. When I'm able to get off the mattress, I grab the piece first.

"Please," she begs.

"You were very difficult," I tell her, pointing the barrel at her head.

"Please. You kill me and Jimmy..."

"Yeah, yeah. Jimmy'll come find me. But I've got news, Helene. I'm going to find your boss first. You know why? Because he planted a cunt like you on me, gun in handbag. That was unnecessary. Especially after all the money David Crowley made for him. I expected a nurse, not a jailer."

"Please don't."

"That all you got?"

"Ben. Please don't."

"Very clever. Call me by name. Personalize this so I won't look upon you as an object. You've been reading JAMA, haven't you."

"Ben..."

I shoot her twice in the forehead, and her head bounces twice from the shots. There's a mess of red, pink and white underneath the back of her head, and the blood is pooling beneath her skull—or what's left of it.

She was right. Twenty-twos make a very big mess, even if they are small caliber.

My shoulder is indeed stiff, but it has healed nicely. Helene was very good at stitching, and the anti-biotics have all kicked in fully by now.

I find my clothes in the closet, and I dress quickly. She calls in to someone every half hour, so I haven't got long before they know something's wrong here. Then Z's people will swarm the place, and I can't beat his numbers. No, I've got to meet with Jimmy Z one-on-one.

I take Helene's Camry into the city. I've got to unload it and buy some new wheels in a hurry. The car I was driving before I was shot by the FBI woman is of no use. Zagnarelli has made that vehicle, so I need to buy a new car, preferably a junker. Something an old man might drive, like a Buick. Something unobtrusive. Something the cops wouldn't be expecting me to wheel about.

I stop at a neighborhood lot in Tinley Park after an hour's drive from the near-Joliet location. They deal in cash. I can't trade in the Camry, obviously, so I purchase the Ford Fairlane for a grand. I give the salesman two hundred to expedite the paperwork, and I'm out of there in under an hour.

Jimmy Z is a creature of habit. I've dealt with him since I was in college. The old fellow, David Crowley, introduced us several times when we visited Chicago. I've always been a student of human nature. I watched him carefully, and I found out that he had a penchant for strippers who were also whores. He cannot resist the pole dancers.

So I go into a joint in Cicero not run by Zagnarelli, and I make conversation with an Asian bar-girl because I know Z really digs Asians. I pay her five hundred dollars to skip tonight's performance in Cicero and for her to go to Zagnarelli's home bar of Pennyloafer's in Berwyn. She agrees when she sees the cash and when I tell her I'll give her another five bills if she gets Zagnarelli to a motel room three blocks from Pennyloafer's. (It's a convenient four-hour-nap joint on 22nd Street.)

She asks me what's going on, and I explain I'm working for Jimmy's wife in a divorce situation. I tell her I'm going to take pictures. She asks where my camera is, and I tell her it's out in the car. She acts as if she's done all this before, so I don't get an argument from her.

I follow her over to Z's home pad. She drives a beat-up Thunderbird, but the black shorts and black haltertop she's wearing ought to work. She gets out of the car and enters Jimmy Z's bar.

Forty-three minutes later, she's coming out of the place. But he's not with her.

However, she drives the three blocks to the Pleasant Hill Motel, home of the "nap," and within ten minutes, here comes Zagnarelli in his black Lincoln. He has only one bodyguard, riding shotgun next to him. He must feel like he's in his neighborhood, in his comfort zone, and he knows he's a made man, too. No one fucks with a made man, especially in his own home territory.

I wait ten minutes before I approach the car with the bodyguard. He's still sitting in the passenger's seat when I tear open the door, and while he tries to blink, I hit him squarely on the bridge of his nose and shove the flat of my palm at his head. The blow doesn't kill him, but it stuns him. I drag him out of the car, and then I see he's a tall, thin man. He's got a shoulder holster and an automatic in the sheath. While he's on the blacktop next to the car, lying flat on his back and bleeding profusely from the nostrils, I stomp on his throat three times, quickly and furiously, and then he stops moving. And breathing. I haul him into the back seat and shut the door behind him.

I wait until they're in Room 106 for about twenty minutes. Just enough time for foreplay and for getting naked. I've got Helene's .22 in my jacket pocket, and I park the Fairlane right next to the black Lincoln.

It's rather late. Probably 1:30 a.m. I don't have a watch on. So I go to the door and knock. She's been told to answer the knock, and she does. When the door cracks open, I shove her back inside and quickly close the entry.

No Jimmy Z.

"He's in the can," the lush-lipped Asian girl says.

"Thank you," I tell her.

"Where's my money?" she asks.

I remove the .22 from my jacket pocket. Just when she's about to scream, I shoot her in the jaw. The jaw comes unhinged, and then she falls flat on her lovely ass.

I rush to the john door. I open it to find Jimmy Z whacking himself while sitting naked on the commode.

"No! No!" he cries out.

"Helene was more polite. She asked please. But she never had time for the thank you."

I shoot him twice in the throat, and the shots throw him to his right, against the bathroom wall. He slumps, and then I see the arterial spray.

I walk over to him.

"You fuckin'…"

He can barely whisper, but he still has a voice.

I watch his eyes. They are the windows to the soul, the philosopher says. The lights are dimming in his attic. He's bleeding out on the john floor.

I don't have much time to linger because the popping sound of the pistol might draw some attention in a fuck flop like this. But I have just enough time to watch his eyes lose their light.

I have just enough time to watch my dad's old mob buddy die.

36

Jimmy Zagnarelli's people react as you would suppose they would. They're hitting the streets and the pavement with a vengeance. They've found the car that Jimmy supplied Anderson with, and we've found the body of Helene Markham, the "nurse" who supposedly watched over Benjamin in some safe house far southwest of the city, somewhere in the Joliet environs near the house we previously raided looking for the ex-Marine killer.

"Why's he kill one of his buddies?" Pete asks us as we walk on Michigan Avenue on our lunch break. We're working days this week, so we eat and sleep pretty much when normal people do.

"Pete," I tell him. "You got to get beyond motive with these guys. That was our mistake when we started all this. First it was the oil bullshit, and then he created a new scenario in Mexico, according to the cops down there. Mexican nationalism or fanaticism, depending on whom you believe. Now he whacks a wiseguy from Chicago's outfit, and we all wonder *why*. In my primitive understanding of the criminal mind, I have to believe this guy just kills for the hell of it. I think he has a genuine feel for it, a taste for it. Women don't appeal to him much, except as targets. Money doesn't mean shit, unless he needs it to operate."

"You're telling us he's the pure sociopath," Jack Clemons says to Pete and me.

We're walking "The Golden Mile" in the downtown area. It's April, but the thaw hasn't arrived yet. The temperatures are hovering near freezing, but there's been no snow or ice, thankfully. April can be a slippery bitch in this city.

We can see our breaths as we walk amid the streams of sidewalk traffic.

The thought of our child growing inside Hannah causes my stomach to twitch, the way it always twitches when I think of them.

"Psychology still hasn't caught this prick. How many shrinks have we talked to, the last month?" Jack asks.

We don't answer him because it was just a thought Clemons made audible. He already knows we've been to four psychiatrists, two of whom work for the CPD; the other two are in private practice, and they both consult for us, occasionally.

"You'd think the guineas could locate him and shoot him."

"Give them time," Jack tells Pete.

"I don't have time," Donato counters. "I'm going to be called back to ship eventually. My stay here is limited. He'll become a cold case again soon, it looks like."

I stop in my tracks.

"We need to keep squeezing the Italians. They're the only ones who've come in recent contact with Anderson."

"We tried that," Jack says.

"You have a better idea?" I ask him.

We talk to the guy in Tinley Park who sold him the car after the used car salesman recognizes Benjamin Anderson from *Eyewitness News* on TV. The salesman's name is Kerry Daniels. He's a good looking black man who stands at least six-six. He tells the three of us he played basketball at DePaul in Chicago about twelve years ago.

He tells us he sold Anderson a Ford Fairlane. He also shows us the paperwork, and Jack calls in the information for an all points, even though we know it's likely our boy has already ditched the Ford. He hasn't made stupid mistakes yet.

But the half million he robbed from Crowley's safe in LA won't keep him in cash forever if he's trying to go subterranean, as he usually does after he snuffs anyone. We can only hope it hasn't been convenient for him to get rid of the Fairlane yet. The nurse and Jimmy Z have only been chilling for seventy-two hours or so.

The Outfit actually reported the two murders. Remarkable. But I think they want us to help them locate Anderson. It just increases the chances of his being grabbed. It's gotten to the point that they want him in a cage before he kills any more made men, just for laughs, the way he smoked Jimmy in the motel.

It was a ballsy move. But Benjamin counted on Jimmy's hubris. It was Zagnarelli's ego that got him shelled. He felt too comfortable in his own territory. He couldn't conceive of anyone fearless enough to reach out and touch him. And Anderson apparently knew Jimmy Z's true weakness—Asian strippers. I feel bad for the stripper. She's the "innocent" member of the dual murders. She didn't deserve to go down. He can't care about witnesses anymore, but his old habits of purging his kill zones must die hard or not at all.

It's pretty clear that Benjamin Anderson has a death wish, himself. It doesn't take an MD or a psychiatrist to come up with that analysis. He's burned all his bridges and all his escape routes too. Now he'll want to come after me before he goes down courtesy of the dagos, the FBI, or the Chicago Police Department.

He has to make the grand exit before he finally gives it up.

I warn my dad to be extra vigilant. He's got the .45 war souvenir close at hand wherever he goes. It isn't licensed, but I don't give a shit at this point, and I'd like to see a cop prosecuting him for illegal possession of a firearm. He's the father of a Homicide detective, and that ought to be worth some consideration for my old man.

Sammy is packing again—this time, it's a .32 snub nose that he purchased legally in Champaign. He's still with Megan, and he never lets her go out alone anymore.

Hannah has her weapon as well.

All of the above disturbs me greatly. My family was not the NRA type until this business with Anderson occurred. Now they're all well-heeled in the gun department. They all take target practice at least weekly.

The worst part is that they fear to go out of the house, especially at night. And I'm frightened for them all, twenty-four-seven. They have cops looking in on each of them, and a pair of plainclothes is still tailing me, but it pisses me off that I've caused them all to live like fugitives. I know I should aim my anger at Anderson, but I feel guilty in spite of reason.

There is barely a pooch in Hannah's tummy. She's told me she doesn't want to know the sex of our baby, and I go along with her wishes. We've told the OB/GYN we don't want to know if she finds out if we've got a pointer or a setter. When I joke about pointer or setter with Hannah, she frowns, so I don't repeat the gag.

"When will we be free?" she asks in bed.

She already knows the answer as well as I do.

"We're doing everything we know how to do," I reassure her.

"I know. I'm sorry, Will."

"If you weren't anxious about all this, then I'd really be concerned about you."

She tries to smile. It doesn't come off very well, here in our dim bedroom.

"You haven't slept at all the last two nights. I hear you rolling and turning all night, Will."

"If it keeps you up, I'll sleep on the..."

"Don't you even say it."

I smile at her.

"I was hoping you'd say that," I tell her. "But I'll try real hard to keep still for you."

"*I'll dream of the day we're free of Benjamin Anderson,*" she smiles warmly.

Then she closes her eyes.

I know I won't sleep again tonight, but eventually my eyes will have to shut. And in ten more minutes, they do.

I dream of playing football in high school. I dream that my brother Sammy is playing on the same team with me. Which he didn't, being three years younger than I am.

But we're in some big-deal contest in Soldier Field. It must be for a trophy, because there's an overflow crowd.

We're winning. We're romping and stomping, as a matter of fact. Sammy opens up gaping holes for our running back, and I catch two TDs.

Then the clock on the far end of the field holds up the game because it stops running. The refs catch the busted timepiece, and there's a very long delay. The crowd becomes hushed at the stoppage, and I find myself looking for someone in the crowd of 60,000. I'm looking for George Koehn. I'm looking for my father. And when I can't locate him, I look for Hannah and the girls. None of them appears.

Then I notice my boss, Captain Pearce, stalking our sideline. He stops and waves to me. I see a smile on his face.

But then I see someone in a ball cap and aviator sunglasses coming up fast behind him. The guy in the shades is carrying a k-bar, but he's making no effort to conceal the blade. There are uniforms and security all over the place, but Benjamin Anderson is rushing Captain Pearce and no one's doing a damn thing about it.

Anderson stabs my boss in the back, but I don't hear any screams or outcry from the stands. Security still has made no moves toward the ex-Marine, and the crowd is more interested in the delay of the game. Everyone's heads are turned toward that stadium clock. They don't notice that Captain Pearce has fallen. No one but me seems to notice the policeman's collapse on the sideline.

I try to rush to Benjamin even though I know I'm too late. And Anderson stands behind the fallen, immobile police captain. He's unashamed and in no hurry to flee.

I look at my feet, suddenly, and I find that my cleats are missing. I'm standing barefooted on the turf of the football field.

Then I look up, and Pearce and Anderson have both quietly vanished. The time clock is still broken, however.

And I awaken to a sound from downstairs in Hannah's Oakbrook home. I bolt out of bed, but when I look down at my wife, I see she's soundly asleep in spite of my jerking upright and then springing off the mattress.

I already have the weapon from under my pillow in my hand. I see that the digital clock reads 2:16 a.m. I have only boxer shorts on. I normally throw on sweats before I walk out into the house from the bedroom. I don't feel right, waltzing before two young girls in my skivvies.

But I don't have time for the amenities. I hurry out the bedroom door. Then I peek inside both of the girls' bedrooms. It's still dark, and I'm not going to wake them by flipping on a light. Everything seems in order, but it's really too dark to tell for sure.

I tell myself that I'm overreacting, and that overreacting is precisely what Anderson wants me to do. That's part of his power thing.

I walk softly down the stairs from the upper floor, nine millimeter firmly in hand, safety off. When I reach the main floor, I do a room by room, saving the kitchen for last.

There is no light in that kitchen save for a nightlight that Hannah always leaves on. I see the dim glow through the crack in the swinging door. I've been here once before, I remember.

I throw the door open, and I find Beth on the floor, sobbing.

Then I click on the overhead fluorescents.

"What's wrong, honey?" I ask as I kneel down next to her in front of the kitchen sink.

She just looks at me with a glance of hopelessness. She doesn't say a word, but now it's down to a sniffling.

"Don't tell Mom I was down here, okay?" she asks.

"Of course I won't."

I feel awkward, sitting next to her in my underwear, but I'm not about to leave her here alone.

"He's taken our house over," she says. "First he kicked down the door. He or that other guy. And now he's got us living like *we* did something wrong."

"He's the bad guy. We're not. You have to remember that. And remember that the house is being watched, every day and night. And they've got people following me and the three of you, and they're watching my family too—I mean my dad and brother."

She sniffles briefly again.

"Do you feel safe, Will?"

I look at her, but I don't answer.

I find myself at the target range whenever I have a free hour. I empty load after load into the bulls-eyes, and my accuracy has never been truer. I have higher scores now than I had as an expert marksman in the Corps. My skills degenerated slightly when I went into NCIS. I improved again when I went into the Academy here at the Police Force, but Homicides don't get much opportunity to fire their side arms. We investigate a whole lot more than we get into gunfights. Gunplay is the aberration; it's the exception to the routine. We deal with guys who are already dead, but there are moments when we have to make arrests that can turn very dicey. We wear vests and we take precautions, but all that doesn't help you with a shot to your melon. Headshots mean vegetation or death, most of the time.

I prefer neither.

However, I continue to improve as long as I keep shooting. We're required to hit the range regularly, but I've exceeded my number of visits to this firing area.

I picture his face on the targets. I superimpose them over the paper bulls' eyes. Then I take aim for his forehead and his eyes. I'm not going to give him the chance to survive a headshot. If I place one in his mid-forehead or through one of his white orbs, he's meat. If I shoot him in the cheek, he might survive. Should I hit him in the chin, he has a chance too. In the eyes or below the hairline, his odds decrease dramatically.

In the Corps they taught us to aim at the torso on the first volleys, and then you aimed around the knees on the second burst, the idea being to finish him on his way down. I can't depend on that reasoning. This has to be a one shot deal, maybe two at most. I have to hit where I aim. I can't let him make it to trial if he gives me the opportunity. If I can find that feverish brain, I have to plant one deep inside so that it eradicates Benjamin Anderson irrevocably. It has to be a one shot blast. Nothing else is acceptable.

I have to be perfect with my marksmanship. When the moment arrives, I cannot fail.

37

April finally lets go, and we're in May. It becomes warm and fragrant, even by the Lakeshore in this first week. Easter was a few weeks ago. I haven't been a practicing Catholic—the trip to confession a while back was my first foray into the Roman ritual in a long while. I never attended mass while I was in the Middle East, being a cop in the NCIS, or even when I was in my four year hitch in the Marines. The Marines always had to know what religion or denomination you were because it was the military and it was a formality, so I never denied being baptized in the "old, corrupt faith of Rome," as Mr. Hawthorne called it in The *Scarlet Letter.* I've never thought of my religion as corrupt. Certainly it is no more polluted than the evangelists and their ilk on TV. But I've just never had any real interest in spirituality, until recently.

I've gone to mass the last few Sundays in a row, but Hannah is an Episcopalian, "Catholic light," as we call it, and she doesn't attend with me. I go early anyway, to the 6:30 a.m. masses, and that's way too soon for Hannah to rise on Sundays.

However, Barbara has gone with me both times. She says she'd like to "explore the faith" with me, as she put it. So I agreed after asking Hannah if it was all right.

"You can get either of them in a church," she told me, "and you're a better man than I am, Gunga Din."

So Barbara is my bodyguard, along with the two plainclothesmen who shadow me everywhere during their rotating two-man shifts. The morning guys meet the late shift guys just after we get into mass this third Sunday. Easter is past, as I say, and Barbara is still fascinated by the Resurrection. She wants to know if I really buy into it.

"Yeah. It's like part of the deal," I tell her. We walk out into the early morning rays. It's still very chilly out here in front of St. Stanislaus.

"I find it kind of hokey," she smiles as we walk to my Cavalier. I wave to the two plainclothesmen parked next to me in the church's lot. They both wave back, but neither is smiling. I'd be pissed too if I had to do surveillance on an early Sunday a.m.

"Why do you think so?" I ask her as we get in the car.

"Ghost story."

"Yes, it is. But then there were lots of other miracles, too, in that book."

We arrive at Smiley's Pancake House on Fullerton on the North Side. I'm taking her to breakfast, since she made the grand effort of rising as early as I do for a mass.

We sit in a booth. The waitress has taken our order.

"You believe in ghosts?" she asks.

She'll be as pretty as Hannah in a few more years when she blooms. She's already a dazzling young woman. They're both gorgeous, in their own ways.

"I guess I do. Otherwise I'd sleep in on Sundays, don't you think?"

"You might just be going because of all this...trouble."

I look at her wise young face. She looks fresh, the way most kids do to me. Not the wiseass fresh, but fresh like the morning breeze.

"You're right. That's part of it, I suppose."

"Don't you find that a kind of shaky reason for going to church?"

"I can see why you'd think so."

271

"I'm not trying to be snotty, here, Will. I just really want to know."

"When I was your age, I never had time for mass. I just had my own life. That was the way it was all through college and the military, too. But now I feel helpless, sometimes. In the Marines they used to say there were no atheists in foxholes. I never fought in combat, but I saw a lot of it from the convoys we tagged along with in Iraq.

"I don't much want to repeat what I saw. I hope you never witness the evil I saw as a cop, especially, in the Middle East. You might have read about it or seen some of it on TV, but it's not the same as *smelling* it."

She looks at me intently, listening to every word.

"Smelling it?"

"The stench of death. It's intolerable. Not even doctors can hack it for very long without gagging. As a cop, I was supposed to get used to it, but I never did. And I'm not used to it now, on the force, either."

She seems to sense my frustration at explaining myself, but, as usual, she is patient with me. There is only calm on her pretty face.

"We were talking about ghosts, Will. You're avoiding the issue," she grins.

The waitress gives us our orange juice. I don't drink coffee, but Barbara opts for a cup with her juice.

"Stunts your growth," I tell her.

"Come on, back to the part about ghosts."

I look down at my hands on the tabletop.

"All those dead guys I was telling you about, they remind me of resurrection. Because if there really is no afterlife, all this seems… It just seems futile, pointless. Does that make any sense to you?"

"Sure. Life's too short. I've heard that over and over again from Mom and my dad."

"They're right, Barbara."

"I suppose, but it seems awfully long to me right now."

"This'll be over soon. Look, I just needed to feel like there's some logic to what I'm doing, to everything that's going on. I used to think I didn't need anybody's help, but I'm finding out I was wrong. I need your mother. I need you two, you and Beth. But I needed something else. Mass supplies some kind of need I never even knew I had until all this crap."

"It makes sense that there's a God. I'm talking strictly logic, here."

"Yeah? How's that?"

"In English class, we talked about dichotomies. Everything comes in twos: large and small, skinny and fat. You'd have no notion of tall unless you had short to measure tall by."

"Yep. I get it."

She fiddles with her bacon and eggs. She pokes the yellows with the prongs of her fork, and her upper lip twitches, nervously, from time to time. She's concentrating so *hard*, it makes me tense, too.

"So if there's a devil, there's got to be a God to give us an idea of how evil Satan's supposed to be."

"Heavy stuff from such a young babe," I smile at her.

"I'm serious."

There's no doubt about *that*. Her eyes almost pierce mine as she drills her gaze at me.

"So am I."

"Benjamin Anderson is evil, isn't he, Will?"

She puts her fork down and stops stabbing the yolks.

"You could say."

"Then we can't judge Anderson unless there is also good in the world, right?"

"There you have me."

"That's because cops see so much shit out there."

It shocks me slightly to hear her use profanity, but I keep my mouth shut.

"Can't have one without the other. Right?"

"Yes, Professor," I smile.

"I'm serious, Will."

"I know you are, kiddo."

A pout crosses her face.

"Don't call me that. My dad calls me kiddo, and he pisses me off when he does."

"Okay, sorry."

I put a finger over my lips.

"I'm not stupid."

Her brows furrow, now, with intensity.

"I know you're not. Take it easy, kid—Whoops."

She has to grin.

"Tell me why you believe in ghosts."

"I read Walt Whitman. That's why," I smile again at her.

"The poet?"

She watches me intently. She's like her mom—patient with me.

"Yes. The very man."

"And what's he got to do with believing in ghosts and God?"

"You've read *Leaves of Grass?*" I ask.

"Some of it, in our anthology in high school."

"Whitman said that dying is not the end and that what happens after death is far more wonderful than anyone can suppose."

"Really? That part wasn't in the anthology."

"Neither was all his stuff about sex."

"I must have missed that, too," she says.

She appears mock-disappointed. She purses her lips.

"He was saying that there's an afterlife, and that this is not all there is."

"Really," she repeats.

"Yes. You have to have something to anchor the ship, kid—Barbara."

"You can call me kiddo if you have to."

"No. I like your name better."

"You really going to get married again in the church in June?"

"Yes, we are."

"Which church?"

"Your mom doesn't want to get married in hers because she told me she thinks the reverend there is a dotty old coot."

"So it's St. Stanislaus?"

I nod.

"Good. I like that church. It's prettier than the Episcopalian place."

"You think your mom or Beth would like to come to mass with us?"

"No. You go too damn early," she grins.

While we're driving to Oakbrook from the North Side, Barbara looks out the passenger's window pensively.

"You think there's really a hell?" she blurts out of nowhere.

"Huh?"

"You think this bastard Anderson is really going to hell?"

"If there is one, yes."

"I don't think God's vindictive, though. What's the point of punishing him, Will? Those people are dead, anyway."

"Justice."

"Justice?"

"Yes. The punishment fits the crime. I think *He* knows what's happening down here, and I don't think *He* lets anything slide."

"So it's pitchforks and sulfur?" she asks.

"No. I don't think so. I think maybe Anderson gets to *feel* the weight of what he's done to all those people he's stolen from."

"Stolen?"

"He's stolen their lives and their innocence. He's stolen them from their parents. He's taken everything from them all."

"I know. I see what you're saying."

She looks back out the window.

"How can you really believe all this when you deal with the skuzziest human beings on this earth?" she wants to know.

"It's a struggle, Barbara. It's a real challenge. No one said it would be easy."

"But why's God got to make it *impossible*?"

"Now there's a great question. Someone a lot smarter than me might take a shot at it."

She smiles warmly at me and looks out the window of my Cavalier. I look into the rearview and see that my tails are right behind me.

"I love you, Will."

I look over at her, but she's still staring out the passenger's window at the sidewalks and houses flying by us and behind us.

This Sunday we go out to a fancy restaurant after mass, all four of us, Hannah, Barbara, Beth and me. We're going to my father's for dinner at 6:30 tonight, but we're having brunch together after the 8:00 a.m. service. This was as early as I could finagle them all into getting up. I would have chosen the 6:30 again because there is less of a crowd, and today is unusually crowded for post-Easter.

I suppose I'm angrier with non-attendees, now that I've returned to the church.

All that talk about ghosts with Barbara has stuck inside my head. I've been mulling it over ever since we had breakfast together after her initial mass at St. Stanislaus.

"The only reason I'm here is to get a lay of the land for the wedding in June," Hannah beams at me. She's sitting next to me here in the last pew on the left side. The place filled up in a hurry today, but we arrived a half-hour early, to be safe. It's jammed inside here.

The first-shift surveillance guys are outside in their car, of course. They'd come in, but they have to pack weapons and they don't like bringing guns into church even though neither of today's escorts are Catholics. One's a Jew and one could give a shit about religion. I know them both pretty well from Homicide.

"That's up to you, darling," I smile at my civil-law wife.

She squeezes my hand.

The mass is over in fifty minutes and we're on the way to brunch. This time it's at Mandretti's near the Loop. It's an Italian restaurant, but it serves a full menu, along with Sunday-morning brunch. It's packed, and it's a good thing I made reservations for us.

We have a booth, and I sit next to Hannah, opposite Beth and Barbara.

I feel like I have my own family at this moment. I felt like an outsider to the girls for months, but ever since we went to Vegas and came back home, I've felt like a part of the three of them. Now I think I've really arrived with the girls as well.

I look out the window onto the Loop avenue. I see a man in a ball cap and aviator shades wearing a leather flyer's jacket walking by. I only catch the back of his head, but I think it's Anderson.

I'm wondering where my two plainclothesmen are, and I'm thinking maybe they figured they owed themselves a Sunday nap.

I get up without a word and I rush to the door.

"Will?" Hannah cries out after me.

But I keep on moving out the entrance, and when I'm out into the cool Sunday-morning Easter air, I see him moving down the block, perhaps one hundred yards in front of me.

I look around, but I can't see the unmarked police car.

I take off after him. I've got the nine millimeter palmed in my right hand. There are a few pedestrians on the street, but most people are indoors, away from the chill. I sprint after him now, but he's not running away from me, and it worries me.

I cock the piece in my right hand, but I let it point toward the sidewalk, my arm fully extended.

I get the gap between us down to twenty yards.

"*Stop!*" I yell out.

There are perhaps a dozen people on the sidewalk with us. They all halt.

"*Put up your hands, Anderson!*"

They all reach for it, men and women and a few kids too.

The guy in the ball cap and shades and flight jacket spins around on his heels, and I raise the gun and aim for his face. A couple of women shriek when they see the piece in my hand.

277

"*Are you talking to me?*" the guy in the leather asks.

It isn't Anderson. Same height and weight. Same general build. Similar facial appearance. But it's not Benjamin Anderson.

"I'm sorry," I sputter, and then I lower the nine millimeter. "I'm sorry. All of you. I apologize.... Police officer."

I show them my ID and badge.

"Sorry. Everybody. I'm very sorry."

"Have a nice day, asshole," a very pretty teenaged girl says as she passes me on the sidewalk.

38

"He is staying in a room in Evanston," Kormelov tells Pete and Jack and me in yet another get-together in Arkady's favorite tearoom near the Loop.

"Why are we hearing this from you instead of from the goombahs?" Jack wants to know.

Arkady Kormelov smiles.

"Because I am the good citizen."

"Why?" Jack insists.

"There are so many cops on the street that no one can do proper business. Things are as tight as a twelve-year-old girl's ass."

"That's why? Because you can't do business?"

He looks at me now.

"Jimmy Zagnarelli was my friend and associate. I want to piss on this Anderson's grave."

The tea arrives with our soft drinks, and the interview is over ten minutes later.

The FBI and our SWAT team will surround the Evanston apartment building.

"He's not inside," I tell Pete and Jack.

We're all dressed in our vests. It's a warm May dawn, upper fifties.

"How can you be sure?" Jack asks.

"Don't ask," Pete warns him. "I've seen this precognition shit of his in action before. He doesn't do it often, but when he says shit like this, it always seems to come true."

The SWATs hit the ground running. We didn't have enough time to clear all the neighbors. We didn't want Anderson to slip off again, but I know we won't catch him this morning.

The FBI agents wait at the entry of the three-flat apartment building. We're about a half mile from Northwestern University. It's a nice neighborhood, and all the college kids and university professors aren't notorious early-risers anyway. We hoped they'd stay out of the way, and there are only a few pain-in-the-ass observers out on the sidewalks. The uniformed cops are keeping them away from us.

The SWAT team walks out, and you can see they're severely disappointed. They enjoy doing their things, and it's like no one showed up to play, as far as they're concerned.

"Nothing," Captain Pete Brannon tells us and the FBI guys. "It's as if he knew we were coming. The place was clean.... Except for the busted-down front door on that second floor."

Brannon walks away from us, his face sour.

"That building manager is going to be pissed at us," Jack grins.

"The local hardware chain stores will love us again," I remind him. I can imagine all the doors they have to replace for the CPD or the FBI.

We interview the manager of the three-flat. He's not the owner, because the owner owns five of those three-flat buildings on the same block in Evanston.

He claims Anderson never contacted him or paid him. He claims it was some wiseguy that he recognized from the neighborhood. The wiseguy's name is Sal Frangella.

We pick up Frangella three hours later and we drag him downtown.

"Hey. I was just the bagman."

"For Jimmy Z," Pete says.

"Yes. We're associates," he smiles.

"You were. Jimmy Z's dead," Pete reminds him.

"Yes. I recall hearing that."

"You recall what accessory to murder means?" I ask him.

He drums his fingers on the table. Sal's a young turk, maybe thirty-five. He's about five-eight and faintly reminds me of Al Pacino.

"Look. I just fixed somebody up with a place to crash. Jimmy didn't tell me it was this guy you got a hard-on for."

"Currently our collective stiffy is aimed right at you, asshole," Pete tells him.

"Take it easy. There's nothing else I know about it."

"You're a lying piece of shit," Jack grins.

"Do I need a lawyer?"

"Of course. This is America," I tell him.

"All right, all right. He never stays more than two days in one place. He's a slick prick. But I only laid eyes on him once. That was when Jimmy was still alive. Jimmy dealt with him because Anderson has a book on our crew. He's got that book with some lawyer. We've been trying to find out who it is, but Anderson is a bit too sly for us, so far. We'll find out eventually, and then we'll kill him and you guys'll be what they call redundant."

"Big word, shit-for-brains," Jack says.

"You don't need to disrespect me. I'm trying to be helpful."

"Where's he headed?"

Sal looks at me with a feigned hang-dog look of concern for my fucking welfare. He's close to breaking out in a big, greasy-goombah grin.

"Word is he's headed right for you."

They double the surveillance on Hannah's house. They've got her and the kids surrounded, and me too.

We find the car, the Fairlane, that he bought for cash. It's been ditched on the far southwest side. He's either purchased a new ride or he's stolen one, I figure. I call Car Theft/Burglary and I ask them to be on the lookout for a boost in the neighborhood where we found the Ford Fairlane. They come up with a possibility almost immediately. A Chevy Lumina has been stolen only three blocks from the location of the Ford. We put out an all points on the Lumina. It's black and it's slightly banged up, the Burglary dicks inform us. The plates are made and the number goes out to every squad and every swinging dick with a badge in Cook County.

There's no sighting of the Chevy for two hours, but then the call comes through, and the three of us are speeding toward the Eisenhower Expressway.

It's 1:46 p.m., and the Eisenhower is medium-clogged. In other words it's moving, but it's moving at about 40 mph top speed. The driver of the Lumina is headed toward the Loop, and there are several squads waiting to block him off.

When we get to the end of the Eisenhower, we don't see the squad cars or the Chevy. We get a call that Chicago P.D. is in pursuit of the black Lumina.

We have our lights on, and we increase our speed. I'm behind the wheel because Jack doesn't like to drive.

We hit State Street and turn left, following the uniform on the radio's instructions. He and another cruiser are in pursuit, and they're perhaps two miles ahead of us, racing down State Street. Maybe "racing" is the wrong word because traffic is so heavy that you can only go 30 mph on this artery in the downtown district. Any faster and you'd be in a multi-car pileup already.

We see the squads and the black vehicle pulled over on the curb a block ahead of us, right at Monroe Street. We literally have to creep up on them because traffic is at a near-standstill. The traffic coppers call it "gaper's block." Everyone has to have a look at the guy pulled over to the curb.

They've got him stretched over the hood. His face is aimed at the black surface beneath him.

"It's just some greaser booster," the uniform explains as we pull over and approach the Chevy Lumina.

"You mean a person of Hispanic origin," Jack corrects him.

"Yes, I'm sorry, Sir."

"Don't worry about it," Jack tells him, and then he pats his shoulder. "You'll get the idea after your first suspension for harassment."

We look the Mexican kid over. He can't be more than seventeen. He's got no clue why all these cops have been chasing him. Later on he might even feel like a celebrity. He was simply a city booster, and suddenly he's got most of the city's law enforcement chasing after him. He might even tell the tale to all his booster pals—how the cops thought he was Chicago's Most Wanted Fugitive, Benjamin Anderson. Some day he can tell his grandkids, if he's out on parole before a heart attack, or old age kills him.

"He doesn't eat where he shits," I tell them.

"Meaning he left the scene with the paid-for car, he took a cab or a bus, and then he boosted a ride in a different neighborhood," Pete says.

So we try the cab companies. We contact the CTA, the bus people. The bus people have no way of recognizing Anderson as a rider even if we narrow the time frame for them and even if we focus on certain routes. Their drivers usually don't look at faces unless they feel threatened, and no one recalls picking up a fare that resembles Benjamin

Anderson on the day in question. Their riders stream by the drivers, anonymous and unseen, for the most part.

We get lucky with the cab companies. City Lights cabs has a driver who recollects someone who looks like our guy. He remembers him because the rider was a very good tipper—he left him a sawbuck. The rider could fit the ex-Marine's description, but the cab driver is not certain. He does know that he left this fare off at 82nd and Kedzie.

We drive to that location, and then we begin canvassing the few blocks in the vicinity. There are grocery stores and bars and dry cleaners. We show Benjamin's photos to as many people in the neighborhood as we can, and finally, a coffee-and- doughnut shop counter-girl recognizes him.

"He was here," she says. Her name is Julie. She's nineteen, and she's a college student at Loyola downtown who's trying to make a few bucks for school here.

"He had coffee and a danish. He didn't say anything. Just ate and drank and left. I remember him because he was kind of hunky," she smiles. "I didn't know he was some kind of creep."

"It's all right. You've been a big help."

All she knows is he turned left and walked north when he left the doughnut shop.

The three of us walk outside. Jack bought a coffee and a doughnut. He couldn't resist. He has a sweet tooth.

It's cooler, now. The wind comes out of the same direction Anderson headed, the north.

"We concentrate patrols on a six-block perimeter," I tell my partners.

"Is he here?" Pete asks me.

"Is your ESPN working again?" Jack teases me.

"I think he is. I really do," I tell them both.

We check a car dealership a half-mile down the street. No one resembling our photo has come in to buy a ride, the manager says after he asks all his salesmen and after he shows them all our boy's photo.

His presence seems to dim on me suddenly, but I have to think he's somewhere close. It's like hearing footsteps in a football game. You're about to catch a touchdown pass and there's no one near you, but you can only sense the approach of a murderous, vicious, headhunting tackler coming up right behind you. Anderson's the tackler, and the hair on my neck is standing straight up.

We have three times the usual number of cruisers patrolling this stretch of neighborhood. If Benjamin shows a hair on his ass, we'll spot him. At least, this has been our best opportunity to make a sighting on him in the last few months.

He's here. I know he's here.

He's been excommunicated by the Outfit. He's killed most of his own confederates and a number of innocents, too. He's murdered an exotic dancer and Jimmy Zagnarelli. He's wiped out several families, here and in the Middle East and in Mexico as well.

It's time for his spree to end. It's time to put this mutt to sleep.

I take a route with Jack on the same night as we got the information from the kid at the doughnut shop. Pete has to sleep off a slight case of the flu, so he's gone to the apartment he's renting, courtesy of the NCIS.

We circle the six blocks, heading north and then returning south. Then we head west and come back to the east. We hit the route over and over, and nothing comes up on our figurative radar.

We stop at the doughnut shop, but the good-looking college girl's not on shift. It's 4:22 a.m. There are only two more hours left of our shift. Pearce doesn't want us to work too many overtime hours because he doesn't want his people frazzled with exhaustion. When you're fatigued, you fuck up. Pearce wants clear heads and minimal fuck-ups.

"Time to catch this bad boy," he told us yesterday morning.

Jack orders another coffee and doughnut. I order a Diet Coke, hoping the caffeine will rouse me.

"When does this fucking nightmare end?" he asks.

We're the only two patrons in the joint. It reminds me of the painting *Nighthawks*. The bar slab is white and porcelain. The walls are painted white. The floor is black and tiled and lustrous, with a fine waxing. Immaculate, like the painting. I think the original might be in the Art Institute.

"He ain't showing tonight," Jack laments. "You agree?"

I nod.

He isn't showing. Not right now.

The hair on the back of my neck has settled. No one seems to be coming up on me.

39

*I*t is difficult finding my way to Will Koehn, but it is not impossible. I assume they're still looking for a vehicle to which to attach me. And I also assume they've noticed that I don't wear disguises—at least, I haven't been. So, like a baseball pitcher who only shows a fastball to the hitters, it's time for me to go off speed, or to use my curveball. I have dyed my hair black from its lighter brown color. I have also grown a mustache and goatee, and I wear a bush hat from Desert Storm. Few vets wear those things once they leave the shit. Mostly, kids wear them, and cammies too—camouflage shorts and pants. They're very popular with punks who've come only as close as a theatre screen to a real war. So I feel safe wearing the cammies and the bush hat, along with my expensive aviator's shades.

I've got myself a flop on the Southeast side of the city, near the Lake. They take cash, and no one ever looks you in the eyes, so I feel confident I haven't been spotted by our landlord in this two-flat building. He only notices the green of my dollars, and he doesn't like conversation either.

I'm riding a bicycle because I don't feel safe in a car anymore. Too many cops. Too many opportunities to fuck up behind a wheel. The bike will serve my purposes, and it offers good exercise.

My shoulder has healed nicely, and I've had no episodes with infection. Apparently her antibiotics weren't placebos. I only feel a little discomfort in the mornings, but the pain is easing every day.

I've been cramped in this Southeast-side apartment for a few weeks, now. I only venture out late at nights, and sometimes around dawn. I ride the bike on the Rainbow Beach sidewalk, near 76th Street. It is fairly exhilarating in the morning air, peddling close to the beach and the water. There are few people out at this hour, and I like the opportunity for solitude. It helps me plan better than sitting around at home. I have a small TV that I purchased, and the apartment has cable, so I'm not cut off from the world. It seems that my trail has gone cold, and I haven't heard mention of my name on the air in over a week. The bigger story is some Hollywood actor coming out of the closet. Also, some media darling has wound up in the alcoholics' tank in California. The rest is just talk and talk and talk.

I won't be out of the news very much longer, however. The plans are made, and all that remains is the execution.

I'm riding west through city traffic. I was so close to the Lake that it'll take a while for the May breeze to stink of concrete and blacktop instead of lake water and dead perch. I miss the shore already as I cross Ashland Avenue and turn right and head north. I've bought a four-speed bicycle to keep things uncomplicated. The kids get more exotic bikes, but I just wanted simple transportation. And who's on the lookout for a slightly older-than-usual throwback to the '70s? That's the way it looks when I see myself now in the mirror. The mustache and beard have been dyed to match the raven-colored topknot. It's a fair job of hairstyling, I must admit.

After an hour of pedaling past city traffic and tie-ups, I'm close to my destination. I have my gear stowed in the backpack on my back. The straps tend to bite my shoulders, but I have ignored that discomfort. I let them bite. It keeps me alert.

Helene's .22 is in the pack. I've bought some fresh shells, but I've worked on them myself. I've rigged them into hollow points with a few tools I bought at the local hardware superstore. They will make gaping holes in whoever is shot with them. I have a few people in mind as targets.

I arrive in Bridgeport after an hour-and-forty-five minute ride. I notice the unmarked squad right away. I'm riding on the sidewalk, as you're not supposed to do, but the cops aren't very strict about bike riders on the walks. I'm pedaling slowly, anyway, almost casually. It's just past eight in the morning, and these two plainclothesmen are settling in for an eight-hour stint. Must be awfully boring.

I go right by them without catching their eyes, and then I pull into the driveway alongside George Koehn's next door neighbor. I've been here before, the night I trashed the old man's house just for giggles and shits. I noticed an old lady going into this house by herself at about midnight. I saw her out George's front window. I was concealed by his blinds. The old girl never saw me.

I'm betting the old bitch lives alone. This neighborhood seems to belong to geezers. George lives alone, too.

I go around back, and then I stand still. I listen. I don't hear anyone stirring in the vicinity. I smell the air, but I don't know what kind of scent I'm expecting to pick up.

Then I hop the old lady's fence and land in George Koehn's back yard. I look over his back fence, but I see no one parked in the alley behind his home. The cops can't afford more than the two-man surveillance out front.

I proceed to Old Man Koehn's back door. It's a storm door and it's locked, so I get the pick out of my backpack after I get out of the straps. I take the .22 pistol out of it as well and lay it on George's fine little backyard lawn. He's been cutting it already, and you can see it's well-manicured.

I'm past the storm door, and then I have a deadbolt to pick. After the deadbolt is popped with my burglar's helper, I contend with a chain. I'm able to use pincers to disconnect the chain, and then I'm inside.

I don't hear a dog or any alarms, and I'm greatly relieved.

I don't see George in the kitchen, either. Perhaps he's a late riser. I move on to his bedroom. I know the room because I spent a lot of time and effort redecorating it last time I was here.

He's under the covers. Snoring, sound asleep.

I walk right up next to him. I nudge his face with the barrel. Then he opens his eyes, and slowly the shock and fear gathers in his weathered face.

"All right. Tell me where it is," I command.

"Where what…"

"Don't play stupid or I won't let you see your son's execution."

He bolts up.

"You worthless piece of…"

I prod him in the forehead with the barrel of the .22.

"Come on. Where you hiding it, George?"

He nods toward the nightstand, right next to the bed and us. I open the top drawer, and there it is. A .45 relic, from World War II, I'm guessing.

"Ooh. A big one," I smile as I lift it out of the drawer.

I check to see if it's loaded, and it is. Clip intact. Safety on.

"There are two cops sitting out..."

His face darkens angrily, and I can feel him tightening as if he's a snake ready to spring up at me.

"I know. I rode right past them both into your neighbor's backyard."

I smile haughtily at him. But he refuses to wither. He refuses to reconcile himself to defeat.

"You don't look..."

His brows furrow with interest.

"I know. I rather fancy it. You like my new look?"

"Why don't you get out? You're not going to make it out of here, whether you kill me or not. And Will's not dumb enough to walk into this."

His face tightens even more. His color has gone white with rage. I'm watching him very closely, now. I don't want to kill him, yet.

"I bet he is. Want to bet?"

The old World War II vet remains mum.

There is a rotary phone on the nightstand. It's black. Everything about Mr. Koehn, Senior, is retro.

I dial the number in Oakbrook. I know he doesn't go on shift until this afternoon. I've pedaled past the CPD building in the Loop on my forays, and I've watched him for the past few days, courtesy of my altered state.

Hannah Menke's number is still in the book, and she's been stubborn enough not to change it. It might be because I've never called over to harass her or him there. Too fucking tacky. I like to be the phantom when it comes to hassling targets. I like to stay in the background until it's time to acquaint myself with the vic.

She answers on the third ring.

"Is your husband there?"

I can barely restrain my glee.

"Who's this?"

Her voice is solemn, concerned, but not yet hysterical.

"An old, old friend."

I wonder if she can visualize the wide grin on my face. She must have hit the wall of anxiety, by now, however.

She goes for her hero immediately.

"Yes?"

"I'm at Dad's."

I can barely keep my good humor to myself. I'm on a roll, now. I'm the stage comedian who's got them crying, they're laughing so hard at all my great mirth.

"You're where? Who…"

"You know who this is, Will. I'm pointing a .22 with hollow points right at his venerable nose."

I show his old man a sobering glance. No more fucking around.

"Leave him…"

"No time for idle talk, Will. I might let him live if you show up all by yourself."

My cheeks are aflame for a killing. I feel the adrenaline coursing through me.

"There are cops right outside his…"

"I noticed as I went right past them."

"What do you want? Meet me alone. You don't have to…"

"I do. I do. It's in my nature. You should know. You've read all those profiles about serial killers, Detective."

"You hurt him, and I won't kill you but you'll wish I did."

"You haven't got it in you. Come alone, and we'll discuss it."

Then I hang up.

"Why're you going after my son? He's just doing his job."

"It really shouldn't have become personal, I know. I'm not a personal kind of guy. It's just that he's so goddamned tenacious, George. I'm sure you must know that about your own son."

My smile has returned. I'm having fun, now. I'm being jovial, even amusing for old George, here.

"He knows shit when he smells it."

The old man flashes anger at me.

"Very good. Very funny."

The smile disappears on my lips. The fury returns, and I'm suddenly at boil, with this ancient prick, this relic of the 1940s.

"I wasn't joking."

He's got murder in his eyes. I can almost feel his heat rising.

"I gathered that, George. You don't graduate Magna if you're dumb."

"How'd they fuck up with you, then?"

He gives me a one-up kind of grin, the old prick.

"Is your boy as badly mannered as you are?"

"Worse. And he won't be coming alone."

He's still smiling at me as if he's whipped me in chess.

"I think he will be. I think you mean too much for him to chance it and for him by fucking with me."

I'm in command again. My voice has leveled itself back to pure calm. I won't let this goat rattle me. No, I will not.

"Wait. See."

The grin is gone. George Koehn has gone dead serious on me.

"Indeed."

He lies back with his head propped up on the pillow.

"I did my homework on you and your boy, too. Quite a few decorations in that historic conflict, yes, George?"

He doesn't acknowledge my question.

"There's no need to be humble. You're a brave man. I can tell."

"What would a cowardly puke know about bravery?"

"I was decorated, myself."

"Who fucked that up?"

He's got that smiling, leering look on his senior-citizen face.

"It's amazing how paperwork can lie. I was decorated, yes. But the reports were greatly--embellished, shall we say. It all looked great on my fucking resume."

I glare at him as if I've returned serve when he never expected the ball back on his side of the court.

"You're on the bottom of the ocean, just like whale shit, aren't you."

He thinks he's really winning. It's painted all over him, the old bastard.

"I was improperly raised, George."

"You have someone to blame, of course."

"Sure. It's the times. None of us in the' 90s accepts responsibility, George. Haven't you read the news or watched the media? They'll tell you. We're the new Lost Generation. Lost in materialism. Lost, without direction or goals or values."

"Don't you bore yourself?"

Now he looks bored *with me.*

"Very astute," I have to laugh. "Maybe I'll kill you anyway. I haven't decided. If I leave you alive, then you'll have to relive all this, endlessly. Now there's terror for you, George old boy."

"I've finally met a crack baby."

He gives me a look of real sympathy that I cannot bear.

"My mother was not a drug addict."

There has to be venom dripping from the corners of my mouth, at this precise moment. I loathe George Koehn. I loathe his son. I hate his whole fucking family.

"No. I meant you were the product of a wad that slid down the crack of your mother's ass. That's what I meant, Benjamin."

He grins yet again. I think I want to waste him now.

"You know my name! I'm so honored!"

The flush of genuine anger is rising in my cheeks, and I can feel it soaring.

"You're like an empty fucking barrel. Nothing inside at all."

"You're trying to arouse my anger, aren't you? I'd expect *that tactic from a defenseless man. There is no hope, George. I don't provoke.... What movie'd that come from?"*

I am provoked, *however, and this old prick* knows *it.*

He doesn't answer. This time he remains silent. I don't feel like messing with him until his son arrives, anyway.

I pass the wait by remembering Officer's Training in Quantico. It was where I first met Carl and Philip, before we reunited twice in Kuwait. The three of us were part of the youngest and the brightest. We were gung ho. We were killers and lean green fighting machines, and all the other assorted horseshit with which the Corps evangelizes the troops.

I was a killer before I met Carl and Philip. They'd never killed anyone, yet. I explained how I shot up my foster mother with a lethal dose of digitalis. Lethal, but the coroner and the Medical Examiner managed to miss it. It was all just a natural heart attack, the report read.

Thomas and Brandon looked at me in awe when I told them the tale at the Officer's Club in Kuwait City.

"What does it feel like?" Carl asked.

"You're like God," I told him.

Brandon literally had his mouth open.

The oil scenario fascinated them both when we discussed it on the internet. Oil was the hook and bait. I knew I couldn't kill a whole family by myself. Not in the middle of a fucking war. There were other rapes and other murders by other killers over there while I was still in uniform, but they were sloppily executed killings and assaults. The point was not to be caught.

After the second family, I became bored, although I had more than a year to go on my hitch. I just couldn't see finishing it all out stateside, waiting for the days to dwindle, so I got out with a little help from David Crowley.

My foster father knew I was twisted, but I don't know if he knew what I was really up to. He might have suspected drugs and such, but I don't think he ever wanted to really believe I was a murderer.

It's been a half hour. Will Koehn should be approaching Bridgeport, if I'm not mistaken.

I return to the interview with the father of Detective Will Koehn. I can't resist trying to somehow win back all the points I've seemed to have lost.

"They say that blood tells, George. Is that really true?"

"Why do you ask?"

He looks at me as if he's finally interested in anything I say.

"Because I never had real parents. I keep hearing it's different, if you're raised by your biological parents."

"You having a moment, here, Benjamin?"

The wise-ass smiled has returned.

"I could just shoot you now and wait for your son to come after me so I can kill him, too."

"You're not leaving here alive today, Anderson. You're already dead and you don't even know it. I saw guys die on beaches in France. They always looked surprised, just the way you're going to look, real soon."

"I know."

He looks at me quizzically.

"You know?" he asks.

The interested expression is on him again.

"Yes. I'm going to die. I'm not afraid. I was never afraid in Iraq or Kuwait, either."

He seems stunned, briefly. But then his pugnacious grin reappears.

"If you ain't afraid, there are only two possibilities."

"Which are, George?"

"You're insane, or you're bone fucking stupid."

I slap him hard, but he never flinches. Then I slap him again, and there's still no overt reaction. Same smile. Same unflappable stare.

I'm becoming bored with him, *now.*

"You're proud of Will, aren't you?"

He doesn't answer. He's telling me he's through talking to me.

"He was everything you wanted in a son, right?"

Still no reply. The air is becoming too thick to breathe. I feel as though I'm going to start gasping soon. I want to kill George Koehn now, but he's the bait for the detective son outside, somewhere.

"It must be comforting to know your boy has become an honorable man."

"You don't know a goddamned thing about honor, you pathetic puke of a human being."

I slap him again. But this time, real rage shows in his eyes. He wants to come up at me and tear out my throat.

"Give it up, Benjamin. Just walk outside, throw down the gun, and get yourself a comfortable cage to live in for the rest of your life. Go on! You don't really want to die, today."

I look at him, my ears burning for his blood. And for the blood of his honorable *son.*

"Did you ever have a friend, Benjamin? A man or a woman?"

Now I'm the one to refuse talking back to him.

"I don't need this, George. I really don't."

"What's the matter? Mommy didn't breast-feed you long enough? She never bought you a fucking pony?"

I aim the gun at his forehead.

"Bettter men than you have pointed a piece at me. They're dead, at Normandy."

I lower the gun. Then I smile. It takes every ounce of strength that I can muster, but I radiate at George Koehn. I remember, now, why I came here in the first place. I came to explode into flames, like the Phoenix.

Will Koehn. The good boy. The good and honorable son.

The dutiful son. The honorable man. The brave soldier and honest policeman.

He is everything in this world I despise and still hate. He was my brother, Abel.

My name? Cain, naturally.

40

One of our SWAT guys is an ex-Marine sniper who was in Desert Storm around the time I worked for NCIS. His name is Bailey Jackson. I knew him at the Police Academy here in Chicago, and I've stayed in touch with him as I got my shield and as he went into SWAT. He killed men from unbelievable distances when he was in the Crotch. I also used to think those Marines exaggerated what they could do, until I saw the bodies that resulted from some of their handiwork over in Iraq.

"Get him by the window, the front window," Bailey tells me.

"The shades are shut," I explain.

Bailey is a big, athletic man. He is African black. There is almost a blue sheen to his skin. He is a very handsome young man. He's also married with three young children, two of whom were conceived just before he left for the Middle East.

"Makes no difference. Get him close enough to the center of that big bay window as you can. We'll call your dad's number. If anyone answers, say his last name as loud as you can, and then make sure you and your dad are nowhere in front of that bay window. And if he doesn't get hit, you're going to have to try and knock his ass down until we come through that window and the back and front door.... Remember, if he answers the phone, say his last name as loud as you can. He won't have time to move. Just get the fuck out of the zone, my man."

"I'll try.... What if he doesn't answer the phone?"

"Count ten slow after the fifth ring. On ten, you better be out of the way. Please, Will. After ten, he's never going to hear another count in his lame fucking existence. Just make sure you're out of the line of fire. Please, because we're going in, one way or the other. This guy don't walk, today."

I nod, and he cuffs me warmly on my right shoulder.

I proceed toward the door. I knock when I arrive in front of it.

"You unarmed?" he bellows behind the entry.

"Yes."

"You better be, Will, or I'll shoot your father first, and then you."

"I'm unarmed."

"Tell your SWAT friends that they're unwelcome here!" he shouts through the door.

He couldn't have seen them through my father's windows. They were all parked a good half-block south of here. And the block on either side has already been quietly vacated. No cop has come within one hundred yards of my father's home here in Bridgeport. He's trying to anticipate me.

"I came alone, like you said."

"Really, Will? You wouldn't lie to me, would you? Because this .22 has a hair trigger."

"Are you going to let me in or not?"

The door cracks open.

I go inside, and then he slams me against the entry and frisks me. He doesn't have a gentle touch.

"You came alone? Truly?" he whispers in my ear, the barrel of the .22 pressed against my temple on the left side.

"I came alone."

"Why do I doubt you, Will?"

"Because you don't trust me. I wouldn't."

"Very candid."

My father is sitting on the sofa. He has duct tape over his mouth, and I assume his hands are bound behind him with the same stuff that covers his lips.

He appears to be just out of range from the front window. You can't be certain where their fire will travel. They didn't set up until I got to the door. They understood Anderson's demand that I come alone, but they weren't going to let it happen. I had to fight with Pearce to be allowed to come inside, but he gave in when I explained my father was dead for sure if I didn't enter as asked. He retorted that both of us would be killed if we went along with Anderson, but I finally convinced him that I had to get in there to try and get between the Captain and my dad. He wanted to plant a weapon on me, but I convinced him that Anderson would find it right away and use it on me or my dad or both of us.

Then I explained the plan Bailey Jackson and I concocted. I told Pearce that it was the only chance my father really had with this mutt. We both knew that SWAT would storm the house regardless of what Benjamin Anderson did, but I had to be inside to try and somehow distract him so SWAT had a chance to kill him clean. Pearce eventually gave in to me.

"You get killed and I'll be very displeased," he said before he shook my hand and okayed the plan.

So now I'm inside and face to face with the man I've been hunting since that brief war in the most volatile, violent spot on earth.

Bailey is giving me a few minutes to see what's going on before he has his tacticals make the phone call. He'll allow me to try to maneuver my dad away from his fields of fire. Snipers don't normally shoot blind at a subject, but the spray—it'll come in three volleys, we agreed—is what will give me just a second or two to knock Benjamin Anderson down and try to overpower him and disarm him before SWAT bursts in and finishes him, regardless of whether my dad and I are still breathing.

"We finally meet," he says as he releases me and walks over by my father.

There is a phone here in the living room. It sits on a table next to the couch where my father is strapped and gagged.

It's the old rotary kind, and it's black like the one in his bedroom.

"You came close. More than once," he smiles.

"Let him go. He's a civilian. You don't need to kill him, too."

"So you're planning on dying, Will?"

"Everyone does. The game is fixed."

"Yes. Indeed it is…. Don't you want to know why I killed all those people, before I kill you both?"

"No. Go fuck yourself."

"Will, such a negative attitude. Wasn't I your worthiest adversary?"

"You're just a rich punk who has a taste for killing. You'll be on my solved board in the morning. And pretty soon after that, no one will remember who the hell you were. You're just another savage that needs to wind up in a cage, Anderson."

"I thought we'd have more mutual respect. I thought I really was a worthy adversary, Will."

"Don't call me anything but 'Detective Koehn,' you sad piece of shit."

My face burns with the desire to shoot out his eyes.

"You chased me all over the country. You had at me, back in the Middle East. Surely you have to admit I was a challenge. Maybe even the greatest challenge you've had as a policeman?"

"What do you want? Hugs and kisses. I'd shoot you in the eye and fuck your skull right now, if I had the opportunity."

He looks almost disappointed with me, at the moment. He's got a sour, nearly-sad expression on his face.

"I thought we had a *connection*, Will."

"I'd like to connect your nose to the muzzle of my piece. That's the only connection I want with you, asshole."

"I can understand why you're angry. I mean with your father, ready to die with you, now."

I feel the anger flush my own cheeks, again.

"Walk out. Dump the pistol. Live the life of a celebrity in jail. Think of all the books you can write, inside the slammer, dickhead."

"No. It ends today. It ends right now."

"It isn't going to end the way you think, jackass."

He blinks, and then his eyes widen. He knows what's coming.

The phone rings.

"*You lied! They're here!*"

"No. It has to be someone else. Pick it up and see if I'm telling the truth. I came alone."

He looks at the phone on the third ring. I'm standing by the front door, now with my shoulder blades against the wall.

He looks over at me.

"It's them, isn't it."

"Only one way to find out," I tell him.

I grin at him, my eyebrows raised as comically as I can manage. I'm trying my damnedest to make him go for that phone.

I eye my father. He should be safe where he's sitting.

Then Anderson picks up the phone. The count is already at seven. Eight, nine...

"*ANDERSON!*" I yell out as loudly as I'm able.

I hit the floor as the shots pulverize the front window into flying shards. I cover my head and count the bursts. When I hear three volleys, I jump up, and I find Anderson scrambling to his feet as well. I notice my father slumped over, on the couch behind him.

I race toward the ex-Captain, and I lower my shoulder into his lower abdomen. I hit him and knock him against the wall next to the couch. He manages to hang onto the gun after the collision, but I knock him to the floor, and we struggle hand-to-hand for possession of the handgun. We roll over twice toward the center of the floor, and then I try to lift him up so I can wrench the gun free.

But he forces me back to the blown-away window, and suddenly we're leaping together, clutching each other, out the gaping hole in the wall of my father's living room.

We plummet to earth, and the concussion of hitting my dad's front lawn separates us and I roll away from him, waiting to hear the explosions of gunfire. As I rise to my knees, I see Anderson standing, his gun pointed my way.

There are six SWATS standing behind him with armed assault rifles pointed at him.

"DROP THE WEAPON!" someone yells.

But Anderson points the weapon at me, and now I know I'm dead.

I hear the crack and then the boom of a high-caliber slug, but it can't be the pop of a .22.

Anderson flies to his right, and his head explodes. He flops on the grass heavily, and then I see the arterial spray the slug has created on my father's aluminum siding. There is white and pink gray matter beneath the blood on my dad's front wall, and Benjamin Anderson's skull looks like a hollowed-out coconut. His eyes have almost popped out of their sockets, and there's a terrible grimace on what's left of his face.

Bailey charges over to check me out. I have several pieces of glass stuck in my back and on the backs of my legs. The shards are sticking out of my trousers and leather jacket. He calls out for medical help, and there are already paramedics and a doctor on the scene.

"Get to my father," I tell them, as the paramedics look me over.

My father has been hit with a bullet that careened off something in the living room, and it has struck him in the right shoulder. The good news is that it's not life-threatening, but he'll be in the hospital for a few days at least since he's lost considerable blood.

Pete Donato, Jack Clemons and Captain Pearce are all at the hospital with me.

"I still kick myself in the ass for letting you go in alone with that asshole," Pearce admits.

"He would've killed my father before the SWATs hit the doors and the windows," I remind him.

"Maybe you're right. You're both still alive, so who the fuck cares? Am I correct?"

"Yes, Sir."

"You ever pull a John Wayne again, and I'll shoot you myself, bub," he winks.

Then he walks toward the hospital exit.

Pete and Jack and I sit in the waiting room to hear how George Koehn, my dad, is doing. I made the call to Sammy in Champaign, and he's on the way here with Megan. Then I call Hannah. She curses me for going inside the house against Pearce's better judgment, but then her relief at the demise of Benjamin Anderson rushes over her, and she weeps over the phone.

Anderson has no family, no one to take the body. He will be buried by the County at the taxpayers' expense. Since he's a deserter, the military will have nothing to do with him, nor would they, given that he's a mass murderer. Arlington will not have him, naturally, even though he's formally a "war hero."

I go into the Medical Examiner's when they perform the autopsy. It's cut and dried. Bailey performed a signature headshot, and Anderson was dead before he flopped. All there was left of him was splattered against my father's wall. I hosed the goo and crap off the siding the same night Bailey wasted him.

Two families in Kuwait demolished—at least two we're sure of, now that we can't interrogate Anderson. And Thomas and Brandon are unavailable for comment, also. Gerald still survives, but now that he has no leverage by squealing on the ex-Captain, we're not sure how much talking he's likely to do. The State gains no benefit by not prosecuting him to the limit after the demise of Anderson.

It was never about oil, in Kuwait or here in Chicago. It was never about patriotism in Mexico. We know all that now. It was always about the same element.

It was always about *evil*.

I have to ease myself back into my caseload. There are other killers to be caught.

Pete Donato will return to *The Intrepid* and his job at the NCIS. Jack Clemons and I return to our routine of finding braindeads who continue to be braindeads. They club each other to death over the price of a Big Mac. They rape those who are unable to defend themselves. They steal because they are too stupid to engage in the labor of the world. Murder goes on and on, and we'll always have job security in Homicide.

I still have nightmares about Desert Storm. I wasn't an official participant. I somehow missed the only war I'll likely be eligible to fight. At least, I hope I've missed my turn at war. Finding apeshit killers is war enough for me. I don't feel as though I missed my chance at combat. I was well-trained when I was in the Marines, and I know I would have done my duty. I was always serious about my commitment to my country and to the Corps. But I don't feel as though I missed the opportunity of a lifetime, the way some guys bemoaned missing Vietnam, now that they're sixty and they avoided the shit over there. No, I feel as though I got lucky that I never had to kill anyone in the heat of battle and that I was even luckier that I didn't *get* killed in Desert Storm. I'm hoping that if Hannah and I ever have a son that he never has to bear arms against his fellow human beings. Maybe we'll finally get smart and stop doing that silly shit.

But probably we won't.

Benjamin Anderson will be buried in what they used to call a "pauper's field." It's where they plant the indigent, the poor. He wasn't poor, but we never found the stash he took from David Crowley's incinerated Beverly Hills pad. We never found the book of names he supposedly heisted, either. We found the place he lived at on the southeast side by the Lake because the landlord finally came forward and spilled that Benjamin Anderson was his one-time tenant.

His bicycle goes into Property, and his file goes into a cardboard box in the bowels of Property, as well. The rest is history. The papers and the TV media will have their day with this dog, and then I hope his name will be forgotten forever.

Epilogue

We get married again in June and on schedule. The baby is on the way.

Hannah is showing proper color in her face these days. She's a normal, healthy, pregnant woman, with nothing on her mind except her due date. She has cravings, but nothing extreme. She loves cucumbers and chocolate milk, but not together.

My father has recovered well, but my mother slowly declines in the nursing home. My brother Sammy is due to receive his MBA from Illinois next summer, and then he has plans to wed Megan.

I'm the one who has bad memories. But I don't let them get in my way. I have the future. I have a life with Hannah. I have a life with her two girls.

Jack Clemons makes nice progress with the INS agent he's been seeing, but no engagement is imminent, he murmurs embarrassedly.

Captain Pearce is busy with other murderers, as Jack and I are, and I suppose Pete Donato is still pursuing AWOL sailors and Marines, along with assorted violent criminals too. I've heard from him a few times since he returned to *The Intrepid*.

We planted Captain Benjamin Anderson in County ground with no one in attendance except for Jack and me and the gravediggers, who used a Cat to burrow into the six feet of earth. We saw them put him down, but I have a feeling Anderson isn't done descending quite yet.

None of my current cases seems inclined to make a personal attack upon me. I find it relaxing to know that they're doing their best to avoid me. It's the way it's supposed to be. They hide and I seek.

Years have gone by since the adventure in the deserts of Iraq and the murders in Kuwait City. Months have passed since the Milan family in Chicago has been laid to rest.

I've visited some of their relatives to let them know directly from me that the killer has been put down forever. It wasn't required of me to contact the Milans—I did it for my own peace of mind, and for closure.

Not all my cases have an ending. Not all of them are neatly tied up by one bullet from an ex-Marine's sniper rifle. That would make life too simple, of course. One thing that life is *not* is uncomplicated.

Hannah makes my existence seem that way, though. At least when I'm with her it becomes easier. The girls are a source of great happiness, too.

And then there's the baby, waiting to enter our world.

Now *there's* a complication to my life that I can look forward to.

Author's Note

Forty-five caliber handguns are atypical for officers who fought in Desert Storm--they used nine millimeter weapons, for the most part, I was told by a veteran of that conflict. As is usually the case with fiction writers, we make stuff up.

Acknowledgements

Much can be learned by reading *The Yellow Birds* by Kevin Powers and *Billy Lynn's Long Halftime Walk* by Ben Fountain. They both have much to say about American soldiers under great duress in the Iraq conflicts. The author hopes that *Desert Storm Heart*, in its own humble way, will honor the veterans of those two wars.

Also by Parkgate Press (Dionysus Books)

www.parkgatepress.com
www.dionysusbooks.com

Thomas Laird

THE UNDERGROUND DETECTIVE

Danny Mangan of Chicago Homicide is on the trail of a
serial killer...while his own life is falling apart.
By the author of CUTTER, SEASON OF THE
ASSASSIN and BLACK DOG, reviewed by
The Washington Post, The Chicago Sun-Times
and *The Independent on Sunday*.

Katharine E. Willers

WHAT TOOK ME OUT TO THE BALL GAME

The Determinants of Attendance of
Major League Baseball Games from 1989–1999
and the Implications of the 1994 Labor Strike

About the Author

Thomas Laird has published five novels: *Cutter* (2001), *Season of the Assassin* (2003), *Black Dog* (2004), *Voices of the Dead* (2006), and *The Underground Detective* (2012). The first three books were co-published in London and New York by Constable & Robinson and by Carroll & Graf (Perseus), the fourth in the Czech Republic by Domino Publishers, and the fifth by Parkgate Press. The books received favorable reviews from the *Washington Post*, the *Chicago Sun-Times*, *Publishers Weekly*, *Library Journal*, the *Independent on Sunday* (UK) and *Crime Time* (UK).

Thomas Laird lives with his wife Marsha (Masha) near Germantown Hills, Illinois. He also shares his residence with Mick the Australian Shepherd, Jimmy the alley cat, and Tar (Tarzan) the Amazon Yellow Nape parrot. He teaches English part-time at Bradley University in Peoria, Illinois, the hub of the arts in central Illinois.

This title is also available as an ebook from Parkgate Digital.

www.ingramcontent.com/pod-product-compliance
Lightning Source LLC
Chambersburg PA
CBHW070547130626
46556CB00001B/43